She was pleasant and charming and an absolute master at avoiding talking about herself. Richard tried to look into the pale blue eyes, but they were like mirrors—reflecting what was around them, revealing nothing.

"How long have you been dealing in antique clocks?"

She arched a brow. "A number of years. You know, you ask a lot of questions."

"I'm interested," Richard said.

"In what?"

His gaze leveled on her eyes. "Where you come from. Who you are. What makes the lady with the clocks tick . . ."

Intrigue. Passion. Deception.

The greatest secret of all lies hidden . . .
SOUTH OF PARADISE

She was a woman under suspicion.
He was a man seduced by curiosity.
Nothing would stop him from
learning her secrets . . .
why she kept moving from town to town,
changing her identity, stealing from
those who adored her . . .

NO ONE CAPTURES THE EXCITEMENT, THE EMOTIONS, THE ROMANCE OF SOUTHERN LIFE AS DRAMATICALLY AS MARCIA MARTIN!

Jove titles by Marcia Martin

SOUTHERN NIGHTS
SOUTHERN SECRETS
SOUTHERN STORMS

SOUTH OF PARADISE

MARCIA MARTIN

JOVE BOOKS, NEW YORK

SOUTH OF PARADISE

A Jove Book / published by arrangement with
the author

PRINTING HISTORY
Jove edition / June 1993

ISBN: 0-515-11123-6

Jove Books are published by The Berkley Publishing Group,
200 Madison Avenue, New York, New York 10016.
The name ''JOVE'' and the ''J'' logo
are trademarks belonging to Jove Publications, Inc.

PRINTED IN THE UNITED STATES OF AMERICA

10 9 8 7 6 5 4 3 2 1

For all the children

Acknowledgement and thanks to

SHERRY CARLSON
Psychologist

CHUCK COLE
Cole Computer Graphics

JOHN GARVEY
Cummins Atlantic, Inc. (Marine Division)

JAY HOWARD
Jay Howard Production Audio, Inc.

=PROLOGUE=

April 1976
McLean, Virginia

It was almost easy now—to escape at will, retreating to an inner sanctum that was hers alone, feeling and seeing only those things she selected.

The ruffled curtains billowed like flags at the open window, pink and white, pink and white, shifting lazily against the gray light of evening. From the lawns below came the scent of cherry blossoms, and from the ornate clock next to the bed the precise *tick . . . tick . . . tick . . .* of Swiss movement.

The cadence was interrupted by the horn of a passing car, and a trailing chorus of laughter. She could well imagine who it was. John Harrod had picked up Elaine Taylor. George Morehead and Kitty Cox were probably along for the ride. That's what the well-bred sons and daughters of the exclusive suburb did on a springtime Saturday night—went cruising in somebody's flashy new car. Except for her, of course. She'd stopped being one of them long ago—long before she ever reached her teens . . . back when Mother died . . . back when bright, girlhood days turned suddenly, irrevocably dark.

She closed her eyes, refusing to see anything but the shifting pink and white of the curtains at the window, refusing to hear anything but the lulling rhythm of the clock. *Tick . . . tick . . . tick . . .* She sank into the dream.

The curtains disappeared in a cloud, and then . . . *he* was there. She knew he would be—walking toward her through the fog, his smile shining like the sun. She couldn't say what color his hair or eyes were. But his smile was unmistakable. There

1

was a warmth within it that could melt a frozen heart. He extended a hand. She knew it almost as well as his smile. It would be strong, but incredibly gentle, and cool to the touch—

Reality rammed through the mist, threatening to drag her back with sweaty palms. She bit her lip and squeezed her eyes tightly shut. Still, the room closed in; as if from a distance, the sound of heavy breathing barreled toward her. Tears gathered behind her straining eyelids.

Who was she trying to fool? There was no salvation! No prince to come to the rescue!

The friendly image began to dissolve, his smile melting like sunbeams in the rain.

Damn you! she silently shrieked. *I see you, and I know what you are! You're nothing but a fairy tale, and . . .*

Don't go away. Don't leave.

Please . . .

Oh, God, please take me with you into the fog.

=ONE=

November 5, 1988
Devil's Rock, North Carolina

The chamber was spacious—nearly a full quarter of the ground floor of the Skinner mansion—but veiled and closed off as it currently was, the wood-paneled study grew increasingly dark and pressing with afternoon shadow.

From her vantage point at the desk in the corner, she cast a hooded look at the neighboring lectern that was a dozen feet long if an inch. A Tiffany chandelier suspended at midpoint provided the only artificial light in the room. Beneath the lamp the mahogany tabletop shone with the gloss of a century's worth of polishing and reflected the images of the seven men seated along its border.

They called themselves the "Big Boys."

The name was legend in the northwest mountains of North Carolina, and had been ever since the half-dozen charter members banded together in the 1880s to carve the future of a good fifty-mile stretch of the Blue Ridge. From them had come electricity, paved roads, telephone lines . . .

And, she thought, *a system of power that bordered on feudalism.*

Beneath lowered lids her gaze moved from one to the next—Cal Stevenson of Parkersburg, Ralph Tuttle and Tyree Boggs from Silverton, Angus MacGregor and his nephew Harley from Millview, and of course District Court Judge Ray Skinner and his son, Kyle.

As personal assistant to the Judge, she'd handled correspondence to all the out-of-towners, but today's big meeting in the

Skinner house was the first time she'd seen them in the flesh. Stevenson was slight and silver-haired; Tuttle overweight and balding; Boggs huge and hulking and embarrassingly deferential to the preeminent member of the Silverton delegation. The MacGregors were tall, lanky, and redheaded, though Angus showed a gray streak at the temple as well as facial creases and hollows that made the angle of his nose appear even more hawkish than it was. Rounding out the group were the Judge and Kyle, the senior and junior members of the group—the first ruddy and broadening about the middle and crowned with snow-white hair; the latter svelte and muscular, his slicked-back hair black as a raven's wing.

Over the course of a century the names may have changed, but these were the descendants of the original Big Boys. Like titles of nobility, seats at their meeting table had been handed down from generation to generation; and like their medieval counterparts, the modern mountain lords ruled with all the arrogance of noblesse oblige.

Gray light sifted through the shuttered windows, illuminating the smoke of the Judge's cigar in shifting bars, enhancing the notion of castles and dungeons and impending doom as yet another shabby subject walked into the room. Worn overalls hung from the man's frame; his face was lined and weathered, his hands gnarled. Obviously a farmer, he looked more than seventy, though she'd bet he was twenty years younger.

"I ain't got the full amount," he announced with some hesitation.

The suspended lamp threw a circle of light on the hardwood floor, its boundary edging across the scuffed toes of the man's work boots. Silence ensued, and her gaze dropped to her notepad. It had been like this for hours—people filing in, filing out, groveling before the men at the table as though entire futures hung in the balance. Indeed, she supposed, that's the way it was. The Big Boys held the deeds to farms and homes, the notes on businesses, the policies on people's lives.

Moving her pen meaninglessly across the page, she pretended to make a note of the farmer's transgression. In truth her sober thoughts hovered on the seven-man tribunal he faced.

Five weeks had passed since she first saw the Judge's advertisement; additional days had lapsed as she traveled and investigated; now, after several weeks in Devil's Rock, she'd learned how things stood. In the rugged hills bordering the Tennessee state line—where townfolk lived modestly, farmers eked by, and backwoods families struggled in poverty—the Big Boys resided in ancestral splendor and controlled every major artery of commerce that passed through their heartland. Utilities and commodities, manufacturing and banking, transportation and education . . . They ran it all.

"I'll have it for ya next week," the farmer added.

"Next week is far away," came the stern reply. Kyle, the dark prince, had spoken.

"Ya can count on me, Mr. Skinner. Ya know ya can."

"I hope so, Jonas. I'd hate to be forced to repossess that new tractor when spring planting is just around the corner."

"No, sir! Like I said, I'll have it next week."

"See that you do, Jonas."

Shoulders slumping, the farmer shuffled out of the room. She glanced along the table. They approved Kyle's action; it showed on their smug faces—Stevenson, Tuttle, Boggs, the MacGregors, even the Judge, who was more often likely to oppose his son than side with him. Bastards.

Her damning thoughts darted to last night when she had worked late with the Judge, making preparations for today's "review," as he called it. It was half past ten when he excused himself to go to the washroom and asked her to locate a certain document while he was gone. She'd been searching through the bottom cabinet when she spotted the drooping corner of a manila file taped to the top of the drawer.

Before she heard the Judge's returning footsteps and hastily replaced the secret file, she'd had time to see the Big Boys for what they really were. On the public stage they made deals to build highways and hospitals and schools; behind the scenes they ran operations ranging from bootlegging to gambling to something that looked revoltingly like white slavery.

The Judge caught her eye and winked . . . while fondling that damn marble-headed gavel of his. He was always touching it, stroking it. She smiled as her stomach turned.

"Vanessa, my dear," he said, "it seems we have a break before the next client is due. How about a round of coffee?"

"Certainly, Judge." With measured tread she escaped the

chamber, ignoring the scorch of male eyes as she walked away.

Passing Tibbs in the foyer, she gave the ancient butler a smile. He returned it with a comradely salute, and she continued along the hall, thinking how empty the house seemed. That morning Kyle's wife, Jeanette, and their two daughters had left for an overnight holiday miles away in Boone. Actually they'd been sent away, along with the servants, purportedly to safeguard the privacy of the Big Boys. The only people remaining to serve were Tibbs and herself.

She turned through the kitchen doorway with a frown. She didn't relish the idea of being alone in the giant house once the meeting was over—just her, Kyle, the Judge, and a poor old black man who couldn't hear fireworks if they were set off under his chair.

Facing west, the kitchen caught the afternoon light. Compared with the cloistered study, the room was sunny and free of smoke and tranquilly deserted. As the coffee perked she stood by the sink and gazed out the window.

Devil's Rock. She could see it there in the distance—an odd formation of stone suggesting horns and slanted eyes and a pointed chin. Despite the malevolent-looking landmark from which the town had taken its name, Devil's Rock had appeared to be such a sleepy little place—lofty old houses facing quaint shopfronts along a main street called Sky Road . . . a town hall that unified every conceivable public service from fire department to town morgue to the housing of a negligible police force chiefed by a middle-aged man who seemed to move with the sloth of one who hadn't been called on in any official capacity for years.

Her gaze shifted across the sweeping grounds of the Skinner estate to the expansive garage with the cupola on top.

From a distance the setup had looked ideal—a widower judge with a fleet of expensive cars living with his son, daughter-in-law, and two granddaughters in a secluded family estate on the outskirts of a remote town. Plus, the Judge had been obviously smitten from the first time he saw her standing on his doorstep, newspaper advertisement in hand. She'd taken the live-in post thinking it would prove the easiest job yet.

But she'd been wrong. She hadn't counted on the Judge being part of a power conglomerate, nor on his temperament.

She'd seen him insult Jeanette until she was reduced to tears, bluster at his granddaughters until they scurried in fright, harangue the servants until several had quit. As for herself, of course, he had only smiles and winks and pats on the back that invariably strayed to forbidden zones.

In addition to the Judge, she'd had to put up with the unanticipated burden of Kyle. Young, bold, physically powerful, in many ways he was worse than his father—his inherited meanness typically couched behind a hard smile that made one wonder exactly what he was capable of.

He'd been a thorn in her side ever since she arrived. Having sampled the wares of most single ladies in Devil's Rock—notably the voluptuous widow Mavis Brewer—Kyle had descended like a hawk hungry for untasted meat, his leading remarks and stolen caresses making each day increasingly intolerable. He didn't seem to care if his wife or father took note; in fact, on one occasion when the Judge called him down for some lewd comment, the two men had ended up squaring off and nearly coming to blows.

Usually she took things slow and easy. This time—despite the breathtaking magnificence of the Blue Ridge setting—she'd been itching to get away by the end of the first week.

At least she'd been right about one thing: the Skinner garage was a veritable horn of plenty—a brand-new Lincoln limo, a late-eighties Mercedes, a classic MG, and more. Both the Judge and his son were car hounds, and a few days ago she'd derived pleasure from pilfering the spare set of keys to one of Kyle's favorites—a vintage Corvette that could bring as much as fifty thousand dollars from the right collector. She'd made a couple of calls and was waiting only for the right connection. . . .

Then last night the Judge made his move—a heavy-handed embrace while he pressed slobbering lips on hers.

"Come now, Judge," she'd said, fending him off with a coy smile. "A lady needs time to be courted, you know."

He'd backed off reluctantly, as others had, promising with his eyes that he'd not be put off for long. The smell of cigars had remained in her nostrils long after she bathed.

She didn't care if she had to settle for half of what the Vette was worth. She was getting out tonight. No more fake charm.

No more forced smiles. No more Vanessa Blair. By this time tomorrow, Vanessa would be a fading memory—as would the lustful leer in the Judge's eyes, the lascivious hands of his son, and the ugliness of what "big boys" could do behind the righteous guise of leadership.

By this time tomorrow her life would be her own again—*where* didn't matter much, as long as it was someplace fresh and free and far away from the haunting stench of cigars. Maybe the coast . . .

Eyes fixed unseeingly out the window, she conjured a vision of a windswept beach. The water sparkled in the sun, the surf roared in her ears, and she was filled with the peace of aloneness.

Kyle forced himself to wait a full fifteen minutes before exiting the study and slipping down the hall to the kitchen door. She was staring into space, completely still. He'd seen her do it before. At the moment her preoccupation gave his eyes the chance to crawl over her inch by inch.

Tall and slim, Vanessa Blair robed her seductiveness in high-collared dresses, pinned-up hair, and tortoiseshell glasses. The efforts only tantalized a man with half an eye. Her copper-colored hair was thick and glossy and called to be released from its pins. Beneath the conservative dress, her body was that of a temptress; behind the glasses her eyes were riveting—so pale a blue they were almost silver . . . like ice.

He'd come to think of those eyes as a symbol; for he'd never come across a woman who could inflict such frigid distance with a simple look. The challenge of her had crawled under his skin, the sensation heightened by the way his father drooled over her like an old, toothless dog.

All she needed was the touch of a real man. She might fight it; in fact, he hoped she did. But once he had her firmly in his grasp, Kyle was confident he could melt the ice. Then everything would be right. He could put his mind back on business, and the honorable Judge Ray Skinner—son-of-a-bitch—would be put soundly in his place.

Kyle moved quietly into the room, his gaze narrowing on her hips, his hands following to make contact as he came up behind her. She jumped, and he laughed as she sidled away.

"Don't ever lay a finger on me again," she said, and reached for the coffee maker.

"Or what?" he retorted. "You'll slap my wrist? Tell my wife? Call the cops? Go ahead, Vanessa. Do your worst."

"I wouldn't invite that if I were you, Kyle."

She turned, steaming pot in hand, her icy eyes meeting his. "Those who play with fire are liable to get burned," she added.

He arched a brow and stepped closer. "Are you threatening me?" he demanded.

"Oh, no." Turning smoothly aside, she began filling the silver service on the counter. "Ladies don't threaten."

He laughed once more. "I wish you'd stop with this 'lady' act. There's nobody here you have to pretend for."

She went about her business without commenting. Kyle took another swaggering step toward her.

"That reserve of yours might work on my father, but not me. I see it for what it is—a little window dressing to make the wares more enticing. What do you want out of the old man anyway?"

"I have no idea what you mean."

"I mean, what does he have to do to get under your skirts?"

She hesitated for a mere instant in the midst of her pouring. Other than that, she surrendered no reaction.

"For that matter," Kyle added, "what do *I* have to do?"

"You're disgusting," she murmured.

"I've pleasured too many women to believe you mean that. Look me in the face and say it."

Setting the coffeepot aside, she turned and looked up with those freezing eyes. In spite of himself Kyle felt a chill.

"You're disgusting," she repeated in the same soft tone.

Gathering swiftly in his loins, the chill turned into erotic pounding. Kyle's smile drained away. "So cool and contained," he said, his heated gaze roaming the smooth perfection of her face. "I'll wager that when you're on your back under a good man, you sing a different tune."

"Even if that's so, *you'll* never hear it," she replied, and started to turn away.

Catching her arm, Kyle yanked her back. "Don't bet on it,

honey.'' Her eyes lifted to his, the cold rejection within them firing his blood all the more.

"Your father and the others are waiting," she said. "Would you kindly release me?"

Kyle stared a few seconds longer. The urge to take her was strong, but now was not the time. "For the moment," he answered finally, and with a parting squeeze of her arm, let her go.

As she picked up the coffee service and walked away, Kyle leaned back against the counter, watching the sway of her hips and imagining them straining beneath his own.

"But only the moment," he promised himself when she was gone.

Adjusting the hardness in his trousers, he followed her path back to the study.

Late in the day a woman strode into the meeting room. Though her hair was gray and her widow's weeds outdated, she emitted an air of confidence, even superiority—a dramatic departure from the piteous chain of humanity that had crawled before the Big Boys' bench.

"Why, Mrs. Faber!" Kyle exclaimed, rising to his feet. "We didn't expect to see you today. The business we have—"

"The business we have is over," the woman broke in.

"What do you mean, 'over'?" Kyle asked after a moment.

"Over as in concluded, finished . . . just like my husband."

Kyle held up a peacemaking palm. "We're all very sorry about Lucas, but that doesn't change the fact that . . ."

He paused as she sent a check sailing to the surface of the mahogany table. "What's this?"

"Payment in full," the woman announced.

Kyle's smile waned. "It can't be."

"It is," she returned, folding her arms in a show of satisfaction as he grabbed for the slip of paper. "The Big Boys no longer hold any claim whatsoever on the lodge, or as you may prefer to call it, 'Faber's Folly.'"

Kyle stared wordlessly at the bank draft as a flurry of whispers swept along the meeting table. Realizing her mouth was hanging open, Vanessa looked down at her notepad and hid a smile.

"Let me see that," the Judge muttered, and snatched the check from his son's hand.

"It's all there," the woman said with a lift of her chin. "Including this month's interest."

The Judge set his cigar in the brimming ashtray and squinted up at the woman. "Where did you get this, Molly?"

Ignoring his question, she speared the panel of men with a look as hard as iron. *"You,"* she muttered in a sneering tone. "My man believed in the lot of you. He accepted it when you didn't bring in the highway you promised. He understood when you opened a competitive ski lodge a mere few mountains away. He believed you when you explained away continuing failure with talk of recessions. For thirty years he took your word!"

"We did what we had to do, Molly," the Judge said.

"Fine. I'm doing what I have to do, too, Judge. I've sold Faber's Folly, and for a handsome price the likes of you wouldn't dream of paying."

"Sold it to whom?" the Judge demanded.

"The son of a good friend of Lucas's. As a boy he used to visit Black Top Mountain most every summer with his folks. He's always had a great fondness for the lodge."

"I repeat: *who is it?*"

"He's not from around here, Judge. He's from Charlotte, and if I were you, I wouldn't think of trying to manipulate him. Richard Adams is a brilliant and wealthy man. If you tangle with him, you'd best have your legions in order."

The Judge's rubbery lips formed an empty smile. "We will, Molly, I assure you. Thanks for the check. Tibbs will show you out."

The woman walked staunchly to the door and turned. "I'd like to say one last thing before I leave these mountains and never look back. There didn't have to be a Faber's Folly. I know it, and you know it. In life poor Lucas was too goodhearted to stand up to the likes of you. I only hope he can see me now as I invite all you Big Boys to go straight to hell."

After Molly Faber's spectacular exit, the study erupted in surprised turmoil. But as soon as the next debtor filed in, the

atmosphere of the room returned to supercilious normalcy—
except perhaps that Kyle remained uncharacteristically silent.

Vanessa Blair took notes, replenished coffee, emptied ash-
trays, one level of her mind maintaining the facade of charming
aide, another reflecting on the truth that despite the rare
sunburst of a rebel like Molly, the Big Boys held their corner
of the Blue Ridge in dark submission.

Interrupted only by supper, which was catered by an
indebted restaurateur, business continued into the evening. At
eight o'clock Tibbs appeared at the doorway to announce that
everyone was gone but "the folks from Shine Valley."

Shine Valley . . . she'd seen the name on the secret
ledgers.

"Vanessa, my dear," the Judge said. "It's been a long day.
Why don't you retire and leave this last piece of business to
us?"

"Of course," she replied. "I'll tidy the kitchen before I go
up."

Pocketing her pad and pen, she retrieved the coffee service
and sent a parting look around the table. "Nice to have met
you, gentlemen."

The typical polite remarks followed her to the doorway. It
wasn't until Tibbs closed the sliding doors behind her that she
heard the burst of guffaws from the other side.

Nearby, Tibbs stood like a statue—and was just as deaf.
Across the foyer a group of rough-looking mountain men were
gathered near the door, the brims of their hats hiding their faces
as they stared at their feet. With a dismissing glance for the lot
of them, she leaned back and pressed her ear to the study door.

"So, where did you find *her*?" Cal Stevenson asked.

"Newspaper," came the Judge's voice.

"Can I subscribe?" Tuttle said in his distinctively coarse
voice, punctuating the question with a sound that resembled a
cough more than a laugh.

"She can take notes for me anytime."

Angus MacGregor. She could picture his hawk-nosed face
creased in a sharp smile.

"Hold on, boys," the Judge cautioned. "Let me stop you
before you get out of line. I should tell you I intend to ask the
little lady to be my wife."

A series of exclamations echoed from the other side of the door. Vanessa hardly noticed as she backed quickly away and headed for the kitchen, more determined than ever that tonight was the night.

Pulling on rubber gloves, she began by collecting every cup, glass, and utensil scattered about the kitchen and loading them in the dishwasher. Then she fetched the silver polish and started on the coffee service. She'd nearly finished when a woman walked in.

"Excuse me, ma'am. Could I trouble ya for some water?"

As Vanessa turned she saw it was no woman, but a girl wearing a clinging red dress as gaudy as her makeup . . . and black spike heels that wobbled dreadfully as she took a few tentative steps.

"Of course," Vanessa answered. "But would you mind helping yourself? As you see, my hands are full of silver polish at the moment. There's a glass in the cabinet to the right of the sink."

As the girl filled the glass with water Vanessa studied her. The light brown hair was swept up in a mature, hairsprayed twist, the rouge meant to cover a sprinkling of youthful freckles. She couldn't have been more than sixteen. Taking a long drink, she dabbed at the corners of her mouth with brightly painted fingertips.

Picking up the polishing cloth, Vanessa began buffing the silver bowl. "Who are you?" she asked.

"Darlene Potter. Hey, thanks for the water. It was a long, dry ride from Shine Valley."

"Is that where you live?"

"That's where I *used* to live. As soon as the meetin's over, I'm movin' to Parkersburg with Mr. Stevenson."

Vanessa looked up. There was a glow of excitement about the girl's face.

"You're moving to Parkersburg?"

"Yes, ma'am! Mr. Stevenson's going to fix it so I live in a big house, and have plenty to eat, and wear store-bought clothes!"

"It sounds very nice, but . . ."

"But what?"

"Well," Vanessa began, hesitating as she chose her words. "I was just wondering what you have to do in return."

Darlene's expression dimmed. "Be friendly. That's all."

"Be friendly," Vanessa repeated gently. "With men, you mean?"

The girl shrugged. "It'd happen anyway down in Shine Valley. Might as well get something out of it."

"Those are not your only choices, Darlene."

"They're not?"

"No. You could go away, get a job."

"I ain't got no money to go away, and I ain't got no schoolin' to get a job."

"All right, then, you could go back home."

"Home!" Darlene stared with disbelief. "Beggin' your pardon, ma'am, but I reckon you ain't seen Shine Valley."

"No, but is it really so bad?" Vanessa questioned, her gaze narrowing to the girl's hazel eyes. "So bad you'd rather let the Big Boys drag you down this way?"

A sudden proud look came over the young face. "Nobody's draggin' me down. I'm steppin' up. All the girls in Shine Valley want the chance to go with the Big Boys, and I got picked!"

Vanessa released a heavy breath. Generations of brainwashing couldn't be undone in the space of a conversation. Besides, this was none of her business.

"I'm sorry, Darlene. I didn't mean to insult you."

She broke into an easy smile. "Hey, that's okay. You never been to Shine Valley, right? You didn't know."

At that moment one of the mountain men appeared in the doorway.

"Darlene?" he rumbled. "Get on out here, girl."

Setting the glass on the counter, she turned and gave Vanessa a bright look of cheer. "Well," she piped in a childlike tone, "wish me luck."

Vanessa mustered a smile. "Good luck, Darlene," she said, and watched the girl do her best to walk gracefully from the room on the high, wobbling heels. When she reached the doorway, the waiting man took her firmly in hand and out of view.

Telling herself to forget about the girl, Vanessa went back to her chores, though she couldn't quite swallow down the sour taste in her mouth. When the silver was sparkling, she scrubbed the counters and sinks, collected Darlene's glass, and turned on the dishwasher. With a last scrutinizing look about the kitchen, she crossed the room and flipped off the light switch before removing the rubber gloves and tucking them in the pockets of her skirt.

She touched nothing on her way upstairs.

The meeting broke up after ten o'clock. Having changed into black tights and turtleneck, Vanessa stood in the dark by her bedroom window, watching as limousines appeared in the drive below, listening as the sound of voices rose from the foyer. She was still observing when Cal Stevenson led Darlene Potter to the backseat of a long, white Cadillac.

Turning from the window with a grimace, Vanessa crossed to the bed and crawled beneath the covers. A quarter of an hour later, the expected knock sounded on her door.

"Vanessa?" the Judge called.

He knocked once more. She lay silently in the darkness. Despite the fact that she must obviously be sleeping, the old goat tried the knob anyway. She rolled her eyes to the ceiling, waiting impatiently until she heard retreating footsteps.

Except for the sheets, the room and adjoining bath were clean. Swinging her legs over the side of the bed, she slipped stockinged feet into soft-soled boots. Next she tucked her hair under the knit cap and finally pulled on leather driving gloves. Carefully stripping the bed, she bundled the linens in her duffel bag, zipped it up, and sat down to wait.

It was just past eleven when the hall light went out. She made herself sit still until midnight.

Slipping into her jacket, she shouldered the bag, picked up the cases, and crept to the door—unable to avoid a slight creak as she pulled it open. The hallway was deserted, though she could see at the end that muted light still showed beneath the double doors to the Judge's chamber. He'd probably fallen asleep in front of the television.

Locking the bedroom door behind her, she proceeded noiselessly down the stairs and kept her eyes and ears sharp for signs of Kyle. She assumed he was in his rooms in the other wing, but she didn't want to go anywhere near to make sure.

The downstairs was silent and dark, but for the moonlight filtering through the windows. She went out by way of the kitchen and moved purposefully along the rear of the house to the utility box. The night was cold and clear, her breath emerging in frosty clouds. She would have wished for less of a moon.

Reaching into her jacket pocket, she withdrew the penlight and wire cutters, opened the utility box, and swiftly clipped the phone lines. Then she moved like a fleet shadow across the moonlit grounds to the garage. Producing the purloined set of keys, she let herself in the side door.

The cavernous structure was freezing cold and black as pitch. Once again flipping on the penlight, she made her way to the Vette, stashed her bags in the back, and reached inside her jacket for the tire gauge. It took just under twenty minutes to flatten the rear tires of the other vehicles.

Settling into the Vette, she placed the key in the ignition, reached for the remote to the garage door, and . . .

Finger on the button, she paused. She was home free now. Even if Kyle and the Judge walked in this second, there would be little they could do to stop her.

Releasing a frustrated breath, she peered into the impenetrable darkness. She shouldn't be thinking what she was thinking, but ever since she watched Darlene stumble away in those ridiculous high heels, the idea had been nagging at the back of her mind.

There was proof of the Big Boys' corruption . . . tangible evidence that they bought and sold young girls the same as moonshine whiskey. And she knew where that evidence was. *She couldn't go back. She was crazy if she went back!* Yet with each passing second the impulse grew stronger.

"Dammit," she muttered finally, and climbing out of the Vette, ran swiftly back to the house.

Hesitating inside the kitchen door, she confirmed that the house remained quiet and slipped down the hall to the Judge's study. Though he'd been gone for hours, the place still reeked of his cigars. Creeping quietly across the hardwood floor, she quickly removed the file from the bottom cabinet and was preparing to leave when the staircase lights came on. Seconds after that she heard footsteps. Hugging the file close, she darted behind the drapes at the nearest window and scarcely gained the meager cover before the Judge walked in and flipped on the Tiffany lamp.

Vanessa held her breath as her ears strained to determine what he was doing. He stopped at the meeting table. Carefully turning her head behind the heavy drape, she saw through a two-inch gap at the end that he was dressed in his smoking jacket and had opened his cigar box. As she barely dared to breathe he went about the business of selecting a smoke and trimming the tip.

This was what she deserved for getting involved. *Get your damn cigar and get out,* she thought fervently, her heart sinking when Kyle stomped in after his father.

"Let me put it *this* way," he barked. "I won't *let* you do it."

The Judge turned and leaned back against the mahogany table. "Sounds like you're entertaining delusions of grandeur, Kyle. You're my son, not my keeper. Besides, it's not really Vanessa that's got you in such a stew. It's Molly Faber."

Eyes straining, Vanessa watched Kyle's hands clench into fists.

"Against my advice you bought up every available parcel of that damn mountain," the Judge went on. "And now, without Faber's acreage, it's not worth a plug nickel. A heliport on Black Top Mountain. I always knew it was a fool idea."

"It's not a fool idea," Kyle answered rigidly. "The Boys pioneered railways and highways. The next logical step is flight. A heliport would open a whole new age for these mountains. It would make millions, and you know it."

The Judge snorted. "Pipe dreams, Kyle. Just like always. You're always grabbing for glory and falling short."

"Maybe if I'd had a little support along the way—"

"Support!" the Judge boomed. "Who paid off all those reckless-driving and speeding tickets? Who bought your way out of a dishonorable expulsion from the academy? You've been nothing but a disappointment since you were old enough to spit!"

"And what of you, old man?" Kyle blazed. "Do you think you're such a gift? The high-and-mighty Judge. I've known what you were ever since I first caught you with that whore from Shine Valley! But this time you're going too far. If you have to take Vanessa Blair to bed, then take her to bed! But for God's sake, don't marry her! Can't you see her for what she is? A gold digger! And I'm not about to share what's coming to me with her!''

"You'd best take care you don't get cut out of my will altogether, boy!'' came the loud reply.

"So, there it is again!'' Kyle spat. "You've been holding that will over my head my entire life!''

"Only way to keep you in line!''

"You think that keeps me in line, old man? Well, here's a news-flash for you! I've already *had* Miss Prim-and-Proper Blair!''

"You're a liar!''

"Any way I wanted!'' Kyle bellowed. "And she begged for more!''

"You're a damn liar!'' the Judge thundered once more, and lunged out of view.

Vanessa strained to see past the edge of the drape as the sounds of a scuffle ensued. When the men next came into view, Kyle had his father by the lapels of the smoking jacket. The Judge seemed unable to do anything to prevent it as his son threw him backward across the tabletop and fell upon him.

Kyle's arm rose, and just as she caught sight of the marble-headed gavel, he brought it smashing into the Judge's face—and then again!—the Judge's head jerking with the first blow, morbidly still after the second. Vanessa clapped a hard hand over her mouth as it opened to scream, watching with shocked eyes as Kyle backed off the table and dropped the gavel to the floor.

"You pushed me too far, old man," she heard him say. "Too far and too long."

Her gaze darted to the Judge. She could see blood now, streaming down the side of his face, streaking into the snow-white hair. Her breath came and went in frantic gasps through her nostrils.

Oh, God. Oh, God. Oh, God, she thought over and over again—the chant more an expression of horror than a prayer. She failed to notice until it was too late that the forgotten file folder was slipping from her grasp. In a matter of seconds it was sliding down her body, across the toes of her boots, out from under the drape with a faint rustle that might as well have been a gunshot.

Kyle's head swiveled. She sensed more than saw that his eyes narrowed on her hiding place. He started slowly toward the window, bending to pick up the file when he came to it, then tossing it nonchalantly to the floor behind him. With contrasting swiftness he lunged for the drapes and ripped them aside.

"Well, well." He sneered. "What have we here?"

When she tried to dart past, Kyle grabbed her by the arms and spun her around. Hauling back, she attempted to drive a knee into his groin. But before she could connect, he grabbed her leg and yanked her off her feet. For a horrifying instant she was in the air. Then she crashed, the back of her head hitting the hardwood floor with a deafening bang. Everything went black.

When she came to minutes later, Kyle had her jacket open and his hands under her sweater. She lurched up, arm swinging, gloved fist striking him hard across the cheek. A split second later his hand was around her throat, forcing her down, threatening to crush her windpipe as he straddled her hips and pinned them to the floor.

She pulled futilely at his iron grip as he grinned down at her, black eyes glittering.

"Sweet Vanessa," he muttered, his free hand moving familiarly over her breast. "You couldn't have picked a better time."

She tried to slap his roving hand. His hold on her throat tightened, cutting off all but a trickle of air.

"What were you doing down here, huh?" he questioned breathlessly. "Ripping us off? I believe you were. I believe the Judge came in at the wrong time, and you killed him."

Kyle started unbuckling his belt. Vanessa's bulging eyes locked with his, and she saw once and for all what lay behind those glittering black eyes. Evil without conscience, without limit. Evil that stopped at nothing. He'd just killed his own father, and as soon as he finished raping her, she would meet the same fate.

Terror gave her strength. Vanessa twisted in his grasp, her gaze flying across the floor, lighting on the gavel. She flailed an arm in its direction, her fingertips falling centimeters short. Planting her boots on the floor, she put all her power into a lunge that moved their two bodies scarce inches across the floor. But it was enough. Her hand closed about the handle, and as Kyle reached for his pants zipper she swung.

The marble smacked him just above his right brow, a glancing blow that wrenched the gavel out of her hand to fall clattering across the floor. And suddenly the crushing pressure around her throat was gone. Kyle rolled off, catching himself with one hand when he would have fallen, his other rising to his temple.

Vanessa started scrambling backward on her bottom, pushing herself with legs she could barely feel as scalding breaths tore up and down her aching windpipe. She was several yards away when she gained her footing only to fall again as she stumbled over the sheaf of papers that had lured her into a web of death.

She glanced over her shoulder as Kyle brought his hand away from his head and looked at it. It was covered with blood. With a rasping groan she grabbed the file and ran.

Kyle stared at his bloody fingers. Stunned into immobility, he sat there on the floor, distantly aware that Vanessa Blair was leaving and that he should do something about it. He shook his head, and though it hurt like hell, his vision gradually cleared.

"Damn," he muttered, pushing to his feet and stumbling out of the study. By the time he reached the front door and burst into the cold mountain night, he was back in full stride. He rounded the corner just as she came roaring down the drive in the Vette.

"I'll get you, bitch!" he yelled, brandishing a fist as she passed. Pouring every bit of speed he had into his legs, he raced to the garage, searched in his pocket for keys, and jumped into the Mercedes. Shifting into drive, he floored the accelerator. The car dragged its rear end ten clattering yards before he slammed on the brakes. The tires were flat.

"Damn!" he exploded.

Leaving the Mercedes heedlessly running, he hurried back to

the garage, checked the Lincoln . . . darted to the MG. She'd disabled the other cars as well. He took off for the house. Matthews and his deputies could catch up to her. She wasn't out of reach yet!

Heaving for breath, Kyle galloped into the foyer, grabbed the phone, and dialed. Nothing.

"Come on, come on," he muttered, angrily punching the button and dialing again. Still nothing.

It took a few seconds for the realization to dawn.

When it did, Kyle threw back his head and howled, his cry of rage blasting through the halls of the mansion, where neither the deaf nor the dead paid it any heed.

The sky was pink, the edge of the sun peeking over the mountaintops, when the ambulance drove away with the body of District Court Judge Ray Skinner.

Inside, Kyle paced the floor of the kitchen, slapping away Tibbs's hand when the old man offered a bandage for his temple.

"How many times do we have to go over this?" Kyle demanded, his eyes flashing to the chief of police. "She was dressed in black like a cat burglar. Maybe she was after the cash box. I don't know. But Dad must have caught her in the act. I came downstairs just as she was leaving, tried to stop her, and got bashed in the head for my trouble. That's it! Now, instead of asking the same thing over and over, why don't you get your butt out of here and catch her?"

John Matthews tipped his cap back on his head. "You estimate it took you about an hour to get to a phone, Kyle. That means that if she was traveling fast—and I imagine she was—she had about a sixty-mile head start in any direction you want to pick. I've put out an APB, notified the state boys in Tennessee and Virginia, as well as North Carolina. There's nothing more I can do."

"Nothing *more*? I don't see that you've done a blasted thing since you got here! What the hell do we pay you for?"

"Me and the boys have combed the house, Kyle—searched high and low for anything that might give us a clue as to where she's gone . . . who she is. There's nothing. Not a hair, not a fingerprint. It's as if she was never here."

"She was here, all right. I've got a dead father to prove it."

Matthews studied the younger man's angry face. Kyle Skinner had always had a temper, but he'd never seen him quite this worked up.

"Can you describe her, Kyle?"

"I've already told you what she looks like!"

"In detail, I mean. They've got one of those police artists over in Boone. If you really want to try and nail her—"

"Try?" Kyle interrupted with a snort. "Trying has nothing to do with anything."

Moving restlessly to the window, he looked out across the dawn-lit grounds, his mind re-creating the image of the Vette's taillights disappearing into the darkness.

"I *will* nail her, Matthews," he added in a tone of deadly earnest. "One way or another. Count on it."

Later that day Vanessa Blair was officially charged with grand theft auto, assault with a deadly weapon, and—at the top of the list—murder in the first degree.

=TWO=

June 22, 1991
Black Top Mountain

Richard had just stepped out of the shower when the phone rang. Of course no one in his odd household could be relied upon to be up at this early hour, much less do anything so responsible as answer a phone. Grabbing a towel, he trotted across the floor.

Damn, it was cold. It might be June, but the sun was barely up, and mountain mornings continued to be chilly.

"How's the hillbilly?" the voice at the other end said.

A born-and-bred city slicker, Bill Honeycutt had given him a hard time ever since he bought the old ski lodge in the Blue Ridge and left Charlotte behind.

"Extremely cool and comfortable," Richard returned. "I'll bet you poor folks are sweltering down there in the Piedmont."

"Summer has dawned. That's for sure."

"How are you, Bill?"

"Good. Real good."

"What's up?"

"Two things. First, I couldn't resist calling when I saw the morning paper. Your picture is all over the front page of the business section."

"What is it this time?"

"That deal you made with the Japanese. Here, I'll read part of it: 'Inventor extraordinaire, Richard Adams, has done it again. In an age when Japanese technology has come to be revered, one of Japan's foremost computer manufacturers has turned to an American and labeled the new Adams circuit as

23

revolutionizing. One of Charlotte's most famous native sons, Adams first made national news at the age of seventeen with a high-school science project that drew the attention of the National Aeronautics and Space—''

"Okay, okay."

"But that's not all! The society columnist ran a sidebar with another picture. 'Thirty-eight-year-old millionaire Richard Adams, long considered one of the South's most eligible bachelors, recently attended a fund-raiser for the North Carolina Museum of Art in Raleigh, causing quite a stir when he showed up with psychiatrist Sheryl Fontaine on his arm. That's the latest of several sightings in the past months. Could wedding bells be on the horizon for the lovely doctor and the elusive scientist?'"

"Oh, man."

Bill laughed. "How about it, Richard? The columnist and I were just wondering."

Richard ran the towel over his wet hair. "Give me a break, Bill. Sheryl and I have been friends since college. We're just good friends. You know that."

"Yeah. But does *she*?"

Richard frowned into the phone.

"I can see your expression right now," Bill added. "Okay. I'll let you off the hook."

"Thanks very much."

"Anyway, I'm getting ready to give you a chance to roast *me* for a change."

"Oh?" Richard supplied with a grin. "I can hardly wait."

"There happens to be a new lady in *my* life. In fact, I'm thinking of asking her to marry me."

Richard's grin faded. Bill's wife had died years ago. Even so, it was a shock to imagine him with anyone but Ann.

"Richard?"

"Yeah? Sorry, Bill. You kind of took me by surprise."

"I was taken by surprise, too. I never expected to feel this way, but from the moment she moved into the house—"

"You're *living together*?"

"It's not like that, Richard. She's my personal secretary, Valerie Blake."

"Personal, huh?"

"Like I said, it's not like that. I wish it were."

"And . . ." Richard prodded.

"And what?"

"Is she tall, short? Blond, brunette? Fat, thin? What?"

Bill chuckled. "She's a little taller than average, I guess. Slim, with dark hair and the palest blue eyes you've ever seen."

Richard whistled.

"She's a beauty, all right, and smart! She has the most amazing ability to anticipate me. I can't think of a request before it's been answered, a task before it's been accomplished. And she does it all with a kind of soft-spoken charm that lights up a room. I hadn't realized how empty the house had become until she walked into it. She's brought me back to life, Richard."

"Then I'm glad. When do I get to meet the lovely lady?"

"When are you coming to Charlotte?"

"As a matter of fact, I need to drive down on business in a couple of weeks. How about if I drop by?"

"Great. I . . . well, I suppose there's something I should mention up front. You see, Valerie's a good deal younger than I."

A note of warning sounded in Richard's mind. "How much younger?"

"To be frank, she's about half my age."

Richard cocked his jaw as his thoughts clicked away. At the age of sixty-two, Bill was a distinguished-looking man with a constant suntan from time spent on the golf course. Still, it was tough to picture him with a thirty-year-old beauty, and Richard found himself considering the prominence and wealth Bill had achieved as one of Charlotte's leading attorneys. He was a catch. No doubt about it. Just the kind of target a pretty young thing might set her sights on.

"So, how long have the two of you been seeing each other?"

"I can't really say we're *seeing* each other. I put an ad in the paper sometime back. A month ago Valerie appeared on my doorstep. I hired her immediately."

"Where's she from?"

"Someplace in Virginia."

"Someplace?"

"Some little town. I can't remember the name right now. Listen, Richard, Do me a favor, okay? When you come by the house, make a point of *not* noticing the age difference. I think she's uncomfortable about what people might think."

Richard reached for his appointment calendar. "Let's firm up a date," he replied evasively. "I arrive the fifteenth. How about supper at your place the next evening?"

Hanging up the phone, Richard walked thoughtfully into the bathroom and lathered up for a shave. Bill Honeycutt had been his father's best friend as well as his law partner. Richard had grown up regarding "Uncle Bill" as family, and still did, especially now that his parents were gone. He'd always considered the man to be exceptionally wise, but even wise men could be foolish sometimes.

Valerie Blake. The razor to his cheek, Richard drew a smooth stroke. Maybe she was just what Bill described— beautiful and charming, his last chance for true happiness.

Rinsing the razor, Richard peered into the mirror and tried to imagine a pretty face with the palest blue eyes he'd ever seen—the face of a woman from "someplace" who "appeared" on a doorstep and turned a man's life upside down in a matter of weeks.

Miss Blake was something special, all right.

The straight blade flashed as he put it to his throat. Exactly what kind of special, he intended to find out.

Afternoon sun filtered through the pines, glistening on the mountain stream and the back of the naked man standing at its edge. At forty-two, Kyle might be showing some silver in his ebony hair, but he had the toned body of a man years younger— due, she imagined, to his obsessive workouts in his downstairs gym.

It was a habit he picked up at the academy, he'd once said. Mavis had known better than to pursue the subject. There had been some sort of scandal about his leaving the exclusive school just before he was to graduate, something that forever altered his plans to become an Air Force officer and pilot. Not that she'd ever been able to picture Kyle in the military. She couldn't imagine anyone giving him orders—except maybe the

Judge, whose commands had been met with fiery belligerence more often than not.

Kyle had gone on to get his private license and maintained a sweet little Cessna at an airstrip near Boone. Still, sometimes when he was drunk, he complained about the lost opportunity to "get jets."

Her eyes moved appreciatively over his muscular physique. Whether he admitted it or not, Kyle had come away from the academy with *something*. Mavis took a leisurely drag off her cigarette.

"Councilman Skinner," she purred. "My, my. If the town council could only see you now, not to mention Jeanette and the girls."

"Shut up, Mavis," he said without turning.

She lay back against the mossy slope, relishing the cool cushion against her bare skin and the warmth of satisfaction coursing through her veins. Kyle Skinner might be the most heartless bastard she'd ever known, but he was one hell of a lover—if undeniably rough at times. In a town the size of Devil's Rock, she was lucky to have him.

Her eyelids drifted along with her thoughts. Men . . . She'd known quite a few before hitting town and hooking up with Harry Brewer, and she'd known quite a few since. Poor Harry, God rest his soul. He'd been sweet and trusting, and had smelled of the must of the feed store. Her lips curved in a smile. On the other hand Lloyd, the trucker, smelled of gasoline; Curt, the pool lifeguard, of suntan oil; Kyle, the councilman, of expensive cologne.

Then there was Richard Adams, whose clean scent reminded her of a rainy day in the pines. Fabulously wealthy, incredibly handsome, and single to boot, he'd appeared on the scene a couple of years back, having bought up the top of Black Top Mountain, lock, stock, and barrel. The talk was he paid Molly Faber a fortune.

Kyle had never gotten over it. He'd had plans for the Black Top, which unlike the rugged peaks surrounding it for miles "was sheared," he said, "as if to specification in near-perfect flatness." Following the building of the heliport would come the renovation of the sprawling lodge, and then the development of shops, restaurants, theaters . . .

The picture he painted was such a vivid one that Mavis herself had invested in preliminary land purchases meant to pave the way. In fact the very glade in which she currently lolled was part of the initial parcel. Cool and secluded, it had become a favorite summer rendezvous point, but was good for little else. As Kyle often pointed out, until they got hold of the top of the mountain, the land they owned was nothing but dirt.

"*Until,*" he always said. Kyle still hadn't given up on his dream, though Richard had proved just as stubborn in blocking it. With a subtlety and patience Mavis had never seen in Kyle, he'd courted his adversary—inviting Richard to parties he never attended, tendering offers that were consistently refused. Soon, Mavis knew, Kyle's placating veneer was bound to crack.

But she didn't want to think about Kyle. Now—while the sound of the stream mingled with that of rustling leaves, and the sun dappled the naked length of her body with sensual patches of warmth—she preferred to dwell on Richard.

Mavis sighed as his image took shape in her mind. He was about her age, tall and broad-shouldered, with the sun in his hair and a smile that made her heart race. She remembered the first time she set eyes on him. She was late for a hair appointment and had been hurrying along the sidewalk toward the salon when he came out of Dell's Sporting Goods.

"Mornin'," he offered, and she'd stopped in her tracks.

"Good Lord!" she'd exclaimed, her eyes racing over him. "Where did *you* come from?"

When he smiled, her pulse had started fluttering like that of a young girl with a first crush.

Since that meeting they'd developed a comradely friendship, although months could pass without their seeing each other. Hell, the man took off across the country the way somebody else might take an afternoon jaunt, and when he was home, he tended to seclude himself atop the mountain with a household staff of misfits. She ran into him most often when he came to town for hiking or ski supplies. Sometimes they'd end up having lunch together, and it wasn't unheard of for her to drop in unannounced at the lodge and demand that he offer her a drink. Half the time he was there; half the time his cross old housekeeper, Hilda, turned her away.

Taking a last puff, Mavis reached out and stubbed her cigarette into the moss. She and Richard were friends, all right, and she knew he liked her. But she wanted more than to be liked. She wanted to be possessed. She *ached* to arouse his passion, to feel his touch. But despite her best efforts, she'd been unable to seduce him beyond friendship. So far.

The crunching of nearby pine needles broke her reverie. Mavis opened lazy eyes as Kyle came to stand at her feet.

"Hear that?" he demanded.

"What?"

"Plane."

Sure enough, she heard the distant noise of a motor, though it was so far away it seemed more like the buzz of honeybees. She shielded her eyes and looked up. Scant seconds later the sound reached a crescendo as the small plane flashed overhead, its echo swiftly falling once more to a buzz, and then silence, as it passed out of view toward the north. She settled back against the bank, her gaze shifting to Kyle.

"But for Adams," he said in a grim tone, "that could be a helluva lot more than a damn pleasure craft. It could be one of our own choppers."

"*Our own?* How very flattering." Mavis smiled, but Kyle didn't seem to notice as he continued to stare into the sky.

"Mountain rescues, hospital runs," he muttered absently. "There's no end to the emergency relief we could provide."

"Emergency relief!" Mavis chuckled lightly. "Nice talk for a councilman, Kyle. But that's not what your dream is about, and we both know it."

He cast her a cutting look. "How the hell do *you* know what I dream about? Get dressed. I've gotta get back to town."

A quarter of an hour later she was following his fast lead down the trail to the flatland where the car was parked. As she climbed into the passenger seat of the Mercedes, Mavis thought of the times the leather seats had seen the two of them entwined—wild, crazy, drunken nights when there had been no place to go but Sky Road Point, no bed but the backseat of a car.

She looked Kyle's way with the beginnings of a smile that quickly died. The lines of his face were hard as rock, his brooding gaze turned sharply up the mountain. Though the forest hid the turreted shape of the lodge two thousand feet above them, she knew he was seeing the interloper planted on Black Top Mountain, the peak he himself had claimed.

"Damn unwanted, uninvited, do-gooding carpetbagger," Kyle muttered in the quietest of tones, and threw the Mercedes in gear, sending dirt and gravel flying.

Thrown back against the seat, Mavis grabbed for the door handle to steady herself and said nothing.

Someday, she mused with shivering premonition, the two mountain rams were going to lock horns, and only one would walk away.

July 16
Charlotte

The elevator began its purring descent from the forty-second floor. Richard loosened his tie and shrugged out of his jacket. The business meeting had taken all day, with sandwiches shipped in at lunchtime. He'd gotten the feeling his financial advisers were afraid to let him out, lest he bolt like an uncaged animal.

God, he hated all that stuff about corporate strategies and financial portfolios, investments and shelters, on and on. They knew he hated it, too. That's why when he occasionally agreed to come to town, they gathered at his heels like a pack of hounds.

The elevator doors opened with a soft *whoosh*. The elegant lobby was deserted, most people having left the bank tower an hour ago. Richard walked out front, where his pickup was parked in a space reserved for VIPs. It looked about as out of place as he felt.

Tossing his jacket in the passenger seat, he rolled down the windows and cruised onto Tryon Street, where tower after tower speared the sky, shining in the late-afternoon sun. Charlotte had long been one of the biggest banking centers on the East Coast; in the few years he'd been gone, it had started looking like one. He drove away from downtown thinking that his hometown had changed. But then, so had he. At the moment he felt, not like himself, but a collection of faceless corporations. Turning onto Kings Drive, he headed into the illustrious Myers Park section.

It was after six, but the pavement still radiated heat. Sunlight washed through the trees, aromas of new-mown grass and flowers filled the air, and stately homes greeted him with familiar faces. Richard's spirits began to lift. Flipping on the radio, he found some beach music and turned up the volume. Settling back, he let the wind rip through his hair and drew a contented breath. Now *this* was summertime in Charlotte.

He was smiling by the time he merged onto Queens Road West, where mansions faced each other through twin arches of gigantic water oaks. Newcomers stared in awe the first time they drove beneath those leafy canopies. Slowing the truck, Richard turned in the well-remembered drive and killed the engine. Bill's house looked just the same, just as grand, fronted by two levels of verandas, surrounded by gardens. As a kid he'd spent nearly as much time here as at his own childhood home mere blocks away. He got out and scaled the terraced walk to the front door.

"Mamie!" he exclaimed, capturing the ancient housekeeper in a hug before she could skitter away.

"Lord have mercy! Here you are, bigger than ever, and still no more than a spoonful of manners! Let me loose!"

"Only if you take me to Bill," he replied with a laugh.

"Well, I'll be glad if you can pry him away from that dining-room window," the black woman muttered as she led the way. "A grown man standing 'round and moonin' like a schoolboy." With a flick of her hand toward the open door to the dining room, she continued along the hall, shaking her silver head as she went.

Richard paused at the doorway and saw what Mamie was talking about. Bill was propped by the window, shoulders slumping, the picture of dejection. When he became aware of Richard's presence, he hurried across the room, greeting him with an exuberant handshake and smile. But his expression was strained, and there were circles under his eyes.

"So," Richard said after a few minutes. "Where's this mysterious lady of yours?"

Bill moved restlessly back to the window overlooking the garden. Richard followed. She was there among the roses, close enough so he could tell Bill hadn't been exaggerating about her beauty. Slim and long-limbed, she was dressed in green and almost blended into the foliage, but for the mass of dark, waving hair that shone like blue fire in the sun. It wasn't so much her physical attributes that held his eye, however, but her stance. Chin lifted, she presented a perfect profile as she stared into the distance, so still that she gave the impression her thoughts were miles away. Realizing with a start that he was staring, Richard turned.

"What's the story? I get the feeling all is not happy on the home front." Bill continued to peer bleakly out the window.

"Two nights ago I asked her to marry me," he said.

"That's great."

"Not so great. All she'd agree to do is think about it. She's still thinking. It's driving me crazy."

"Come on, Bill. Women take time—"

"It isn't just that." Bill's voice fell as he added, "She won't let me touch her. At first there were a few kisses, but now . . . nothing. No contact whatsoever. And I know as surely as I'm standing here that if I push her, I'll lose her."

Richard looked once more into the garden. Valerie Blake seemed not to have moved a muscle. There was something eerie about the way she stood there like that—eerie . . . and mesmerizing.

"Sounds like the lady has a mind of her own," he murmured.

"I never realized how much. Have a drink with me, Richard. I need something to take the edge off." They retired to the study.

"It's amazing, really," Bill went on as he poured a couple of brandies. "Her work and manner are impeccable. She smiles and chats as gracefully as always, but then she's gone. Out of sight, out of reach. She's avoiding me, I know, but she does it with such aplomb that I can't seem to catch her at it."

Taking the brandy, Richard sank into a leather chair. "I can't tell you what to do, Bill, but if it were me, I'd confront her."

And so the secluded conversation about Valerie Blake went on. Richard asked questions; Bill answered, but grew notice-ably flustered as it became apparent just how little he knew about the woman who'd infiltrated his home, his life, and his heart.

"Damn, Richard!" he exclaimed at one point. "I'm one of the best criminal law attorneys in town. Why don't I know more than I do?"

By the time they came out of the study a half hour later, Richard was more intrigued by the woman than when he went in.

It was well past seven. Still, the soft light of dusk filtered down the hallway where Mamie was lighting the lamps.

"Have you seen Miss Blake?" Bill asked.

"I ain't studyin' Miss Blake," she replied. "I got my hands full with supper and everything else without tendin' to Miss Blake." With that Mamie bustled off toward the kitchen.

Bill shrugged. "Shall we have a look in the garden?"

But Valerie Blake wasn't in the garden. Nor was she in any of the rooms on the sprawling main floor.

"Probably in her room freshening up," Bill commented, and climbing the stairs, he tapped at a door on the second floor.

There was no answer. Waiting below, Richard peered up the graceful, spiraling staircase. With each passing second the feeling that something was wrong became more acute. Bill opened the door and disappeared inside the room. A moment later he was back at the head of the staircase. Even in the dim light Richard could tell his face had turned ashen.

"She's gone," he muttered.

Richard took the steps two at a time. The bedroom was impeccably neat, the bathroom spotless. He opened the closet door. Empty.

"There's nothing of hers left here," Bill mumbled. "Nothing."

A further search of the house and grounds revealed that Bill's Mercedes convertible was also missing.

"I gave her a key," he admitted. "She was always doing errands."

"Call the police," Richard advised.

"No! Not yet. Maybe . . ." Bill rubbed his forehead. "It's only been an hour or so. Maybe she'll be back."

"Bill," Richard murmured, placing a comforting hand on his friend's shoulder. "Think about it. All her things are gone. Do you really believe she's coming back?"

Despite Richard's logic, Bill held off until eleven o'clock before allowing the police to be called in.

"Can you tell us about the Mercedes, Mr. Honeycutt?" one of the officers asked.

"You've got the tag and serial numbers. What else can I tell you? It was white. Brand new. Loaded with everything."

"Quite a valuable piece of merchandise. Obviously we're looking at grand larceny. Smooth job, too. Any idea where this Blake woman might have headed?"

"No," Bill replied in a hollow tone.

Shortly after midnight Richard left the mansion on Queens Road West feeling as though he were about to explode. He hated the pain Bill was feeling. But maybe more than that he hated the way Valerie Blake had taken the both of them—slick as a whistle, smooth as glass—like a pair of prize turkeys at a county fair.

July 17, 2:00 P.M.
Salisbury

It was hot as blazes in the garage, and the damn paint gun didn't help any. Taking a break, Jake Isley stepped back from the Mercedes convertible, which was now half-white, half-red. Passing a sleeve across his brow, he cast a furtive look in her direction.

She was a looker, all right, blond and long-legged, all decked out in a fancy dress and high heels. But there was something weird about her—showing up out of the blue, announcing she'd grown tired of her car. She'd wait for the job, she said.

He'd have thought a classy dame like that would have better things to do. But she didn't seem to—just sat there on the bench under the trees, staring off into space. Weird.

An hour later when she tipped him a hundred and smiled, Jake forgot all thoughts of weirdness.

Tucking the money in his pocket, he watched her drive away and thought of how he'd dream about her for months to come—a long-legged blonde in a red convertible, disappearing toward the sun while her hair trailed in the wind.

4:00 P.M.

Richard walked into Bill's study, releasing a heavy breath as he took in the scene. Empty bottles sat on the table, and Bill hadn't changed clothes. It looked like he'd been up all night drinking.

"You're not doing yourself any good, you know," Richard said, taking a seat across the table.

Bill smiled wearily. "I know. I've already been to raging drunk and back again. Don't worry. The binge is over."

"Glad to hear it. Listen, Bill. My business is done, and I'm heading back to the mountains. Why don't you come with me? A change of scene can't do any harm."

"Thanks, but no. I want to stay here. Who knows? Maybe . . ."

His voice trailed off, and Richard looked away, unable to bear the look of hope that climbed to his face.

"You know what the worst part is?" Bill asked after a moment. "I don't even give a damn about the car."

Feelings from the previous night swamped Richard anew— frustration, resentment, even a taste for revenge. "They'll find her, Bill," he promised grimly. "Sooner or later they'll find her."

But he was wrong. Months passed. A year went by. And neither Valerie Blake nor the Mercedes convertible in which she disappeared was seen again.

=THREE=

October 23, 1992

The mountain morning was clear and crisp, sunlight flooding the roadside vista of rolling hills and fall colors. Richard stretched an arm along the back of the car seat, his gaze sweeping appreciatively over the driver. Mavis Brewer was a good-looking woman with shiny chestnut hair, big brown eyes, and an hourglass figure. Today she was dressed to kill in a clinging, black sweater dress that bared her legs halfway up the thigh.

"Thanks for offering to take me to the airport," he said.

"My pleasure."

"What was it you wanted to talk to me about?"

She slipped him a smile. "First you have to promise not to scowl."

"Now you've got me curious. What's on your mind?"

Reaching inside her purse, she handed him an envelope. Richard read the contents, a frown gathering on his brow.

"Oh, man," he murmured, stuffing the paper back in the envelope. "Can't he take a hint? How many times does this make?"

"I believe this is number eight. He says it's his last."

"Hallelujah."

Mavis glanced aside. "At least you must admit it's a very attractive offer. Kyle said it's triple the land's worth."

"It wouldn't matter if he offered ten times this much," Richard replied in a weary tone. "I don't want to sell."

"Did you notice he's revised the terms? You wouldn't have to give up the lodge. Just the rest."

"The *rest* is the whole top of the mountain, Mavis. It's a wildlife sanctuary, and has been for nearly four years."

"I know," she said with a sigh. "And I know the sanctuary means a lot to you. But forget the animals for a minute and think of the *people* of the mountains. Helicopter service would open up a whole new world for these parts. It would mean quick rescue for climbers and skiers, emergency service to hospitals. Doesn't any of that strike a chord?"

Richard cocked a brow. "So, now he's turned you into his emissary. What did he think—that you could squeeze a better response out of me?"

"Was he wrong?" Mavis returned, relaxing a bit when she saw a small smile.

"No," Richard answered. "You're a very persuasive go-between."

"Thank you, sir."

"But I can't forget that it's Skinner who's behind the whole thing. And I can't help but think there's bound to be an angle."

"It would mean new jobs," Mavis countered. "New money."

"A lot of it to go in Skinner's pocket, I imagine."

"Would it make a difference if I told you I'm a partner in it?"

Richard looked at her with surprise. "You? Why?"

"Harry left me with a big house, a feed business that runs itself, and nothing to do with my time. Devil's Rock isn't exactly the most exciting place in the world, you know. The idea of something new going on has a definite appeal."

Richard shook his head. "As much as you'd like to see something new in these mountains, I'd like to see them stay the way they are. And what of Hilda and Eric, Miles and Gertrude and the Chef?"

Oh, God, Mavis thought. *Here we go with the misfits.*

"The lodge is their home as well as mine," Richard concluded.

"Like I said, Kyle has cut the lodge out of the proposal. It wouldn't be touched."

"But everything around it would change. The sanctuary would be demolished, the trees mowed down. I'm sorry, Mavis. I just—"

"Don't say another word. How long will you be in Atlanta?"

"Through the weekend."

"Can I at least tell Kyle you're thinking about it?"

"What good would that do?"

"For one thing it would make for a more cheerful weekend."

Richard gave her a long assessing look, his gaze trailing over sooty lashes, a pert nose, generous red lips. The Widow Brewer was undoubtedly the most flamboyant figure in Devil's Rock, and the most incorrigible flirt he'd ever met. But the free-spirited way she had about her was impossible not to like.

"How did you get mixed up with a guy like Skinner?" he asked.

"Oh, he's not so bad."

"He's a small-town big shot who uses his council position to further his own ends. I don't know how he keeps getting elected."

"There's been a Skinner on the council ever since the town became a town. Kyle's dad was district court judge; his grandfather, the mayor; and so on. Besides, Kyle's one of the Big Boys. They swing a lot of weight, you know."

"Then how about the fact that he's a married man?"

Mavis shrugged. "Jeanette only cares about her garden parties. And besides, if it wasn't me, it would be somebody else. Kyle has always played around."

"You could do better, Mavis."

"Could I?" She looked over with dark, serious eyes. "If I thought so," she added, "I'd drop Kyle like a hot potato."

Richard arched a brow, his expression at once scolding and smiling. "Tell him I'll think it over while I'm away," he said, and stuffed the envelope in his breast pocket.

Minutes later they turned up the rutted, rural road to the airport. Pulling over in front of the small terminal, Mavis cut the engine. Richard reached for the door handle.

"Well—" he began.

"Don't be in such a hurry," she objected. Slipping out of her seat belt, Mavis leaned over, caught his jacket lapels, and pulled him to her.

Richard's brows went up as she planted her mouth on his.

Her tongue moved against his lips, seeking entry. Closing his eyes, he leaned back against the headrest and opened up to her, going with the feeling as her practiced mouth drew his tongue into play. His hand rose to cup her jaw; hers strayed down the front of his jacket to his belt.

"I'm going to miss my plane," he mumbled into her mouth.

"I got the impression you were already flying," she replied.

Backing away, he reached down, captured her wandering hand, and raised it to his lips.

"You owe it to yourself to give me a shot, Richard."

He brushed the back of her hand with a kiss and looked up. "You could be right about that," he said.

His brown eyes were warm and shining, glimmering with golden lights. Mavis's gaze moved over him. Though short in the front, his sun-streaked hair grew long in the back. Paired with the dark leather jacket he was wearing, it gave him the look of a rebel, though his perfect features were those of an aristocrat.

"Let's make it soon," she urged.

With a brief, ambiguous smile he got out and retrieved his bags from the backseat, leaning in to say, "Thanks for the ride. I'll talk to you when I get back."

She watched until he passed out of sight in the terminal. He had a swaggering walk. Confident. Sexy. But then everything about the man struck her that way.

His parting remark could have been merely that, but Mavis preferred to think it was more. She knew he'd been looking at her legs, and she knew a hot kiss when she got one. Feminine instinct said things were finally going to click when he returned from Atlanta, and a respondent heat flooded her female core.

Turning off the bumpy airport road, she drove back along the mountain highway with a sensual smile curving her lips.

If she could have Richard Adams, she wouldn't waste a minute telling Kyle exactly where he could stuff his precious choppers.

October 24
Atlanta, Georgia

The chandeliers suspended from the ceiling of The Ritz-Carlton's ballroom were aglow, along with candelabra spaced among a periphery of tables covered in white linen. From the west end of the room came the strains of a minuet, courtesy of a chamber group dressed in traditional black. To the east a platform draped with gold bunting accommodated a microphone for the inevitable speeches. Between these points strolled a good number of the most prominent philanthropists from three states.

Richard adjusted his black tie as he passed a gilded mirror. He didn't mind that the annual affair was designed to gouge their wallets. The Scholarship Foundation was a worthy cause, they always put on a good party, and he liked Atlanta.

What he didn't much care for was the flurry of widows, divorcées, and hopeful mothers—with single daughters in tow—who hovered about any man who happened to show up stag. Since arriving an hour ago, he hadn't had a minute's peace. But it really wasn't so bad. For the most part the ladies were a treat, all decked out in their formal gowns, pretty smiles, and Southern charm. He could think of worse ways to spend an evening.

Another half hour went by. He found it unnecessary to visit the elegant spread of hors d'oeuvres and canapes. Women kept coming over and offering him selections he "really must try." He was sampling a stuffed shrimp from the plate of a Mrs. Henderson when he happened to glance toward the entrance just as a late-arriving couple walked in.

The man, silver-haired with a matching mustache, wore a black tuxedo in striking contrast with the white gown of the lady on his arm. She was nearly as tall as he, and younger, her auburn hair pulled back with a ribbon and cascading halfway down her back.

They moved into the room. Richard's eyes moved with them. Something about the way she carried herself seemed familiar. Did he know her?

"What do you think, Mr. Adams?"

He turned to Mrs. Henderson with a blank look.

"The shrimp!" she exclaimed with a scolding smile. "Isn't it heavenly?"

By the time he responded with due politeness and glanced back, the couple had blended into the crowd.

A short while later the chairman of the foundation took the

platform and made an eloquent plea for support. The crowd applauded. The music resumed.

As the night wore on, Richard spotted the couple from time to time—at the bar, near the bandstand, always surrounded by a circle of which the silver-haired man appeared to be the smiling center of interest. In contrast, the woman seemed to shrink away from such attention, generally standing in somewhat concealing fashion behind her escort, so that Richard found it difficult to get a clear look at her.

He went about the business of writing out a generous check to the foundation and accepting the enthusiastic handshakes of several board members. Through it all his gaze kept returning to the auburn-haired woman across the room. He happened to be looking when she separated from the group surrounding her companion and walked off on her own.

Richard followed at a leisurely pace, greeting a few people along the way as he traversed the ballroom, his eyes targeting her over the heads of the crowd. She was heading for a quiet far corner, where a set of French doors opened onto a terrace.

Backtracking to a relatively deserted corridor behind the serving tables, Richard moseyed in the same direction and was awarded an unobstructed view as she stepped into the doorway and halted. He hung back on the fringe of the crowd and studied the length of her. She was slim, her sleeveless white gown baring slender arms and a long, graceful neck. There was definitely something familiar about her.

His gaze lifted to her profile. A breeze stirred her hair, yet she remained perfectly still, staring into the night as though she longed to become part of it, as though her thoughts were . . .

"Damn," Richard mumbled as it hit him.

Valerie Blake! No! It couldn't be! But yes, it was. The longer he absorbed the sight of her standing there, the more certain he became. Her hair was a different color, but he was looking at the same woman he'd seen a year and a half ago in Bill's rose garden.

Richard was still gaping when she came to life and moved, her face turning in his direction. Frozen to the spot, he watched her gaze sweep toward him . . . and pass him by. Seconds later she was on her way back the way she'd come.

By the end of the night he'd learned that she was calling

herself Veronica Bates, and was personal assistant to her escort, District Attorney John Renfield.

When the couple said their good-byes and left the ballroom, Richard meandered into the hotel lobby, watching from near the concierge station as they passed through expansive glass doors to the front drive. Renfield spoke to the doorman. Moments later a sleek black Jaguar sedan was delivered.

"Good evening, Mr. Adams."

Richard looked around with a start. It was the concierge—Peters or Peterson or something. "Evenin'," he returned absently.

"I understand you're leaving us tomorrow. I certainly hope you've enjoyed your time here at The Ritz-Carlton."

"Yes," Richard murmured, his gaze drifting back to the glass doors as the Jaguar rolled away. "In fact, do me a favor, will you? Extend my reservation. I think I'll stay awhile."

"Hello, handsome."

Richard looked around in surprise. "Sheryl?"

"Yes?" she replied, her smile turning into a chuckle as he gathered her in a quick embrace.

"For crying out loud, this is a surprise. Let me take a look at you." She complied with a slow turn that gave him ample opportunity to survey the petite figure in the classy black dress, the shapely legs set off by matching heels. Her dark hair was cropped short, her dark eyes shining with the light of her smile.

"Beautiful as ever," Richard murmured.

"Gallant as ever," she returned.

"How long has it been? A year?"

Sheryl arched a brow. "Closer to *two*."

"Come on," he complained. "I know we've talked more recently than that."

"Over the phone, yes. But not in person. It seems you became extremely tied up with business soon after the society columns started linking us as a couple."

Richard's face turned warm. "Are you scolding me?"

"Would it make an impact?"

He smiled into the dark eyes. "Coming from you? Always."

Sheryl shook her head and sighed. "You're the most shameless charmer I've ever known. The first time I laid eyes on you in college, I knew I was in trouble."

Richard laughed. "What are you doing here in Atlanta?"

"Psychiatric conference. I'll have you know Dr. Fontaine just delivered an exceedingly well-received paper on agoraphobia."

"I don't doubt it. You always were exceedingly bright."

"Never in your league, Richard. How about you? What are you doing here?"

"The Scholarship Foundation had its annual bash tonight."

"That's right. You're a generous supporter. I should have remembered when I saw the sign at the ballroom."

"Are you staying here at the hotel?"

"Yes. Until tomorrow. My flight's at noon." Sheryl's eyes widened. "I've got an idea. The foundation thing is over, right? Why don't you come back with me to Raleigh? The practice is slow this time of year before the depression of the holidays hits. We could tour the museums, get reacquainted."

The thought of Veronica Bates returned. "Not this time, Sheryl. There's something here in Atlanta I've got to take care of."

"Some*thing,* or some*one*?"

"A kind of . . . puzzle that needs solving."

"I know better than to try and compete with a puzzle." Her gaze moved caressingly over his face. "All right, then, you won't be going back with me, but one thing you can't deny."

"Yeah?"

"We've got tonight."

His expression turning serious, Richard looked into her eyes. "Is that all right with you?"

Sheryl grimaced. "Still the straight shooter with all his cards on the table. No, it's not all right. But I'll take it."

Breaking into a smile, Richard offered an arm, and they strolled off toward the elevators.

With a towel wrapped around his hips, Richard walked out of the steamy bathroom. Morning light seeped between a break in the drapes and fell across the bed, limning Sheryl's bare shoulders and sparkling in her partially opened eyes.

"Do you know anything about the female criminal mind?" he asked.

She shifted to prop herself on an elbow, her lids lifting to release a look of impatience. "Here I am, basking in afterglow, and you're already back on the trail. That's it, isn't it? This criminal female is the puzzle you mentioned last night."

Richard moved to the bed and stretched out beside her. "I'm sorry," he said. "I didn't mean to be abrupt, or to demean what just happened between us."

A smile curved Sheryl's lips. "I know you didn't. You are who you are, Richard. A lady can't keep that mind of yours occupied for long when there's a mystery lurking in the back of it. What's your question again? Do I know anything about the female criminal mind? Yeah. Enough to know there's usually a damn good reason she turned to crime," she concluded with a light laugh.

"I'm serious."

Her expression of merriment faded. "I see that you are. Okay, yes. I know the textbook scenarios. Sometimes they apply. Sometimes not. Give me a rundown."

"Let's say an attractive young woman latches onto an older man, gains his trust, and ends up using that trust to steal from him. What would you say about a woman like that?"

"More than once?"

"Maybe. Why?"

"Because a pattern suggests something different from an isolated act. You'll have to be more specific."

Richard smiled. "I can't be. Not yet anyway."

"So this mystery woman . . . she's the reason you can't come to Raleigh with me?"

He shrugged. "Yeah. I guess so."

"I hate her already," Sheryl commented. Reaching out, she ran a palm over his wet hair. "I suppose if you were less complicated, I wouldn't feel the way I do."

He caught her hand and pressed a kiss in her palm. "We're special together, Sheryl. We always have been."

"Then why haven't we stayed together?"

A frown knitted Richard's brows as he stared wordlessly at the small hand resting in his own.

"Why, Richard?"

"You know if you ever needed me, I'd be there," he rumbled.

"I know. But that's not the same as committing."

"God," he mumbled after a moment. "I hate that word. It sounds like someone's being sent off to an asylum."

"Now *I'm* the one who's serious. You ran off eighteen months ago just like you ran after college. Why can't you just settle down?"

Looking up, he met the dark, searching eyes. "I don't know, Sheryl. Really I don't. I love being around you. I love making love to you. There's just so much out there to do and see—"

"So, the boy explorer is still alive and kicking," she said sharply.

Drawing her hand from his grasp, Sheryl turned and would have climbed out of bed, but he caught her by the shoulder.

"There's nothing I want more than for you to be the happiest you can be," Richard said to her back.

"Coming from the footloose wanderer who holds my heart, that's rather a taunting remark."

"Sheryl, look at me."

When she finally turned, Richard lifted a hand to her cheek.

"If I'd known our being together would make you unhappy, I never would have come to your room."

"Oh, shut up, Richard. I told you I'd take it. No strings. Just like always. I only ask one thing in return."

"What?" he murmured, his thumb descending to the tempting corner of her mouth.

"When you decide to grow up, let me know. All right?"

Richard smiled, his gaze fastened on her parting lips. "You'll be the first," he whispered, and buried his mouth on hers.

November 1

It was just past seven, the clouds muting a newly risen sun. Another gray Atlanta morning.

The hotel parking deck was deserted as Richard approached the rented sports car and tossed his satchel in back. Following the winding path down the ramp, he turned onto Peachtree Street and headed in the familiar direction of Buckhead, wondering what the day held in store.

A week had passed since he spotted the woman. That first

night, after Sheryl went to sleep, he'd lain awake thinking about phoning Bill. If he were in Bill's shoes, he'd want to know that the vixen who'd stolen both his car and his heart had finally turned up.

But the haunting image of Bill's face stopped him. The experience had scarred the man—not so acquaintances might notice, but friends did. Bill put up a good front, but there were times when he could be caught staring into the distance with an expression of utter bleakness, times that hadn't been there before Valerie Blake.

Picturing that look, Richard couldn't bring himself to dial the number. Bill would have to be told, but it didn't have to be now.

His thoughts had switched to the police, and at one point he'd gone so far as to pick up the phone before putting it down again. Valerie Blake was a wanted felon. Was he certain Veronica Bates was Valerie Blake? Yes. Did he have any proof? No.

The remaining course was clear. He'd track the woman himself—at least until he had more to offer than speculation.

In the ensuing seven days he'd learned that Veronica Bates had moved to Atlanta from "someplace in Maryland" a month ago, and Renfield had hired her on the spot. Residing in the widower's mansion in prestigious Buckhead, she accompanied him on both business and social occasions.

On Thursday they'd stopped for lunch at a sidewalk café. Even from a distance Richard had been able to see that the district attorney's interest in his secretary was more than professional. Yet for every move on his part, she had an evading one; for every thrust, a parry. As Bill had confided long ago—all grace and smiles, she managed to fend off any approach.

The situation was identical to what Bill had described—a pretty young secretary moves into the home of a wealthy older man, gets him to fall for her . . . and then what? Would she complete the pattern and simply disappear one day along with Renfield's silverware? Richard was betting she would, and the possibility she might prove him right any day had him primed to a keen sense of alertness.

Bill once mentioned that she had an amazing ability to

"anticipate." Now the tables were turned. Anticipating *her*, Richard had been carting his luggage around for a couple of days. Today was Sunday. Chances were nothing would happen, but a gut feeling said the lady was about to make her move, and he intended to be ready.

Making his way along the elegant, oak-lined lanes of Buckhead, Richard cruised past Renfield's house, turned around, and parked a short distance down the street. At nine-thirty a limousine arrived. The district attorney came out with Veronica Bates. She was dressed in a dark suit with a white ruffle at the neck, her hair pinned on top of her head. She stepped smoothly away when Renfield attempted to give her a parting embrace.

He got into the waiting limo. She returned to the house, never looking back as the car pulled away. A half hour passed before she appeared again in the doorway, this time with a load of luggage.

Richard straightened in his seat, watching with sharp eyes until she passed behind a screen of trees. She was heading toward the garage. Pulse quickening, he started up the sports car and was ready when the black sedan crested the drive.

He shouldn't have been surprised when she hightailed north on I-85. But he was, just for the second that it became clear she was leaving Atlanta . . . in Renfield's Jaguar. Richard thought of Bill's Mercedes. The names the woman used might be different, but her modus operandi didn't change much. As she continued north mile after mile he passed the time theorizing her next move.

An hour had passed when the Jaguar's turning signal came on and she took an exit for Athens. Proceeding to the outskirts of the city, she turned into a car dealership and went inside. Richard parked near the drive and reached for the notepad on the neighboring seat. He'd been keeping the journal since the first day—dates, locations, hunches, questions . . . disparate fragments until now. Now everything was coming together.

Sterling Imports, he wrote. *Athens, Georgia.*

When Veronica Bates reappeared by the sleek black sedan, it was to unload her baggage. Leaving the Jaguar behind, she drove away in an unassuming Volkswagen.

So that was it, then. She traded the luxury import for the cheapest lemon on the lot and pocketed the profits.

Tossing the notepad aside, Richard shifted into gear and followed her back onto the interstate.

She continued north, crossing out of Georgia and into South Carolina, bypassing Anderson . . . Greenville . . . Spartanburg . . .

Just outside Spartanburg she turned off the highway and took a service road that circled to the back of a shopping center. He watched from a distance as she tossed a couple of suitcases out the passenger door and then screeched off, apparently leaving the baggage to whoever cared to claim it. He thought of going down to collect it, looked back to the fast-disappearing rear of the Volkswagen, and headed off once more.

Hours drained away, along with the sports car's fuel, as Richard kept stubbornly to his post far behind her. A mere few miles south of the North Carolina line, she exited the highway and turned into a motel.

He pulled onto the shoulder of the road as she parked the Volkswagen in a secluded spot behind a dumpster at the rear of the lot. When she emerged, she was wearing a dark cloche that hid her hair and a trench coat that muffled her figure. Easily managing the two bags she had in tow, she moved swiftly across the parking lot and, without so much as stopping by the office, produced a key and let herself into a second-floor room.

Richard sank back against the leather seat. Obviously she'd lined up everything in advance—the car dealership, the motel, everything—like a chain of dominoes set up and waiting simply for her touch before falling into motion. Grand larceny in grand style.

What now? Did he call the local authorities and send them storming on her motel room?

He glanced at his watch. Five o'clock. Everything was shutting down, and he was tired and hungry. The bottom line was he didn't feel like seeing it through at the moment.

He found a matchbook in the glove compartment and waited a quarter of an hour before pulling into the motel parking lot. Leaving the engine running, he swiftly climbed the iron stairwell to the second level and propped a matchstick at her door—no hindrance if she decided to go anywhere, but he'd know if she did.

It took less than a half hour to gas up at the station across the street and grab a hamburger from a fast-food joint. Still, by the time Richard returned to the motel and rented the room next to hers, he was squirming to make sure the bird hadn't flown.

Taking the metal steps with long, noiseless strides, he confirmed that the matchstick was in place, breathed a sigh of satisfaction, and let himself into the neighboring room. It was small and sparsely furnished, just what he would have expected from such a nondescript motel—not what he would have expected from a woman who just got away with a fortune.

But maybe she'd thought of that.

Dropping his satchel on the bed, Richard went into the bathroom, reached for the sink faucet, and halted. From the other side of the thin wall came the sound of a running shower. The image of her naked, beneath a cascade of water, crashed into his mind. There was no face, of course—he'd never been close enough to really see it—but he knew her height, her shape, the way she moved . . . Turning on his heel, he strode out of the bathroom. He had no business thinking about such things.

Stretching out on the bed, Richard rested a forearm over his eyes. *What now?* he thought again.

He'd witnessed her unloading a stolen car, made a note of the time and place. Surely that was enough for the authorities to act on. He ought to get up off his rear, pick up the phone, and call the police.

Yet he continued to lie there, eventually convincing himself that he was simply too weary to deal with it tonight . . . that tomorrow was soon enough. It wasn't until the end of his silent monologue that the truth whispered to the surface.

Somewhere along the line of the day's events, the case of Valerie/Veronica had taken on a new dimension. Behind the pale blue eyes Bill described long ago, a steel trap lurked, and Richard couldn't help wondering what she was going to do next.

The distant hum of running water ceased. He pictured her climbing out of the tub, reaching for a towel, and grew uncontrollably hard. The intrigue was getting to him. Pushing off the bed, he stripped down and took a cold shower.

He spent the night fully dressed, sleeping in spurts in the chair by the window, waking to step outside and make sure the matchstick was still in place. He couldn't afford to lose her now, not when he'd decided to keep what he knew to himself for one more day. It was early morning when she emerged, suitcases in hand—her hair shorter by six inches and a rich honey-blond color.

Springing out of the chair, Richard waited until she cleared the stairs before hustling down to his car. Ignoring the Volkswagen parked by the Dumpster, she walked around the corner of the motel. He backed out, cruised slowly around the building, and stopped when he spotted her getting into a black BMW across the parking lot. She took a back road away from the motel.

Damn, he thought. *New hair. New car. New identity. Just like that.* The BMW had a good hundred-yard lead when he fell in behind it, shaking his head in self-derision. Although the press was kind enough to use the term "eccentric," Hilda was fond of saying he was "just plain crazy as a bedbug." If she could see him now, he'd never hear the end of it.

Yesterday the mystery woman had headed steadily north. Today she traveled southeast by way of solitary country roads that demanded he keep a distance. Miles flashed by; hours crawled. She stopped for lunch. Richard grabbed a sandwich and cold drink at a gas station.

When she came out of the restaurant, he half expected her to change course once more. After all, since leaving Atlanta yesterday morning, she'd zigzagged across two states. But she kept to the winding roads and their southeasterly path. It was midafternoon when they reached the South Carolina coast. Turning onto I-17, she bypassed Myrtle Beach and headed south. They continued past Surfside Beach, Garden City, Murrells Inlet.

How much longer can this go on? Richard was thinking when she slowed and left the highway just north of Pawleys Island. Flanked by cedar and live oak draped with Spanish moss, the road she pursued curved languidly through the collection of rustic buildings that composed the town. To the left, beyond a stretch of marsh, he saw the ocean. To the right, the inland waterway. Traffic was nonexistent.

Richard hung way back, speeding up when the BMW took a turn away from the beach. He pulled over at the intersection and peered around a thicket of cedar. Halfway down the sandy road, the BMW had stopped in the drive of a two-story house overlooking a finger canal to the waterway. She got out of the car, the front door opened, and a dark-haired girl ran to greet her.

The blonde put an arm around the girl and hugged her, the first show of affection Richard had seen her display. The girl picked up a suitcase, they walked to the house together and disappeared inside. The scene had all the appearances of a homecoming.

After a few minutes Richard drove down the canal road. There were no other houses, the road ending abruptly to leave a strip of untamed shoreline to the inland waterway. Turning back, he came to a halt. The afternoon was drawing to a close. He had the feeling Veronica Bates—or whoever she was—was in for the night.

Richard set his jaw, his gaze sweeping beyond the walls that secluded her, across the finger canal, and on to . . . a house. The drapes were pulled. No cars in the drive. It looked vacant.

Shifting into gear, he headed back to the main road.

The Shoreline Realty Company was deserted but for a gray-haired woman with an eager smile who leaped to her feet when he came in.

"Hello. I'm Norma Trippley. Can I help you, Mister . . . ?"

"Adams. Richard Adams. I was hoping you could help me find a place to stay."

"Thank heaven!" she exclaimed with a theatrical hand to her throat. "I'll confide, Mr. Adams, that you're the first soul who's set foot in this office all day. We have a hundred-day season here. Memorial Day to Labor Day we're booked solid. But after that . . . well, there's just the occasional fishing party. Is that by any chance what brings you here? Fishing?"

"That's right," Richard agreed readily.

"Do you prefer surf or deep-sea?"

"What?"

"If you prefer surf, I'll show you beachfront. If you like deep-sea, I'll show you the canal homes bordering the waterway. I can even line up one with a boat and dock if you like."

"Deep-sea," he answered. "In fact I happened to notice a house on the canal that had your sign out front. . . ."

The sun was going down when Norma led the way to the tall, contemporary beach house complete with fenced-in lawns and a dock. Following her up the front stairs, Richard took a deep breath of the salty air. Fresh and brisk; there was no denying its appeal, nor that of the quaint stretch of coast on which he found himself.

"It's rather spacious," Norma said as she unlocked the door. "Are you expecting others?"

"No," Richard replied. "Just me."

Luxuriously furnished with thick cream carpet and rattan furniture, the place featured a cathedral ceiling, four bedrooms, and three baths. It was more house than he could possibly use—he moved to a south-facing window—but it offered a perfect view of the place across the canal.

"I'll take it," he said.

"For how long?"

"How do you usually arrange it? By the month? The season?"

At his last words the agent became noticeably animated.

"Naturally I'd prefer to lease it for the season—"

"Why don't I write you a check for that amount?"

"Why, of course, Mr. Adams!"

When the paperwork was done, they walked down to the dock.

"I can have a boat delivered from the marina," Norma suggested.

"Good."

"And you'll need a guide. Believe me—if you plan on deep-sea fishing, you don't want to be going out in these waters alone. I happen to know one of the best men in the business, Henry Deese. He's part owner of the marina, very reliable, and his latest charter party left just a day or two ago. Shall I have him come by to see you tomorrow morning?"

"Fine," Richard answered, his gaze turning across the canal along with his attention.

The boat at her dock was covered with canvas, but from a distance it looked a lot like a boat a friend of his used to keep out at Lake Wylie—a wooden Chris-Craft cruiser, a kind that hadn't been made in years even back then.

"Who's my neighbor?" he asked.

"Victoria Blackwood, though I doubt you'll see much neighborliness from her."

"Oh?"

"Well, she's practically a hermit," Norma went on with pursed lips. "She's been leasing that house from me for the past four years, and the only times I've had so much as a conversation with her have been when she renewed her lease."

"She lives alone, then?" Richard asked.

"Except for the young housekeeper she took on this summer."

"Victoria Blackwood," he repeated quietly.

"Very pretty, though decidedly unusual. If you want to catch fish, you can't do any better than she does," the chatty woman went on. "And right off the back of that old tub she reclaimed from Henry Deese's shipyard. I hear she scuba dives, too."

"Really?"

Norma nodded. "Quite the sportswoman, but I still say she's odd—disappearing for months at a time the way she does. An antiques dealer, they say. And when she's here, she keeps so to herself. A number of local gentlemen, including my son, have invited her out. She turned down every one of them."

"Is that a fact," Richard murmured.

"To my knowledge, Victoria Blackwood hasn't been out socially since she arrived here. Of course, now that I think about it, that's not quite true. She's active at the school. That's the only way people have gotten to know her."

"School?"

"The Dalton place down the causeway. They call it a school, but I suppose it's really a home for problem children—you know, runaways, orphans, delinquents, and the like. Seems Miss Blackwood has more a taste for *that* sort of folk than the rest of us."

When Norma Trippley ran out of gossip and left, Richard lingered on the dock, gazing through the fading twilight at the house across the canal. One by one the lights blinked on in downstairs windows.

Valerie Blake. Veronica Bates. Victoria Blackwood.

A dealer of antiques, Norma had said. *Gone for months at a time.*

Not a bad ruse to mask a master thief and femme fatale.

Darkness fell swiftly, the seaside air taking on a nighttime chill. Planting his hands in his pockets, Richard started up the stairs to his new domicile.

The decision to stay in Pawleys Island had been made on impulse, without plan, based on nothing more than being caught up in the chase. Now he found the plan had materialized on its own.

He'd tracked her to her lair, and come hell or high water he'd meet her face-to-face.

Morning sunlight poured through the east-facing windows, casting columns of gold across the hardwood floor. Arms laden with fresh linens, Victoria moved along the upstairs hall with a light step.

It was wonderful to be home, feeling infinitely comfortable in her most faded jeans and oldest sweatshirt, her thick hair pulled casually up in a ponytail. She walked into the master bedroom, humming under her breath. Darcy was perched on the seat at the bay window.

"What on earth are you doing?" Victoria scolded with a smile. "You were supposed to be stripping the bed."

"Just taking a little break. After all, we've been house-cleaning all morning."

"Hardly all morning," Victoria tossed.

Setting the linens aside, she went to the bed and turned back the multicolored quilt. The wedding-ring pattern had been hand-stitched with loving fingers some fifty years before, a gift from a mountain bride to her groom.

One day years ago, as she explored the Blue Ridge, she'd come across the run-down shanty with the "Antiques" sign out front. The old woman who lived there had been alone and terribly poor, offering little of value in her makeshift shop except the hand-stitched quilt Victoria spotted in a small anteroom as she prepared to leave. She'd offered a handsome sum for the coverlet, then added another twenty when she saw the sheen of tears in the old woman's eyes.

Victoria hugged the quilt close, soaking up the familiar scent of cedar before piling it on the nearby rocker. It was wonderful to be home, she thought again. Stripping off pillowcases, she moved to the top sheet, and became aware of Darcy still peering out the window.

"What's so interesting?"

"We've got a new neighbor across the canal," Darcy announced in a lilting voice. "Mr. Deese just brought him a boat, and they're down there on the dock. Boy, is he ever something!"

Victoria chuckled.

"What's so funny?"

"You're always saying that about some man."

"This time it's true," Darcy said defensively. "Come here and look."

"No, thank you."

"Then I'll describe him for you. He's tall, blond, wearing jeans and a navy-blue parka. Nice shoulders. Long legs. Definitely an athletic build. I'll bet he plays some sport."

"I'll bet he has a wife," Victoria offered.

"I don't see one."

"She and the children are probably inside."

"No kids. There's a little red sports car parked in the drive. No room for kids."

"You've got him all figured out, huh?"

"No," Darcy admitted with a sigh. "But I'd like to. From here he looks about perfect."

"Looks can be deceiving," Victoria warned with a grin. "Besides, Bill Jacobs would be jealous. Ten-to-one he asks you to the Dalton dance."

She straightened with the pile of sheets and glanced over, expecting Darcy to be beaming, finding instead that her lively expression had drained away.

"What's the matter?" Victoria asked. "You told me long ago how much you like Bill."

"I *do* like him. That's the problem."

"What problem? As security guard at the school, he's got a steady job. I know he's a few years older, but I get the impression he's been waiting for you to grow up enough to—"

"He isn't that much older," Darcy interrupted. "He's only twenty-three."

"Well, then?"

"Even if he *did* ask me, I wouldn't go."

Victoria dumped the sheets on the floor with a frown. "You're not making sense."

"Yes, I am. You know how it's always been with me. A guy takes me out once or twice, and that's it. No one ever lasts."

"The right one will," Victoria responded, not that she believed in such fantasy, but it seemed the thing to say.

Darcy's expression remained glum. Victoria gave her a swift once-over. Tiny and raven-haired with huge brown eyes, Darcy was only eighteen and didn't look even that. Yet she'd experienced more than many women did in a lifetime. A runaway of fifteen, she'd been about to be drawn into prostitution by some sleazy character when Anita Dalton spotted her and brought her to the school. Victoria and Darcy had become friends at first sight, and when Darcy graduated in the spring, she'd offered her a job.

Despite blows that had been dealt her at a time when she should have been doing no more than playing with dolls, the girl retained an impish optimism toward life at which Victoria marveled. Moving around the bed, she placed a tender hand on her shoulder.

"What's the matter, Darcy? You like Bill. There's no reason you should turn him down if he asks you to the dance."

"I'm not like other girls. You know that. I never learned to play the game, and when it comes to Bill . . ." She shook her head. "I wouldn't want to screw it up like the others."

Victoria made herself smile. "Come on. Where's the old Darcy I've always known? Lighten up, kiddo. Take a chance."

Darcy gave her a solemn look. "No offense, Victoria, but you're one to talk. You haven't been out with a single man who's asked you since I've known you. Why don't *you* take a chance?"

With a sharp lift of her brows, Victoria stepped around and started spreading the new sheet on the bed. "You're right. Let's make a deal. I won't give you advice, and you won't give me any. Look . . . why don't I finish making the bed, and you go downstairs and brew a pot of tea, hmm?''

After Darcy left, Victoria finished tucking in the sheets and started toward the dresser for the pillowcases. As she passed the window she glanced out at the dock across the canal. Henry Deese was there with a big, flashy *Hatteras* and . . . the new neighbor. She stepped curiously to the glass.

As Darcy had said, he was tall and fair. No . . . his hair was light brown, with sun streaks that glistened as they shifted with the breeze. And she supposed he did look rather athletic, particularly in the sort of cocky way he was standing, his weight shifted to one leg and his hands in his pockets so that his elbows were at right angles. A basketball would look right at home within the crook. . . .

Suddenly he turned, and though a substantial distance separated them, Victoria got the impression he looked directly at her.

Richard's breath halted as he spotted her at the window. An instant later she was gone, but there was no doubt it had been she. A shiver raced over him. After days of watching the lady, it was startling to glance up and find her returning the favor.

''Mr. Adams?''

''Yeah.'' He turned briskly back to Henry Deese.

''I was sayin' we can work this a couple of different ways. I can bring the boat on the days we go to sea, or you can lease her—*if*, that is, you can handle a forty-five-foot sportfish.''

Richard grinned. ''It's been a while, but I think I can hold my own. I'd like to lease the boat and go fishing several times a week, your schedule permitting.''

Henry shrugged. ''Right now I'm free as a bird.''

''Good. What kind of catch are we after?''

''Spanish and king mackerel. Blues and dolphin. Maybe grouper.''

''You gonna clean them up for me?''

''I'll clean 'em, fillet 'em. All you'll have to do is take 'em out of the wrapper.''

''Mmm-mmm.'' Richard briskly rubbed his palms together. ''I can already smell them sizzling in the pan. How soon do we go?''

"Tomorrow's forecast is fair."

"Let's do it!"

Henry grinned around the stem of his pipe. "Best warn you we'll need to leave early. It takes an hour and a half to get fifteen miles out, and that's just a start. Dependin' on how the fish are running, we *might* get a good day in . . . *if* we leave at sunrise."

"Sunrise it is. Who furnishes the coffee?"

"I'll bring everything we need. You just be ready and dressed warm. And one more thing, Mr. Adams." Henry cast a reticent look at the *Hatteras*. "You *sure* you can handle a forty-five-footer?"

Richard gave him a merry look. "Want to go for a spin?"

Dropping into the boat with a sure step, he started up the engine and cast off. It had been a number of years since he'd been behind the wheel of a boat, but back in his teens he'd been one of the most-sought-after ski pullers on the Catawba River. Richard backed smoothly away from the dock, content with the way the feel of the water came rushing back.

Shifting out of reverse, he started at a respectful pace toward the inland waterway, unaware of Henry Deese's swift glance of approval as his interest returned to the house across the canal. The second-floor window was now vacant, but minutes ago she'd been watching. For the first time since this escapade began, she'd actually *looked* at him. He shrugged off the idea that the thought shouldn't give him quite such a thrill.

Facing ahead, Richard smiled into the wind. The air was crisp, the water sparkling in the sun, and the deck of a good boat was beneath his feet.

Damn, life was good!

=FOUR=

November 4

The early-autumn morning was brisk anyway, but at sea the air carried a penetrating chill, the briny wind chaffing skin continually dampened by ocean spray. Richard huddled in his canvas windbreaker, his gloved hands buried deep in his pockets.

"There they are, Mr. Adams!" Henry called. Springing across deck with a lithe step, he pointed off stern.

The deep Atlantic was a murky gray, the chum line streaking behind the boat like a red tail. Sure enough, fifty yards back the water was churning, the sunlight flashing off surfacing mackerel. Richard took his place by the outrigger and began reeling in. Minutes later he had a strike.

By the end of the day they had a respectable catch of eleven Spanish mackerel and a half-dozen king. One of the first things he noticed as they cruised into the finger canal was that Victoria Blackwood's Chris-Craft was gone. Confirming that the BMW was still in the drive, Richard turned his attention to pulling alongside the dock and securing the lines.

Henry transferred the cooler of fish to his modest outboard and looked up. "You did real good today," he said.

Richard smiled down from the dock. "Once I got my sea legs."

"I'll clean and package these back at the marina. They'll be ready in an hour or so if you want some for supper."

"That's all right. I think I'll let somebody else do my cooking for me tonight."

"Right tired, are ya?" Henry questioned with a grin.

"Right tired," Richard agreed.

"Think you'll be ready to go at it again tomorrow?"

Richard looked across the canal. It would be interesting to see if she went out every day in that boat of hers and, if so, where.

"How about we wait a day or two?" he suggested.

Henry nodded and started up the outboard motor with a practiced yank. "It's supposed to be fair all weekend!" he called over the noise. "I'll be in touch!"

With a parting wave, Richard started up the stairs to the house. His arms and shoulders ached, his face stung, and the chill of the sea was in his bones. After a long hot shower, he began to feel human again, though his cheeks continued to radiate with windburn. Dressing in the comfort of sweat pants and T-shirt, he went down to the kitchen, put on a pot of coffee, and looked across the canal. The Chris-Craft was back.

As the coffee perked he moved barefoot across thick carpet to the expansive stereo center in the deserted, cathedral-ceilinged den. The reception in Pawleys Island wasn't the best, but he found some jazz, turning up the volume when he heard the wail of a sax.

The sexy, brass notes filled the beach house as Richard wandered into the Florida room, where west-facing windows featured a spectacular sunset. One of the legendary "Pawleys Island hammocks" had been mounted in the corner to afford a comfortable view.

Sinking into it, Richard pushed absently back and forth as he took in the panorama. Beyond the waterway the dusky flat-lands stretched as far as the eye could see. Above them the sky was like a painting—purple dusted with pink giving way to red streaks, and ultimately at the horizon a bright wash of orange where the sun melted into misty treetops.

It was pretty, all right, but the very flatness of the land made him think contradictorily of home. How different the sunsets were there—the sun sinking behind the western mountains, silhouetting the rolling peaks of the Blue Ridge. The smell of wood smoke would be on the air, mixing with the scent of pine.

Richard closed his eyes and imagined the lodge. Eric was outside somewhere, probably tracking the perimeter of the sanctuary. Cainey was, more than likely, tinkering with the ancient generator he allowed no one else to touch. Miles was sequestered in the greenhouse; Hilda and Gertrude setting the dining table; Chef Renault bustling about an aroma-filled kitchen.

Pushing out of the hammock, Richard returned to the kitchen, poured a cup of coffee, and picked up the phone. "How's everyone doing?" he asked Hilda.

"Cainey's ornery as ever," the old woman chirped. "Spent all afternoon messing with that generator."

"I figured that."

"Everyone else is fine. Oh, and Mavis Brewer came by today. She was so disappointed to have missed you," Hilda continued in a singsong voice. "'I understood he was to have been back by now,' says she. 'And so did I,' says I. 'Whatever is he doing in Atlanta?' says she. 'Whatever he likes, I expect,' says I."

"You're shameless, Hilda," Richard said with a laugh.

"You know I can't tolerate that woman, Mr. Richard."

"Mavis is all right."

"What she *is* goes without saying," Hilda returned. "But she did have a point. Whatever *are* you doing down in Atlanta for so long? You said you were only going to stay a few more days."

"That's why I called. My—uh—business has turned out to be more complicated than I expected. In fact, I left Atlanta a couple of days ago."

"Where are you, then?"

"The South Carolina coast. Pawleys Island."

There were a few seconds of silence. Richard could picture the sharp look of curiosity on the old woman's face.

"What *are* you up to, Mr. Richard?"

Turning his head, he looked across the canal. "Fishing," he answered with a smile. "These are interesting waters, Hilda. There's no telling *what* I might catch."

The next morning he was dressed and ready to head for the boat if Victoria made an appearance on her dock. He envisioned calling a friendly hello across the canal, striking up a conversation. But morning turned into afternoon and finally dusk, and she never emerged from the house.

The next day she came out dressed in a sweatsuit and got in

the BMW. Richard followed at an inconspicuous distance as she drove south, ultimately turning in a drive with a sign announcing DALTON SCHOOL. He took an interested look as he drove past, but could tell little of the distant buildings backing up to the causeway.

The following morning he went fishing with Henry, returning late in the afternoon and puttering into the canal just in time to see her finish tying up the Chris-Craft. By the time they docked, she was gone, proving herself once again as elusive as Norma Trippley had claimed.

Thanks to a "get-acquainted" fish fry Norma insisted on throwing that Sunday evening, Richard met a number of the townfolk. They were down-to-earth and friendly, pointing out favorite fishing spots, the best shops and markets, landmarks that shouldn't be missed, and so on. After supper, the group gathered around the huge fireplace in the Trippleys' basement and exchanged tales.

The region was rich with folklore, the legends ranging from a haunted bell tower at the old fort in Huntington Beach, to "the gray man" who supposedly walked Pawleys's beaches to warn of approaching hurricanes, to an unfortunate Southern belle named Alice whose spirit continued to roam Murrells Inlet in search of her engagement ring.

That night Richard returned home and looked across the canal. No less haunting, he thought, was the mystery of Victoria Blackwood.

A week and a half passed, and he lived the life of a Pawleys Island fisherman. Weather permitting, he and Henry went to sea every other day, and the downstairs freezer began to fill up with mackerel and bluefish. Other days he roamed the coastal area both by car and on foot.

He liked Pawleys. Its beauty was rustic and peaceful, untainted by the fast-lane commercialism of the beaches farther north. Instead of high-rise hotels, the sandy roads were lined with live oak and cypress. Instead of condominium towers, there were sprawling homes of natural wood, along with splintering cottages that had stood for seventy years. Instead of a carefully combed strand, there was an untamed shoreline of inlets and marsh.

But although he enjoyed the people and life-style of Pawleys, Richard was growing increasingly impatient. On the morning that marked three weeks since his arrival, he hadn't so much as set eyes on Victoria Blackwood in four days. She might reside just across a strip of water, but she was as far removed as ever.

That afternoon when he and Henry returned from sea, they pulled into the canal as she was leaving. Richard raised the shipboard hand of greeting, but if she saw him, she made no show of it. He cast a sharp glance astern where Henry was gathering lines.

"Tell me something, Henry," he snapped. "What's her story?"

Henry straightened and cast a glance at the departing Chris-Craft. "Who? Victoria?"

"Yeah. What do you know about her?"

Henry moved forward. "Ever met her?"

"No."

"Handles that Chris-Craft like a real captain, don't she?"

"Seems to," Richard replied shortly.

"She showed up at my shipyard a couple years back, wanting to buy that old boat. It hadn't been run in ten years. I figured it'd never run again and told her so. She just smiled and said she'd take her chances." He shook his head. "You wouldn't think it to look at her, but the woman's some kind of wizard with engines. Inside of a week she had that thing up and running like a top."

Henry looked over his shoulder. In the distance the Chris-Craft kicked up a wake as it entered the waterway. "She's a strange one, all right," he added. "Cool and back-offish. Almost like a statue sometimes. But ya know what?"

"No. What?" Richard supplied as Henry turned back with a grin.

"She's got a smile that melts a man clear down to his toes."

That night Richard's mood turned steadily morose. A scrap here. A scrap there. Three weeks on Pawleys Island and scraps from other people were all he had to show for it. The time of hoping for a spontaneous encounter was past.

"Enough," he muttered to himself, and went to bed.

The next morning he called the Dalton School.

November 25

Anita Dalton was watching from the window when he pulled into the school parking lot. The flashy sports car didn't mesh with what she knew of Richard Adams; the casual ensemble of a leather jacket and jeans did, as did the confident stride that took him steadily up the path and out of her line of vision.

She crossed the office and opened the door. Seconds later he rounded the corner and started up the corridor, swiftly removing aviator glasses as he saw her waiting in the doorway. He was taller than she'd expected, at least six-one, maybe six-two. As he joined her at the doorway he offered a hand and a smile.

"Mrs. Dalton?" he queried.

His voice, deep and manly, was laced with a Southern accent, and when he smiled, his dark eyes sparkled with the golden lights that danced in his hair. She'd seen several newspaper photos. His clean-shaven, rosy-cheeked face was far more handsome in person.

"Come in, Mr. Adams."

Gripping his hand in a firm shake, she drew him authoritatively inside. With a surprised lift of his brows, Richard followed her lead. The headmistress of the Dalton School was a heavyset woman of about fifty, with curly red hair and a no-nonsense manner.

"Sit down," she directed, motioning to a chair as she rounded her desk to face him. Feeling a bit like a schoolboy, he complied.

"I understand you arrived in Pawleys a few weeks ago," she said.

"That's right."

"How do you like our little island?"

"Very nice," Richard tendered with a smile.

She didn't return it, but only regarded him with a piercing look before saying, "I don't intend to beat around the bush, Mr. Adams. Your reputation precedes you. I know who you are, where you come from, and that a number of worthy causes are in your debt. What I don't know is why you're interested in looking around the school."

Richard spread his palms. "From what I hear, you've managed to turn around the lives of quite a few kids out here. I'd call that pretty worthy."

"Are you saying you might want to contribute to the school?"

"I might," he returned slowly. "I like to back the good guys, Mrs. Dalton. From all appearances, you seem to be one."

A smile spread across her face, and all traces of abruptness disappeared. "We're having a fund-raiser Saturday night," she said. "Our goal is to pay off the final bill on our new gymnasium. I'd like you to attend. But in the meantime, come along. I'll show you around."

Originally an inn, the school had a main lodge with classrooms, cafeteria, and chapel, plus two wings of bedrooms. Along the halls, they passed groups of children ranging from the age of nine or ten on up into the teens. Fresh-scrubbed faces and smiles greeted them, and it occurred to Richard that none of these kids looked as if they came from the problem backgrounds reputedly associated with the Dalton School.

"They look surprisingly . . ." He trailed off, unsure of the adjective he wanted to use.

"Normal?" Anita supplied. "I hope so. That's what we're after—giving children who've grown up in abnormal circumstances the chance to be normal, develop their own talents, achieve their own goals. Take Bobby Shaw, for instance."

Pausing at an open door, she gestured inside a classroom, which at first glance appeared to be empty. Then Richard noticed a teenage boy bent over a computer.

"Bobby never knew his father," Anita continued. "His mother died when he was ten, and he was sent to live with an uncle who beat him regularly until he ran away at the age of fourteen. When he came here, he barely talked and had the education of an eight-year-old. Despite all that, Bobby has shown remarkable potential. In three years he's managed not only to catch up to his junior year level, but also to win a state award in math. I got that old computer secondhand from a public school in Georgetown. It's hopelessly outdated. The only reason it runs at all is because of him. That's Bobby's gift. Somehow he and computers seem to understand each other."

About that time the boy slapped the machine and cursed it.

"It doesn't seem so at the moment," Richard said with a smile.

"Did I mention he has a temper?"

Richard's grin broadened as he turned from Anita and walked into the classroom. "Hi, kid," he greeted. "What seems to be the problem?"

The boy straightened with a start. He was tall and gangly, wearing long hair and a silver-studded black jacket undoubtedly meant to make him look as tough as the look in his eyes.

"What do you care?" he countered.

Richard shrugged. "I used to work with a computer like this a while back. If you're having trouble with system errors, I might be able to give you a hand."

"You think so, huh? You think you know more about it than I do?"

Richard regarded him placidly. "Mind if I take a look?"

When the kid folded his arms and said nothing, Richard bent over the circuit board Bobby had removed from the computer. "Yep," he murmured. "This is the same thing that used to screw me up all the time. Do you chew gum?"

Bobby's arms unfolded as he looked down with surprise. "What?"

"I asked if you chew gum," Richard repeated, extending a palm in his direction. "If you do, I could use a piece."

Slowly the kid reached inside his jacket, withdrew a pack of gum, and offered a stick. Unwrapping it, Richard popped the gum in his mouth and began tearing and molding a portion of the wrapper.

"What the hell are you doing, man?" Bobby demanded.

"You need a brace," Richard replied.

Tearing and folding the waxed paper into an appropriate size, he looked up to find the boy staring—virtually dumbfounded.

"You can't let any of the foil remain exposed," Richard explained. "Nothing that will conduct a current."

Bobby nodded and bent behind his shoulders for a closer look.

"This circuitry has a fatal flaw," Richard went on. "The casing wasn't designed to live as long as the machine, and after a year or two's use, it doesn't handle the load. The plastic gets cured to the point that it becomes brittle and breaks, just like it did here. What you need is a little leverage." He deftly tucked the wrapper between the second and third memory chips. "And then you bypass the bottleneck."

Reaching over, Richard pushed the start button. The computer spat several bleeps and settled into a purring sound of readiness.

"See what I mean?" he asked.

"That is *radical,* man!" the boy exploded.

"But only temporary," Richard warned. "You need a fan. Keep the unit cool and you'll have fewer problems."

The kid extended an eager hand. "I'm Bobby Shaw. Who are you?"

"Richard," he replied, joining Bobby's hand with a smile. "Now that you know the trick, I'm sure you can fix it yourself anytime you have a problem." The boy looked pleased at that.

"Go ahead," Richard suggested. "Sit down. Get back to work. I've got to finish my tour with Mrs. Dalton."

"What are you doing with Mrs. D, anyway?" Bobby asked as he took his seat.

"Just looking around. I like your school."

"Yeah," Bobby admitted with a grin before he turned to the computer screen. "Me too."

"That was great," Anita whispered as Richard joined her.

"Was it?" Richard replied with a questioning look.

"Radical!" the woman confirmed as she strode toward the doorway. Melting into a new smile, Richard followed her outside.

"How many students do you have?" he asked as they proceeded into the bright afternoon sunshine.

"Fifty-two," Anita answered. "Up from a mere nineteen a few years back when the state almost yanked our certification."

"But they didn't?"

"No. We were lucky. Very lucky."

"What happened?"

She gave him a Mona Lisa smile. "I'm not what you'd call a religious woman, Mr. Adams, but I'd have to say God sent us a guardian angel."

With that tantalizing comment, she stalked ahead, so that Richard lengthened his stride to keep up with her.

Outside grounds included soccer and football fields, a playground, and a brand-new gymnasium. Following Anita Dalton through swinging doors, he stopped just inside and was assaulted by the smell of new paint and the exuberant sounds of kids at play. Beyond the basketball court, a group of teenagers were in the midst of a hot volleyball game.

Richard's gaze swept the gym. Bleachers shone with fresh varnish; the chrome of new equipment sparkled in sunlight pouring from tall windows. Along with the basketball and volleyball courts there were parallel bars, a trampoline, vaulting horse, rings . . . Not bad. He'd seen much less at much bigger schools.

"Nice," he pronounced.

"Yes, it is," Anita confirmed. "A few years ago I never would have dreamed we could have such a facility."

Richard's gaze returned to the volleyball game, scanned the players, and came to a skidding halt. Blond hair up in a ponytail, she was wearing shorts and a T-shirt, and at first glance had blended in with the teens. His stomach did an undeniable flip.

"The blonde over there," he murmured.

"Yes?"

"She looks like my neighbor, Victoria Blackwood."

"That's her."

He was still watching when she spiked a setup and won a point. The kids on her team surrounded her, the boys patting her on the back, the girls enfolding her in gleeful hugs.

"Tell me about her," he prompted.

"I thought you said she's your neighbor."

"She is."

"Haven't you met?"

Finally looking away from the game, Richard met Anita Dalton's lively eyes. "You'd have thought so, wouldn't you?"

"Maybe not," she admitted with a faint grin. "Considering who we're talking about. All right, I'll tell you about Victoria, and the first thing I'll say is that I love her like a daughter. The school was about to go under when she came on the scene a few years back. From where I don't know or care. Since then the rooms have been renovated, the cafeteria opened, and the counseling staff expanded. We needed an infirmary; she made it happen. This gym, too, which *now* she's decided needs a weight room. To shorten a long story, although she keeps most of her donations anonymous, Victoria Blackwood is the guiding hand behind this school.''

As Anita talked a feeling of warmth had risen in Richard until he could feel its heat in his face. "So *she's* the guardian angel?" he surmised in a low tone.

"That's right."

He glanced back across the gym, where the woman he'd labeled a thief, a femme fatale, a calculating heartbreaker was cavorting with the carefree abandon of her teenage playmates. God . . . what had he stumbled across?

"Well, Mr. Adams?"

Anita's brisk tone drew his eye.

"Have I piqued your interest to the point that you'll come to our fund-raiser?"

"Will *she* be there?" Richard parried with a light smile. He didn't say the name. He didn't have to.

"Most assuredly. She planned the whole thing. All I did was take orders. 'Yes, Victoria, I called the caterer. . . . Yes, Victoria, the decorations are ready. . . . Yes, yes, *yes,* Victoria!' ''

He laughed, and the sound was so pure it reminded Anita of a happy child. Oh, but she liked this man, and he was the most handsome thing she'd ever seen. If only she were twenty years younger . . . like Victoria. Anita gave him a sly look.

"I believe I read that you've never married," she said.

He looked surprised as he answered, "That's right."

"How is it a nice catch like you has managed to slip through the net?"

He laughed again. "You know the old saying. Never met the right girl, I guess."

"But you *do* like them," Anita pressed. "Girls, I mean."

One of his brows arched high as a church window, but he continued to regard her with unequivocal friendliness. "Oh, yeah. I like them. Maybe that's the problem. Maybe I like them too much to narrow the field to just one."

Anita fired a sidelong glance in Victoria's direction. "You

seemed to have no trouble narrowing the field a minute ago.''

His cheeks grew a little rosier, but he shrugged and said nothing.

"Be here Saturday night at eight o'clock, Mr. Adams."

"Yes, ma'am," Richard returned with a smile. "What kind of party is it?"

"A formal dance here in the gym. Black tie. Long gowns. The works. Victoria's philosophy is that the more dressed up people have to get, the more money they're likely to spend."

"She sounds very wise," he commented on a chuckling note.

They left the gym, and Anita walked him to the parking lot.

"Any questions?" she asked as they paused by his car.

"Can't think of any."

"Then I'll see you Saturday night."

With a parting salute to Anita Dalton, Richard drove away, the phrase echoing in his mind. *Saturday at eight.* Finally the long-awaited meeting was at hand.

That night he sprawled across the foot of the king-size bed in the master chamber of the lofty beach house.

Founded in 1984 and fully accredited by the state of South Carolina, the Dalton School appears to be an institution deserving of support, he wrote in the leatherbound journal. After a thoughtful pause he added, *As for the lady, she unfolds like a thorn-studded rose, revealing hidden petals of beauty. . . .*

Stopping abruptly, Richard scowled at the page. What the hell was he doing now? Writing damn poetry about her?

Tossing the pen aside, he rolled onto his back, peered up at the ceiling, and tried to picture a face he'd never seen.

November 28

Victoria fluffed the full skirt of ivory, watermarked taffeta.

"Stop fidgeting, Darcy! I can't check the hem with you bouncing around like a flea on a hot brick!"

Victoria stepped back and gave her a head-to-toe look. After much urging, Darcy had agreed to accept Bill Jacobs's invitation to the dance. Since then it had been nothing but chaos.

"I have nothing to wear!" Darcy had wailed.

At the back of her storage closet Victoria found a gown she'd worn one time some five years ago.

"But it doesn't fit!"

With infinite patience Victoria had tucked and pinned, revved up the old sewing machine in the spare bedroom, and altered the ivory gown to Darcy's slight frame. Now, with her hair pulled up on the sides with combs, the girl was a vision.

For some reason Victoria felt her eyes fill with tears. "You're beautiful," she said in a husky voice.

"You're the one who's beautiful," Darcy retorted.

Victoria glanced down and saw the familiar sheen of the long-sleeved, ice-blue silk. She'd forgotten what she was wearing. It seemed unimportant in the face of Darcy's debut. "Nonsense," she muttered.

"It's true," Darcy insisted, her eyes large and bright. "It fits you perfectly, and it's almost the exact shade of your eyes, and . . . Oh, God, he's going to be here any minute. Are you sure I look all right?"

"You look perfect," Victoria said with a smile. "This gown looks far better on you than it ever did on me. Stop worrying!"

Yet when Bill rang the bell, she found that *she* was the fidgety one—looking on like a nervous mother, shivering with excitement when the young man was struck speechless at the sight of Darcy.

"I have flowers," he announced after a moment, and thrust his hand forward.

With trembling fingers Victoria affixed the orchid corsage to the shoulder of Darcy's gown.

"Are you ready?" Bill asked, his eyes only for Darcy as he offered an arm. She tucked a gloved hand in the crook and glanced over her shoulder.

"See you there," Darcy said nonchalantly, and waltzed out on Bill's arm with all the grace and poise of a consummate debutante—as though she'd never suffered a nervous moment in preparation for this night, much less turned both their lives upside down the past weeks.

Victoria watched with a fixed look of surprise.

See you there?

As the door closed behind the couple she released a shaky breath and laughed aloud.

* * *

Everything was going splendidly. The lighting, the music, the decor of shiny leaves that made the gym look like an autumn forest . . . everything was perfect. Between seventy and eighty people had shown up, more than Victoria had expected. And the school secretary, who was sitting at the front and taking pledges, had confided that the financial goal was well in sight.

Victoria sought out a few of the guests who'd been regular contributors to the school. But for the most part she stayed on the sidelines, checking with the caterer or bandleader, making sure everything was going smoothly, noting over the course of an hour that the tall stranger was undoubtedly watching her. Spotting Anita near the front doors, she moved to join her.

"We've never had such a turnout for any event," Anita said in greeting. "Who'd have thought old Pawleys would be so hungry to dress up?"

Victoria smiled.

"And Darcy looks positively radiant," Anita added. "I declare poor Bill is hopelessly smitten."

Following her line of vision to where Darcy and Bill were swaying to a slow romantic melody, Victoria noted the man once more as Norma Trippley drew him onto the dance floor. "I saw you talking to someone earlier," she said with a nod in his direction. "That man over there, the one—"

"I know, the one in the white dinner jacket," Anita broke in. "Kind of stands out in a crowd, doesn't he? His pictures don't do him justice."

"He rented the house across the canal from me. Who is he?"

"Richard Adams. They say he's a bona fide genius, if a bit eccentric. He made his first million with the invention of some valve or other before he turned twenty-five. A few years back he retired to the North Carolina mountains, bought a ski lodge, and turned it into a wildlife sanctuary."

"How do you know all that?"

"He's a celebrity, Victoria. Haven't you read about him?"

"No."

"Well, my dear, Richard Adams is a multimillionaire with a string of patents and a reputation as a philanthropist. Best of all, he's expressed an interest in the school. He visited us the other day. Bobby Shaw was positively enthralled—''

"Bobby Shaw!"

"That's right. Richard walked right in and fixed Bobby's old computer with a gum wrapper. It was *something*! From there we continued to the gymnasium." Anita thought of the volleyball game and Richard Adams's pointed interest, but said nothing.

"By the way," she added, "I mentioned your latest idea concerning a weight-lifting room."

"Did you?" Victoria murmured absently, her gaze lingering across the way. "I wonder what he's doing here in Pawleys."

"Came for the fishing. I get the impression Richard Adams goes and does as he wants." Anita's gaze darted from Victoria to the man and back again. "Kind of like you," she went on. "In fact now that I think of it, the two of you have a great deal in common—both of you young, successful, terribly attractive. He's never been married either," Anita concluded, and received an arch look.

"Anita . . . do I detect one of your matchmaking fits coming on?"

"You've been alone since I met you, Victoria, and Richard Adams is the most charming man I've ever come across. Besides, he was asking about you the other day."

"What?"

"I think he likes the looks of you," Anita replied, undaunted. "And I can't say I blame him."

Victoria had gone instantly on guard—her back rigidly straight, jaw firmly set. Anita had seen the look before.

"Come now, Victoria," she urged. "Think of the school. Richard Adams isn't a threat, he's an ally. You know that exercise room? If he took a notion, he could buy us ten! Be nice to him."

"I'm sure my being nice has no bearing on whether Mr. Adams decides to support the school."

"I wouldn't be too sure about that," Anita returned knowingly.

Pursing her lips, Victoria turned, her gaze skimming the crowd, lighting on the man in question just as he looked in her direction. Across the distance their eyes met, and a strange feeling brushed over her. He smiled, and her skin tingled again.

The music ended. The dancers applauded. Richard Adams said something to Norma Trippley, stepped away, and started toward the front of the gym. The queer feeling escalated, her heart pounding a warning beat. Something about him spawned the urge to escape, and Victoria had long ago stopped questioning such instincts.

"I think I'll call it a night," she said.

"Not already!" Anita objected.

"As you said, everything's going wonderfully. You don't need me here any longer, and I have a bit of a headache."

Victoria glanced beyond Anita's shoulder. Richard Adams was halfway across the gymnasium floor, still moving unmistakably toward her.

"See you later, Anita."

Grabbing her purse and wrap from a table near the door, Victoria walked rapidly out of the building and along the walk to the drive. As she opened the door to the BMW she heard a man call her name. For a split second she experienced a startling impulse to stop and turn.

But she didn't. Starting the car with a swift hand, Victoria wheeled out of the parking spot and sped into the cover of night.

=FIVE=

November 29
Devil's Rock

The ring split the quiet like the shrill of an alarm. Wrenching around, Kyle grabbed the phone and jammed it to his ear.

"Hello?"

"Hello to you. What are you doing? Sleeping?"

He glanced at the bedside clock. Three in the morning. He rubbed at his eyes with irritable knuckles. "Of course I'm sleeping. What's wrong?"

"Nothing's really wrong," Mavis replied, curling her finger about the phone cord. "I've just been thinking about Richard."

"We talked enough about him yesterday, and you're only supposed to call me here if there's an emergency. Go to bed, Mavis."

"I *am* in bed. Stark naked. Does the image do anything to wake you up?"

Casting an eye at Jeanette's softly heaving back, Kyle swung his legs over the side of the bed and sat up. "All right," he whispered tersely. "Get it over with. What the hell do you want?"

"Not so much. Just the chance to handle Richard my own way."

"Your own way? What does that mean—land him in the sack and turn his head with your charms? You've been trying to get Adams into bed for four years now and haven't made it to first base. What makes you think you can handle him now?"

The treasured memory flared into her mind—his mouth opening beneath hers, his hand on her cheek. She hadn't been wrong about the electricity that passed between them. She knew it!

"I got him to agree to think over the offer, didn't I?"

"So you said. You also said he'd be back after the weekend. It's been over a month."

A frown knitted her brows. "Okay. I admit he's been gone longer than anticipated, but there's bound to be a good reason."

"I don't give a rat's ass about the reason. I told you when he left that this was my final offer. As long as Adams is sitting on top of that mountain, the land at the bottom is nothing but a loss. He isn't going to change his mind, Mavis. He'll have to be forced out. And that's the end of it."

She caught her lip as reality stung. The past few years she'd viewed the whole thing like a little girl caught up in a fairy tale, captivated by the contest, thrilled as the white knight consistently held his fortress against the onslaught of dark power.

But now playtime was over. She sensed it as surely as she'd sensed the building of Kyle's wrath, like a hurricane gathering force for a strike. And the target was Richard.

Picturing his flashing smile, she remembered his touch . . . and taste. God, she wanted him.

"Just give me a chance, Kyle. Wait until—"

"I'm sick of waiting. And so are the Boys. I'm the one who pitched this proposal. I'm the one who's responsible. And all of us are losing money with each day that goes by. It makes me look bad, Mavis. And I don't like looking bad."

"Well, you can't do anything until Richard gets back, right? Besides, maybe he'll surprise you. Maybe he'll take the offer. At least give me the chance to ask his decision."

A moment of silence passed.

"All right, then," Kyle agreed, his voice low and deadly. "Take the chance. Give him your best shot. But if you come away empty-handed, I'm taking over. Is that clear?"

There was a sharp click and then a dial tone. Hanging up the phone, Mavis switched off the bedside lamp, settled back against the pillows, and peered into the darkness.

Come back soon, Richard, she prayed. *And come back to* me.

Pawleys Island

The sun was on the rise, the light soft and dreamy. Although his eyes were on the dark windows of the house across the way, Richard's mind re-created her image from last night.

Dressed in a flowing gown, her hair pinned up in a shining twist, she'd been a portrait of elegance and beauty. Flashing at her earlobes were diamonds . . . or some stone. He'd never gotten close enough to determine what the jewels were, or if the pale blue cloud of a dress matched the color of her eyes.

On a couple of occasions he'd maneuvered close enough to consider approaching her, but each time—as though she could sense his intent without a glance—she'd slipped away, gracefully putting distance and the obstacle of milling guests between them. When he realized he'd watched her do the same kind of thing with John Renfield, his patience had come to an abrupt end.

During the dance with Norma Trippley, he'd sought Victoria and found her looking his way. When their eyes met and held, he could have sworn something sparked between them. But if it had, she obviously wanted no part of it. No sooner had he started in her direction than she fled.

He'd pursued her out of the building, called to her through the darkness, stood there like a jilted groom as she drove out of sight. With grim determination he'd returned to the gym and solicited her phone number from Anita.

The sun continued its ascent, heralding a clear autumn day. He waited until nine o'clock to call.

"May I speak to Victoria Blackwood?"

"This is she."

"My name is Richard Adams. We haven't been formally introduced, but I've rented the house—"

"I know who you are, Mr. Adams. What can I do for you?"

It was the first time he'd heard her voice. It was soft and definitely Southern.

"I was hoping to meet you last night," he said.

"Oh? Why is that?"

"I hear you're the chief benefactor of the Dalton School."

"I do what I can."

"I'd like to help."

"I'm sure Anita will be happy to—"

"She's the one who suggested I talk to you." It was a lie, but a small one.

"About what?"

Richard perused the ceiling. "Your vision, ideas, things the school needs, directions it should take. What do you say? Are you free for dinner tonight?"

After weeks of subterfuge, the simple question seemed a brazen overture. She said nothing. Richard winced, expecting any moment to hear a rejection. And then it came.

"Thank you, Mr. Adams, but I really must decline."

"Must you?"

"Yes."

"Why?"

Turning at the kitchen window, Victoria directed a sharp look across the canal. "I simply don't have the time."

Her gaze traveled along the face of the house across the way, halting on the second level, where a light from within silhouetted the man at the window. A pang shot through her, the same kind of thing that had started her heart pounding the night before.

"If tonight isn't good for you, we could make it another night."

His voice couldn't have been more gentle; ironically it only heightened her sense of alarm.

"Timing has nothing to do with it," Victoria announced to his shadow. "I'm certain we can discuss the school quite adequately over the phone."

"We could do it more pleasantly in person."

"That's a matter of opinion, Mr. Adams."

There was a wounded silence from the other end of the line. Victoria pivoted, her bathrobe swirling about her legs as she turned her back on the window.

Well? What did he expect, pushing her that way? This was *her* place, *her* time. She didn't have to do a damn thing she didn't want to.

Still, in the hush that fell between them, she pictured him smiling from across the gym and felt a surprising stir of regret.

"Are you sure a simple dinner is out of the question?" he asked.

"I'm sure."

"Well, then, I guess I've no choice but to respect your wishes."

"I'd appreciate it."

"No problem. After all, what are neighbors for?"

Once again the gentleness of his voice rumbled into her ear and went shivering down her spine. Her arms broke out in goose bumps. Victoria stared at them with disbelief.

"You said we could talk over the phone," he added. "Maybe I'll give you a call some other time."

"Fine."

"Fine," he returned quietly.

"Fine!" she repeated sharply. "Good-bye, Mr. Adams."

Victoria slammed down the phone and cast a panicked look across the room. Somehow, he reminded her. There was something about the way he looked or smiled, or the timbre of his voice, something that tore away veiling cobwebs from corners she'd vowed never to look in again. A cloud must have passed over the sun, for suddenly the bright kitchen seemed filled with creeping shadow.

She swept out of the room toward the staircase, running from chilling feelings that overtook her anyway. She'd buried the past, entombed it in a dark reach of memory that had nothing to do with Victoria Blackwood. Yet something about Richard Adams took her back to the girl of long ago.

The unsettling sensation stayed with her through the day, leaving her preoccupied and short-tempered. By late afternoon Darcy had had enough and announced she was taking the car and having supper "with civil people" at the school.

"I'm sorry!" Victoria called as the girl pranced to the door.

Darcy turned and gave her a wary look. Victoria tucked her hands in the pockets of her jeans.

"Truly. I *am* sorry."

The indomitable smile returned to Darcy's face. "Don't worry," she said as she walked out. "Everything's all right."

Is it? Victoria wondered as night closed in along with a sense of vulnerability. She moved through the downstairs, lighting lamps, adjusting blinds, pausing by the front door to scan the deserted road. Outside, a lively breeze stirred the dark shape of a palm; inside, the living room was silent but for the friendly ticking of the clocks.

Victoria turned and leaned against the door, her gaze wandering over the timepieces. The rustic grandfather clock in the corner was the oldest, handmade by a mountain craftsman at the turn of the century. She'd found it in Memphis, the porcelain on the sideboard in Charleston, the intricate cuckoo by the stairway in a little import shop in Savannah.

There were fifteen in all, each a special find, each voicing the same message: *Time is passing. All is well.*

The comforting sound of ticking filled the room, but tonight she found it wasn't enough to drown out an echo from the past.

She heard Darcy come in around ten. Long after that Victoria stood by her bedroom window. The canal below shone with moonlight, and the wind sang around the eaves of the house. Everything was as it should be in her safe and peaceful harbor, except she couldn't dispel the notion of a threat rippling across the water.

She'd spoken to Richard Adams once. There was no logical explanation for the eerie instincts that had her spine tingling, strange intuitions that whispered they'd met before . . . that they were somehow linked . . . that something was about to happen over which she had no control. The sound of a man's voice had cracked the shell of Victoria Blackwood, and she couldn't fathom why.

The next morning she was eager to escape the confines of the house. By eight o'clock she was dressed and on her way down to the boat, determined to go out, though a cloudy sky threatened rain. Richard Adams's fancy *Hatteras* was gone.

Looking determinedly away from the facing dock, Victoria started up the Chris-Craft and pulled away on water smooth as glass. Sometimes before a rain it was like that. There was the expected choppiness where the causeway merged with the sea, but once that was cleared, the Atlantic was calm, a gray undulating sheet.

The wind rushed by with a roar, dimming the sound of the motor and the cries of gulls. She'd bundled herself up from head to toe—long johns, jeans, sweater, galoshes and gloves, a fleece-lined windbreaker with a hood that cinched to cover everything but a porthole for her face. And over it all, of course, the canvas life jacket. Still, the ocean air was cold and wet, and her cheeks began to sting. Her head began to clear as well.

The smell of the sea filled her nostrils, its salty taste burning the back of her throat. Victoria relaxed her hold on the wheel, her gaze wandering across the watery expanse that stretched far as the eye could see. She was a couple of miles offshore when she began losing power, looked swiftly over her shoulder, and saw the smoke billowing from the rear of the boat.

Shifting into neutral, Victoria moved astern, lifted the engine hatch, and was sprayed immediately with a flume of fuel. She jumped back, sputtering and swiping at her eyes as she hurried to shut off the engine.

The fuel line was broken, the old tubing having snapped like a brittle twig. She wrapped it with electrician's tape and started the motor, breathing a sigh of relief when her patchwork held. There was no choice but to go back. She headed for shore, but had gone no more than a half mile when the smoke appeared once more.

Victoria shut down the engine, expecting the worst this time and finding it. The old line had fallen to pieces. There was no way to patch it. She was considering her next move when the wind picked up. Glancing at the sky, she was awarded a few fat drops before the rain began to fall in earnest. She scrambled down to the shelter of the galley, yanking back her hood as she moved to the radio, feeling a stab of desperation when the old CB delivered only static.

A quarter of an hour passed as the rain poured down, pounding on the roof, stirring the sea into two-foot swells. Finally it began to slow, then gradually faded to a drizzle.

Watching from the galley door, Victoria checked her watch. It was just past nine. The morning was young, the sea relatively calm, and the shrimpers came and went along this channel. Someone would be along to give her a tow. She was in no real danger . . . unless the current turned strong and started drawing her out to sea.

She tried the radio again. Although the old box sounded a little stronger, there was still nothing but static.

Replacing her hood, Victoria reached for the box of signal

flags, selected the four she needed, and went topside, where she ran them up the outrigger. Against the meshing grays of rain and sea, the banners flapped with bright urgency—the top one red and white, then blue and red, yellow with black checks, and at the bottom blue with a white bar. Not a very modern cry for help, but it was the best she could do.

"Dammit," she muttered, and making her way surefootedly across the rocking deck, knelt beside the motor.

Richard scanned the western horizon through binoculars as the boat headed in. The rain had let up. There was no reason to cut the day short, but—hell!—he didn't need any more damn fish! In fact, he'd started giving the catch to Henry days ago.

He glanced aside and caught Henry in the midst of a sour, sidelong look. He couldn't blame the man. Richard had met him at the dock with a short greeting, complained over the coffee, maintained a stony silence as the morning progressed and they threw out the chum line.

Henry, of course, wasn't the problem. The problem was himself. He'd been feeling like a fool ever since Victoria Blackwood had taken off from the school dance, and he couldn't abide the feeling. Just what was he trying to prove, anyway? He didn't have to meet her to turn her in—in fact, Henry had once mentioned that one of his card buddies was the chief of police. All Richard had to do was say the word. He couldn't rationalize holding off any longer . . . unless he faced the truth.

Raising the binoculars, he stared once more into the distance. The truth was it had turned into something personal. Despite her aberrant behavior—or perhaps because of it—the woman was the most challenging enigma he'd ever come across. The lure of figuring her out had him hungry and ill-tempered.

Ultimately he'd apologized to Henry for his black mood and suggested they call it a day. Now they were on their way back. *Back to what?* Richard wondered somberly. *More charade?* His musings halted as he saw the signal and recognized the boat bobbing on the horizon. "Trouble starboard!" he called.

Henry appeared swiftly beside him. "What is it?"

"Distress signal. Looks like Victoria Blackwood's cruiser."

"Victoria?"

"Yeah," Richard mumbled. Adjusting the focus on the binoculars, he swept the lines of the Chris-Craft. "Don't see her on board, though," he added. "What do you say we get this boat moving, Henry?"

Victoria straightened as she heard the engine. Peering astern, she waved her arms at the approaching craft, her relief overwhelming a flash of surprise as she recognized the *Hatteras*.

"Ahoy, Victoria!" Henry Deese greeted as they idled up. "What's the trouble?"

"Busted fuel line! Can I get a tow?"

"Sure!" Henry yelled down.

Seconds later Richard Adams appeared at deckside, a coiled rope in hand. "Ready?" he called.

Victoria nodded, and he pitched her a line, which she deftly secured. The boats pulled alongside.

"Mind if I come aboard and take a look at your fuel line?"

Victoria shielded her eyes from the light rain as she looked up. "No offense, Mr. Adams, but there's nothing you can do."

"You never know until you try," he returned.

And then he was hoisting a leg over the side, shimmying down the ladder, dropping onto her deck. Victoria backed away a few steps, a feeling of breathlessness sweeping over her as he approached through the mist.

"Hi there," he said with a smile.

And it struck her—a smile that beamed like sunshine through the rain . . . a handsome face blurred by swirling fog . . .

A buzzing sound exploded in her ears and filled her head. Victoria could see he was speaking, but didn't hear a word as she lost herself in the old, forgotten dream.

Richard mentioned something about its being a lucky thing they crossed paths, but drifted into silence as she stared wordlessly up at him. He could see no more than a circle of her face, and it was wet with rain. But there she was after all this time.

In the space of seconds, a dozen impressions slammed into

him—how much younger she was than he'd thought, perhaps not even thirty . . . how her eyes, as Bill Honeycutt had said, were like shining pools . . . how her brows curved in dark arches above them . . .

With a sudden move, she turned her back and stepped away.

"If you insist on taking a look at the motor, it's over there," she said with a nod of her head.

"Sure," Richard mumbled, and moved astern.

The fuel line was blown, all right. A toolbox lay nearby, along with an assortment of rubber tubing, some of it sporting bands of electrician's tape. Apparently the lady had been hard at work. He had to admire her ingenuity, but could see at a glance that none of the pieces had fit. They were all too big.

Rising to his feet, he found Victoria still rooted to the spot across deck, although she had—at least—turned so that she faced him. Richard took a few steps in her direction as he scanned the boat. Mounted neatly on the sidewall was a collection of rods and reels and . . . scuba gear.

"I think I can fix you up with a fuel line," he said.

"A simple tow will do," she replied. "I'll have it fixed when I get back."

"Why not now? It would only take a few minutes."

"How would you fix it, Mr. Adams?" she asked pointedly. "I've been working on this motor for more than a half hour, tried every piece of hose on board. All of them are too big."

"Is that right?"

"Yes, that's right," she returned stiffly.

The rain had more or less stopped. Richard loosened his hood, pushed it back, and ran a hand over his hair. "I tell you what," he began. "I'll make you a deal. If I can fix it, you'll let me take you to dinner tonight."

She gazed at him with shimmering eyes he couldn't read.

"Come on," he urged. "Where's your gambling spirit?"

"I'm not much of a gambler, Mr. Adams. I prefer to plan things out before I make a move."

"I heard *that*," Richard muttered under his breath.

"What?"

"Look," he said, spreading his palms. "What have you got to lose? At worst, you end up with a functioning boat motor and a chance to ply me with your ideas for the Dalton School."

He thought he saw the flicker of a smile before she looked away.

"I don't believe you can make the motor function, Mr. Adams, but go ahead and try if you like."

Bending to the toolbox, Richard took out a fishing knife and moved across deck. She was silent until he stopped at the scuba gear and removed the regulator from its mount.

"What are you going to do with that?" she asked.

"I think this might work."

"But that's my air hose," she objected.

"I'll buy you a new one," he replied casually.

He sensed that she was looking on in horror as he sliced the tube in half. But she said nothing. Within minutes he'd spliced the hose into place, anchoring both ends with tape.

"Go ahead," he suggested. "Give it a try."

His eyes roamed over her as she walked away. Even muffled in the bulky clothes of a fisherman, she was something to see. She turned the key, and the engine started with a roar. She gunned it a few times. It revved in response, the rigged fuel line holding like a charm. Richard waited for her to look around. When she didn't, he moved in her direction.

"Still want a tow?" he asked the back of her windbreaker.

With a shake of her head, Victoria turned and looked up. "Thanks," she said.

"No problem."

He gave her another of those glowing smiles.

"You owe me an air hose," she managed.

"And you owe me dinner. Is seven all right?"

"Seven?"

"Is that a good time for me to pick you up?"

"Mr. Adams, I really can't—"

"Don't tell me you're a welsher," he scolded. "We made a bet, remember?"

"A bet," she repeated dazedly.

"That's right. Seven is good for me. I'll see you then, okay?"

By the time she found her tongue, he'd backed into the mist. Victoria busied herself with casting off as he climbed to the towering boat alongside.

"We'll follow you in just to make sure there's no trouble!" he called from above.

"That isn't necessary!" she returned.

"My pleasure, ma'am!"

Pulling away from the sportfish at a respectful idle, Victoria soon pushed the throttle full speed and sent a white wake sailing behind the Chris-Craft.

She *never* went out with men when she was home! *Never!* Yet somehow it was coming about . . . with a smiling stranger who seemed to have stepped from the fog of her dreams.

Her instincts last night had been on target. They'd warned of something strange in the offing, and now she sensed a chain of events unfolding, sweeping her along like a cork in a stream. It was a helpless feeling she couldn't—in fact, *wouldn't*—tolerate. The days of helplessness were long over.

The wind raced by, blocking all sound, sealing her in the isolated speed of the boat. Gradually the shakiness of the past hours died away, overcome by a steadying resolution. Now she knew why Richard Adams struck her so oddly. He called to mind a fantasy from another lifetime. That was all. And like Father always said, *"Only the unknown need be feared."*

Her face took on a hard look as Victoria stared toward the dark shape of land spreading across the horizon.

It was just a dinner, and Richard Adams was just a man. All she need do was take control . . . like always.

By the time she docked well ahead of the *Hatteras,* she'd attained a sense of distance from it all, and by nightfall was once again the woman of cool poise who had successfully handled a hundred such evenings.

Richard had changed twice, ending up in khakis, a ski sweater, and a leather jacket. When he pulled up behind the black BMW, he was still early. The dark-haired girl answered the door.

"Hi. I'm Darcy."

"I'm Richard."

"I know," she said, surprising him with a flirtatious wink. "Come on in."

Richard stepped inside and momentarily stopped in his

tracks, his attention arrested by the room's unquestioned focal point. Clocks. There were more than a dozen of various shapes and sizes, their syncopated ticks filling the air, pendulums swinging, faces staring. It was as though the room were alive. And then suddenly they began to strike the hour; a chorus of chimes and tin melodies erupted, accented with the song of a cuckoo. Richard stared around with wide eyes.

"*That* was interesting," he mumbled when it was over.

"What?"

"The clocks."

"I'm used to them," the girl said. Circling around, she gave him an unabashed once-over.

Richard glanced over his shoulder. "Is everything okay?"

"Looks good to me," Darcy answered with a grin. "Pardon me for checking you out, but you *are* something of a rare bird."

"Yeah?"

"The first guy I've ever known Victoria to go out with."

"I'm honored."

"You should be. Mind if I ask your intentions?"

"My what?" he said with a chuckle.

The girl's expression turned serious. "Let me tell you something, Richard. Victoria puts up a tough front, but she's not so tough. When I graduated last spring, I had no money, no place to go. She took me in. Oh, she prefers to say she 'hired' me, but the truth is she gave me a home and I love her like a sister; so I figure I've got the right to ask what's on your mind."

"Just . . . dinner?" Richard responded with a lift of his brows.

The girl studied him for a moment and relaxed into a smile. "I can tell," she said. "You're a good guy. Want some advice?"

"Sure."

"Take it nice and slow."

Richard smiled. "I'll keep that in mind."

"And I'll tell Victoria you're here."

Darcy sprinted for the staircase. Richard meandered in the same direction, his eyes turning past Oriental rugs and antique furniture to return to the clocks. Some stood on the floor;

others were mounted on the walls. Several had figures that moved and twirled like parts of a calliope. Altogether, they made the room the most unusual place he'd ever stumbled into.

But then, he supposed, he shouldn't expect anything usual from Victoria Blackwood.

"Victoria," Darcy sang. "Your date is here."

Running a brush through her hair, Victoria glanced across the mirror to Darcy's reflection. She was grinning from ear to ear.

"He's not my *date*," Victoria replied crisply. Rising from the vanity, she surveyed herself. Dressed in tan corduroys, white turtleneck, and navy blazer, she was comfortably understated.

"What is he, then?" Darcy pressed.

"A dinner partner. That's all. Strictly business." Picking up her purse, Victoria approached Darcy, who continued to beam.

"It seems a shame to waste something that good-looking on 'strictly business.'"

"Darcy."

"Well, he's *gorgeous,* Victoria," the girl went on, undaunted. "Any woman in the world can see that!"

"I'll be sure and tell him you think so," Victoria returned. Walking swiftly out of the room, she headed for the staircase.

"If you don't want him, can I have him?" Darcy entreated as she scurried along behind.

"Bill won't like it," Victoria tossed over her shoulder in a lilting voice.

Darcy stopped cold. "You're right," she said. "Forget it."

Victoria couldn't help but laugh, and so her face was wreathed in smiles when she looked below and saw Richard Adams waiting at the foot of the stairs.

Richard looked up just as she started down—fair hair floating about her shoulders, eyes sparkling. She was smiling.

On the boat she'd been bundled up against the rain. Now he could really see her for the first time. High cheekbones. Delicate chin. Her finely drawn features resembled those of a porcelain doll, though her skin glowed with the blush of the outdoors. As for the smile, Henry was right. You felt it down to your toes.

No wonder she gets away with what she does, Richard thought fleetingly. *The poor guys never had a chance.*

"Hello," he said as she joined him at the foot of the stairs.

"Hello," she returned.

Richard glanced about the room. "Interesting place. I see you're a collector."

"Just a hobbyist, really."

"What is it about clocks that you find so intriguing?"

"Nothing at all," she replied. "I simply like to keep track of the time. Shall we go?"

They went to a seafood house she recommended. Papa Doc's Low Country Café was a sprawling, rustic place filled with the aroma of broiling seafood and the chatter of a sizable dinner crowd. A waitress showed them to one of several small candlelit tables by a bank of windows overlooking the marsh.

As Victoria bent over her menu her hair swirled forward, catching the light of the candle, shining like gold. She was a beauty, all right.

"You're a local," Richard said. "What do you recommend?"

"At this time of year the oysters are exceptionally good."

"Want to order for us?" he suggested.

They had oysters on the half shell for appetizers, followed by broiled seafood platters. During the meal they talked easily, though each time Richard tried to steer her to personal ground, she turned the subject adroitly back to the school.

"That accent," he said at one point. "Virginia, isn't it?"

"Yes," she admitted.

"Whereabouts in Virginia?"

"I grew up in Richmond. Now, about the weight-lifting room. The gymnasium is a wonderful addition, but I feel the older students would benefit immeasurably . . ."

"I understand you're an antiques dealer," he tried later.

"That's right."

"Do you have a shop, then?"

She shook her head. "I have a number of regular clients. I know their tastes and have the authorization to buy when I come across something special."

"Where do you find these specialties?"

"Auctions. Buying trips. Speaking of buying, did I mention I've contacted several sports-equipment manufacturers? One of them offers below-wholesale prices if we take a package. . . ."

She was pleasant and charming and an absolute master at avoiding talking about herself. Richard tried to look into the pale blue eyes, but they were like mirrors—reflecting what was around them, revealing nothing.

When they finished eating, he pushed his plate aside and propped his arms on the table, watching her movements with the attentiveness of a zoologist confronted with an unknown species. Placing her silver noiselessly on the dish with her left hand—the fact that she was left-handed was the only personal thing he'd discovered about her—she dabbed her mouth, folded her napkin, and tucked it sedately by her plate.

Her manners were impeccable. They spoke of a refined upbringing, as did everything else about her. She looked up and caught him studying her.

"What?" she asked with the wisp of a smile.

"How long have you been involved with the Dalton School?"

"Three years. Soon after I came to Pawleys I met Anita. She's so caught up in the school, I guess I got caught up with her."

"Where were you before you came to Pawleys?"

"North," she answered after an instant of hesitation.

"How long have you been dealing in antiques?"

She arched a brow. "A number of years. You know, you ask a lot of questions."

"I'm interested," Richard said.

"In what?"

His gaze leveled on her eyes. "Where you come from. Who you are. What makes the lady with the clocks tick."

Though her face remained flawlessly composed, her cheeks flooded with color. "We're here to discuss the school, Mr. Adams."

"We're here because you lost a bet," he reminded with a smile.

Interrupting the moment, the waitress appeared at the table

and started clearing the dishes. "Can I get you folks anything else?"

"No, thank you," Victoria answered smoothly. "We'll take the check."

They rode in silence on the way back. The evening was drawing to a conclusion, as were Richard's sober thoughts.

It had been a month since he first saw her in Atlanta—a one-dimensional, cold-blooded figure . . . faceless and heartless. Now it was different. Now he knew her other life as benefactor of the Dalton School, befriender of lost kids like Darcy. He glanced Victoria's way. She was staring out the window, still and pensive, unaware that she was sitting beside the one man who knew her secret . . . the man who could send her to prison.

Richard looked back to the road. She was the criminal, but suddenly he felt like the felonious one.

Anita loved her like a daughter, Darcy like a sister. He pictured their horrified faces if he were to throw Victoria to the wolves—he knew he couldn't do it. Regardless of the way she'd hurt Bill, he couldn't just drop her in the lap of the police. Not anymore. He had to talk to her, tell her what he knew, give her a chance to . . . what? Explain? There was no way to explain away grand larceny. *Why?* he demanded silently. Why would a beautiful, intelligent woman choose to lead such a double life? There had to be a reason.

The night was clear and brisk, the sky speckled with stars.

"Did I make a case for a weight-lifting room?" Victoria asked as he walked her to the door.

"Very admirably."

"Does that mean you've decided to help?"

"Most probably."

"Well, then. I suppose the evening has been a success."

"In a way," he replied.

If the remark was meant to draw her eye, Victoria resisted. Focusing ahead where porchlight beckoned, she fished her keys out of her purse. When they reached the door, she turned to face him and offered a hand.

"Thanks for dinner."

He took her hand in both his own, folding his fingers around hers. They were firm and cool to the touch. Taking a quick backward step, Victoria pulled away from his light grasp.

"Could I come in for a minute?" he asked.

"Tonight isn't a good night," she replied.

"When is?"

"I can't say."

Tucking his hands in his pockets, he leaned a shoulder against the door. It was a casual stance. It also blocked her exit.

"I need to talk to you, Victoria."

"About what?"

"You," he responded quietly.

A tremor of warning flashed along her spine. "I really don't see the point of—"

"There's a point."

The light of the door lantern shone on his hair, glistened in his eyes, glanced off cheeks streaked with windburn. *Gorgeous,* Darcy had said. *Dangerous,* Victoria thought. She'd known it from the first time their eyes met.

"It's important, Victoria."

"I can't imagine what could be so important," she retorted. "After all, we hardly know each other."

"You may think that, but that's not quite the way it is."

Her pulse began to pound. "What can you possibly be saying? We met this morning."

"In one sense."

"You mean we've . . . met before?"

"I mean we need to talk. Privately."

The determined voice echoed in her ears with the portent of doom. Victoria took a deep breath of the salt air, looking for a steadiness that failed to come, noting the rustle of the wind in the palms and the distant slap of water on the shore. The peaceful night sounds were the same, but all sense of peace had flown. As long as Richard Adams remained in Pawleys, it could no longer be her haven. She knew it as surely as she'd known that somehow the man before her was going to change everything. A lump of sadness rose to her throat.

"Well?" he prodded.

Victoria summoned a pleasant expression reminiscent of other times . . . other men.

"All right, then, we'll talk, Mr. Adams. If you insist. But not tonight. Tomorrow will have to do."

"What time tomorrow?"

"I'll expect you for tea."

"Tea?" he echoed.

"Three-thirty sharp. And now if you'll excuse me, it's getting a bit chilly out here."

He backed reluctantly away from the door. Victoria sensed he was considering a way to call her back as she turned the key and stepped swiftly inside.

"Good night," she tossed over her shoulder. Closing the door, she leaned back against the barrier.

"And good-bye," she murmured to the clocks.

=SIX=

December 13
Raleigh, North Carolina

The Chamber of Commerce dinner had dragged on longer than Sheryl anticipated. Now, as she drove away from downtown, the streets were dark and slick with the freezing drizzle that had fallen most of the day. By the time she reached the fashionable district of town houses on the fringe of the city, it had turned to sleet. Chilled to the bone, she burst into the cozy shelter of the kitchen and made a beeline for the stove, putting on the teakettle before shrugging out of her coat and checking her answering machine.

There was a message from her mother . . . and a dinner invitation from Bob Taylor. Sheryl rolled her eyes. He must be the most persistent man she'd ever known. How many times did she have to turn him down before he got the message? And then—

"Sheryl? Hi. It's me."

Her heart skipped as she recognized Richard's voice.

"I could definitely use the input of my favorite brilliant psychiatrist. Call me back collect, okay? It doesn't matter how late. I'll be here all night."

The number he left had a South Carolina area code. As she copied it down the kettle began to sing. Setting it aside, Sheryl turned off the stove and went upstairs. She didn't feel the need for tea anymore; suddenly she was warm through and through.

Flipping on the bedroom light, she crossed to the cheval mirror, her gaze lifting from the note in her hand to her reflection. But it was his face that she saw, his breaking smile. *Beautiful as ever,* his voice echoed in her memory.

She hadn't spoken to Richard since their evening in Atlanta. It was what she'd told herself to expect, but she hadn't been able to quell the hope that maybe this time . . . Turning away from the mirror, she stepped out of her pumps and began to undress. The hope had gradually hardened and crumbled, leaving her with the same bitter emptiness she'd first known when he walked off the Duke University campus eighteen years ago.

Having aced a four-year physics program in scarcely more than two, the scientific genius had been drafted promptly into a classified government project that took him to Washington. The night before he left, the physics department threw a going-away party attended by hundreds of students, and faculty as well. Everyone loved Richard—the eggheads for his brain; the coeds for his charm; the jocks for his easygoing expertise in one sport or another. Richard was the true Renaissance man, and as Sheryl made the rounds of the party on his arm, she'd forced herself to smile through a daze of shock and pain. His intellect was a powerful part of what drew her; she'd never stopped to think of how it would set him apart . . . and take him away.

When he returned from Washington eight months later, it was for a brief stop before accepting a grant from M.I.T. When she graduated Duke, he was in Germany; when she finished med school, Japan; when she opened her practice, back in D.C. Each time he'd sent a congratulatory note that moved her to tears.

Since then they'd continued to stay in touch, mostly from a distance, although occasionally—like two years ago—the old romance flared to life, filling her with the same foolish hope she'd felt in Atlanta. You'd think she'd have learned by now. Richard was like an eagle flying high and solo. She knew it. She shouldn't set herself up for the painful longing that consumed her each time he soared through her life.

Yet she knew she'd keep right on doing it. He'd broken her heart, spoiled her for other men, and somehow through it all managed to remain the best friend she'd ever had.

When last they met, he'd said he'd be there if ever she needed him. The opposite was true for her as well. She'd always be there for Richard. No matter what. No matter how it hurt. She guessed that was what love meant. Slipping into a fleecy robe, Sheryl sat down on the bed and dialed his number.

"Hello, handsome," she greeted.

"Hi, Sheryl." She could hear the smile in his voice. "Thanks for calling me back."

"Sure. Where are you, anyway?"

"Pawleys Island."

"What are you doing down there?"

"That's part of the story, but before I get started, I need to ask you to keep this in strict confidence. For the space of this conversation, I'm talking to Dr. Fontaine. All right?"

"If you say so. Now you've really got me curious. What's going on, Richard?"

"Remember the night we met in Atlanta? I'd just spotted someone, a woman I'd seen more than a year before at Bill Honeycutt's. . . ."

As the fantastic tale unfolded it struck Sheryl on an emotional as well as an intellectual level. This woman had captured Richard's interest two months ago, and she continued to hold it.

"When I showed up at her place the next day," he said ultimately, "she'd been gone for hours. Darcy said she received an urgent business call and had to leave immediately. But that wasn't it. I'm sure I scared her off. I didn't say much—just that I needed to talk to her. But apparently it was enough."

There was a note of desperation in his voice that Sheryl didn't like at all. "Richard," she began firmly. "You say you're certain this woman—what's her name, anyway?"

"Call her Victoria."

"Okay. Are you absolutely certain this Victoria is the one who stole Bill's Mercedes?"

"Yes."

"And you watched her take off with Renfield's Jaguar, right?"

"Right."

"Then why didn't you just turn her over to the police?" With each second that he hesitated, Sheryl's feminine instinct sounded a louder warning.

"She turned out to be different from what I first thought," he said eventually. "As Victoria she helps run a school for damaged children. She takes in a young girl who has no place to go. I don't get it. How can the same woman do these other things? *Why* does she do these other things?"

"I imagine the money is a great incentive," Sheryl quipped.

"Money is an incentive to a lot of people, but not many commit grand larceny to get it. This woman is extremely intelligent. It's not as if she couldn't make a living some other way."

"So, what do you want from me?"

"I was hoping for a diagnosis," he answered quietly.

"Diagnosis?" Sheryl repeated, her voice uncontrollably sharp. "How can you expect me to diagnose someone I've never even met?"

"In Atlanta you asked if the behavior was a pattern or an isolated act. I know now it's a pattern."

"That's still not enough, Richard."

"Just hypothesize, okay?"

"All I could possibly give you would be hunches," she said after a moment.

"I'll take them. If I could get a line on what drives her, maybe I could get a feeling for where she is."

"It doesn't matter where she is, Richard! Don't you see? This thing has already gone too far. You're permitting a criminal—"

"Sheryl," he interrupted in that same quiet, rumbling voice. "I screwed up. I can't let go without trying to fix things. Come on. Help me."

Swallowing down an ache of jealousy, Sheryl did her best to shrug out of the skin of a woman and into that of a physician.

"Okay," she said finally. "There are several ways to look at this woman. The most probable explanation is that she is, quite simply, a thief. There *are* thieves in the world, you know—people who opt to take from others to get what they want."

"What else?" Richard prodded.

"The other ideas are more clinically based. You say she changes her name, hair color, her entire identity. That could suggest a multiple personality disorder. Maybe Victoria is unaware of what her thieving alter ego is up to."

"No. That doesn't feel right. It was Victoria I threatened that night, Victoria who ran. She knows exactly what she's doing."

"All right, then, here's one last idea. Look at the similarities between Bill Honeycutt and John Renfield—both widowers, both older men, both in the legal profession. She seems to choose her targets very carefully. Maybe along with their cars, she's getting away with revenge, the smallest part of which might be connected to the immediate victim."

"Who else would it be connected to?"

"Someone from her past. Someone she punishes over and over again. I'm talking about a compulsive personality, someone triggered by deep-rooted trauma to commit an act again and again."

"So she could be out there right now setting up another mark," Richard commented after a moment.

"*If* she's compulsive, I guess she could be."

"But where?"

"How the hell should I know? But I'd be willing to bet she won't be showing her face in Pawleys Island for a while . . . if ever."

"Her things are here. Her life is here. Surely she'll come back sometime."

"Surely?" Sheryl repeated. "Can you be sure about *anything* to do with this woman?"

"No," he admitted slowly. "I guess not. Man, I sure as hell didn't mean for things to turn out this way."

"How *did* you mean for them to turn out?" she asked pointedly.

"I don't know. Not like this."

Slumping back against the pillow, Sheryl closed her eyes. "Ten-to-one this woman is a common thief—good at what she does perhaps, but common nonetheless. You scared her, and she's lying low. Enough is enough, Richard. You know very well that by withholding what you know, you're putting yourself outside the law. It's time to tell the police everything and get the hell out of it."

Silence.

Her eyes opened. "Richard?" she questioned. "That *is* what you're going to do, isn't it?"

"I guess I'll have to," he answered finally.

"But you don't want to?"

"I want to understand, Sheryl."

Her eyes searched unseeingly across the room as she imagined the expression accompanying such an intense tone. "Why?" she asked. "So you can redeem her?"

"Maybe. Is that so wrong?"

Sheryl caught her lip as she considered her reply. "You've always been able to fix anything," she said. "A computer with nothing more than a hairpin . . . an engine with a rubber band. But a human being is different. Whatever this woman's problem is, it started long before you came along. She could even be dangerous. Forget her, Richard. Pack your bags and go home."

A heavy breath of defeat came over the line. "Sounds like good advice, Doc."

"Do you intend to take it?"

"I'll let you know."

"You'll call me when you get back to the mountains?"

"Sure."

"If you don't, I give you fair warning I'm liable to show up unexpectedly on your doorstep."

He laughed, and her heart melted like always.

Long after Sheryl turned out the light and curled up under the covers, the name of Victoria buzzed like a nagging insect through the shadows of her mind.

December 16

Anita looked up from the check with shining eyes. "This is far more than I ever would have dreamed, Richard."

He shrugged. "It's enough for a weight room, I think. And a computer system. I'd like to see what Bobby Shaw can do with a decent piece of equipment."

Anita's gaze drifted back to the check. "First Victoria. Now you. I guess I'm going to have to start believing in the idea of blessings from heaven."

"Still haven't heard from her?" he asked. "Victoria, I mean."

"No, but that's not unusual. Sometimes she's gone for—"

"I know. Months at a time."

Two weeks had passed since she fled Pawleys Island. *Never to return?* Richard wondered. Looking at Anita, he found it hard to believe but . . . possible.

"When do you leave?" Anita asked.

"Tomorrow." Henry had already taken the *Hatteras* back to the marina. Norma was picking up the house keys in the morning. There was no point in staying.

"I wish you wouldn't go, Richard. Couldn't you wait long enough to see the fruits of your generosity? The computer at least? I know Bobby would love it."

With a small smile he shook his head. "Bobby will do just fine on his own. And to be truthful, I'm ready to go. Seems like I've been away from home an awful long time."

"Feeling a little homesick for the mountains?"

"Yeah. I guess so." Reaching across the desk, Richard handed her his card. "Stay in touch, Anita. I want to keep track of how Bobby's doing . . . and Victoria. Give me a call when you hear from her, will you?"

The woman's sharp eyes moved over his face. "You care for her, don't you?" she asked.

"Let's just say I have her interests at heart," he replied.

It was late afternoon when he left the school, remembering the first time he trailed Victoria to the place . . . the day he spotted her playing volleyball . . . the night he tried to catch up to her outside the gym. Elusive as she was, she'd drawn him into the Dalton School as surely as she'd enmeshed him in her own mystery.

Richard drove along the sunny road, pursued by the shadows of guilt and self-reproach that had haunted him since she disappeared. Looking back to the beginning, he saw his actions as direly irresponsible. He should have known better. He should have acted sooner. He couldn't recall ever having been so wrong about anything—except that time thirty years ago when he was dead sure the compound he was mixing was stable, and the chemistry set blew up in his face.

Sheryl was right. Once again, in his insolence, the boy genius had taken things too far.

The result was he'd let Bill down, he'd let himself down, and in a way, Victoria as well. She might be smart and quick, but the life she led was a reckless race along the brink of disaster. She needed to be stopped; instead he'd driven her on a wild flight back to the edge. He felt guilty for that, too.

Richard grimaced. Whatever he felt, the matter had been taken out of his hands. She was gone, and there was no way of determining where. It was entirely possible he might never see Victoria Blackwood again.

On the way home he stopped by her house to say good-bye to Darcy and found the girl lugging a box twice her size across the lawn. Pulling into the drive, Richard got out of the car.

"Need some help?" he called.

"That would be great!" Darcy returned enthusiastically.

Shoving up the sleeves of his sweater, Richard took firm hold of each side of the heavy box and dragged it to the roadside as Darcy walked along beside him.

"What's in here, anyway?" he asked.

"Newspapers and more newspapers," she said with a groan. "I don't know how Victoria finds the time to read them all, but I guess she does."

Setting down the carton, Richard glanced inside. "She subscribes to the *Washington Post*?"

"Um-hmm. Along with a half-dozen others from other places."

Richard straightened as Bill's voice blasted into his memory— *I put an ad in the paper, and she appeared on my door-step. . . .*

"Newspapers," he mumbled.

"The subscriptions are always changing," Darcy said. "I guess it has something to do with buying antiques."

"Which ones does she subscribe to now?" Richard quickly asked.

"There they are. About a month's worth."

"Mind if I look through them?"

"Help yourself," Darcy answered with a shrug, then looked on curiously as he proceeded to unload the entire contents of the box into the back of the sports car. "You are one crazy guy," she said when he finished.

Richard grinned. "So I've been told."

With an energy he hadn't felt in days, he sat on the floor of the den that evening, sorting through the finger-blackening newsprint, culling the issues of the past two weeks and building a sizable pile of discards.

He'd invested several fruitless hours when he came across a three-week-old issue of the *Columbia Sentinel* that grabbed his attention. The classifieds were folded back to the legal section. Richard scanned the listings and halted.

Retiring judge needs help with memoirs . . . The ad went on to list a name and address, and the concluding line: *Apply in person.*

He stared at the type, willing himself to see into the past, envisioning Victoria reading the ad, folding back the page.

It was a long shot, and he guessed he was as crazy as everyone said. But the next morning when Richard left Pawleys Island behind, he headed west, toward a retirement resort on the outskirts of Columbia.

December 17

The Crystal Lake Country Club was an exclusive development of luxury homes, rolling golf courses, and an entrance patrolled by a security guard. If your name wasn't on his list, you didn't get in. Richard took a room at a nearby inn and made an appointment for eleven the next morning with the Crystal Lake sales agent.

He arrived early. The guard opened the gate with a friendly salute. The entrance to Crystal Lake was bordered with cedar, flanked with rolling lawn that merged in the distance with the greens of a golf course. Ahead on the left was a massive white-pillared building Richard assumed to be the clubhouse. On the right the lake sparkled in the winter sunlight, overlooked by the swell of a forested hill and the faces of lofty mansions.

He glanced at the newspaper on the neighboring seat. The name in the ad was Warner; the address 300 Lakeside Lane. He found the street marker just opposite the turn to the clubhouse.

Lakeside Lane was lined with oak, its towering houses sitting well back off the road and secluded by iron fences. The number 300 was on the third gatepost. Just after Richard drove by, a silver Cadillac emerged and turned in the opposite direction. Continuing up the street, he checked his rearview mirror. He couldn't be sure, but thought there were two people in the car.

At the appointed time he met Jack Fisher at the clubhouse, noting the Cadillac parked across the lot. A slight, fast-talking man, Fisher had done his homework on Richard Adams, and plunged into an arduous examination of three expensive houses.

As the tour expanded to the tennis courts and a golf-cart jaunt about an "award-winning course," Richard held his tongue against a mounting sense of impatience. The man was only doing his job, he knew, but now that Fisher had gotten him inside Crystal Lake, he was anxious to test his theory. Would the long shot pan out? If not, he had two choices—abandon Victoria Blackwood to the realm of chance that their paths might cross again someday, or go to the authorities with his journal. He didn't like either option.

Finally returning to the clubhouse, Fisher led the way to the terrace overlooking the golf course. The December day was pleasantly cool, the nip in the air mellowed by bright sunshine. The patio table umbrellas were up, and a number of people seated beneath them. Waiters in livery moved among the tables.

"Luncheon on the terrace is one of our most popular amenities," Fisher said, almost preening himself. "The weather is beautiful nearly all year round, and our chef . . ." He kissed his fingertips.

Richard looked away, his glance moving across the flag-stoned terrace.

"You can see we offer only the finest here," Fisher added. "As a result, we draw only the finest people."

"I'm sure," Richard murmured, looking from one patio table to the next, passing and then returning to one across the way where a couple was seated—a white-haired man in a dark suit and a brunette in a blue dress. His gaze lifted from the sweater knotted about her shoulders, and a charge ran through him. The color of her hair might have changed, but her profile was unmistakable.

"Who's that?" Richard asked with a nod in her direction.

"Why, you've noted one of our foremost residents, Mr. Adams. That's Judge Archibald Warner, a brilliant and prominent man. He often takes lunch on the terrace. The lady is Vera Blaine, his personal secretary. Shortly after the Judge retired, he hired Miss Blaine to help with his memoirs. He's positively mad about her. Come along. I'll introduce you."

The man was off like a shot. Richard followed at a lazy pace, his gaze targeting Victoria. She had yet to notice their approach. They'd come within a few scant yards before she turned, spotted them, and froze. At least he thought she froze. A heartbeat later she'd lifted a hand and donned dark glasses, effectively hiding her eyes as he and Fisher stepped up.

"Hello, Judge Warner," the agent greeted. "And Miss Blaine, so nice to see you. Forgive me for interrupting your lunch, but I wanted to introduce Richard Adams, who's looking into our club in terms of a winter home."

Stepping into the shade of the umbrella, Richard offered a hand. "Nice to meet you, Judge Warner," he said, his gaze sliding to Victoria as he straightened. "Miss Blaine," he added.

With a passing nod of acknowledgment, she leaned toward the Judge, murmured something, rose, and left the table. Without a word or backward glance. Slick as glass.

Richard watched attentively as she glided away toward the clubhouse, her skirt shifting with her gait. She thought he hadn't recognized her. Little did she know how transparent were the layers of silence and dark hair and glasses. Her walk gave her away. She moved like no one else.

"Have a seat, why don't you?" the Judge invited.

Fisher sat down with obvious eagerness, Richard with reluctance. Victoria wouldn't return as long as he remained at the table. He should go after her—

"So you're thinking of buying into our little community, eh?" Judge Warner asked.

"It certainly has its appeal."

"I must say I'm extremely happy here—close enough to the

city to go in from time to time, far enough out so that I feel I'm living in the country. The best of both worlds, you know."

The Judge, who appeared to be in his late sixties, had a pleasant smile, a heavy Southern accent, and a penchant for soliloquy. On and on he went, extolling the virtues of Crystal Lake. If he happened to pause, Jack Fisher swiftly brought up a new topic that would get him going again. Richard was looking for an opportunity to break in when a waiter approached.

"Excuse me, Judge Warner. Miss Blaine asked me to tell you she recalled an urgent errand and will return shortly."

Richard's gaze snapped to the waiter as the Judge chuckled indulgently.

"Urgent errand?" he repeated. "Probably more file folders. I swear that girl is going to have me organized in spite of myself. I'm beginning to believe those memoirs of mine are going to get written after all."

Fifteen or twenty minutes had elapsed since she left. Was she merely steering clear of the table? Or was she bolting?

Richard rose to his feet. "Excuse me, gentlemen," he said. "This talk of urgency has reminded me of a call I need to make."

"But, Mr. Adams!" Fisher sputtered as he strode away.

"I'll be in touch," Richard called. Circling the clubhouse to the parking lot, he confirmed that the Judge's Cadillac was gone.

"Damn," he mumbled, and ran for his car. Roaring away from the clubhouse, he down-shifted as he approached the intersection with the main drive and would have turned toward the Warner house. But just then the silver sedan sped by on its way toward the entrance. By the time the security guard opened the gate and let him through, she was disappearing up the public road. There was access to the interstate a few miles north.

"Damn," Richard muttered once more. He was unprepared for this, his bags left at the inn, his gas tank less than half-full. Minutes later he was following her west on I-20.

As soon as she stopped at a damn car lot—hell, as soon as she stopped for anything—this whole damn fiasco was going to end!

But an hour passed, and she stopped for nothing. They crossed the Georgia line. Richard continued to hang back, his eyes locked on the distant sedan. The needle of his gas gauge was hovering on E, and he was considering driving up beside her and trying to make her pull over, when she took an exit in the middle of nowhere.

There were a mere three buildings clustered about the exit ramp—a gas station, a diner, and a motel. As she had done before, she pulled into the motel and parked in an inconspicuous spot. As before, she produced a key and let herself into a room.

Having watched from the roadside, Richard drove determinedly into the parking lot and got out of the car. A sour taste filled his mouth. The past few weeks he'd begun thinking of Victoria in the light of Pawleys Island and the Dalton School. Today had reacquainted him with her dark side—the phantom who had drawn him into this in the first place. Now the reckoning was at hand.

Running a restless hand over his hair, Richard climbed the stairs and knocked on her door. No answer. He tried again. The door opened enough to reveal a chain lock and a strip of her face.

"Hello, Victoria." The one vivid eye he could see blinked. "Or is it Vera until you wash that color off your hair?"

"You must be mistaken," she said, and started to close the door.

"I wouldn't do that if I were you."

She hesitated, the space through which she viewed him no more than a fraction of an inch.

"I only want to talk to you," Richard added quietly. "But I'm tired, and I'm irritated, and I'm liable to cause a god-awful scene if you don't let me in."

Silence.

"I know what's going on, Victoria. And I'm willing to bet you wouldn't welcome a lot of attention."

Seconds ticked by. When she finally opened the door, she stood barring his way. "How did you get here, and what do you want?"

"Obviously I got here by following you. As for what I want, I haven't quite decided."

"You *followed* me?" she echoed in something like a hiss. "Of all the underhanded—"

"Underhanded!" Richard broke in with a laugh. "*You're* calling *me* underhanded? Excuse me, Victoria."

Brushing past, he walked in and looked around. It was a typical cheap motel room—chair, dresser, TV, bed. She'd emptied her handbag across the bedspread. His gaze swept a litter of wallet, keys, hairbrush, tissues, and stopped on an array of identification cards laid out in a neat line.

Flashing a look in her direction, Richard saw she'd closed the door but continued to stand woodenly by it. He took a step toward the bed, and she darted in front of him—grasping up handfuls of things and stuffing them into her purse.

"I repeat," she said sharply, "what do you want?"

Loosening his tie, Richard walked slowly to the chair and sank into it. "To begin with, I want to know why you left Pawleys so suddenly."

"Is that all?"

Propping his elbows on the armchair, he made a temple of his hands and studied her over his fingertips. "No, that's not all. But it's a place to start."

Having tucked every stray item out of sight, she dropped the handbag on the bed, straightened, and faced him. "I was called out of town unexpectedly," she offered.

"You could have let me know. We had a date for tea, remember?"

She tossed her head. "Sorry. I'm unaccustomed to making dates with men, much less breaking them."

"It doesn't appear that way to anyone who cares to look."

"What do you mean by that?"

"I mean, Victoria, that you play men like a gifted artist, a veritable master."

"I'm not enjoying this little cat-and-mouse game of yours, Mr. Adams! Get to the point. You said you know what's going on. What exactly is it that you know?"

"I know you left Judge Warner high and dry without his Cadillac."

"I borrowed the Judge's car," she replied. "That's all."

Richard frowned. "You didn't borrow the Caddy, Victoria.

You stole it, you crossed state lines with it, and now you plan to sell it. I'll bet you've already got the fence picked out.''

She searched him with a pale, penetrating gaze. Beneath her scrutiny he felt both a chill and an uncontrollable warming.

"What is it you want me to do?" she asked after a moment. "Give it back? If that's what it takes to make you forget this, then that's what I'll do. First thing tomorrow morning, I'll drive to Crystal Lake and give the Judge his car. Will that square things?"

"For him, maybe. But what of the others?"

"Others?" she repeated in surprise. "Surely you're not saying you think I've done this sort of thing before!"

"Sweetheart, I *know* you've done this sort of thing before."

An angry flush stained her cheeks. "You're wrong, Mr. Adams. The school needs a weight-lifting room, and I intended to provide one. That's all there is to it. I've never done such a thing before, and don't plan to again."

"Victoria, Victoria," he murmured scoldingly. Releasing a tired sigh, Richard rose from the chair. "I knew you were a thief, but I had no idea you're such a little liar."

She swept him with a look of outrage as he walked past. Crossing the room, Richard picked up her purse and dumped its contents on the bedspread.

"What do you think you're doing?" she cried, springing toward the bed.

Richard stepped in her way and began sorting out the cards he'd seen earlier. There were more than a dozen—driver's licenses, social security cards, credit cards . . . all bearing different names.

"You have no right to go through my things!"

She attempted to snatch them from his hand; he lifted them out of her reach, staring as he thumbed through the stack. Vera Blaine. Veronica Bates. Richard paused when he came across Valerie Blake, picturing Bill's face, remembering how devastated he'd been when he faced the truth. God, was there a Bill Honeycutt for every one of these cards?

"Would you give those to me, please?"

Her tone was cold as ice. Richard turned. So were her eyes.

"I don't think so," he replied, and tucked them in his jacket.

"What makes you think you can come in here and treat me this way?" she demanded. "I won't stand for it."

"I'm afraid you'll have to stand for it, Victoria. I caught you fair and square, and now I'm calling the shots—unless, that is, you relish the idea of police involvement."

"Police? You must be insane!"

"Am I?" Richard cocked his head to one side as he studied her. "Do you remember Bill Honeycutt?"

Though she said nothing, the high color of her cheeks went a shade brighter.

"Charlotte?" he prodded. "Your name was Valerie Blake then."

"I don't know what you're talking about."

"Give it up, Victoria. I've got a card with the name on it right here in my pocket. Besides, I saw you in Charlotte. And then I saw you again in Atlanta."

"Atlanta?" she questioned hesitantly.

"I also know about District Attorney Renfield. Apparently you specialize in the legal profession. Tell me, Victoria. Just how many have there been?"

Spinning around, she presented him with her back. "You mentioned police," she said to the wall. "Is that what you intend to do? Turn me in?"

Richard's gaze swept the length of her. The dark hair still startled him, and the silky dress didn't look like the kind of thing Victoria Blackwood would wear. But there was no mistaking the proud stance, the curve of her back, the long legs . . .

"For Bill's sake, that's what I *should* do," Richard replied huskily. "But it isn't what I *want* to do."

She turned, looked at him, and must have read the warmth in his eyes. A moment later she shocked him by stepping forward and looping her arms around his neck—a kind of closeness she'd never before allowed, much less offered.

"Let me go," she pleaded, her eyes plumbing his. "I swear I—"

"Shhh," Richard interrupted, pressing a finger to her lips.

His gaze followed the movement. Her lips were slightly open, her mouth warm and moist against his fingertip. Silence fell as the touch became electrifying. Richard traced the lines of her lips, scarcely aware he was doing so until they began to shake.

"Shhh," he murmured once more, his fingers cupping her chin.

He kissed her gently. Her lips continued to tremble. Richard moved his tongue caressingly over them, his hand traveling along her jaw, fingers threading into her hair. He was dimly aware that she remained motionless, unresponsive. But once his mouth was on hers, he couldn't make himself stop. He had no concept of the time that went by before she grasped his neck and started kissing him back, her lips parting in welcome.

Richard's arms went around her, holding her close as his tongue filled her mouth. Desire washed over him in a hot shower, his senses flooded with the taste, the scent, the feel of her. His hands roamed her back, tracing her shape, feeling the warmth of the flesh beneath the dress. He shifted his face across hers, gaining a fierce new kiss that tipped her head. As he lifted an arm to cradle her the other slipped down to her hips and pulled her tightly against him.

She broke away and, taking swift backward steps, put a brisk distance between them. Richard regarded her in silence, faintly smiling as he lifted a hand to his tingling lips.

"Does this mean you'll let me go?" she asked.

Her voice betrayed a lingering breathlessness from the kiss, but she looked mad as hell. His smile spreading, Richard shook his head.

"You needn't be so infuriatingly smug about this! I want to know what you're planning to do, Mr. Adams, and I want to know now!"

Richard's arm fell to his side as his smile faded. "My given name is Richard. Unlike you, it happens to be the only one I have, and I'd like you to use it."

"All right then, *Richard*. If you're not going to turn me in, and you're not going to let me go, what *are* you going to do?"

"I'm working on it," he returned, his gaze moving over her angry face. God, she was beautiful . . . and dangerous.

"Why?" he asked. "You're a lovely, intelligent woman. Why do you do it?" She looked pointedly away. "There must be a reason," Richard added. "I want to understand."

"My life is my business and no one else's," she said, still facing away from him.

"Forgive me, Victoria, but you lose a certain right to privacy when you start committing grand larceny for a living."

Her head snapped around, though she only glared at him in silence. The idea that had been flickering in the back of Richard's mind flashed suddenly forward.

"Do you have family?" he asked.

"They're dead and have been for years."

"Any husbands or boyfriends tucked away?"

"Don't be ridiculous."

"You mean you're all alone in the world?"

"I like it that way," she snapped.

"Ever been to the Blue Ridge Mountains?" She didn't reply, only watched him with narrow eyes glinting like strips of silver.

"I have a place," Richard went on, a smile creeping to his lips. "A lodge. My family is gone, too, but I've got some good friends there, and we've turned the top of the mountain into a wildlife sanctuary. It's something to see. A few years back a boy from down the mountain brought me a raccoon who'd gotten her leg caught in a trap. So I took her in, bandaged her up. The next week it was a hawk that had been shot by a poacher. To make a long story short, I now have a greenhouse full of birds and a house full of animals. Some people call it a zoo."

"Why are you telling me this?" she demanded.

With each passing second Richard's thoughts became less clouded, the course of action more clear. "It's obvious you can't be left on your own," he replied. "I guess I'll have to take you home with me."

"You can't be serious."

"Why not? The mountains are a great place for sorting things out. If we leave by noon tomorrow, we can be there for supper."

"I don't require any sorting out. And I don't intend to go anywhere with you, least of all to your mountain retreat."

"Think before you speak, Victoria." Richard lifted a hand to his breast pocket. "Are you willing to risk having all these identities tracked down? I imagine it would be fairly easy. Computers can do anything these days."

She stared at him, outrage radiating about her like a halo.

"It's your choice," he added. "Which do you prefer? The custody of the police, or mine?"

"Blackmailer," she whispered.

"I guess so," he admitted, his eyes moving between hers. "My car is rented. I'll arrange to have it picked up, along with the Judge's Cadillac. We'll take your BMW. Am I right in assuming it's parked somewhere nearby?"

"Would you please leave?" The barely audible request issued from between gritted teeth.

Richard gazed at her steadily. "Not a chance," he said.

"I'll do as you say. Just go."

Ignoring the command, he crossed the room, dragged the chair to a barricading position at the door, and sat down. She took a frustrated step in his direction.

"You can't stay here."

"Where did you think I would stay?"

She lifted her palms. "How would I know? Any number of places! Get yourself a room!"

Clasping his hands behind his head, he leaned back. "This chair is just fine."

"I told you I'd go with you," she repeated in exasperation. "Don't you trust me?"

Richard chuckled wearily. "I'm tired. And I trust you about as far as I could throw this motel."

"I refuse to share this room with you overnight!"

His reply was a questioning lift of his brows.

"If you're afraid I'll run away, I won't. What good would it do me? You know where I live, after all."

"I have a hunch you might live any number of places, Victoria. It wouldn't surprise me to learn you've got two or three completely separate lives going on out there."

Richard shrugged out of his jacket and tucked it behind his back. She peered at him in stony silence, hands clenched at her sides. Leaning forward, he rested his arms on his knees and gave her a long searching look.

"I'd like to help you," he added quietly. "If you'll let me."

"I've been getting along on my own since I was seventeen. I don't need any help."

"And how have you been getting along? By stealing a fortune in cars from aging attorneys and judges?"

"They were insured," she replied stiffly.

"Do you call that an explanation?"

"I don't have to explain myself. Not to you."

"You're wrong, sweetheart. That's exactly what you have to do. Explain yourself. To me."

She shook her head, her face a mask of defiance. "Not a chance," she said in a low voice.

"Then it looks like we're in for a long siege," Richard responded in a matching tone.

She looked as though she could kill him. It was hard to believe that mere minutes ago he'd been kissing that angrily set mouth.

"You are the most insufferable human being I've ever met!" she exploded. "And don't call me sweetheart!"

With that she stalked into the bathroom, slammed the door, and locked it. Settling back in the chair, Richard eyed the barrier thoughtfully.

No doubt about it. He had a tiger by the tail, and there was no telling if he'd get his eyes clawed out before it was over.

The supper hour came and went without notice. Victoria couldn't have forced anything down her throat anyway.

Long after she washed the dark rinse out of her hair, she remained in the bathroom, dressing once more in the only garment she had. All her clothes were in the other room, but so was *he*. From time to time she heard him moving around. A while back he'd turned on the TV, making himself perfectly at home in *her* room, *her* place.

She peered blindly into the mirror, unable to decide what appalled her more—the way he'd trapped her, or the fact that she hadn't seen it coming. He knew about Bill Honeycutt. And John Renfield. And somehow he'd found her with Judge Warner—forcing her to make a hasty, unplanned departure.

He'd done the same thing at Pawleys. That night on her porch she'd felt danger emanating from him like the scorch of a fire. Now she realized she'd had no concept of just how dangerous he truly was.

The thought of Pawleys brought a stab of sadness. Folding

her arms across her chest, Victoria paced the narrow confines of the bathroom floor. She'd planned to stay away a few months, enough time to be certain her canal neighbor was long gone. Now she could never return. Richard Adams would find her if she did.

How long, she wondered, would he continue looking for her after she escaped? For, of course, she *would* escape; it was just a matter of when.

The reviving thought pierced her state of shock. Escape! Yes! Late tonight after he went to sleep. He was blocking the door. It would have to be the window, and she wasn't even sure it would open. But that was her only alternative.

She jumped as a knock sounded on the door.

"Victoria?"

She didn't answer.

"Victoria, it's nearly nine o'clock. Come on out."

"No, thank you."

A moment passed, and she pictured him frowning.

"I wish you'd reconsider."

"I could say the same to you," she returned.

"Can you come up with a better solution?" he asked, his voice low and gentle and sending shivers up her spine like before.

"Victoria?"

Eventually, when she didn't answer, she heard him move away from the door. A short while later he made a phone call to someone named Hilda and announced he'd be arriving at the mountain house the next afternoon and was bringing a guest.

The hours crept by. Sometime after eleven Victoria turned off the bathroom light and pressed her ear to the door. From the adjoining room came the low-pitched hum of the TV, but nothing else. Biting her lip as she released the lock with a click, she drew open the door and peered around its edge.

The lights were out, the room illuminated by the mere glow of the TV. Across the way he was sprawled in the chair, his eyes closed. Her gaze shifted to the window. She had to pass within two feet of him to get there.

Tucking her shoes in the pockets of her skirt, Victoria tiptoed to the bed and slung her purse over her shoulder. She held her breath as she slipped past the man, her eyes locked on his motionless form. Releasing a sigh of relief as she sidled up to the window, she reached behind the drapes for the latch.

"It's painted shut."

She spun around with a start. His eyes were wide open. In the dim light it appeared as though they twinkled with amusement.

Sweeping past in an angry swirl of blue silk, Victoria returned to the bathroom and locked the door between them.

=SEVEN=

The next morning Richard was awakened by a sharp nudge to the ribs. She was blond again, and looking wickedly fresh in a starched white blouse and navy slacks.

"I'm hungry," she announced.

He rubbed his eyes. "Can you be good long enough for me to take a shower?"

"What do you think?" she responded.

He did without the shower, but put away a huge breakfast in the diner across the road. Shortly thereafter they were heading north in her BMW, the sun bright as a penny above them.

"We've got a few hours," he said after a while. "Would you like to talk?"

He'd insisted on driving. Tossing him a glare from the passenger's seat, she turned and looked out the window.

"Come on, Victoria. Take it in stride."

"Come on?" she repeated sharply, her head swiveling so that her pale eyes speared him. "You break into my room, take over my life, and tell me to take it in stride?"

Richard shrugged. "It's your best choice. I'd hoped you'd be more adaptable."

"Adaptable!"

He couldn't help but smile at her shrill tone.

"You are—"

"I know," he broke in, still smiling. "The most insufferable human being you've ever met."

"That's right!"

He laughed. God, why was he laughing? Here he was—unshowered, unshaven, and speeding along the highway in the getaway car of a woman capable of who-knew-what!

116

He's spent two weeks scolding himself for being irresponsible, telling himself that if he were ever given a second chance, he'd approach the matter with the sobriety it deserved. But he didn't feel like behaving soberly, or solemnly, or particularly responsibly. She was beside him, and he felt alive in a way he'd never experienced . . . except maybe as a boy when confronted with a great puzzle that demanded all his powers for the solving.

Richard glanced in her direction. "Maybe we could start with something simple. How do you get rid of the cars so quickly?"

She gave him a look that said he was crazy for asking.

"I saw what happened with the Jaguar. It was gone in the blink of an eye. How'd you manage it?"

She only peered at him, silent and stubborn.

"This whole thing will be resolved sooner if you condescend to explain a few things," he suggested. Looking back to the road, he kept her within his peripheral vision.

"I set it up beforehand," she murmured after a moment.

"What?"

She met his questioning glance with blatant irritation. "I went in the week before, said I had a luxury car I wanted to trade. We did the paperwork, lined up the money. Do I have to spell it out for you?"

Richard shook his head. "You really are brilliant."

"I'm so happy you're pleased."

He laughed again—the sound erupting from deep inside, expressing a crazy joy. Limits had been violated. Lines had been crossed. He was running away with Victoria Blackwood, and the challenge showed no sign of ending.

The hills rolled away from the road, swelling to a spectacular chain of peaks against the western horizon. Emphatically ignoring the man who sat a foot away, Victoria peered ahead and maintained a cool facade of silence that masked her rising spirits. The mountains had always done that to her. When she looked at them, she couldn't help but feel the uplift of their grandness and timelessness. Against the Blue Ridge the ugliness of mankind seemed small, fleeting, hardly worth noting.

The last time she'd been anywhere near this part of North

Carolina, the forested hills had been ablaze with fall colors of scarlet and amber. Now the deciduous trees had lost their leaves. Close up you noticed the black, barren branches; but from a distance the towering firs and spruce and pine painted the ancient mountains a smoky evergreen.

She remembered hiking the trails along the Blue Ridge Parkway, the air crisp and clean as it flooded her throat, the trees thick and tall around her, blocking the sun but for shifting beams that dappled moss-covered rock and a carpet of pine needles. She remembered the quiet majesty of it all.

Much as she loved them, she'd planned never to return to the spellbinding mountains of the Blue Ridge. Until yesterday . . . when Richard Adams smashed into her carefully controlled world and blew it to smithereens.

Beneath hooded lids, her eyes cut in his direction. His left elbow propped casually on the doorsill, he drove with one hand and looked entirely at home behind the wheel of her car. But then she fancied he'd look at home most anywhere. There was an air about him, a kind of easygoing confidence that made him seem to fit in—whether on the deck of a stricken boat or the dance floor during a formal soirée.

Having discarded the tie from yesterday, he wore the same dark leather bomber jacket, the open collar of a white shirt showing at the throat. Her gaze lifted. Though it grew long in back, his sun-streaked hair was clipped on the top and sides, dusting his forehead in short wisps and layering back to frame a perfect ear. As for his face, she supposed Darcy was right. Sandy brows that arched above the corners of twinkling eyes, a perfect nose with a slight tip at the end, lips that glowed with the same rosiness as his cheeks . . . Except for the dark shadow of a masculine beard, he was downright pretty.

Of its own accord Victoria's gaze drifted back to his mouth. The fiery feeling returned, the same flare of femaleness that rocked her last night when he kissed her. She looked swiftly ahead. It had happened that morning, too. He said something about a shower; she made a smart reply. And then he looked at her and smiled. "I like you better blond," he'd said.

She'd known many men in her life; no one had come close to stirring the sensations he provoked with such seeming ease.

But then he was the man of her dreams . . . as well as her captor.

Victoria's eyes turned his way once more, this time with a sharpness that searched beyond surface attributes. Behind that perfect face was the mind of a genius. Anita had said so. Why hadn't she paid attention?

"How long have you been following me?" she asked.

He looked her way, confronting her with the twinkling eyes. "I spotted you at the Scholarship Foundation dinner in Atlanta."

"You were there?"

"Yes," he replied.

"That was months ago."

"I know."

"You've been tracking me since then?"

He nodded. Victoria stared. How could she have failed to notice him? *How?*

"You mean you came to Pawleys and set up house across the canal not for the purpose of fishing, but because of *me*?"

"Yes," he said again.

She thought of the morning Darcy announced they had a new neighbor, the night of the school dance, the day he fixed the engine on the boat. All those times he'd been watching her with spying eyes.

"Don't you have anything better to do?" she snapped.

He cracked one of his brilliant smiles. "Not really."

As he turned toward her Victoria looked out the window.

"Are you in the mood to talk now?" he questioned.

"Not really," she returned curtly.

She stared through the glass, watching the panorama of undulating hills, thinking that she must be losing her edge, vowing to herself she'd get it back.

An hour passed. The sun was low over the mountaintops when things began to look suddenly, alarmingly familiar. She gave Richard a sharp look.

"Exactly where is this ski lodge of yours?"

"Black Top Mountain."

"Where the devil is Black Top Mountain?"

He smiled again. He was the most damnably cheerful person she'd ever met.

"Interesting choice of words," he answered. "It's just beyond a little town called Devil's Rock. In fact, that's where I do my shopping.''

He turned a casual glance her way while Victoria's blood seemed to stop flowing.

"Ever been there?" he added.

"No," she mumbled, her blood coming abruptly back to life, racing and pounding at the walls of her veins. *Devil's Rock!*

The section of the Appalachian Mountains known as the Blue Ridge stretched hundreds of miles from Virginia, through North Carolina and into Georgia. There had been no reason to think . . . no possible reason to suspect!

As they crossed the town limits, she sank low in her seat, her eyes peeping over the ledge of the window, confirming that in four years not much had changed. The small mountain community was still charming, the houses on the outskirts clinging to the side of the mountain, peaked rooftops level with the road, chimneys issuing gray tendrils of wood smoke.

In town the air of mountain rusticity continued, the familiar buildings peering from the roadside with rough-hewn familiarity—Dell's Sporting Goods, Murphy's Grocery, Brewer's Feed and Hardware, the town hall. She held her breath as they approached the outskirts of town, but it didn't prevent the voices thundering in her mind as they passed the impressive markers at the head of the Skinner drive.

I've already had Miss Prim-and-Proper Blair!

You're a liar!

Any way I wanted, and she begged for more!

You're a damn liar!

Victoria's eyes slammed shut against the images that began racing before her—the Judge's snow white hair streaked with blood . . . Kyle's evil mouth grinning down at her . . . his charging form running toward the Corvette.

I'll get you, bitch!

She'd driven most of the night, finally stopping at an out-of-the-way place deep in the heart of Tennessee. Later she read that Kyle Skinner had accused Vanessa Blair not only of stealing the Judge's car, but also of his murder.

Even after the BMW left the village miles behind, Victoria's heart continued to thunder. Four years was a long time. Maybe

Kyle had left Devil's Rock. Maybe he was dead. Maybe even if he saw her, he wouldn't recognize her. Vanessa Blair was a redhead who wore horn-rim glasses. . . . Catching her lip, she stopped herself. Regardless of the time that had passed or the color of her hair, Kyle would know her at a glance.

Several miles beyond town Richard turned onto a narrow road that inclined so sharply that she fell back against the car seat. Victoria's ears popped. Her stomach churned. Still, they ascended through a bank of pine that crowded the roadsides, past occasional secluded chalets that thinned away to nothing.

The damn lodge must be on top of the highest peak in the Blue Ridge, she thought numbly.

But it really didn't matter where it was. All that mattered was that she had to get away.

She looked up and saw it. Sprawling around the side of Black Top Mountain, the ski lodge was a stone fortress surrounded by towering fir, bordered with turrets at the north and south ends, fronted with a series of arched, cathedral windows already aglow with light. Despite the welcoming lights, the place emitted an overwhelming impression of the Dark Ages.

"Oh, God," Victoria mumbled.

"What?"

"Dracula's castle."

"Yeah," Richard agreed with a smile. "Isn't it great?"

Bypassing stone gateposts, they continued up the mountain. Forests of fir and pine sequestered the road that turned into a cobblestoned drive, then flared into a parking courtyard where Richard stopped the car. Victoria got out to the sound of the calls of birds and the chill of mountain altitude.

Richard opened the backdoor of the BMW. Matching the gesture on the other side, she retrieved her bag and jacket just as he reached for them. He gave her a frown, but said nothing.

They passed through arched double doors and entered a huge receiving room, its stone floor repeating in a giant hearth where a fire blazed, its walls sporting crimson tapestries, shields, and crossed lances. Staircases ascended on each side of the hearth, leading to a second floor where doors began opening and faces appearing. Within minutes a half-dozen people had converged on Richard, enfolding him with hugs and handshakes.

Victoria stood aside, watching from a self-conscious distance until Richard motioned in her direction.

"Victoria, I'd like you to meet the members of my household."

Eric Ryan, a Nordic blond of about her own age, was introduced as "slopes manager." Beside him Miles Norton, who looked about ten years older, appeared slight and mousy.

"Miles is the ornithologist who manages the greenhouse I told you about," Richard said. "And this is Cainey Wilson."

An ancient-looking man with a white beard tipped his hat.

"Cainey keeps everything running around here," Richard said. "And Chef Renault here feeds us as if we were royalty."

A lithe, dark-haired man with a mustache gave her a short bow as Richard continued with Gertrude Little, a plump brunette in her twenties who kept casting dimpling looks at the chef, and finally Hilda McCoy, who was small and bent and wearing a somber black dress that resembled service livery. Gray hair framed a face wizened with age, but her dark eyes glittered like shiny beads.

"Hilda, of course, keeps all of us in line," Richard concluded.

A moment of silence fell as the group stared at Victoria with blatant curiosity.

"It's been ages since Richard brought home a girlfriend," Gertrude piped up with a giggle.

"I'm not a girlfriend," Victoria snapped.

"Miss Blackwood is a highly regarded consultant on antiques," Richard said, arching a sharp brow in her direction. "She's been kind enough to agree to look the place over, make a few suggestions."

"Since when have you been interested in antiques?" Eric asked on an obviously teasing note.

"It came on quite suddenly," Richard replied with a grin. The look of mirth was gone by the time he met her eyes once more.

"Maybe you'd like some time to yourself before supper," he said.

"That would be most welcome," Victoria replied.

"I'll take your bag."

She reached down and grasped the handle. "Don't bother."

"All right, then," Richard responded slowly. "I'll see you at supper. Hilda? Could you show Miss Blackwood to her room?"

As they ascended the stairs Victoria cast a glance over the rail. Richard was watching. She made a point of looking away and concentrating on the back of the small woman ahead, who opened the door to spacious quarters on the second floor furnished with the same opulence as the room below.

Stepping inside, Victoria surveyed the chamber. An elaborate French Provincial dresser stood across the way, topped by a huge mirror and flanked by a massive stone hearth in which a fire was laid. A graceful love seat, as well as a four-poster, canopied bed, were done in scarlet velvet. In the far corner a tea table was set with silver service and attended by slender chairs. Lining the west wall was a series of arched windows crisscrossed with lattice, which was meant to be purely decorative but—in the face of her current situation—impressed her as prisonlike.

Dropping her bag at the foot of the bed, Victoria tossed her purse on the velvet spread.

"I'll go ahead and light this for you," Hilda said, and moved to the hearth, which was big enough to accommodate several Yule logs.

"Nights up here on the mountain get nippy," the old woman added. "And the sun's already on its way down. Might as well go ahead and chase the chill away before it comes."

Victoria wandered to the dresser. In addition to a gilded vanity set of brush, comb, and mirror was an exquisite porcelain carousel, a small clock embedded like a jewel in its center. Her fingers trailed absently over the shapes of painted horses while her thoughts churned.

"Do all of you . . . live here?" she asked after a moment.

"Oh, yes, miss. This is home sweet home. Our rooms are just across the landing."

"Are there any more of you?"

"No. You met the lot of us downstairs."

The lot . . . Neither Hilda nor the old man nor the dimpled

young woman should prove a hindrance. But there were three able-bodied men in addition to Richard.

Having started a crackling fire, Hilda approached.

"That belonged to Mr. Richard's mother," she said, alluding to the carousel.

"It's lovely," Victoria murmured.

"Yes, but not nearly as lovely as she was. I watched her grow up, you see, and then moved with her when she married Mr. Adams. How happy the two of them were! They've been gone a long time, but I still remember."

Withdrawing her hand from the carousel, Victoria turned to look down at the old woman. "How long has it been?" she asked.

"Nearly seventeen years to the day. In fact," Hilda added with an assessing look, "I'm real pleased you've come. Christmas can be a sad time for Mr. Richard."

Victoria pictured his smile, glowing as if some special inner light were impatient to be shared. "It's hard to imagine him sad," she said. "He's the most invariably sunny person I've ever met."

"Ah, but don't we all have dark corners, miss?"

Victoria met the beady eyes and found them perusing, probing.

"I'm sure you'll help keep him cheery through the holidays," Hilda concluded with the hint of a challenge in her voice.

"I don't think I'll be here that long," Victoria answered.

"Oh? When Mr. Richard called, he gave me the idea you'd be staying awhile."

Victoria tried a smile and hoped it didn't look as brittle as it felt. "I have obligations of which he's unaware," she said.

"I'm sorry to hear that," Hilda replied. "How long *will* you be staying, then?"

"It's a little early to tell."

"Is it?"

The sudden look of suspicion on the old woman's face was as sharp as her tone. Victoria arched a brow.

"Yes," she confirmed. "It is."

For a few awkward instants the two women regarded each other in adversarial silence. Finally Hilda turned away.

"I'm sorry, miss. I don't mean to pry. You see, I've known Mr. Richard since he was a baby. Sometimes I still find myself acting the nanny."

"He's lucky to have someone looking out for him that way," Victoria said.

The old woman stared for a moment. When she surrendered a smile, she nearly managed to hide it as she moved spryly toward the door.

"Well, I should think you'd be wanting a bit of privacy now. Your bath is through the door by the hearth. Is there anything else I can do?"

"No."

"Then I'll be seeing you downstairs at seven. Supper's in the banquet hall. You can't miss it."

"Hilda!"

The old woman looked over her shoulder.

"Thank you," Victoria added, gaining another fleeting smile before the door closed and she was left alone in the scarlet comfort of her captor's den.

Crossing the room, Victoria stared out the west-facing window. The sun was halfway down, a flaming circle dying inch by inch behind the purple silhouette of the Blue Ridge. She folded her arms and leaned against the cold glass of the arched window, considering her position as darkness fell on the mountain, black and freezing.

Setting off on foot was out of the question, even in daylight. She needed the car, and of course Richard had retained her keys. But he didn't know that she'd been perfectly capable of hot-wiring a dash since she turned seventeen.

She must wait until all was still.

Though he kept his face turned to Eric and Miles, Richard's eyes cut to the staircase as Hilda descended. She seemed to cast some sort of accusing look in his direction before turning along the corridor toward the kitchen.

"The poachers are growing bolder by the season," Eric was saying. "They know the sanctuary isn't being regularly patrolled, and they're taking advantage of it."

"Maybe we can give them a surprise tomorrow, huh?"

Richard responded. "But right now I need a shower and a shave."

Eric and Miles walked off with a parting chorus of "Welcome home," and Richard picked up his bags and climbed the stairs. Glancing at the door of the guest room as he passed, he shook his head as he proceeded along the hall to his own chamber.

He'd been away too long; the room felt chilly and empty. Crossing to the hearth, Richard lit a fire before moving to the foot of the bed and wearily shrugging out of his jacket. As he did so he felt the unfamiliar bulk in his breast pocket. Withdrawing the cards, he tossed the jacket aside and spread the IDs so all the faces were showing.

Settling on his haunches by the bed, he scanned the collection. The obvious connection among them was the initials V.B. What else? Gradually his gaze narrowed on the four driver's licenses. They all listed the same birth date—May 30, 1960. His mother's birthday was the end of May. If one believed in such things, the date fell under the astrological sign of Gemini. The Twins.

Twins, he thought wryly, and headed for the shower. *Not even close.*

That night at supper Victoria wore a mask of courtesy, responding politely, if not talkatively, to the odd assembly's questions. They were all there—Richard, Cainey, Eric, Chef Renault, Miles, Gertrude, and Hilda—all grouped about one end of a banquet-sized table that could have seated thirty.

Candlelight flickered on the table. Firelight glowed from a hearth overlooked by a giant family crest. Facing the hearth was a cabinet of weapons including everything from medieval-looking axes to modern rifles. If ever she might have pictured a dining hall in a nobleman's castle, it would have looked like this.

The fare was a feast of French onion soup followed by stuffed chicken, yams, peas, and the lightest biscuits she'd ever put in her mouth. Chef Renault was overtly pleased as Victoria dug into her portion, and yes, she was glad to eat, but also it gave her an excuse for short answers to an onslaught of questions.

"Where do you come from, Miss Blackwood?" Miles asked.

"Virginia."

"Oh? I thought Hilda said Pawleys Island."

Heat rushed to Victoria's face. She was right. She could never go back. "Virginia, originally," she amended, and speared a yam with her fork.

Gertrude propped an elbow on the table. "How did you and Richard meet?" she asked on a sighing note.

"Through a mutual friend."

"Your life must be so exciting," Gertrude went on. "Antiques consultant! Imagine! I suppose you get to travel all the time."

"I've been a few places."

"Ever been to Europe?"

"Once," Victoria answered slowly.

"I'd love to hear about it sometime, Miss Blackwood!"

"I'm going to be here for a *short* while," she replied with a meaningful glance to the head of the table. "Call me Victoria."

Richard smiled. He'd been sending her smiling glances all through supper, apparently pleased with her show of civility to his staff. Little did he know that as soon as the time was right, she'd be gone like a puff of smoke.

Victoria looked back to her plate as the tingling sensation beset her anew. Having cleaned up, he was dressed in a bulky white sweater and jeans, and was sensationally handsome. She supposed the fact that she found him attractive shouldn't shock her anymore. But it did.

She picked at the last remnants of chicken on her plate.

Anyway, it didn't change anything. As soon as she left tonight, Richard Adams would be a thing of the past.

After supper Richard came around to Victoria's chair and offered an arm. She hesitated, and he knew she'd have liked to refuse, but she acquiesced—more, he imagined, for the gain of a graceful escape from the table than anything else. They climbed the stairs arm in arm, followed by the interested looks of the supper crowd, who peered unabashedly from the banquet-hall doorway.

"I think you'd have to agree they're a nice bunch," he said.

"Oh, yes," she responded. "Charming." Pulling away, she opened the door to her room and would have stood in his way.

Richard pushed past and stepped inside. "Are you comfortable?" he asked.

"As much as I can be." She remained by the door, holding on to it as though she'd like to hit him with it.

"Can we talk for a minute?"

"Indeed we can. Now that you've got me locked away in this mausoleum, I'd like to know what you intend to do with me."

Richard released a heavy breath. "You're not locked away, Victoria. You can roam the lodge as you will. There's a great deal to do here. Until the snow comes—"

"Until the *snow* comes?"

"Then we open the slopes," he said.

"Do you really think I care about the sports you have to offer?"

"Then, of course, there's the mountain. One of the hiking trails goes by a waterfall—"

"*Or* the scenery?" she broke in vehemently. "You've brought me here against my will, Richard."

"That's nice." She looked at him as though he'd lost his mind. "You called me by my name," he explained with a smile. "I like the sound of it."

She shook her head, eyeing him as though he were a creature from another planet. "Then I'd like to say good night . . . *Richard.*"

He stuffed his hands in the pockets of his jeans. "Don't make this so hard, Victoria. It doesn't have to be this hard."

"Good night," she repeated sharply.

His eyes moved between hers. They were mirrors once more.

"If you need anything, I'm at the end of the hall," he offered.

She looked away, and as soon as he crossed the threshold, she closed the door. Long after he left, Richard continued to see her standing there, defiant as a warrior, beautiful as a goddess.

Victoria waited until after midnight when she hadn't heard a sound for at least an hour. Bundling herself in everything warm she had with her, she slung her bags over her shoulder and crept to the head of the staircase.

The entrance hall below was quiet and deserted, the coals of the fire casting eerie shadows on the walls. Hurrying noiselessly down the stairs, she slipped out the front doors and was confronted with the freezing night. A biting wind ripped her hair as she ran across the cobblestones for the shelter of the BMW.

Banging the door closed behind her, she removed her gloves, rubbed her hands, and reached for the dash panel. Her breath puffed in frosty clouds against the darkness as she removed the encasement and selected the wires with knowing fingers. She brushed their ends, and the engine coughed.

She tried again. It responded with a fruitless whir.

"Dammit," she muttered.

Leaning over to the glove compartment, she fished out a flashlight and climbed out of the car, once again beset by the whirling cold of the mountain night. Switching on the flashlight, she lifted the hood. It didn't take long to determine the trouble. The distributor cap was gone. Victoria spun to face the macabre shape of the lodge looming behind her.

"Damn you, Richard Adams!" she cried, the curse no sooner shrieked than swept away on the stinging wind.

Grabbing her bags, she stalked back inside, gaining steam like a locomotive as her fury mounted.

The end of the hall . . . Despite the weight of her burden, she took the stairs two at a time. Passing by her bedroom door, she peered down the corridor. At the end were double doors; beneath them, a strip of muted light.

Shedding her bags, Victoria swept down the hall, threw open the doors, and walked in. She was met by the glow of a dying fire . . . and the warning growl of a wolf.

Victoria stopped in her tracks. He'd been lying at the foot of the bed, but now he crouched ready to spring. Not a wolf but a coyote, his eyes glowing red with the light of the fire.

"Easy, Lobo," came Richard's voice. "Easy, boy."

Victoria's astonished eyes turned across the bed and found the man sitting up, bare to the waist, where bedclothes provided cover.

"I told you this was a zoo. Just be still, Victoria. He doesn't know you yet. His name is Lobo. Why don't you say hello?"

The growling continued as Victoria's sharp gaze darted from Richard to the coyote and back again.

"This is one time you'd better speak up," Richard said quietly.

"Hello . . . Lobo," she murmured after a moment. The growl fell to a hum.

"Out, boy," Richard said. The coyote didn't budge. "Go on. *Out!*"

At that, Lobo slunk to the door and, with a passing sniff of her pants leg, trotted out of the room. Victoria looked back to the bed. Shifting the pillows behind him, Richard settled against an ornately carved headboard.

"Sorry," he said. "I wasn't expecting company. Come on in. I'd stand, but . . . like I said, I wasn't expecting company."

She took a few stilted steps in his direction. The bare skin of his chest and arms gleamed in the firelight. Victoria imagined the rest and felt an undeniable stirring. Undeniable or not, it would never come to fruition.

"Where's my distributor cap?" she demanded.

"How did you know it's missing?" Though he kept the smile off his face, it was in his voice.

"Stop playing games, Richard. Some things aren't meant for play. I *can't* stay in this place. Do you hear me?"

"Why not?"

"I just can't," she reiterated more quietly. "Would you please give me back my distributor cap and let me get out of here?"

"I can't do that."

"Why the hell not? Because of Bill Honeycutt? Is that what this is about? Revenge?"

He studied her with those dark eyes that somehow glowed with the sunlight of a summer afternoon. "Come here a minute," he said, and patted the bed beside him.

Victoria's chin went up as she remained rooted to the spot. "Have you stopped to think," she said briskly, "that the authorities would call this kidnapping?"

"In truth, I guess the authorities would hold me accountable for a lot more than kidnapping. How about withholding information regarding a felony? Harboring a criminal? Maybe even accessory after the fact?''

"Then why are you doing it?" she demanded. His eyes moved over her like caressing hands. "Well?" she added sharply. "What do you hope to gain from this?"

"The truth, I guess," he answered slowly.

"*What* truth?"

"The one about you."

Victoria crammed her hands in her jacket pockets, her heartbeat lurching into a gallop as Richard gathered the covers around his hips and climbed out of bed. He moved toward her, his chest like bronze above the trailing bedsheet. She made herself look him in the eye as he came to stand before her. With so much flesh showing, he seemed bigger than before . . . and potently male.

"When this started, it was about Bill," he said in that spine-tingling voice. "Now it's about you, too."

Securing the sheet with one hand, he lifted the other to stroke her hair. She steeled herself against a startling inclination to lean into his palm.

"There must be a way of setting things straight, Victoria. You can't go on the way you are."

"I'm not an errant child," she snapped. Jerking away from his touch, she took a quick backward step.

"No," he replied softly. "At least not on the outside."

Moving at a slow unthreatening pace, he came close once more—so close her level gaze became fixed on the dark hair curling on his chest and about the base of his throat. His hand rose to cup her chin, gently prodding until she looked once more into his eyes. He bent toward her, and for a split second Victoria almost lifted her mouth. At the last possible instant she tore away.

"Don't do that!" she commanded.

He said nothing as he lowered his arm.

"I have an aversion to that sort of thing," she added.

"Oh?" he responded with an arch look. "You didn't seem entirely averse yesterday at the motel."

A searing heat flooded her face. "That was for a purpose," she said, "not pleasure."

"I see," he said after a moment.

"Don't expect it to happen again."

"Okay."

"I mean it, Richard!"

"I said *okay*!" he shouted.

Victoria started for the door.

"Wait a minute!"

She halted but kept her back turned.

"I'm not going to press you," he said.

She looked over her shoulder. Though his voice had dropped to a silky rumble, his face was a portrait of anger, the sunny smile lost in the storm of a scowl.

"Not about that," he went on. "But I do intend to get to the bottom of Victoria Blackwood . . . or Vera Blaine, or Valerie Blake. Which one is you, anyway?"

She regarded him in smug silence.

"Well, then, I'll just continue to call you Victoria. But in parting, I'd like you to consider one thing—you're going to remain here enjoying my hospitality until you explain yourself. That's my price. How long you take to meet it is up to you."

Turning on her heel, Victoria stalked back to her room and spent the night staring out the barred window into inky darkness.

Richard Adams . . . Richard Adams . . . the name sounded in her head as images flew through her mind. She remembered the night of the school dance when he smiled from across the gym, and the day on the boat when that same smile burned through the rainy mist. He was the only man who'd ever been able to touch her, much less with such a simple thing as a smile. He was also the man who'd placed her in the most perilous position of her life.

Once again the violent scene bloomed in her mind's eye, sweeping aside figments of Richard and girlhood fantasies.

The heavens had begun to grow light when Victoria took a last look across the dark peaks of endless treetops and left the window. Crawling beneath the covers of the unfamiliar bed, she closed her eyes and willed herself to dwell in a meager sense of respite.

The remoteness of the mountain lodge thwarted immediate escape. Maybe it thwarted the likelihood of crossing paths with Kyle Skinner as well.

=EIGHT=

December 20

Victoria heard a knock and the sound of an opening door. She fought to lift her eyelids. No sooner had she caught a glimpse of Hilda's small, black-robed figure than an animal appeared out of nowhere to drop smack on her stomach. Her eyes flew open, and she found herself staring into the face of a raccoon.

"Damnable rodent!" Hilda exclaimed, hurrying forward and flapping her hands. "Down with you, Rosemary! Get off that bed and be gone!"

With a scant glance at Hilda, the animal stayed exactly where she was, studying Victoria with bright dark eyes.

"Does she bite?" Victoria murmured, her face a mask of surprise.

Coming to stand by the bed, Hilda propped disapproving hands on her hips. "Only me," she answered.

Glancing at the disgruntled woman, Victoria released a light laugh. The raccoon stepped onto her diaphragm, stifling the laugh in an abrupt whoosh of breath. Victoria's eyes grew wider still as the animal craned toward her and began sniffing at a lock of hair curling across her shoulder.

"I'm sorry, miss," Hilda said with a shake of her head. "The varmint won't listen to a thing I say. Best to let her get her curiosity out of her system, I guess."

"How long do you think that will take?" Victoria mumbled.

Bursting into laughter, the old woman clapped a quick hand over her mouth, though her eyes continued to dance with merriment.

133

"I'm sorry, miss," she said after a moment. "I don't mean to laugh. It's just that Mr. Richard asked me to make you feel at home, and I'm sure he didn't have anything like this in mind. Down with you, Rosemary! Let the young lady have some peace!"

Casting a disdainful look at Hilda, the raccoon walked across the bed and landed with a thump on the floor. A moment later she waddled sedately out the door.

Shifting up in bed, Victoria brushed a lock of hair over her shoulder, unconsciously smiling at the startling appearance of Rosemary the raccoon, thinking what an odd place Richard Adams called home, remembering with a start where she was, how she'd gotten here, and that she shouldn't be smiling at all.

"What time is it?" she asked.

"Nearly noon, miss. I thought you'd be wanting to get up and about. It's a clear day, though cold as a tinker's heart."

Crossing to the window, Hilda opened the heavy crimson drapes. Sunlight poured into the room, silhouetting the old woman as she returned to the bedside.

"You must be hungry by now. Before he left, Mr. Richard suggested you might like me to show you around the place."

Victoria's gaze sharpened. "Before he left?"

"He and Eric left shortly after sunrise with a packed lunch. I reckon they'll be gone most of the day."

Part of Victoria was annoyed that he'd deserted her; the wiser part was elated at the opportunity to explore options for escape free of Richard's watchful eye. "Where have they gone?" she asked casually.

"To walk the sanctuary. There's always trouble with poachers this time of year."

"I see." Climbing out of bed, Victoria crossed to the dresser and began brushing her hair. "How big is the sanctuary?"

"Why, it's the whole top of the mountain, miss. I doubt they'll be back much before sunset."

Reaching for a rubber band, Victoria secured her thick hair in a ponytail and turned to the old woman with a smile. "Yes, I'd like you to show me around," she said. "And yes, I'm starving."

Hilda looked pleased. "Then meet me downstairs in the kitchen. I reckon the chef has a surprise for you."

Victoria took a quick shower, then pulled on a navy, cable-knit sweater, and rolled the cuffs of her jeans to the top of lace-up boots. She left the bedroom and, upon reaching the landing at the head of the staircase, was struck by the difference daylight made. Sunshine beamed through the arched windows, flooding the halls with golden light, glancing off surfaces of wood and silver. The macabre air she remembered from last night had vanished.

The kitchen added to the cheery atmosphere. Huge and sunny, it was filled with delicious aromas and the lively chatter of Chef Renault, Gertrude, and Hilda. The two women sat down with her at the breakfast table while Chef Renault served up his surprise—a brunch of fluffy cheese omelets, crisp Canadian bacon, and melt-in-the-mouth croissants. Victoria savored every bite.

When she finished, Victoria leaned back in her chair. "That was fabulous," she announced, and the chef beamed.

"Chef Renault studied in Paris and London," Gertrude piped up. "And now I'm his apprentice."

"And a very good one, too," the chef pronounced as he took Victoria's plate and moved away.

"What are you going to do first?" Gertrude asked curiously.

Victoria looked across the table. "Excuse me?"

"Richard said you're going to upgrade the place—you know, with antiques. So, what do you do first?"

"Well . . . first, I simply look around. Hilda has volunteered to play guide, and I suppose we'd better get going." Rising from her chair, Victoria patted her stomach and smiled. "After a meal like that, I could definitely use a walk."

Richard's lodge was a rambling place, the second floor composed of living quarters, the downstairs offering a game room with both pool and Ping-Pong tables, the entrance hall with clusters of tables and overstuffed chairs, and of course the banquet hall and kitchen, the latter of which overlooked rear grounds that stretched to the forested slope of the mountain.

As Hilda led the way she pointed out the animals who claimed the lodge as home. In addition to Rosemary the raccoon, there were a fox and rabbit who had formed an unlikely alliance, and of course Lobo, who was "taken in as an orphaned pup."

"Mr. Richard never has been able to pass up a stray," Hilda added. "Even the two-legged kind."

Victoria gave her a swift look. "What do you mean by that?"

"I mean, miss, that this place is a sanctuary in more ways than one. Take Eric, for example. He was a champion downhill racer until he took a terrible fall. The chef had a nervous breakdown and lost his job. Miles lost his wife and nearly drank himself to death. Cainey had no home. Neither did Gertrude. All of them found new lives here, good lives Mr. Richard gave them. He has the touch, and not just with animals. With people, too."

A moment or two of silence passed, the old woman's eyes glittering up at her all the while.

"I have a feeling you've told me this for a reason," Victoria commented.

"I can see he thinks you're something special," Hilda replied without hesitation. "Reckon I felt like saying he's special, too. You'll never meet a finer man."

"You're probably right," Victoria admitted, her face turning warm as the words rang with truth in her ears. "Let's get going," she added briskly. "I'm sure there's more to see."

They proceeded toward the greenhouse at the south end of the lodge. As they approached, Victoria heard the chatter of birds, but was unprepared for what she found inside. Geese, quail, and other fowl roamed a simulated mountain forest, complete with pine and fern and a waterfall supplying a pool. Miles Norton appeared from behind the curtain of water, smiling in welcome.

"This is amazing," Victoria said.

"Yes," Miles agreed. "It's the most phenomenal aviary in the state. I may take care of it, but I didn't conceive it, so I'm free to brag. Richard designed the entire microcosm."

"Of course," she murmured. "Richard."

As the tour continued Hilda noted ingenious devices ranging from a firewood stacker to a boot warmer to a dispenser from which animals could feed themselves—all invented by Richard, who kept a workshop "in the toolshed out back."

Genius, Victoria thought once more, stifling a feeling of admiration that leaped stubbornly back to the surface when

Hilda led her into the final ground-floor room. Sprawling and furnished with heavy masculine trappings, the multifaceted chamber was at one end a workplace—complete with a huge desk, a sophisticated computer system, and even the necessary equipment to function as a small laboratory. The middle walls were lined from floor to ceiling with shelves bulging with books; the opposite end featured a cozy seating area before a giant stone hearth identical to the one in the entrance hall.

But what caught and held her attention were the elaborate puzzles that provided the only artwork in the room. Some were framed and hanging on the walls. Some looked up from tabletops. A few were constructions that stood on the floor and reached as high as her head. All were testaments to the intellect that had put them together.

"Oh, he's a master of puzzles, miss!" Hilda exclaimed. "I dare say there's not much put before him that he doesn't figure out."

The words struck an icy chord, shattering the lulling sense of warmth that had stolen over Victoria. The lodge might be a fascinating place, but it was still her prison . . . and a formidable genius, her jailer.

"I think I'll go out for a while," she said.

"All right," Hilda agreed slowly. "Though I must say Mr. Richard asked that you not leave the grounds."

"I'm sure Mr. Richard did!"

Her voice resounded in the quiet room. Hilda looked uncomfortably away.

"I'm sorry," Victoria said after a moment. "I didn't mean to snap at you."

"It's all right—"

"No. No, it isn't. I'm afraid I'm not myself today."

The beady eyes bored into her. "What is it, miss? What's wrong?"

Victoria managed a smile. "I've just got a lot on my mind, Hilda. You've been very kind to show me around. I'll see you later, okay?"

Retrieving her jacket from upstairs, Victoria passed through the front doors and into the cobblestoned courtyard. The afternoon was clear and cold, the smell of pine blanketing the air.

With a passing glance for the immobilized BMW across the

way, she headed for the garage backing up to the woods beyond the courtyard. The windowpanes in the bay doors were dingy, but she could see there were several vehicles parked inside. There was also a strange, computerized lock that prevented her entry.

More of Richard's handiwork, she surmised. Circling round with the hope of finding another door, Victoria heard a rustling in the nearby brush. She looked over, saw a face in the pines, and gasped before realizing it was that of a child.

"Hello," she said with a small laugh. "You startled me."

A little girl stepped out of the trees. Her waist-length hair was pale as wheat, her eyes green as mountain laurel. She could almost have been a little angel but for the worn clothes in which she was dressed. The pants were inches too short, the jacket a boy's hand-me-down and way too large.

"Hello," Victoria said once more.

"Hello," came the high-pitched reply.

"I'm Victoria. Who are you?"

"Missy Rochelle."

"Missy Rochelle? That's a pretty name."

Leaving the forest, the child walked toward her. "You're new at the lodge, aren't you?" she asked.

"That's right. I arrived yesterday for a short visit. How about you? Do you live around here?"

"At the foot of the mountain."

"Really?" Victoria murmured. Obviously the child wasn't living in the lap of luxury, but there must be people. And where there were people, there were cars.

"Did you walk here, Missy?"

"Climbed is more like it. It takes me an hour each way, but it's worth it. I come here a lot. Richard lets me pet the animals, all except Lobo, of course. He doesn't like anybody but Richard."

"I see," Victoria commented with a faint smile.

Coming to stand before her, Missy surveyed her with an inquisitive look that seemed to hover on her hair.

"Is something wrong?" Victoria asked.

"How do you get your hair to stay up like that?"

"With a rubber band. Or you could use a clip or a ribbon. It's called a ponytail."

"I've heard of that," she commented in a tone of importance.

"I'm not surprised. You sound like a very bright little girl. How old are you?"

The child looked at the ground. "Nine. But my stepfather says I act old for my age. He says it won't be long now."

"It won't be long before what?"

"I don't know. He just says that."

Victoria cocked her head as she studied Missy. "It's only two o'clock," she said eventually. "Why aren't you in school?"

"We're on Christmas break."

"That's pretty great, huh? A vacation with no school?"

The girl gave her a somber look. "I don't like it when school's out," she said.

"Even for a holiday?"

"No. I'd rather go to school. Who wants to spend the day in Shine Valley?"

"Shine Valley?" The shrill repetition was out of her mouth before Victoria knew it was coming.

"Yes," Missy replied with a probing look. "Have you been there?"

"No, but . . . I've heard of it."

As the child looked away she took on a troubled look too old for her years. "Sure you have," she murmured. "Everybody's heard of Shine Valley."

Victoria studied her. Despite the coarse clothes, there was an air of refinement about Missy Rochelle, something that clashed with the memory of a rough-edged young hillbilly in a red dress.

"You don't sound like you're from Shine Valley," she commented. "I've met a couple of people from there. They had a distinct way of talking that you don't have."

Missy's chin went up. "I didn't grow up in Shine Valley. We just moved there a year ago after Papa . . . died." Once again her gaze fell to the ground. "We didn't have any money. Mama thought she was doing the right thing when Mr. Sweeney came to town and asked her to marry him."

Sweeney . . . Somehow the name rang a bell.

"She didn't know what he was bringing us to," the child

was saying. "She said as soon as we saved enough money, we'd go away. But then last spring she got pneumonia and died."

Victoria dropped to her knees and looked up into the laurel-green eyes. "I'm sorry, Missy." Lifting a hand, she placed a long strand of hair behind the small shoulder. "My mother died when I was about your age," she went on. "I miss her, but sometimes I get the feeling she's still with me. Like she's kind of watching over me. Do you know what I mean?"

The child smiled. "Yes. I feel that way sometimes. You know, Victoria, you're awfully nice. Pretty, too."

Victoria rose to her feet. "Thanks. So are you."

"Do you think you could put my hair in a ponytail like yours?"

"Sure," Victoria answered with a smile. "But I don't have a rubber band or hairbrush with me at the moment."

"I've got a ribbon at home. And a hairbrush, too."

"Okay. Just bring me a brush and ribbon, and we'll have you a ponytail in no time."

"Okay! See you tomorrow! Bye, Victoria!"

With that she bolted for the forest and disappeared into the screen of trees like an elfin creature.

"Bye!" Victoria called, her gaze searching through the swaying branches where the child had passed.

Missy Rochelle. With a lingering smile, Victoria went back to her exploration.

Leaving the garage, she followed a path that curved around the turreted corner of the lodge and continued to the rear of the property. Here, in a clearing threatened with being overgrown by the brush of the mountain, was a toolshed—the site of Richard's workshop, she assumed—and another garage. This one was small and open and had an old pickup parked inside.

Victoria cast a searching look across the back grounds. They were deserted but for Cainey, who was far across the yard at the woodpile, busily at work splitting firewood. Eyeing the truck, she slipped into the garage and peeped through the driver's window. The keys were in the ignition.

Too easy, she thought with a frown.

Backing away, she bent down and looked under the truck.

No wonder. The disemboweled transmission was lying beneath it. The pickup wasn't going anywhere, keys or no keys.

Propping her hands on her hips, Victoria glanced around the garage. An array of tools was pegged neatly on the walls. More were scattered about a toolbox on the counter. There were jacks in the corner, along with a mechanic's dolly, and even a space heater to take the chill out of the place. She stepped over and turned the dial. Gradually the coils of the heater began to glow, emitting a welcome warmth.

Victoria looked from the truck to the tools and back again. Stripping off her jacket, she went to work.

It was nearly five o'clock, the sun dipping toward the mountains as the air turned bitingly cold. Pulling the fur collar close about her throat, Mavis hurried up the walk and rang the bell.

"Afternoon, Mrs. Brewer," the butler greeted.

"Afternoon, Tibbs." Stepping inside, she began unbuttoning her jacket. "Where is everybody?"

"Miss Jeanette and the girls are upstairs, ma'am. Councilman Skinner's in the study. Can I tell him you're here?"

"That's all right," she replied, already on her way.

Pulling open the double doors, Mavis stepped in without knocking. Dressed in a crisply tailored suit, Kyle was seated at the long mahogany table that had been in the Skinner family for generations—pen poised above a pile of documents and looking every inch the dignified councilman. Tossing her a disinterested glance, he returned his attention to the papers.

"Barbara Jessup ran into Gertrude at the grocery this morning," Mavis announced. "Richard's back."

"So I hear."

Stripping off a glove, she tapped it in her hand as she strolled forward. "Did you also hear he brought a woman with him?"

He chuckled dryly. "Sir Lancelot with a woman?"

"I don't find it so funny."

He looked up. Kyle might be undeniably attractive, but he had the coldest, darkest eyes she'd ever seen.

"No. I don't suppose you would, considering your snowball's chance just melted."

"We don't know that yet," Mavis said with a lift of her

chin. "I intend to go up there and see what's going on with my own eyes. Remember, Kyle. We made a deal. I get first crack."

"Then get on with it," he replied shortly. "I told you before. I'm fed up with waiting. The Boys are meeting just after the turn of the year. I *will* have something positive to report, one way or another."

Mavis started to turn, then hesitated and looked back. "Just exactly what are you planning, Kyle?"

"I'm not planning to let a fortune go down the drain because of some eccentric newcomer. I can tell you that."

"Be more specific," she said. "You're always talking about not waiting any longer. Not waiting for what?"

He leaned back in his chair and eyed her. "Why don't you stop worrying about what I'm going to do and just be glad I'm taking care of it?"

"I want to know, Kyle."

Rising from the chair, he circled the desk to stand before her. His face showed absolutely no expression as he said, "They have trouble with poachers up there, and Adams does a lot of hiking. I think a shooting accident will do quite nicely."

Horror closed over Mavis like a cold ocean wave. "That's murder," she said, her voice barely audible.

He cocked a brow. "That's an ugly word. I said accident. What did you think I was going to do—*wish* him off the mountain?"

"I'll have no part in it, Kyle."

There was the warning of a quick, chilling smile before he grabbed her by the wrist, his fingers biting into her flesh.

"You'll have a part in it, all right. You've been in this from the beginning, and you're staying in."

She pried at his fingers, but to no avail. "You're hurting me."

"You don't always seem to mind," he replied, his eyes drilling into her.

"Let me go, Kyle," she whimpered.

Flinging her hand away, he walked around the desk and sat down behind it. "Oh, and Mavis . . . need I say anything about what happens to you should you let any of this slip?"

Rubbing her wrist, she backed silently away, her frightened eyes locked on his face.

"I didn't think so," Kyle commented blandly and went back to his paperwork.

When Richard and Eric returned to the lodge late that afternoon, it was amidst a flurry of activity. A poacher had shot a young doe. Victoria wheeled from under the pickup as they passed the garage, Eric carrying the wounded animal atop his broad shoulders.

People began spilling out of the lodge and converging on the toolshed—Cainey, Hilda, Chef Renault, and Gertrude. Wiping greasy hands on a cloth, Victoria joined them at the door just as the two men placed the deer on the worktable.

The doe squirmed and squealed in terror. Eric held her down as Richard applied a cloth to her nose and mouth. Gradually she went still. Tossing aside a quilted red jacket, Richard rolled up his shirtsleeves and went about the business of cutting a bullet out of her shoulder.

Beneath the spotlight of an overhead bulb, his hands performed like stars on a stage—one steadying the animal, the other wielding a scalpel with practiced sureness against a backdrop of tawny fur. From behind the screen of Hilda and Gertrude, Victoria watched, her gaze riveted on the movements of his long, suntanned fingers, her memory recalling the touch of them in the darkness of her Pawleys Island porch.

She knew men's hands. They were fast and fleshy and damp with desire. Or so she'd always thought. That night Richard Adams had proved her wrong. His touch was neither fast nor damp, but cool and slow and sure of itself—startling in its ability to trigger a longing to remain within his grasp.

Hogwash! she thought, suddenly rearing herself up.

Nonetheless she continued to follow his hands' every move as he set aside the bloody blade and displayed a bullet before dropping it with an irreverent clink to the floor.

"You want to fix a bed out of those blankets over there?"

His voice brought her to attention. Looking up, Victoria saw that Richard's eyes were on her.

"Me?" she asked, her brows rising.

"Just make it soft and warm," he said, and went about wrapping the deer's shoulder with a bandage.

By the time Victoria made the bed and Richard settled the

animal into it, everyone else had returned to the lodge. When they emerged from the toolshed, the sun was disappearing behind the mountain and the temperature was dropping.

"Want my jacket?" he asked.

"No thanks. Mine's just over there in the garage."

"I'll walk you," he said.

"You don't have to—"

"I'll walk you, Victoria," he reiterated.

Side by side they started across the yard.

"Will the deer be all right?" she asked eventually.

"She'll be fine."

"You looked as though you'd done that sort of thing before."

"Removed a bullet? Yeah. Once or twice."

They walked along, Victoria studying the toes of her boots as her mind's eye replayed the sight of his hands on the deer.

"You were great with the doe," she added.

"You think so?"

"She was helpless. You helped. I guess that makes you something of a humanitarian."

"No more than you," he returned, and drew her eye. "Kids and animals aren't very different. They share the same vulnerability to man, the same helplessness. How about all you've done for the Dalton School and kids like Darcy?"

Victoria gazed at him, and a tremor that had nothing to do with the December cold raced over her. Sometimes he made her want to reach out and . . . Looking away, she hugged herself against the trembling.

"I didn't appreciate your disappearing today," she said bluntly.

"Miss me?"

"I missed being able to ask exactly what I have to do to get out of here."

"Just talk to me. That's all."

The gentle words reached through the gathering darkness, urging her to turn. She tried to crush the impulse, but failed. When she glanced aside, he met her look with a sweet smile. His smiles did strange things.

Turning away, Victoria marched into the garage. From the corner of her eye she saw that Richard followed her inside and propped an arm on the bed of the truck. The front end was up on jacks, a variety of tools lying about the floor. It was obvious she'd been tinkering.

"I see you've been making yourself at home," Richard said.

"I had to find *something* to do."

"What do you think of the pickup?"

Shrugging into her meager jacket, Victoria glanced his way. "It would run better with a transmission."

"Think you can fix it?"

"It's possible."

Straightening away from the truck, he stuffed his hands in his pockets, his elbows forming right angles. She was reminded of the first time she saw him, standing on the dock across the canal.

"So, you're going to bolt off this mountain as soon as you can," he said. "Is that the plan?"

In a quick move Victoria zipped her jacket to her chin. "Generally speaking, yes."

"I wish you wouldn't."

The gentleness in his voice washed over her once more.

"How can it be otherwise?" she questioned sharply.

"It just can . . . if you want it to be." He walked toward her, his eyes glowing like foxfire in twilight. "Trust me," he urged. "I want to help."

"By dragging me off to the mountains?"

"By making a plan here in the mountains. Slates can be cleared, Victoria, and charges dropped . . . if reparation is made."

A host of faces flashed across her mind's eye.

"Reparation?" she repeated in a hard tone. "First, there's no one who deserves it. Second, I wouldn't know where to begin."

"Have there been so many?"

"Enough," she replied tightly.

"Do you have to make them all fall in love with you?"

Her eyes snapped to his. "I don't make them do anything," she stated flatly. "They're perfectly eager all by themselves, but not for love. For lust. Plain and simple."

"It wasn't plain-and-simple lust with Bill. He loved you."

Victoria turned away.

"And you broke his heart."

"It wasn't supposed to be that way," she mumbled.

"What?"

She met Richard's eyes with a feral look. "I said it wasn't supposed to be that way. No one asked him to get emotionally involved."

Richard stared. "Don't you have any regrets at all?"

"Yes! I regret that you saw me at his house!"

The look that came over Richard's face was filled with disbelief and disappointment. Catching her lip, Victoria turned her back and bent to turn off the heater.

"You'd go right back to it, wouldn't you?" he asked quietly. "New town. New guy. Same old pattern."

Though she straightened, Victoria kept her face turned to the wall. "At least it's a pattern *I* control."

"Do you? Or does it control you?"

Again she bit at her lip, this time piercing the flesh and drawing a drop of blood. Whatever it was about Richard Adams, it was powerful enough to grope deep inside and make her gnash her teeth for what might have been.

"Whatever the case," she returned coolly, "the die were cast long before you ever heard of Valerie Blake."

"I don't believe that. Things can change. People can change."

"Maybe I don't want to change. Did you ever think of that?"

"Yes. But if that's so, you're not as bright as I thought. I found you, didn't I? Someday someone else would, too—maybe a cop, in which case you'd merely end up in prison; maybe an irate victim who happens to own a gun, in which case you could end up dead. You're living on the edge of a razor, Victoria. One slip and you're done for. Stop it now, before it's too late."

The ungovernable feelings he provoked flared within her until her cheeks felt on fire. Reaching for the light switch, Victoria plunged the garage into near darkness before facing him. "Why should you want to help me after what happened with Bill?"

Through the shadows of the darkened room, she saw his tall shape move forward. "Because I see someone worthwhile in you, Victoria. Someone who doesn't need a reckless alter ego that's only going to destroy her someday. If you really want control, take it now. Work things out—here, where you're safe."

"Safe?" she repeated on a shrill note. "I've never been more unsafe in my life."

"What do you mean?"

In a fleeting instant Victoria imagined telling him about Kyle Skinner, and it sickened her—the unspeakable tawdriness of her past at Devil's Rock . . . hell, the tawdriness of her entire life! It had always been effortless to keep everything separate—to keep the others locked away in a shadowy realm of unreality. But somehow Richard was opening the door on all the darkness; somehow he had from the first time she heard his voice.

Sweeping wordlessly past, she left the sequestered garage and forged into the fast-falling night. He trotted up beside her.

"You were talking to me, Victoria. Don't stop now."

"I don't want to talk anymore."

"All right. If not now, then tomorrow. Go hiking with me."

Accelerating her pace, she stared ahead toward the kitchen lights. His hand closed about her arm. She whirled to face him.

"Let me go, Richard."

"For now, or forever?" he asked with searching eyes.

"Both."

"I can't."

"You *can*! You said it yesterday—you're calling the shots. This is *your* damn game! *Your* damn mountain!"

"Hike it with me," he repeated quietly. "We'll take the north trail over the bridge and up to the falls. Maybe you won't be so anxious to leave when you see what the mountain has to offer."

Victoria snatched her arm out of his light grasp. "You paint a pretty picture, but all you really want is the chance to probe and cut—just like you did with the deer."

"Maybe," he acknowledged. "And she's going to be all right."

Victoria peered up at him, feeling the violent clash of poles pulling one against the other—one force wanting to believe, a stronger one surging forth to deny.

"Come on," he urged. "Let's hike tomorrow. It'll do you good."

"I'm not about to equate myself with a broken animal," she returned in a voice cold as the mountain night. "Nor this escapade of yours with some sort of therapeutic retreat."

Stalking away, Victoria threw open the backdoor and swept through the kitchen, oblivious to the curious stares that followed her as she passed.

Mavis had just walked in when the blonde came barreling out of the banquet hall toward the staircase, snatching off a common, buff-colored windbreaker in the process. A moment later Richard emerged on the same path, taking long strides after her. Mavis's heart sank as she brought a smile to her lips.

"Well, hello!" she greeted brightly.

The blonde looked up and came to a halt. She was taller by several inches, younger by several years, dressed in jeans that hugged slim legs, a sweater that hugged a slim throat. A smudge of grease marred the cheek of an otherwise flawless face, the one of storybook princesses. And her eyes—silvery blue, like an iced-over lake. Never had Mavis seen eyes quite so shocking, although . . . suddenly there seemed to be something familiar about them. She had no chance to consider the notion as the blonde glanced to the floor. The sinking feeling swelled as Mavis offered a hand.

"I'm Mavis Brewer. Please allow me to welcome you to Devil's Rock, Miss . . . ?"

Victoria hesitated for an instant, finally supplying her hand for a brief shake as Richard came up behind her. "Victoria Blackwood," she said.

"Victoria?" Mavis repeated with a lift of her brows. "I love the name. So regal."

Her gaze sweeping to Richard, she strolled up to him, hips swinging. She'd changed outfits three times before settling on the red cashmere ensemble that accented her figure and lit up her complexion. Topped with the sable coat Harry had given her on their final anniversary, Mavis knew she looked her best, and buried the thought that because of the shabbily clad blonde it might all be for naught.

"And hello to you, vagabond," she murmured.

Despite high heels, it was necessary to rise on tiptoe to kiss Richard on the cheek, the stubble of his beard prickling her lips and stirring thoughts that flew beyond the issues of heliports and Kyle Skinner. Rocking back down, Mavis looked for Richard's smile. It came, along with a slight blush.

"Hello, Mavis," he said. "How have you been?"

"Bored," she replied on a sighing note. "But then how could it be otherwise with you gone so long?"

As he caught a sharp look from the blonde, the pink cast of his cheeks went a shade darker. Mavis released an airy laugh.

"Don't mind me, Victoria. Richard and I are just dear old friends, although I suppose at the moment a little business is mixed in through Kyle Skinner. How about the two of you? Have you been—uh—friends long?"

"Not at all," the blonde fired.

"No?" Mavis questioned innocently, although more than anything she longed to reach out and throttle the beautiful woman.

"We met through mutual friends in Atlanta," Richard supplied.

"How interesting," Mavis said as an awkward moment fell. "And are you planning to stay with us for long, Miss Blackwood?"

"A short while."

"Not *too* short, I hope," Richard put in.

Ignoring the remark, Victoria Blackwood slipped Mavis a small smile and started to move away. "It's very nice to meet you," she said. "But if you'll excuse me, I was on my way upstairs."

Richard's arm shot out to corral her shoulders. "Don't rush off, Victoria. Like Mavis said, we're old friends. Why don't we all sit down and have a drink before dinner?"

As the blonde turned to face him her smile broadened, though Mavis had the feeling it was frigid as a winter morning.

"As you know, Richard," she said, "I have a terrible headache and probably won't make dinner, much less a drink beforehand."

Mavis saw the look that passed between them—one indomitable will pitted against another. The woman won out.

"Of course," Richard acquiesced. As he removed his arm

she drew swiftly away. "I forgot you're not feeling well," he added. "Maybe you can join us later."

"Good-bye," she replied noncommittally, and hurried up the stairs.

"Interesting girl," Mavis commented, drawing Richard's eyes from her disappearing back.

"Yes," he agreed.

"How about that drink?"

Shrugging out of her fur, Mavis tossed it to Richard and led the way to the liquor cabinet in the library, giving him ample time to appreciate her shifting walk as he followed. "Brandy?" she asked, picking up the crystal decanter.

"All right," he answered slowly.

She poured two glasses and turned to see that he'd sat down in one of two single chairs by the firelit hearth, leaving the expansive sofa that would have seated both of them vacant. With a determined smile she came to stand before him, handed him the snifter, and offered her own for a toast.

"To good times," she said, touching her glass to his.

They took a drink, and he sat back in the chair.

"So, tell me, Mavis. What did I miss while I've been gone?"

Shifting her weight to one leg, she attained a sexy pose while rolling her eyes coquettishly to the ceiling. "Let's see. Corinne Jessup married Glen Moody, who was wearing the most awful blue tux you've ever seen. Mary Jane Halliday had a baby girl who's bald as a billiard ball. Cody and Brent McAllister got arrested for absconding with old Mrs. Weatherby's cow. . . ."

He laughed, and as she watched, Mavis's smile faded away. He was so beautiful, his hair and eyes gleaming in the firelight. She thought of the times she'd watched him, longed for him, imagined him when it was Kyle on top of her. For the past four years Richard Adams had been a bright dream in her dreary Devil's Rock existence.

All it would take was one time, she told herself. One time and he'd be hungry for more.

Acting on instinct, she took his glass, set it aside with her own, and sank onto his lap, lifting her legs to dangle brazenly over the arm of the chair.

"Have a seat," he said with a light smile, though he failed to put welcoming arms around her.

"I missed you," she murmured, trailing a fingertip along his jaw. "You were going to call me when you got back, remember?"

"Was I?" he replied blankly.

"We have business to discuss. That day at the airport you promised to think over Kyle's offer."

"I forgot—"

"Did you forget *everything* about that day?"

Reaching behind his neck, Mavis pulled him close and kissed him, hoping for the same melting response as before. He mumbled something against her lips. Choosing to hear it as a moan of passion, she went on with the seduction, one hand securing him in the kiss while the other roamed his chest.

He mumbled again. This time she heard her name, but paid it no mind as her body caught fire. God, it was going to be good. She could tell. Her fingers moved steadily down, closing with practiced confidence between his legs.

His head lurched back as he tore away. "Dammit, Mavis!"

Seconds later he'd imprisoned her hands in his own. She looked up to find him scowling down at her.

"Dammit, Mavis," he repeated quietly. "You're a beautiful woman. I know it, and you know it. But we're *just friends*."

"And that's all we'll ever be?"

He glanced toward the hearth. Snatching her hands from his, Mavis climbed abruptly off his lap and glared down at him.

"Look at me, Richard."

He turned her way, the reluctance on his face piercing her heart as well as her pride.

"So, what does it take to get to you?" she asked angrily. "A snooty little iceberg like Miss Blackwood up there?"

"Victoria has nothing to do with this."

"The hell she doesn't! The last time I saw you we made fireworks together. You can't deny it! All the time you were gone I kept thinking about you, waiting, hoping. . . . And all the time you were with *her*, weren't you?"

He frowned but said nothing.

"*Weren't* you?" Mavis demanded.

"This is going nowhere," he answered. Getting to his feet,

he gazed down with an uncomfortable, apologetic expression that crushed her dreams into the dirt.

"Don't look at *me* that way, baby," she retaliated in a near hiss. "You're the one who's missing out."

"Probably so."

With a toss of her head Mavis turned and reached for her coat. "What do I tell Kyle?"

"I think you know what to tell Kyle."

"Yes," she said in a cutting tone. "I guess I do." Slinging the fur over her shoulder, Mavis sashayed out of the lodge before the stinging in her eyes turned to tears.

By the time she reached home, her eyes were dry, if somewhat parched by the burning image of a blue-eyed blonde with grease on her cheek. Closing the front door with a bang, Mavis didn't stop to shed her coat and gloves as she stalked to the phone.

"Go for it, Kyle," she said when he picked up. "The ball's in your court now."

=NINE=

The fire leaped in hot swirls as Victoria stoked the logs, her gaze lingering in the flames as her mind re-created a night more than four years past.

It was Halloween, and the Skinners were having a costume party. Having opened the imposing family home to more than fifty guests, Jeanette played the gracious hostess while her husband slipped upstairs with Mavis Brewer. When they returned a half hour later, Victoria had the bad luck to be standing near the foot of the staircase. Kyle seized the opportunity to introduce them.

"Vanessa?" she'd repeated. "I love the name. So feminine."

Setting the poker aside, Victoria rose to her feet. Years had passed, and on that night she'd been wigged and costumed in the eighteenth-century fashion of Marie Antoinette. Still, Mavis had looked at her in a strange, penetrating way. It was possible she'd made a connection, and if so, she was sure to tell Kyle. The way she alluded to him, she obviously remained close to the man, and after all, Vanessa Blair was his father's alleged murderer.

The image of Kyle's face materialized in the fire, the black eyes glowing with hellish light.

Now she knew with certainty he was still here, still prowling the North Carolina Blue Ridge like a hungry wolf. Whatever prey fell in his path would be devoured—like an unlucky sparrow straying across the path of a foraging beast. She'd been lucky once. She couldn't count on being lucky again.

Seeing Mavis Brewer brought it all excruciatingly close, and dispelled any notion that Black Top Mountain was sufficiently removed from Devil's Rock to offer safety. She must leave, but . . . where would she go?

Victoria stared into the flames, her troubled thoughts turning to Pawleys—the school, the beach house, the sting of brine on her face as she turned the boat to sea. They were all farther away than mere miles now. She glanced across the room to the phone, longing to call Darcy and Anita, knowing the most she could hope for was the boon of hearing their voices. She couldn't ask for their help, and even if she did, there was none they could give.

She was caught, and there was only one way out—the way of burned bridges, unfamiliar streets, unknown faces. The way of starting over again.

Turning briskly from the hearth, Victoria went about the bedroom picking up a sweater here, socks there, and tucking them into her suitcase. She wasn't going anywhere, not tonight. But packing gave her a comforting sense of readiness. Collecting her things from the bath, she stuffed them in her shoulder bag and zipped it up.

There it was, all she had left after fifteen years. Oh, there were IDs Richard didn't know about, bank accounts tucked here and there that would keep her going. But everything that mattered was slipping away. All at the hand of one man.

Sinking down on the velvet cover of the four-poster bed, Victoria released a heavy breath. Richard Adams had tracked her, trapped her, destroyed the only life she'd been able to forge that had any meaning. She should be filled with hatred and rage.

Instead she felt only a consuming sense of loss. In spite of everything, she couldn't bring herself to hate the vision of the prince smiling through the mist.

Rising from his chair at the head of the table, Richard took the plate from the vacant setting and began loading it with portions of veal and rice, green beans and sweet-potato soufflé.

He looked up as the conversation around him dwindled to a halt. His gaze swept from Eric to Miles to Cainey to the chef, and then to Gertrude and Hilda. All six pairs of eyes were staring.

"So?" Richard challenged.

"So, it looks like your appetite has grown since you came back," the chef said with a chuckle. The others joined in.

Richard gave them a sour look. "She didn't feel like coming down, okay? She's got a headache."

"Yes. I've seen that kind of headache before," Miles chimed.

"It seemed to come on about the time Mavis Brewer arrived," Eric said with mock thoughtfulness. "Quite a dilemma, Richard—one you can't get rid of, the other you can't get hold of."

Again the laughter.

"Get outta here," Richard mumbled.

He continued about his task as the others left the table . . . except for Hilda, who remained behind her chair scrutinizing his every move.

"Okay, Hilda," he said finally. "What's on your mind?"

"She's different from the rest of us, Mr. Richard."

"Who?"

"You know very well who. She's no antiques dealer. At least that's not why she's here. The most interest she's shown in anything around the place is for that old truck of yours."

"Engines are kind of a hobby with her," Richard offered evasively.

"She doesn't want to be here," Hilda returned bluntly. "I can't help but wonder why she is."

He glanced up and paused. "That's my affair, Hilda. Suffice it to say I'm hoping to help her with a problem."

"She doesn't seem to want your help."

"Maybe not yet."

Hilda shook her head scoldingly. "She's not a wounded creature you can nurse back to health, Mr. Richard."

"Yes, she is," he replied, decisively returning to his chore. "Something—someone—wounded her long ago. I've just got to find out who and how."

"I see. So now you've turned her into a pretty puzzle."

Richard scowled as the remark hit home. The others came and went from the kitchen, carrying away plates and glasses, chatting as they went. Hilda remained where she was, silent as stone.

"I know what I'm doing, Hilda," he said ultimately.

"Do you? Then I suppose I don't need to tell you that if you load any more vittles on that plate, it's liable to crack."

Richard looked down at the plate in his hand. It was filled to the brim with more food than Victoria could put away in a day, much less a single meal. With an arch glance for Hilda, he procured a serving tray from the sideboard and escaped both the dining hall and the old woman's piercing eyes. As he climbed the stairs Lobo trotted up to join him, watching curiously as Richard balanced the tray with one hand and tapped at Victoria's door. There were footsteps, and then she opened the door a mere crack.

"I thought you might be hungry," he said.

Her pale eyes darted to the tray. "That was very thoughtful," she murmured. Drawing the door wide, she moved aside for him to enter.

"Home, Lobo," Richard commanded, and walking into the chamber, deposited the tray on the tea table. He couldn't help but notice the packed bags sitting by the bed, or that Victoria continued to stand by the open door, wordlessly inviting his departure. Stuffing his hands in his pockets, he walked toward her.

"Did you happen to reconsider about the hike?" he asked. She looked down at her boots as he came to stand in the doorway.

"The weather is supposed to be clear through tomorrow," he added. "After that—"

"Stop pushing!"

Richard's mouth slammed shut as his gaze raced over the recalcitrant face turned up to him. Little by little the angry color faded from her cheeks.

"God," she mumbled in a weary tone. "Can't you just let up for now? It's been forty-eight hours since you showed up at that motel, and I feel as though I've aged a hundred years."

"All right," he replied slowly. "Is there anything you'd *like* to do tomorrow? Maybe drive into Devil's Rock and—"

"No!" Once again a crimson blush flared to her cheeks. "Did your friend stay for supper?" she added sharply.

"Mavis? No. She . . ." Richard paused as the scene in the library flashed to mind. "She left shortly after you did."

"She's very attractive," Victoria said. "Have you known her long?"

"About four years. Everyone around here knows Mavis. She keeps kind of a high profile."

"Does she come to the lodge often?"

"Every now and then," Richard answered, his brows furrowing. "Why all the interest in Mavis?"

Victoria glanced away. "Just curious."

"We're not involved, if that's what you're wondering."

The pale eyes snapped back to his. "I wouldn't presume to wonder. What you do is your business—though I gather such an attitude is quite beyond your grasp. Look, Richard. I appreciate your bringing up the food. But if you don't mind, I'm tired and I'd like to be alone."

"I feel suddenly tired, myself," he returned shortly. "Good night, Victoria."

Stripping off his sweater as he stalked into his room, Richard slung it across the back of the chair, plopped down, and pulled off his boots. Damn, she was infuriating!

Curled in his place at the foot of the bed, Lobo gave a questioning yip as Richard stomped past in his stockinged feet.

"It's a long story, boy," he muttered.

Richard lit the fire, stoked it to a blaze, and sat down on the braided rug by the hearth. Spotting a piece of kindling on the nearby floor, he sent it spinning into the flames.

The fireside was penetratingly warm. Pulling the T-shirt over his head, Richard tossed it aside, inviting the heat to radiate on bare skin as his fevered thoughts hovered on Victoria.

He went back to the beginning, remembering the way she'd stood in Bill's rose garden, staring into the distance as though separated from the rest of the world. Little had he known how intricately their lives would become entwined, though she remained separate . . . unreachable . . . unfathomable.

How long the whole thing could go on, Richard wasn't sure. She was a wanted felon, and he'd absconded with her the same way the McAllister boys had taken off with Mrs. Weatherby's cow. Linking himself with the McAllisters, he had no delusions about the questionability of his actions.

Then there was Bill. He'd spent the last two Christmases at

the lodge, and was probably expecting an invitation for this one. As Richard realized he had no intention of extending it, he felt an upsurge of the guilt that had haunted him for weeks.

Life used to be so simple. He had no excuse for not contacting Bill—none!—except for the tornado of events that had swept him up in Atlanta, spirited him to Pawleys Island, and finally dropped him back on the Black Top . . . bound to a bewildering entity he couldn't reach, but couldn't release.

Richard told himself there were extenuating circumstances. Months ago when he'd started the adventure with the notion of avenging Bill, he'd had no idea of the complexities that lay in store—the paradoxes of a woman who could steal one day and succor abused children the next . . . someone who could drive off in a stolen car without a backward glance, and tuck a wounded doe gently beneath a blanket.

On the one hand she was ruthless; on the other saintly. In either case, if Richard faced the truth, he was obsessed with her.

Lobo moseyed over and hunkered down beside him. Reaching down, Richard scratched behind his ear.

"Nobody said it was going to be easy. Right, boy?" With a grumbling yawn, the coyote settled his chin on Richard's leg and closed his eyes.

"Right," Richard murmured. Burying a hand in the scruff of Lobo's neck, he stared into the fire.

It was only her second morning at the lodge, but as Victoria trotted down the staircase she was struck by the notion that she was no longer a stranger. The golden sunbeams flooding the entrance hall were familiar, as was the cheery air of camaraderie when she entered the kitchen to a chorus of "good mornings" from the lodge folk gathered about the breakfast table. Everyone was there but Richard.

"Will you have some coffee?" Chef Renault asked. "I have a special blend shipped in from South America."

"I'd love it," she replied, drawing a pleased smile from the chef and an enthusiastic invitation from Gertrude to have a seat in the chair next to hers.

"We missed you last night at supper," she chirped.

"Thanks. I . . . wasn't feeling very well."

"So Richard said," Miles commented, his eyes peeping over the tops of his glasses.

"And no small wonder," Hilda put in, "what with the commotion of traveling and coming to a new place and all. How are you feeling this morning, miss?"

Victoria gave the old woman a smile. "Better, Hilda. Thanks. Speaking of Richard, where is he?"

"In the library," the old woman answered with a staunch look. "You should see the correspondence that piled up while he was away. I reckon he'll be there for a week or so."

"We all are going to the farm on the next mountain," Gertrude piped.

"We all?"

"Eric and Miles and me. They have the best Douglas firs in the Blue Ridge, and we're going to get the biggest one they've got and put it smack in the middle of the entrance hall."

"A Christmas tree?" Victoria questioned.

"After all, it's less than a week before the day," Hilda said.

"Care to come along?" Eric asked. "We've got plenty of room."

The thought that slammed into her mind had to do with the possibility of escape, but as Victoria looked at the trusting faces turned her way, the notion fizzled.

"Thanks anyway," she replied. "I have some things to do here."

"Aha!" Gertrude exclaimed. "She's going to work. Soon we'll have all kinds of ritzy antiques all over the place."

Victoria chuckled. "I don't know about that. Thanks, Chef," she added as he placed a steaming cup of coffee in front of her.

"Would you care for breakfast?" he asked. "I'm afraid the rest of us have already eaten, but I've got waffle mix and—"

"Please," Victoria interrupted, raising a palm. "Don't trouble yourself. I'm fine. Really. The coffee smells wonderful."

"We're going to have a decorating party when we get back," Gertrude announced. "We've got strings of lights a mile long, and ornaments, and an angel for the top. And we're going to open a keg of cider. Ever had mountain cider, Victoria?"

"No. I can't say that I have."

"Boy, are you in for a treat!"

"It sounds like it," Victoria admitted, sinking once again into a smile.

She took a sip of the hot coffee, her hooded gaze moving around the circle of people at the table. She couldn't help but be touched by how friendly they were, how welcoming. It would be easy to surrender to the feeling that she'd come to a winter playland fully staffed with playmates, but . . . she couldn't stay.

"Has anyone looked in on the doe?" she asked.

"I checked on her earlier," Miles answered. "The dressing on her shoulder looks good, and so does she. I wager she'll be good as new in a week or so."

Victoria glanced to the table's centerpiece, a bowl piled a half foot high with apples, oranges, and bananas. "Aren't deer supposed to like apples?" she asked.

"Oh, yes," Miles replied. Following the direction of her gaze, he broke into a smile, the expression changing his serious, bespectacled countenance into that of an adventurous boy.

"Want to take her some?" he added brightly.

When Victoria left the kitchen some ten minutes later, it was with a bag of apple carefully sliced into deer-sized bites. She stepped out back thinking she shouldn't be feeling quite as good as she did.

It was nearly eleven. Still, the winter morning slapped her with breathtaking cold. The zippered windbreaker she'd brought from Pawleys was appropriate for a mild South Carolina winter, but sadly lacking for the North Carolina mountains.

She glanced up at the sky. It was brilliant, cloudless, the sapphire blue of postcards and magazine pictures. Fishing dark glasses out of her pocket, she put them on, noting the way her breath clouded the lenses as they passed her mouth. It must be in the thirties, the air clean and sharp and cutting down her throat the way she remembered from long ago. She headed for the toolshed, smiling when she saw Missy Rochelle propped in the door.

"Hi, Missy," she greeted. "What are you up to?"

"Shhh," the child said with a finger to her lips. "There's a hurt deer in there."

"I know," Victoria whispered. "I brought her this."

"What is it?" Missy whispered back.

"Apples. I understand deer—especially hurt ones—*love* apple. How about if you and I offer it to her together?"

Had it been only a matter of hours since she and Richard bedded down the anesthetized doe on the mound of blankets? It seemed much longer. As she and Missy stepped quietly into the toolshed, the animal looked up with wide brown eyes.

"Easy, girl," Victoria said. "We're friends. Aren't we, Missy?"

"Yes. Friends," the child quickly confirmed.

Reaching into the bag, Victoria withdrew a piece of the apple and sank to a crouch as she extended her hand. "Here you go, darlin'," she crooned. "I'll bet you've never had the treat of an apple in wintertime."

The velvety black nose extended. The mouth reached. Seconds later the doe was munching contentedly—if somewhat hesitantly—from their hands. She ate all they had to give and sniffed for more, staying curled all the while in the blankets Victoria and Richard had fixed for her the evening before.

Victoria rose to her feet. "That's all we have," she said, spreading her palms. "But we'll come back later. Won't we, Missy?"

"Yes," the child agreed, her eyes only for the doe. "We'll be back later. I promise."

Closing the toolshed door against the cold, the two of them walked into the clearing. Victoria looked—really looked—at Missy. She was wearing a warm red sweater and matching pants, but no jacket. When she proffered a red ribbon in gloveless hands, something about the look on her face tore at Victoria's heart.

"I have a hairbrush in my back pocket," she said.

"You want me to do your hair?" Victoria questioned with lifted brows. "Okay. Come here. Sit down on this tree stump."

Missy obeyed, and Victoria began brushing through the long, shining tresses, the filaments sifting through her gloved fingers like skeins of gold.

"You have very pretty hair, Missy."

"Thank you."

"You know, a lot of people pay money to make their hair the color of yours."

"They do? Why?"

"Because it's so pretty."

"Where do you live?" Missy asked after a moment.

Victoria grasped the hair in a practiced grip and wrapped the ribbon tightly around it. "The coast. Actually it's an island."

"Is it nice?"

"Yes," Victoria admitted on a wistful note. "Very nice."

"I think I would like to live on an island very much."

"Would you?" Victoria tied the bow with a flourish and left the ribbons trailing. "There now. Let me have a look at you." Stepping around the tree stump, she smiled. "You see? Perfect. How does it feel?"

Missy lifted a hand to the back of her head. "Good."

"Well, I guess I'd better be moving along," Victoria said. "I'm doing some work on that pickup truck over there in the garage."

Missy's perfect little-girl features pinched into an expression of disbelief. "Ladies don't work on trucks," she said.

"This one does," Victoria replied with a smile. "Want to keep me company?"

As she lay back on the dolly and rolled under the front end, Missy sat down on the garage floor and peered beneath the truck with wide-eyed interest.

"What's wrong with it?" she asked.

"The transmission went bad."

"Is that important?"

"Yeah. Pretty important," Victoria answered with a light laugh. "The truck won't run without it. See that wrench over there by the toolbox, Missy? Hand it to me, would you?"

The girl scrambled to do her bidding. "How did you learn about trucks and things?" she asked.

"I just always liked knowing how things work. When I was about your age, I used to love to take my toys apart and put them back together again. Later it was engines."

"Could you teach me?"

"Sure, I could teach you, but . . . well, it would take time, and I don't know how much longer I'll be here, Missy."

"When are you leaving?"

"Soon, I'm afraid."

"How soon?"

Victoria examined the motor above her. Another day's work ought to do it. "Maybe tomorrow night . . . I'm not sure."

"Take me with you!"

The child's words rang as both a demand and a plea. Pushing from underneath the truck, Victoria sat up on the dolly. "What are you saying, Missy?"

"Take me away from here. I want to live with you on the island."

Victoria's heart wrenched at the look of abject supplication on the little girl's face. "Take you? Now, how could I do that? What would your stepfather say?"

"He'd be mad," came the rebellious reply. "But not because he cares about me! Just because . . ." The child's voice broke.

Victoria extended anxious hands, catching her head as she would have looked away. "Because of what, Missy?"

The clear, green eyes lifted. "Never mind. I just can't stay there anymore. Please!"

Though Victoria got the impression Missy was on the verge of tears, there were none in her eyes. "What's wrong, Missy? Tell me."

"I can't."

"Why not?"

"I just can't tell. It's a secret."

Victoria placed tender hands on the small shoulders. "It must not be a very good secret if it makes you so upset."

"It isn't," she admitted, and lunging forward, threw her arms about Victoria's neck. "Please take me."

Victoria cradled her head against her shoulder. "Missy, I . . ." She trailed off as she spotted Richard walking in their direction. At the sound of his footsteps, Missy got swiftly to her feet.

"Don't tell Richard I asked you," she whispered. "Don't tell anyone! Promise!"

"All right," Victoria quietly agreed. "I promise."

As Richard stepped inside, Missy darted past.

"Bye, Richard! Bye, Victoria!" she called, her long blond ponytail streaming behind as she dashed into the sunshine.

"I didn't realize you two know each other," Richard said.

Rising to her feet, Victoria moved in his direction. "Tell me about Missy."

He shrugged. "A nice little girl. She likes to visit the animals and birds. She lives down the mountain."

"So she said."

Richard caught her eye with a sharp look. "Don't go thinking you can find refuge in Shine Valley, Victoria. It's not a nice place."

"Then what's Missy Rochelle doing there?" she challenged.

"What are you asking?"

"If it's not a nice place, and you know Missy is living there, why don't you do something about it?"

Richard spread his palms. "Like what?"

"Like look into it," Victoria supplied. "See if children are being abused there."

"This is the first I've heard of abuse."

"What *have* you heard?" she inquired with the arch of a brow.

"Nothing . . . except Shine Valley is rough and backward and full of miscreants who'd cut a throat for pocket change."

"And you just turn a blind eye?"

"Not a blind eye," Richard objected, his face settling in disgruntled lines. "I just never thought of them before . . . the children of Shine Valley, I mean. Maybe I *will* look into it."

"Well, then," Victoria concluded, "I guess something good has come of my being here, after all."

Stuffing his hands in his jacket pockets, he gave her a long searching look. "You get so fired up about kids getting an even break. Why not give yourself one?"

Sunlight danced on the fair streaks of his hair, glistened in the dark eyes, glanced off cheekbones red with cold. He was tall and masculine and breathtaking. Once again she thought of the first time she observed him from an unknowing distance on Pawleys Island. Even then she'd felt something; now the powerful draw of the man sent charges running through her like so many electric currents. The feeling was exhilarating, dizzying, frightening. With considerable effort Victoria maintained a look of utter calm that masked it all.

"Why don't *you* be the one to give me a break?" she taunted. "My distributor cap would do quite nicely."

"You know I can't do that."

"Then if you'll excuse me, I'd like to get back to work."

He cast a fleeting look to the truck. "Are you planning to put in another day on the pickup?"

She folded her arms as she gazed steadily up at him. "Are you telling me not to?"

"It doesn't do me any good to tell you anything, does it, Victoria? I've told you there's a way to set things right. I've told you I'll do everything I can to help."

Richard's eyes settled on hers, igniting a secret fire of whose existence he hadn't the slightest suspicion.

"My hope is that you'll come to me," he added. "In time."

His quiet words set the inner fire blazing; heat flashed up Victoria's spine and into her face. She fought it down with thoughts of Mavis and Kyle and the urgent need to leave Devil's Rock far behind.

"You're the renowned genius," she returned levelly. "You should know better than to manufacture hope out of thin air."

Cocking his jaw, Richard backed away, though he continued to gaze at her—punishingly—from beneath furrowed brows.

"Have a nice day," he said finally, and turning on his heel, headed off in the direction of the toolshed.

Raleigh

"Thank you, Dr. Fontaine."

Sheryl smiled into the gentle, bespectacled eyes. The only child of wealthy parents who had died when he was a toddler, Theodore had been raised by an embittered spinster aunt who criticized his every move. Tormented by an inferiority complex, paralyzed by introversion, he'd spent the majority of his life sequestered in the old family house, burying himself in books and movies, unable to function in the real world. Now, at the age of fifty-one, he was two months into his first job. And today's session marked the end of three years' therapy.

"I'm very proud of you, Theodore."

Rosy color rushed to the flagging cheeks. "It's not much of a post, I suppose."

"It's an excellent post, and Mrs. Ford's bookshop is one of the most highly regarded in the city. Don't demean what you're doing, Theodore. Mrs. Ford says she doesn't know how she ever managed without you."

His face went a shade brighter as he rose to his feet. "And how am I to manage without you?" he asked. "If not for you, none of this would have come about."

Sheryl stepped forward and shook his hand. "I helped," she said. "But you did all the hard work. Don't ever forget that."

Spotting a glitter of moisture in his eyes, she felt an unprofessional burning in her own. "Now, congratulations and good luck and get going," she prompted. "I'm sure Mrs. Ford is anxiously awaiting your return."

When he left, Sheryl moved to the window and looked down, waiting for him to appear on the sidewalk two stories below. Wreathed in holiday greenery and lights, Hillsboro Street was bustling with Christmas shoppers and office workers embarking on the lunch hour. It was the kind of milling scene that three years ago would have struck fear in Theodore's heart. She watched with immense pride and satisfaction as he merged smoothly with the crowd and disappeared up the street.

She remained by the window, her thoughts gradually drifting to the subject lodged in the back of her mind. It had been nearly two weeks. Richard should have called by now. Each day she'd hoped to hear he was back in the mountains, but there had been no word.

Was he still on Pawleys Island? Had he returned home? And what of the mysterious Victoria?

Losing patience with wondering, Sheryl crossed to the phone and dialed the mountain number. Hilda answered.

"Merry Christmas, Hilda."

"And a very merry one to you, miss. My, it's nice to hear your voice. It's been a long time."

"Yes, it has," Sheryl admitted with a wistful thought of the last time she'd visited the lodge. They'd been a couple then—at least, the closest thing to it since university days. She'd spent the days following Richard's lead about the mountain, the nights in his arms.

"Is Richard around?" she asked.

"He went out back not ten minutes ago."

So! He had *returned home!* Sheryl drew a breath of relief.

"Would you like me to go and fetch him? I believe he went to the garage to see Miss Blackwood."

Her spirits sank like a stone in a pond. "Would that be *Victoria* Blackwood?" Sheryl asked.

"The very same. Do you know her?"

"Not really," Sheryl mumbled, and reached for her book. "Hold on a minute, will you?"

She flipped through several pages. There was an appointment she couldn't miss the next morning at ten. After that, her schedule was cleared for the holidays. "What do you think, Hilda? Can you handle another guest for a few days? I could be there tomorrow afternoon."

"Why, of course! I'm sure Mr. Richard will—"

"Let's keep this between us for now, okay, Hilda? I'd like to surprise him for Christmas."

Hanging up the phone, Sheryl peered unseeingly across the room.

Victoria Blackwood. Thief. Felon. Fugitive from justice. And Richard was harboring her. Had he lost his mind?

Sheryl closed her eyes against the fearful query that dawned. *Or was it his heart that was missing?*

When Victoria ceased her labors late in the afternoon, the pickup's transmission was in working order, though she'd deny it to anyone who asked.

Turning off the heater, she stepped outside the garage and looked up at the sky. Clouds were rolling in, the deep blue bordered to the north by a bank of gray. Richard had said the day would be clear, and it had been. But now it looked as though bad weather was on the way.

Hugging the windbreaker close around her, she started across the yard. The truck was running, ominous weather impending. All signs targeted tonight as the night, and yet as she looked ahead to the lodge where light beamed from the arched windows of the kitchen, she couldn't deny the reluctance that welled up inside her.

The mountain, the lodge, the people within. It wasn't going to be like leaving a bunch of strangers anymore.

Then, of course, there was Richard. With every day she was around him, she felt his impact more deeply. Now it was more than just the physical attraction that startled her, it was feelings as well. Today, with a mere look, he'd made her feel sorry and ashamed. *You're the renowned genius,* she'd quipped. The flip remark had tasted bitter when she caught the look in his eyes, and she'd ended up spending most of the afternoon reviewing the many times she'd snapped at him, rejected him, thrown his offers back in his face.

There was no doubt about it. He was getting to her in a way she'd never dreamed possible—an unexpected, amazing man. Brilliant, as everyone knew. Only this time Richard Adams didn't know what he was talking about. Clear the slates. Start a new life. He made it sound naively simple, but then she supposed, she shouldn't expect the pure of heart to anticipate how morbidly entangled a tainted life could become.

Clearing the slates meant facing the dark—charges of murder, charges of theft, Vanessa Blair, Valerie Blake, and so many more. Suddenly the phantasms took on an unnerving reality.

Accelerating her pace, she hurried through the door and into the kitchen, where she found Hilda putting the last touches on one of several platters of cold cuts. From the front hall came the commotion of voices, laughter, and Christmas music.

"Evenin', miss," Hilda greeted. "How's the old truck faring?"

Victoria shrugged out of her jacket. "It's not in the greatest shape," she answered truthfully. "That looks good," she added, peeping over the old woman's shoulder and changing the subject.

"I'm glad you like the looks of it," Hilda returned with a smiling glance. "I'm afraid this is all there'll be for supper. Everyone else is too busy with the tree to think about food."

"That's right," Victoria said, and draping her jacket about a kitchen chair, came to lean against the table near the old woman. "They got a Christmas tree today."

Hilda nodded. "And a fair party there is out there, too. Music and cider and carrying on. A while back Gertrude actually got the chef to dance with her!"

Victoria laughed. "So that's what all the commotion is about? Everyone's up front decorating the tree?"

"Every one of them," Hilda confirmed. "Except Mr. Richard, of course."

Victoria's smile faded. "Except Richard? Where is *he*?"

"Still in the library, I believe."

"He's not joining the party?"

"Oh, no. It's been many years since he touched a Christmas tree. He doesn't begrudge us having one, but I know he'd rather do without it."

"Why?"

The beady eyes lifted as Hilda turned to face her. "I told you before that Christmas is a sad time for him."

"But you didn't tell me why."

"It's a bit of a story," the old woman warned.

"I've got time," Victoria returned, and settled more comfortably against the table.

Hilda released a long sigh. "All right, then, you may know that Mr. Richard was always terribly bright."

"I got that impression."

"But what you don't know is that from the time he was a boy, people were after him—come here, go there, do this, do that. By the time he was a young man, he was known across the country. And when he graduated from the university, the government snapped him up like a prize plum. After that, he went from one thing to another, one place to another, always hither and yon. . . ."

"Go on," Victoria urged when the old woman trailed off.

Hilda's gaze shifted beyond her. "He was twenty-two," she began, "and in this particular year he was doing work for some institute in the Northwest. The night he arrived home for the holidays, his parents insisted he accompany them to a Christmas party. Mr. Richard didn't want to go, and he made them a deal—if they stopped pushing him, he'd decorate the tree while they were gone. Late that night the police officer came to the door. A drunken driver had crossed the center line and hit them head-on. Mr. and Mrs. Adams died instantly."

"I'm sorry," Victoria murmured.

"It was very sad, but it's long past. Except for the fact that Mr. Richard continues to blame himself."

"For the accident? He wasn't even there."

"He says it never would have happened if he'd gone with them. He'd have been driving, and his reactions were faster. Or his presence would have changed things, and the car wouldn't have been in that spot at that moment. Whatever he thinks, the result is that he blames himself, and for him Christmas has become a time of mourning."

The thought of Richard in pain brought an ache to her throat. Once again Victoria marveled at the effect he had on her.

"Like I said before, Miss, you could help keep his spirits up through the holidays—*if* you had a mind to."

Victoria met the old woman's probing look with the arch of a brow. Still, she couldn't help hearing as a seductive inner voice whispered, *Stay.*

Tonight's the night, the voice of logic rose to bellow.

One more day. What possible difference could one more day make?

All the difference!

"I'll see what I can do," Victoria said aloud. Shifting to her feet, she deftly changed the subject once more. "Now, how about these platters? Can I help you take them somewhere?"

She broke into a smile as they approached the entrance hall. Cainey and Eric were arguing over the opening of a brown keg, presumably of mountain cider, and everyone else was bustling about a giant Douglas fir that filled the entire space between the staircase and hearth, its top reaching well above the railing on the upper landing.

"Isn't it beautiful?" Gertrude called.

"The most beautiful tree I ever saw."

"Help us decorate it!"

"All right. Just let me put this tray down."

Following Hilda into the banquet hall, Victoria set the platter on the massive table, her gaze turning over her shoulder.

"Go ahead, miss."

Victoria glanced back. The old woman was smiling encouragingly.

"I can bring the rest of the things out," she said. "Go ahead. Join the party."

The voices and music clamoring from nearby brought a new smile to Victoria's lips.

"I think I will," she said, and moved into the great hall festively draped with the scent of fresh fir.

Richard continued through the stack of correspondence on his desk, absently listening to the distant voices down the hall.

"Can you help with this, Victoria?"

Richard's ears pricked at the name. Looking up from his paperwork, he peered out the door of the library.

"What do you want me to do?" she asked.

"Take the end of this string around the back of the tree."

"This way?"

As the conversation went on, Richard leaned back in the chair and closed his eyes. He liked hearing her voice in his house. He liked the feel of her sleeping under his roof. Regardless of who she was or what she'd done or how infuriating she could be at times—hell, *most* of the time!—he didn't like the thought of her being anyplace else.

He pictured her from earlier in the day, standing out back, fair hair shining about her perfectly composed features. *You should know better than to manufacture hope out of thin air. . . .*

Damn, he'd never met anyone who could be so defiant and so stone-cold placid all at the same time. It was like a wall closing off the real Victoria—the woman he glimpsed now and then in a rare open smile . . . the woman he was falling in love with.

Richard's hand rose to massage his forehead. God, it was the first time he'd allowed the thought to form, although if he were honest with himself, the seeds of the feeling had taken root long before he left Pawleys Island. He'd called it fascination, intrigue, obsession; the truth was he was losing his heart to a mystery woman he was no closer to figuring out than he'd been a month ago. Hell, he probably didn't even know her real name.

Reaching over, he opened the top drawer of the desk and perused the ID cards scattered within. A driver's license pictured Veronica Bates as a redhead. Another showed Valerie

Blake as raven-haired. The honey-blond image of Victoria danced across his mind's eye.

Who are you? Richard silently demanded, barely completing the thought as he noticed the sound of approaching footsteps. Slamming the drawer shut, he sat swiftly up as Victoria walked in bearing a glass of cider.

"I thought you might like this," she said.

"You did?" he questioned, his voice conveying the astonishment that she should think of him in any way whatsoever. Setting down the glass on his desk, she backed away a few steps.

"After all, you were thoughtful enough to bring me supper last night. It's the least I can do."

"Thanks," Richard said, still regarding her with surprise.

Tucking her fingers in the pockets of her jeans, she looked away, seemingly to study the makeshift lab set up behind him. "Do you still want to go hiking tomorrow?" she asked in a rush.

Richard blinked. "Sure. Did you change your mind?"

"Maybe," she answered, her eyes returning to his. "Maybe I just lost it. Where exactly would we go?"

"There's a trail that leads up to the falls. It's pretty there. I'd like to show it to you."

"Okay," she said, surrendering. Though her mien was calm as ever, the color of her cheeks was high, the pale eyes sparkling.

"What changed your mind?" Richard asked.

"Maybe the spell of the mountains," she responded. "You know there's an old saying about the Blue Ridge—it'll bewitch you if given half a chance." She folded her arms, her sparkling gaze moving over his face as if searching for something.

"Or maybe *you're* the wizard," she added quietly. "From the first time you smiled, I—" A look of amazement filled her eyes as she broke off and turned abruptly toward the doorway.

"Whoa!" Leaping from his chair, Richard strode around the desk and caught her arm. "You can't start something like that and not finish," he chided.

"Let go of me, Richard," she said without looking at him. "I'm not making sense at the moment."

Taking hold of her other arm, he turned her to face him. "From the first time I smiled, what?"

The lovely face turned scarlet as she jerked away. "I agreed to a hike," she threw over her shoulder. "Not an interrogation."

With that she made a hasty exit. Richard watched her go, a slow smile making its way across his face. He wasn't fool enough to think everything had just turned around, but it was a start.

Returning to his seat, he reached for the cider, halting before he touched it as his gaze focused on the glass. Lamplight shifted through the amber depths of the liquid and showcased the smudges on the glass surface.

Victoria's fingerprints.

Pulling a handkerchief from his pocket, Richard surrounded the base of the glass and lifted it to the light. The five prints couldn't have been more clear if placed there on purpose. He gazed across the room, his memory racing . . . searching . . . selecting. . . .

Ben Walters. Ben had been with the FBI twenty years, and he owed him a favor.

The light of the lamp refracted through the cider glass, the shafts glinting with the temptation of secrets soon to be revealed. He had a dusting kit tucked away somewhere in the lab. Setting the glass carefully aside, Richard rose from the chair and started searching through cabinets.

Fingerprints—a long shot admittedly, but then long shots had paid off before.

A great deal of Sky Road Tavern's charm had to do with the fact that it was the only place within twenty miles to get a drink. Plugging a quarter in the jukebox, Mavis made a selection and weaved her way back to the bar. As the strains of an old love song filled the room, she tossed down the last of her whiskey.

"Set me up again, will you, Freddy?"

Picking up the shot glass, the black bartender looked at her with dark probing eyes. "You drivin', Miz Brewer?"

"Not at the moment," she answered lazily. "Go on, Freddy. Fill her up. I'm long past the days of listening to a chaperon."

As Freddy grudgingly poured the whiskey and set it in front of her, the door swung open, sending a blast of freezing air down the length of the bar. Mavis looked around with bleary eyes, breaking into a smile as she recognized Kyle.

"Councilman!" she greeted, patting the bar stool next to her as he approached. "Have a seat! Freddy, how 'bout a drink for my friend here?"

"No thanks," Kyle said curtly. "Looks like you've had enough for both of us. I went by your house."

"Aha! You have a social call in mind?"

As she lifted the glass toward her mouth Kyle reached out and grabbed it, so the liquor sloshed over both their hands. "I might have," he replied in a grumbling tone. "Jeanette's bridge club has filled the whole house with their infernal chatter. I had in mind to drop in on a real woman. But you're no good to me this way."

"I'm good *any* way," Mavis said with a lick of her dripping fingertips. "Drunk or sober, front or back, top or bottom—"

"I'll drive you home, and we'll see."

"Freddy will be glad to hear that. Oh, Freddy," she crooned as Kyle dropped her coat around her shoulders and steered her toward the door. "No need to worry! I won't be driving tonight!"

The night air struck her like a cold slap. Mavis stumbled and would have fallen, but for the fact that Kyle caught her at the last instant.

"For God's sake, Mavis! You can't even walk!"

"Don't get anxious, darlin'," she answered silkily. "You don't want me for my walk."

He supported her the rest of the way to the black limo, tore open the door with obvious distaste, and virtually dumped her inside. Mavis leaned back against the familiar headrest as he circled around and climbed in the driver's seat.

"Wanna know why I'm drunk?"

Kyle started the car and pulled away from the curb. "Not particularly," he said.

"Broken heart," she returned with a heavy sigh. "I was too late . . . too, too late. You should have seen the way Richard looked at her, and her standing there in sloppy clothes, and with grease on her face! Can you beat that?"

Mavis's head lolled as she turned Kyle's way. Without replying, he continued to stare straight ahead. Her eyelids drooped.

"It's her eyes," Mavis went on, the flow of her thoughts coursing unimpeded from her lips. "There's something about her eyes. Something strange, almost scary. They're so pale . . . blue, or maybe gray. Like ice. You ever see anybody with eyes like ice?"

Kyle cut a quick glance in her direction. "Once," he answered. "What about the rest of her? What does she look like?"

"Kinda tall and blond . . . young and pretty." Mavis yawned, her lids succumbing to the irresistible urge to close. "But it doesn't matter. She's not the real reason I'm drunk. It's me."

Turning on her left side, Mavis tucked freezing hands beneath her cheek. "He doesn't deserve it," she mumbled. "Do you hear me, Kyle? Whatever Richard feels for his little blond iceberg, he doesn't deserve to be shot down for it, okay?"

Once again, no reply.

"Come on, Kyle," she urged in a syrupy, if undeniably slurring voice. "Call off your Shine Valley dogs."

"It's too late."

When she lifted heavy lids long enough to catch Kyle's eye, he threw back his head and laughed.

The limo shot through the black mountain night. To Mavis, it seemed they were flying. There was no sound, no light, only the image of the devil for company as she slipped beneath the surface of consciousness.

=TEN=

December 22

The day was cloudy and cold. Though they waited until noon, the temperature remained below forty. In addition to the lace-up boots that were the closest thing to walking shoes she had with her, Victoria had put on jeans, a soft white turtleneck, and two pairs of socks. Tucking the windbreaker in the crook of her arm, she stepped outside the scarlet room.

Richard was waiting in the hall, done up like a seasoned sportsman in a red quilted jacket, water-repellent pants, and black hiking boots. Stretching a bright red knit cap over the top of his head, he swept her with a frowning look.

"Haven't you got anything warmer than that windbreaker?"

"I didn't know I was coming to the mountains, remember?" she replied with the arch of a brow.

"Wait here," he commanded.

Striding down the hall, he returned from his chamber with a dark blue, down-filled jacket and insisted that she put it on. It swallowed her to her knees, hung off her wrists, and wearing it gave Victoria an undeniable, girlish thrill.

They stopped by the kitchen, where Richard filled a backpack with sandwiches, fruit, a thermos of coffee, and a canteen of water, all under the watchful eyes of Chef Renault, Gertrude, and Hilda.

"There's nasty weather brewing," the old woman warned. "See that you don't go far."

"We won't," Richard promised.

Gertrude regarded Victoria with obvious bewilderment. "It's the middle of December. What do you want to go traipsing up the mountain for?"

"Ask him," Victoria said with a nod to Richard.

"It'll be fun," he announced with a smile. Reaching through the straps of the pack, he hoisted it up his back and reached into his jacket pocket. "There's just one more thing."

Producing a dark knit cap with a fuzzy white ball on top, Richard reached over and pulled the thing onto her head, so that it covered her ears and forehead and lodged about her brows. With the merest of grimaces, Victoria peeped up at him in silent obeisance.

"Come on," he said, his smile now dazzling. "Let's get going."

They left by way of the kitchen door, a chorus of good wishes trailing them across the grounds.

The hiking trail began a short distance beyond the small garage where the pickup was parked, swiftly narrowing to a single-file path between looming banks of spruce and pine. Falling in behind Richard, Victoria breathed the invigorating scent of the forest while her eyes were captured by the spectacle of the man ahead. Below the edge of the red cap, his hair dusted the collar of the quilted jacket, which stretched across broad shoulders, which tapered to narrow hips . . . long legs . . .

Looking determinedly to the ground, Victoria turned her attention to the trail. A short way north of the lodge they came to a narrow wooden bridge spanning a plunging ravine. Richard started merrily across while she stopped in her tracks.

"Are you sure this thing's safe?" she called.

He paused and looked over his shoulder. "Perfectly safe. It's been the only way across for thirty years."

"That's very encouraging."

"Come on," Richard urged. "Just don't look down."

Victoria gave him a doubtful look.

"Come on," he repeated. Backing up a few steps, he offered a hand. As soon as her fingers were in his, he drew her firmly onto the narrow thoroughfare. When they were halfway across, he startled her with an abrupt halt.

"Look over there," he said, pointing along the path of the ravine to the neighboring foothill. "That's Devil's Rock."

Following his line of vision, Victoria saw the stone formation. At the crest two jagged rocks speared the sky like horns;

at the bottom another tapered like the point of goatee; and in the middle two dark slabs looked for all the world like evil eyes. Devil's Rock. She'd studied it before . . . years ago, from the kitchen window of the Skinner mansion.

"Let's move on, huh?" she prodded. "I'm not overly fond of this bridge."

Across the ravine, the trail took a sharp incline. To the right, Black Top Mountain dropped away to the valley; to the left, it rose with the steepness of a forested wall. The scenery was breathtaking, the pungent scent of the air like a tonic. Despite the cold that bit at Victoria's cheeks and nose, the churning movement of her legs kept her warm. Nearly an hour passed before fatigue began to set in.

Looking ahead, she watched Richard's loping gait. He was carrying a pack. Even so, his pace was brisk and steady. Injecting speed in her stride, Victoria moved up behind him.

"I suppose you do this a lot," she puffed.

He cast a quick look over his shoulder. "Am I going too fast?"

"Oh, no," Victoria replied, masking her breathlessness with a cheery look. "Lead on."

"Good. I'd like to make the falls before we take a break. They're not much farther. Just over that ridge up there."

As she peered beyond his shoulder Victoria's heart sank. At the moment the ridge in question seemed a mirage dancing farther away with each second she looked at it. Pinning her gaze stalwartly on Richard's back, she did her best to copy his easygoing lope.

Finally the trail took a turn, sloping up and over the infamous ridge. Before they were halfway down the bank, Victoria caught the sound of the water, and when they emerged from the trees into a clearing, she had to admit the sight was worth the hike. The falls spiraled over the top of a rocky promontory, splashing into the pool thirty feet below with a gushing roar. Away from the crashing water the pool was calm and clear as a lake, eventually tapering into a stream that continued down the mountain.

Shrugging out of his pack, Richard turned to her with a smile. "Well? What do you think?"

"It's wonderful," she replied, her gaze roaming appreciatively about the spot.

"The animals come here to drink. Deer. Raccoon. Fox. Bear. It's the most popular watering spot around."

"I can see why."

Having shed the pack, Richard took a few slow steps in her direction, stopping when he stood a mere foot away. "In the summer I use it for a swimming hole," he said. "The grass is green and warm, the water sparkling and cold. There's nothing like it on a hot day."

"Sounds lovely."

"You should try it with me this summer."

The response that sprang to mind was: *We both know I won't be here this summer.* Instead Victoria sat down without comment and turned her attention to her boots. Inside the two pairs of socks, her feet felt as though they were on fire. Propping a knee, she began untying her laces.

"Don't take off your boots," Richard warned. "Your feet will swell and you'll never get them back on."

She glanced up. "Is there a rule against loosening the laces?"

He surrendered a smile. "I guess not. Hungry?"

"Oh, I could eat a wild boar or something. Whatever you have in the trap."

He chuckled at that and went to fetch the pack.

Folding her legs in Indian fashion, Victoria propped her elbows on her knees and surrendered herself to the sensations of her surroundings. The sight of tree upon tree scaling the ancient mountain in a mass of evergreen. The sound of rushing water and the smell of pine. The sting of the cold stirring the blood to her cheeks. It felt clean and pure and like being close to creation.

Dropping down beside her, Richard offered the canteen. "Glad you came?" he asked.

She nodded. "It's like paradise. Only colder." Victoria took a long swig of water, which tasted fabulous. She'd had no idea she was so thirsty.

"Go easy," Richard cautioned. "One swallow at a time."

Taking a few more rebellious gulps, she handed the canteen over to him and wiped the back of a gloved hand across her mouth.

Neglecting to take a drink himself, he gave her a long look. "Do you mind if I ask you a question?"

"So, you seek permission before asking these days?" she returned with the wisp of a smile. "That's a switch. Okay. Go ahead. What's your question?"

"Why are you here with me now?"

Looking into his eyes, Victoria found them serious and searching. "I'm not sure I know," she replied after a moment.

What he might have said at that point would remain a mystery. Three staccato cracks split the air, and before Victoria knew what was happening, Richard had slung himself in her direction and was rolling with her to the ground, effectively knocking the cap off her head and the breath out of her body at the same time.

"Stay down!" he commanded.

She spat a leaf out of her mouth. "What's going on?"

"Sounded like shots."

"Someone's *shooting* at us?" she trilled.

"Some poachers shoot at anything that moves. Just stay put."

Richard rose cautiously to his feet, scanning the trees above the clearing. "Hey, buddy!" he called. "This is a game preserve, and—"

He was interrupted by another volley of shots. This time he could have sworn a bullet whizzed just past his ear. Grabbing Victoria by the neck of her jacket, Richard scrambled with her to the cover of the forest, their flight punctuated by trailing gunfire. Darting through the trees to a fallen pine, they climbed over the massive trunk and hunkered down behind it. Richard's gaze turned up the slope, following the shape of the once-towering tree halfway up the ridge.

"Come on," he muttered. "Stay low." Rustling swiftly along on knees and elbows, they crawled up the bank to the top branches.

"Get all the way under," he urged as he crawled into the bushy camouflage. Grabbing her arm, Richard yanked her to him.

Feet flying, Victoria slammed into him and would have pulled away but for the sudden noise that reached her ears—approaching footsteps crunching along the carpet of dry pine needles. She gasped, and in a split second Richard's hand was over her mouth.

The two men came to a stop scarcely ten feet below them. His hand clamped on Victoria's mouth, Richard peered through the branches of the pine. The shooters were wearing hooded jackets and ski masks. There was no way to recognize them.

"Where did they disappear to?" one of them asked.

"Hell if I know, but the boss ain't gonna like this. He said to make it count the first time."

"He didn't say there would be two of 'em, did he?"

"What the hell does it matter? We get paid to do a job, and we get nothing if we come back empty-handed, which is about what you've guaranteed with your itchy trigger finger."

"Shut up, asshole. I can outshoot you any day."

"Then do it! You head down the mountain along the trail. I'll head up. If you find 'em, fire twice. I'll do the same."

The men split up and headed in opposite directions, one of them scaling the bank and passing not three feet away from his quarry's hiding place.

Seconds took on the breadth of minutes as Richard waited, scarcely breathing as his ears strained for any sound of them. Finally he removed the hand from Victoria's mouth. She looked up with eyes as round and glassy as saucers.

"You okay?" he murmured.

Her reply was a blink of the glittering eyes.

"There's a rescue station not far from here," he added. "If we stick to the trees, we ought to be okay."

"Why can't we just stay here?" she hissed.

"What if they backtrack, Victoria? No. Our best bet is the station. Are you with me?" He offered a hand.

With obvious reluctance she placed her own within its grasp. "Do I have a choice?" she whispered, and shifting to her knees, crawled with him from the cover of the pine.

The station was small and dark, the windows covered with wooden shutters. The only light was the gray stream falling through the doorway. Propping her just inside the door, Richard proceeded across the room.

"As soon as I get the generator going, we'll have some light," he threw over his shoulder.

Remaining stolidly where he'd planted her, Victoria surveyed the room. There was a bed in one corner, a table stacked with provisions in another. A big, homey-looking rag rug was spread before a stone hearth, which was flanked on one side by a single straight-backed chair, on the other by a desk with a CB radio.

A mechanical whir sounded out as Richard cranked the generator, setting a series of wall lamps flickering, and finally flaring to life. Striding back to the door, he swiftly closed and bolted it.

"I'll try to get Eric on the radio," he said. "He was planning to be up here today, and we could use a friend with a rifle."

With that he walked away once more. "Make yourself at home," he said as he switched on the radio and picked up the mike.

"Eric? Are you there? Come in." He released the button, and the sound of static joined the hum of the generator.

"Eric?" he tried again. "This is Richard. Come in."

"Eric here," came the answering voice. "What's up? Over."

"Victoria and I are here at the rescue station. We had some trouble over by the falls. . . ."

Victoria watched and listened as if from a great distance, frozen as much by a dawning conclusion as the cold that pierced her bones. Those gunmen weren't poachers, they were hired killers. The night before last Mavis Brewer had recognized her and told Kyle. He was "the boss," and Vanessa Blair the target.

Moments later she became aware of Richard moving again, this time stooping at the hearth to light a fire.

"Damn, that was strange as hell," he said. "It was like they were gunning for us or something. But don't worry. We've got shelter now, and there's an ax here by the fire if we need it."

Rising to his feet, Richard moved to join her. "Plus a friend on the way who's a crack shot. Are you okay?"

When Victoria nodded mutely, he steered her to the rag rug. Stripping the gloves off her hands, he rubbed them briskly with his own. "That ought to get the circulation going. Here. Sit down," he added, urging her to a cross-legged seat before the fire. "I'll get this stoked up a bit."

Kneeling by the hearth, he threw another log on the flames. That was when she noticed the tear on the right shoulder of his jacket.

"Oh, no," she breathed. Rocking forward, Victoria crept up to him as he turned to look at her questioningly.

"What is it?" he asked.

"Look at this," she urged, pointing to his shoulder. "It's a bullet hole."

Shrugging out of his jacket, Richard held it up. "Well, I'll be damned. I thought one of them sounded pretty close."

"Eight inches lower and it would have been through the heart."

"Now I know why they quilt these things," he remarked blithely, and tossed the garment aside. "Even if one square gets shot out, the rest are still good as new."

"It's not funny!" Victoria objected in a vehement tone.

Richard's brows rose. "Well, it's over now. It won't do any good to get all worked up, will it?"

"How do you know it's over?" she demanded. "What if they follow us here and try to break in?"

"I've never met poachers quite that tenacious."

What if they aren't poachers? the unasked question rang in her mind. Victoria sank back on her heels. "I'm sorry," she said quietly.

"There's no need for you to apologize. It's not your fault."

"Yes, it is."

"Of course it isn't. How could it be your fault?"

"It just is!" Victoria chimed. "I know it! I can feel the whole thing closing in."

"*What* whole thing?"

"Just . . ." Her feverish gaze moved between his eyes. "Just bad luck," she finished lamely. "I'm a jinx, Richard. Ask any one of a dozen men. You'd be wise to steer clear of me."

The fire grew suddenly hot, the room close, and Richard was filled with the throbbing urge to touch her.

"Regardless of how wise that would be," he replied, "I don't seem quite able to pull it off."

Victoria barely heard what he said as she concentrated on his perfect features. She'd told herself a day wouldn't make a difference, and now she'd nearly killed him. God! Unconsciously lifting a hand, she traced the curving shape of his cheek with her fingertips.

"A few nights ago you warned me never to kiss you," he said.

"I remember," she mumbled absently.

"Well, that's exactly what's going to happen if you keep doing what you're doing."

Victoria's gaze leaped to his eyes, and almost as swiftly, her hand flew away from his face.

"I was only thinking you might have been hurt," she said.

"Thanks for the concern." An ambiguous smile played about his lips. "All this time, if only I'd known—all I had to do to capture your interest was get shot."

"Again you make jokes," she snapped. When she started to move away, he caught the sleeve of her jacket.

"Wait, Victoria. I'm just trying to lighten things up, okay?"

Though she pulled no farther away, she didn't look around.

"Come on," he added. "Settle down."

Reaching instinctively about her shoulders, Richard was shocked into staring when—after an instant's hesitation—she turned into his arm and buried her face in his sweater.

"Do you mind?" she asked in a muffled voice.

"No problem," he replied, and drew her close.

Her hair was silken against his neck, her body warm against his side. Richard's gaze rolled to the ceiling as he thought of the few times he'd allowed himself to imagine being close to her. The surroundings had always been custom-made for the occasion—music in the air, champagne on ice . . . a far cry from the floor of the rescue station after they'd been fired on by thugs.

Several minutes passed before he realized she was shaking. Leaning back, Richard caught her chin and tipped her face so he could look into it. There were no tears, but her teeth were chattering like mad.

"I d-don't seem able to stop shaking," she managed.

"It's shock," he replied. "We need to get you good and warm."

Sliding closer to the fire, Richard dragged her matter-of-factly onto his lap and wrapped both arms snugly around her.

"Everything's all right," he added, his lips moving sensually against her hair. "Relax."

"You m-must think I'm a simpering idiot."

"I don't think you're a simpering idiot," he returned. "It's been a rough day. You're doing just fine."

He stroked her hair, and quiet minutes passed. The more her trembling seemed to dissipate, the more acutely aware Richard became of her body—the head lodged beneath his chin, the torso settled within his arms, the thigh resting between his legs. He could do nothing to prevent the gathering hardness there, and was certain Victoria must feel it.

His eyelids drifted, only to spring open as she wrenched out of his arms and shifted swiftly off his lap. In the glow of the fire her face appeared the color of ripe strawberries.

"I think I'm warm enough now," she said.

"Yeah?" Richard caught her eyes and held them, unwilling to apologize for his reaction or let the moment pass. "Then maybe you'd be more comfortable without the jacket."

She didn't move a muscle. Didn't even blink. Leaning forward, Richard reached for the zipper. She remained stock-still as he unzipped the jacket, shifted it off her shoulders, and tossed it across the floor to join his own. Blood thundered in his ears as he studied her—the porcelain face wreathed in rosy color, the pale eyes shining like glass.

"Come here," he said, his voice deep and thick.

"No."

The word was issued so softly, it was almost like a hiss from the fire. Richard cocked his jaw, his eyes boring relentlessly into hers.

"All right, then," he murmured, and shifted forward.

The only hold he had on her was the bond of his gaze. However tenuous that should have been, it seemed unbreakable. Victoria couldn't look away, could only follow the progress of Richard's approaching mouth, her lashes dropping . . . closing . . . as his open lips met hers. Though she'd thought them locked in rigid horror, the traitorous things opened at his touch, responding to his openmouthed caresses, inviting his tongue with sensual play.

He reached around her then, his hand grasping the back of her head, holding her steady as his kiss turned fierce and plunging. Her mouth—as though it secretly had known all along how to do such a thing—stayed with him, caught up in a hot, wet melding that both astonished and seduced her.

He pushed, and they fell back onto the meager pad of the rug, Richard cushioning her head in his hands as his body stretched on top of hers. Victoria waited for the wave of revulsion, but it didn't come—even when his knees moved between hers, even when his weight settled forcefully between her thighs. A far cry from revulsion, she was filled with the most glorious, languorous, consuming drive. . . .

In a distant corner of consciousness Richard expected a denunciation; instead Victoria held him close, one hand closing in his hair while the other traveled his back. A leg bent beside him, the booted foot reaching, the calf curling over his. Breaking out of the kiss, he rose on his elbows and looked down.

"Not that I'm complaining," he managed, "but what the hell's going on?"

"I've never kissed anyone like that," came the breathless reply. "I didn't realize I could."

"Care to find out what else you can do?"

His eyes locked with hers. No longer mirrors, they were filled with firelight, and what appeared to be the glow of desire. Richard lifted a hand to her face and trailed his fingers along the lines of brow . . . cheek . . . jaw. He touched the soft fabric about her throat and kept going, his hand fanning open as it continued its descent. She caught her lip as his hand moved caressingly over her breast on its way to the bottom of her sweater.

Slipping beneath the soft knit, Richard's palm connected with warm flesh. An instant later her hand closed on his wrist.

"Wait," she said.

His hand went still as his gaze lifted. "I'm waiting," he rumbled after a moment.

"There are things you don't know about me, Richard."

"No kidding."

"Things that might make a difference in your wanting me this way."

"Nothing seems to have made a difference so far."

"Like I said, there are things you don't know."

"Want to tell me about them?"

She looked away, and the crackling sound of the fire escalated against the silence. Richard lifted his free hand to smooth the frown from her brow, his fingers moving into her hair and turning her back to face him.

"These things, whatever they are, couldn't wipe out the woman I'm looking at. Not a simple picture, I grant you, but I've learned things about you. It doesn't matter how tough a front you put up, I look at you and I see the guardian angel of the Dalton School . . . the savior of kids with faces like Darcy's."

"Don't you ever see the face of Bill Honeycutt?" she rallied in a last belligerent effort to forestall what seemed to be occurring. It was unprecedented, unforeseen . . . undeserved.

"Sometimes," Richard admitted. "But not as much now as I did before. God help me, but I want you for myself, Victoria. Right or wrong, I do. And I don't think there's anything you could say that would change that."

Lifting swift hands to cup his face, she drew him down to her.

"I thought you had an aversion to this sort of thing," he mumbled against her parting lips.

"I always have," she whispered, her tongue moving against his. "Until you."

"Then tell me I can stop worrying about you disappearing every time my back is turned."

"I can't tell you—"

"Then forget it," Richard broke in. "Don't tell me anything."

He buried his mouth on hers, once again experiencing the mind-blowing shock of Victoria's welcoming response. He reached beneath the sweater, his fingers curling around her side. She pulled his shirttail free, her fingernails grazing across the bare skin of his back. His hand moved to close around her breast, his thumb brushing and circling the nipple, playing until it went rigid beneath his touch. Her teeth closed on his tongue—

Richard halted, his breath coming and going in shallow gasps through his nostrils as she held him captive. Seconds later her searching fingers pried beneath the waistband of his jeans.

With a mindless moan of passion, he tore his mouth from hers and shifted down her body, his open mouth following the upsweep of his hands as he lifted the barrier of the sweater out of his way. When he closed on her breast, she arched beneath him, her hands grasping in his hair, cradling him to her bosom.

He washed the entirety of the soft mound with his tongue, then lavished a trail of kisses across velvety skin to her other breast, once again feeling the shivering stir of her body as he brought the nipple to erection.

Shaking his head free of her massaging fingers, Richard broke away once more and rocked back on his knees, his eyes pinning her to stillness as he captured her arms and gently extended them on each side of her head. Swiftly gathering the folds of the sweater, he spirited it off her body and tossed it beyond the rug.

For a split second she glanced up with shining eyes. Then she looked away, her arms bending and folding like the wings of a bird to shield her breasts from his gaze. With a flickering smile Richard reached behind his shoulders and, in one fell swoop, pulled both sweater and underlying shirt over his head.

"Don't hide from me," he said in a ragged tone.

"I . . . I don't know—"

"Some things you don't know. You just feel."

Catching her by the arms, Richard rolled to his back. She looked at him with surprise, her hands reaching to break a fall and landing on each side of his chest. His glittering gaze swept the spectacle of the woman poised above him—golden hair tumbling beyond bare shoulders to tease the tops of perfect breasts, slender arms framing the curve of a narrow waist, and shimmering about it all a halo of firelight that made her perfection glow like something surreal.

"Come here," Richard mumbled once more, and locking a hand behind her neck, drew her down into a delving kiss.

With slow sensual grace she gradually settled atop him. His arms went around her, one pressing her breasts to his chest, the other pulling her hips tight against his hardness and into an erotic rhythm as he began to move against her.

A nerve-shattering round of banging sounded at the door.

"Richard? Open up! It's Eric!"

As Victoria would have broken away Richard's arms clamped about her. He closed his eyes, willing himself under control as he shook with unbridled desire.

Why the hell did you call Eric? an inner voice boomed. *The rescue station is perfectly capable of sustaining people overnight! That's what the damn place is here for, after all!*

But then he'd been thinking only of the danger of the gunmen, never dreaming of what might come to pass with Victoria.

"Richard!" Another round of banging. "Are you all right?"

Opening his eyes, Richard turned his face toward the door. "We're all right!" he called. "I'm on my way!"

Reaching past his staunch grip, Victoria placed a hand on his cheek. He looked up to find her watching him with the most angelic expression he'd ever seen.

"You must let me go," she said softly.

"I'm not sure I can."

She smiled. Again he thought of an angel, grimacing as Eric's insistent knocking seemed to shake the rafters of the hut.

"Dammit, Richard! Hurry up! It's cold out here!"

"We'll finish this later," Richard murmured to Victoria, and with a rasping groan, opened his arms to release her.

As she moved away he sat up slowly, his glazed eyes locating his clothes a few feet away. Pulling them haphazardly over his head, Richard got to his feet and looked in Victoria's direction. Having donned the white sweater, she was combing her hair with her fingers. Noting his attention, she shifted the tresses behind her shoulders and clasped her hands.

"Ready?" he asked in a hollow tone.

When she nodded, he turned for the door, swiping up the jackets and tossing them at a chair on his way.

"Well, it damn well took you long enough!" Eric blustered. Stamping inside, he brought a burst of wintry air with him before Richard quickly closed the door.

"Hello, Victoria," the tall man greeted. "You all right?"

"I'm fine, Eric. Thanks."

"So what the hell happened?" he demanded, turning to Richard.

"I don't know. They fired on us, tried to trail us—"

"They fired *on* you?" Eric interrupted.

"It seemed that way at the time."

"Have you radioed the police?"

Glancing swiftly to Victoria, Richard saw her stiffen. "I don't think there's any point in that. There's nothing we could tell them. The guys were wearing ski masks, and I'm sure they're long gone by now. I don't guess you spotted anything on the way over."

"Just critters heading for shelter," Eric replied, and started for the hearth. "A storm's heading this way. We'd best be dousing this fire and hitting the trail. Snow's already falling thick as molasses on the north ridge."

Rifle in hand, Eric led the way down the mountain. Richard's gloved hand was wrapped securely about hers as they followed single file along the narrow path. About the time they reached the bridge across the ravine, the snow began to fall, veiling her vision with fluttering white, surrounding her with quiet, numbing cold. But the feeling inside Victoria burned like summer sun.

She loved him.

The wondrous idea of it filled her mind. The wondrous feeling of it filled her heart. As he walked just ahead of her she stared through the snowflakes, watching the way they settled on his hair. When he occasionally turned to give her a smile, she was fascinated by the way they caught on his eyelashes.

She loved him.

It was real. It was true. Beyond the artifice of imagining, fact was more fantastic than fantasy.

The amazing revelation buoyed her along the path . . . until they approached the lodge and she remembered what she was returning to. The night of departure had arrived. Now, more than ever, it was imperative that she leave Black Top Mountain. An icy feeling of dread joined the cold sting of the snowy air.

They entered the back way, at once besieged by the anxious questions of the crowd gathered in the kitchen.

"Is anybody hurt?" Gertrude piped.

"I was getting ready to call the fire department," Cainey announced.

"Thank heaven you're back," Hilda breathed.

"Would you like some soup?" the chef inquired.

"Like Gertrude said," Miles broke in testily, "the important thing is whether or not someone's been hurt."

"We're all right," Richard replied with a calming hand. "I'll tell you all about it. Just give us a minute to catch our breath."

"Look who's here," Hilda then said. "Dr. Fontaine."

Stepping aside, she revealed a petite young woman in plum stretch pants and a beautiful matching sweater seeded with sequins and pearls. Her hair and eyes were black as night, her smile brilliant as she gazed at Richard.

"Hello, handsome," she greeted. "I warned you I was liable to show up on your doorstep if you didn't give me a call."

"Sheryl," Richard mumbled.

"Well, don't I get a hug or something?" she prompted.

Moving forward, he stepped into her welcoming arms. On top of everything else the sight of Richard embracing another woman was more than Victoria could take.

"If you'll excuse me, I'd like to go up and change," she said, and did her best not to notice the kitchen prattle dwindling into awkward silence as she walked away.

Richard slowly released Sheryl, his eyes turning out the doorway where Victoria was fast disappearing up the hall. "I'll be back in a minute," he said, and strode after her, catching up just as she reached the door to the scarlet room.

"Victoria?" She turned to face him as he stepped up. "Is something wrong?"

"No. I'm just chilled to the bone. That's all."

Richard arched a brow. "Your rather brisk exit had nothing to do with Sheryl?"

The shining eyes Victoria turned up to him were impossible to read. "Maybe in a sense," she replied slowly. "I can't help but notice that every time I come in the backdoor with you there's a different woman waiting."

He cracked a smile. "Sheryl's a very old, very dear friend. And I didn't know she was coming."

"Hilda said *Doctor* Fontaine."

"She's a psychiatrist."

"Psychiatrist?" Victoria repeated with obvious suspicion.

"Victoria, I said I didn't know she was coming."

She searched his face, the twinkling eyes, rosy cheeks . . .

"Do you believe me?" he added.

Once again the miraculous thrill enclosed her. She loved him. "Can anyone *not* believe you?" Victoria asked.

Catching her wrists, Richard looped them behind his neck and gathered her close. "Then believe this, too," he said quietly. "You don't need to worry about other women, waiting at the backdoor or otherwise."

He kissed her with languid thoroughness, and it crossed her mind how wonderfully familiar his kiss had become—his lips firm and warm as they moved over hers, his tongue melting her with bold caresses. Reaching into his hair, Victoria clasped him to her.

A long moment later he lifted his head and gazed down at her, his eyes glowing with the fire of new passion.

"We need some time together real soon," he murmured huskily. "Like tonight?"

Victoria managed a small smile as her insides seemed to crumble.

"But for now I guess you want to freshen up." Backing out of the embrace with obvious reluctance, Richard reached around her to turn the knob and push open the door.

"See ya," he said, and with a brush of her lips, stepped away.

"Richard!" He turned and looked over his shoulder, and in that instant a dozen images whirled through her mind—him smiling on the deck of her boat, taking her hand on the porch of her house, laughing as he drove her car along the mountain highway. On and on they went, blurring the current sight of his face . . . the last sight of his face.

"Victoria?" he questioned. "What is it?"

"Nothing," she replied, forcing her stiff lips into an amicable curve. "See ya."

He smiled and started down the stairs. Victoria watched him go, noticing with a start that Dr. Sheryl Fontaine was waiting below, peering up at Richard with the most unabashedly accusing expression. Backing swiftly into the scarlet room, Victoria closed the door, but not before she heard—quite clearly—the female voice demand: "What the hell do you think you're doing?"

Whatever the pretty doctor's relationship with Richard, she seemed perfectly at home in calling him to the carpet. *What the hell, indeed?* Victoria thought. *What the hell is Richard doing with a mixed-up piece of baggage like Victoria Blackwood?*

Spinning away from the door, she eyed the neatly packed bags waiting by the bed. Sheryl Fontaine was the kind of woman he belonged with—attractive, intelligent, accomplished . . . a *doctor,* for goodness' sake! Victoria could easily picture Richard walking into a charity event with the charming doctor on his arm—they'd chat and laugh and end up the most popular couple at an affair where she herself couldn't even dare to show her face.

Victoria hugged herself against a feeling of utter emptiness. She'd never thought she could love any man, and now that the incredible had happened, she had to give him up . . . just like she was giving up everything else.

Maybe her sins had caught up with her; maybe this was her just deserts. But she couldn't help thinking it was a cruel God who gave a taste of heaven only to snatch it away.

Unzipping Richard's jacket, Victoria spread it carefully on the bed and went into the bath. An hour later, as the sound of voices wafted from the banquet hall, she slipped out the front doors and into the freezing silence of the snowy night. There was a new vehicle in the courtyard—a sporty white Porsche that must belong to Sheryl Fontaine. With a quick look of longing at the flashy car, Victoria trotted alongside the lodge wall and turned toward the garage housing the old pickup.

The talk around the dinner table that night was all about the poachers who'd targeted not the game of the wildlife sanctuary, but its owner.

"What could they possibly have been after?" Miles asked.

"I really don't know," Richard replied, his gaze drifting out the door, past the Christmas tree, up the staircase.

"An amazing turn of events," Sheryl commented. "Have the authorities been notified?"

"There was no need," Richard replied shortly.

"No need?" she questioned. "The need seems fairly apparent. Gunshots were fired, weren't they?"

"Calling the police would be an exercise in futility. The poachers are gone, and they were hooded and masked. There's no way to identify them."

"What happened seems pretty obvious to me," Eric put in. "They'd already shot their game and were afraid Richard and Victoria would find them out."

"Speaking of Victoria," Hilda said. "Where is she? It's been a couple of hours since the two of you returned. I'd have thought she'd be down by now."

"Maybe she fell asleep in the bathtub," Gertrude suggested with a giggle.

Richard needed no further prompting. "I'll go see," he said.

Rising from his chair, he strode out of the dining hall, oblivious to the uncomfortable color that climbed to Sheryl's face, as well as the knowing glances that circled the table he left behind. Taking the stairs at a trot, he smoothed a hand over his hair before tapping at her door.

"Victoria?" No answer. He tapped again, and at the negligible force of his knock, the door creaked open. As he stepped inside, the first thing he noticed was his jacket on the bed; the second, that her bags were gone; the third, that the room reeked with the vacuous stench of desertion.

Stalking into the bath, Richard confirmed that all her things had been removed. As he turned he caught sight of his reflection in the mirror over the sink. His face was drained of color—ashen . . . like that of a corpse.

A year and a half ago Bill had looked exactly the same way.

The snow was blizzardlike, and the pickup running rough, its headlights probing negligibly into the darkness. Staring ahead with eyes that burned like live coals, Victoria kept the truck at a crawl as the snow threatened to hide the mountain road beneath a sheet of white.

If she could have cried, she would have. But it had been a lifetime since she cried . . . not since Mother's funeral. Since then, it seemed, she'd lost the knack.

"Dammit," she muttered, her heart aching at a pitch that would have plunged someone else into a fit of weeping. But then someone else could have found release. She had none as the feeling of emptiness grew, swamping her, tormenting her. She tried to picture what Richard was doing, and grew frightened by the dim image she was able to produce. Would it be this way for always?

The pines were dark sentries on each side of the road, defining the expanse between them with disappearing accuracy as the snow filled the mountainscape, blending hill into hill . . . tree into tree. The windshield wipers swept back and forth, back and forth, seeking to clear the glass of flakes that fell too fast to be brushed away. Victoria strained to pinpoint the center of the road as she rounded a curve.

Just when she thought she'd made it one more time, a figure darted into her path. Her heart slamming up to her throat, Victoria stomped on the brakes. The truck fishtailed, spinning a hundred and eighty degrees before sliding to a halt.

It took her a moment to gain her bearings. The front end of the pickup was pointing up the mountain, the rear end lodged dangerously close to the treacherous shoulder. Before she had time to consider anything else, the passenger door swung open and Missy Rochelle climbed in, dragging a suitcase with her.

"Missy?" Victoria voiced in a tone of disbelief. "What are you doing?"

"I was waiting for you."

"Waiting?"

"You said you might leave tonight."

"But . . ." Victoria sputtered to a halt as she took in the sight of the child. Her head was uncovered, her hair wet with snow, and she wearing nothing more than a white dress with a light matching jacket.

"Honey, your legs are bare!" she accused, finally finding her tongue.

"It's my best dress. I wanted to look nice."

"Nice for what?"

The child looked across the cab of the truck. Even in the eerie light of the snowy night, Victoria could see the hope on her face.

"For going to live on the island with you," she answered. "Don't leave me behind, Victoria."

Expelling a deep breath of shock, Victoria shook her head.

"Please," Missy added from between shaking lips.

"You're freezing!" Victoria exclaimed.

"I am kind of cold," she admitted.

Stripping off her jacket, Victoria wrapped it around the child.

"The heater in this truck isn't the best in the world," she murmured. "But at least it's better than being out in a snowstorm. You're a smart girl, Missy. What on earth could have possessed you to do such a thing?"

"I just want to go away," she replied, her teeth knocking regardless of the supportive warmth of Victoria's jacket. "I'm never going back to Shine Valley again. Ever."

Stretching an arm about the girl, Victoria drew her across the seat and settled her against the warmth of her own body. "I'm not sure what to say to that, Missy. But I do know one thing."

"What?" the child asked, her body shaking uncontrollably.

"If we don't get you warm in a hurry, you could get very sick."

Shoving the cranky stick shift into first gear, Victoria started the old truck on the tortuous climb back to the lodge.

Richard knew he'd find the truck gone. But he needed to see it. Grabbing the jacket she'd left behind, he shrugged into it on his way down the stairs. Hilda moved to meet him as he strode toward the door.

"What is it, Mr. Richard?" she asked.

He turned and gave the old woman a burning look. "Looks like you were right, Hilda. She didn't want to be here."

"She's gone then," Hilda murmured.

"That's right," came the tight reply.

"What's going on?" Sheryl asked, stepping up to join them.

"You were right, too," Richard tossed, his face a mask of restrained anger. Providing a welcome break from the all-knowing women, Lobo chose that moment to appear by his pants leg.

"Come on, boy," Richard said, and stepped out into the swirling snow just as the truck came to a slippery halt in the courtyard.

Missy was asleep against her side, though her body continued to shake with tremors that scared the life out of Victoria.

Switching off the ignition, she gathered the child in her arms.

"Come on, baby," she murmured. "Time to go inside and get warm."

"Victoria?" she mumbled. "Don't leave me."

"I won't," Victoria said. "Put your arms around my neck."

"And don't call my stepfather! Promise!"

Victoria hesitated as she kicked open the door of the truck. "For now I promise," she then replied. "The important thing right now is to get you warm."

The snow shrouded them like a cold white blanket as Victoria hurried toward the lodge. Her eyes trained on the toes of her boots, she looked up as she neared the doors, her breathing catching in her throat as she nearly collided with Richard . . . who apparently was starting out with Lobo at his side. As always, the coyote began to growl.

"Hush, Lobo!" Victoria commanded. Surprisingly the animal sank to his haunches, his growl falling to a whine.

"I'll take her," Richard said, extending his hands.

Gratefully Victoria shifted Missy to his waiting arms. "She's got to get warm," she said swiftly. "I thought a bath . . ."

Victoria trailed off as Richard turned his back. Throwing open the door, he stalked into the entrance hall. After a moment's hesitation, Victoria followed the coyote inside and closed the door. Sheryl Fontaine stood mere yards away. Hilda was closer.

"What's happened now?" the old woman demanded.

"Ask her," Richard said with a jerk of his head, and continued toward the staircase.

"Well?"

Victoria met the beady eyes and caught the gleam of hostility within them. "The child was out in the snow," she replied levelly. "She's half-frozen." With that she started up the stairs after Richard, somewhat surprised as Hilda fell in beside her.

"I'll help," the old woman announced, though the companionable remark was devoid of so much as a sidelong glance.

From the foot of the stairs, the pretty brunette watched their ascent with blatant curiosity. Victoria could feel the dark eyes boring into her back.

"Hello, Richard," Missy said.

Victoria looked up, her gaze fastening on the broad shoulders in the jacket she'd worn mere hours ago.

"Hello to you," he replied.

"That's an awful pretty Christmas tree," the child murmured.

After that Victoria heard nothing else.

Nudging the door with his shoulder, Richard strode into the scarlet room and proceeded to the bath. As he and Hilda looked on, Victoria started the water, turning it hot until steam began to fill the small room. Missy continued to huddle in Richard's arms until Victoria stepped up and stroked her hair.

"Time to wake up now, Missy."

Her eyelids slowly lifted. "I'm sleepy."

"But it's best you get good and warm before you sleep," Hilda said, briskly stepping forward.

"Hello, Hilda," she mumbled.

"Put her down, Mr. Richard," the old woman instructed. When he complied, she tossed Victoria's jacket aside and moved on to Missy's light wrap. "We'll just get you out of these wet things and into a warm bath, child. That's the ticket for you."

"Okay," Missy replied with a yawn.

Bending to the child's shoes, Hilda glanced up. "I'll take care of this. I'm sure the two of you have things to talk over."

Victoria turned and walked into the adjoining room. Though she didn't look at Richard, she heard him close the bathroom door and felt the scorch of his eyes as he came up beside her.

"All right," he said abruptly. "What's the story, Victoria?"

She met his eyes with the steadiest gaze she could manage. "I was just starting down the mountain when she darted in front of the truck. She was freezing. I had to bring her here, and she doesn't want to go home."

"She's run away?"

"Yes. And I promised not to call her stepfather."

Richard folded his arms across his chest. "You promised not to call her stepfather. In other words you promised to conceal the whereabouts of a minor from her legal guardian."

"I guess so. At least for tonight. I gave her my word."

"Your loyalty is extremely touching," Richard replied. "And patently against the law, but then what's new?"

Victoria's chin went up. "I have the feeling something terribly wrong could be happening to Missy. Give me the chance to find out if I'm right."

Richard's gaze searched her from head to foot. "Okay," he agreed eventually. "Tonight is no night to be taking her down the mountain, anyway. Only a fool would go out in such a storm."

Victoria continued to look him in the eye, taking his glare of accusation, knowing she deserved it. "Is that your best shot?" she asked quietly.

"What?" he questioned, his brow knitting more fiercely.

"It seems you're in the mood to strike. Surely you can do better than that."

"Damn right I can." Shifting his weight to one leg, Richard folded his arms. "You know, seeing your concern for Missy almost makes me believe you actually have a heart. But then, I believed that once before today. I even believed I touched it."

With stoic calm Victoria stood before him, consumed by memories of how it felt to hold him and be held, to kiss him and be kissed.

"You did," she murmured.

"Yeah. I could tell."

The appalling threat of tears rose to her eyes. *Not now,* she raged silently. *Not now!*

"I thought something happened between us today, Victoria. I actually thought it meant something."

"It did," she mumbled.

"Did it? Funny. It looked an awful lot like the same old pattern to me."

His image was swimming. Turning her back, Victoria blinked secretly, viciously, at the abominable well of tears.

"What do you want from me, Richard?"

"The truth would be a pleasant change."

"I *did* tell you the truth," she stated emphatically. "I said all along I couldn't stay."

"And obviously this afternoon did nothing to change your mind."

"I can't allow it to."

"Why, dammit? What's so impossible about staying here and letting me help you straighten things out?"

Finally the tears receded, leaving her eyes raw, but dry. Victoria turned to face him. "Some things are beyond straightening out," she replied. "Even for you."

"How can you be sure unless you let me try?"

She peered silently up at him. His cheeks were streaked with scarlet, his brows dark and curling over angry eyes.

"This is no game we're playing here," he went on. "You're a wanted felon. I can't just let that slide. You gave Missy a promise. It's time to give me one as well. Stay. Work things out."

"I can't," she whispered, looking away.

"Don't you realize that if you run again, I'll be forced to go to the police?"

Her scalding eyes flashed back to him. "Is that what you want, Richard? Me locked up behind bars? Do you like the picture?"

"You're banking on the fact that I don't, aren't you?"

"Maybe," she retorted.

He shook his head as he considered her. "You're good, Victoria," he said eventually. "Kiss a guy a few times, and he'll let you get away with anything."

Taking long strides to the open doorway, he passed swiftly out of sight. Victoria stood rooted, dizzied by the clashing sensations that took hold—the joy of loving him, the sorrow of losing him . . . back and forth, on and on, turning seconds into hours and the room into a scarlet blur.

Catching her lip between punishing teeth, she bit until she tasted blood.

Richard had no idea how wrong he was about her having no heart. Never had she felt its existence more acutely than now, as it seemed to split within her breast.

=ELEVEN=

Mavis rolled over and reached for her cigarettes, stifling a groan when her punished thighs grazed one another. Her skin felt raw; it always did when Kyle's thick beard had a full day's growth that turned the bristling whiskers into pinpoints.

She'd complained about it before, but of course he never gave the matter a moment's thought. The truth was, she guessed, that he enjoyed it—the power of hurting her and bringing her to climax at the same time.

She lit a cigarette and lay back against the pillows, her gaze shifting in his direction. He was standing by the window and peering absently outside as he tucked the tail of his starched shirt into the waistband of his tailored slacks. It was something she'd seen him do a hundred times—*tonight* was something they'd done a hundred times—but suddenly, after years of being with Kyle, everything was different.

Taking a drag, she blew a long column of smoke into the air. He'd arrived ranting and raving about the foiled attempt on Black Top Mountain. "The damn fools let him get away," he'd muttered as he grabbed her and propelled her up the stairs toward the bedroom. "I guess I'll have to think of something else."

They'd been lovers more years than she cared to count. She should have known the man inside and out by now. But she hadn't. The air of danger surrounding Kyle had always been part of the thrill. Now that she saw through to the absolute evil that lay beneath, there was no putting the blinders back on.

Tonight she'd had to pretend to welcome Kyle's touch, had thought it would be impossible to respond. But then he knew her body too well, after all. Despite her inner cries of revulsion, he'd seduced her to shuddering culmination.

But like everything else tonight, that, too, was different. Instead of feeling satisfied, she felt dirty. Her lover was planning to murder the man she loved. And she was part of it. Forcing down a wave of nausea, Mavis brought a practiced smile to her lips.

"What's it like out there?" she called.

"Sleet's coming down with the snow now. The reports say it'll continue through tomorrow."

Picking up his tie from the back of the chair, he slung it around his neck as he walked to the foot of the bed.

"You were different tonight," he said, his black eyes traveling the length of her.

"Was I?" she replied lightly.

"Almost distant. Almost . . . a challenge."

"Is that good?"

He tossed her the semblance of a grin as he knotted his tie. "It almost makes up for last night when you passed out in the limo."

Mavis put a hand to her brow. "Don't remind me of last night. I can still feel the whiskey banging around in my head."

"And what of your heart?" he questioned with the arch of a brow. "Last night you said it was broken."

"Did I?"

"By Sir Lancelot and his fair lady. What was her name again?"

"Victoria."

Finishing his tie with an expert tug, Kyle reached for his jacket. "He was never for you, Mavis," he added as he shrugged into the sleeves. "Too much of a Boy Scout."

She stubbed out her cigarette and, dragging the sheet with her, shifted up against the headboard. "I'd like to talk to you about Richard," she said.

"Again?"

"I don't like the idea of his being . . . eliminated."

"So you've said."

"Will you reconsider, Kyle?"

"No."

Mavis pursed her lips, then relaxed them in a seductive smile as she allowed the sheet to slip below the peaks of her breasts.

"Isn't there *anything* I can do to change your mind?"

Again, the flickering grin.

"You're the best piece of ass in the Blue Ridge, Mavis. But if you think you can bend my mind, you've lost your own."

Her smile drained as she covered herself once more. "What's so important?" she asked. "You've already got more money than you can spend in a lifetime."

"You're missing the point, Mavis. It's not the money. It's not even the dream. It's the principle. Adams has something I want."

Retrieving his overcoat, Kyle started for the door.

"Isn't there anything you've ever wanted that you didn't get?" Mavis called with intentional sharpness.

He turned and fired one of his cold, dark looks across the room.

"Once," he answered grimly. "And when I find Vanessa Blair, she's dead."

With that he stomped out. Mavis lay a minute more in the bed, listening to the familiar sound of his footsteps going down the stairs. When she heard the bang of the front door, she got up, slipped into her wrapper, and moved to the window. Down below, the headlights of the black limo came on, illuminating the falling snow in shafts of brightness.

How could she fight Kyle? How?

There was no way she could, short of having him killed. And even that wouldn't work. The Big Boys' network stretched leagues in every direction. They always knew everything, and a strike against one brought down the wrath of the others. Mavis pressed her fists against the glass, watching with a feeling of helplessness as the limo turned onto Sky Road.

Should she warn Richard? If she did, she was dead. If she didn't, he was. If only there was some way to get Kyle to back off . . . but there wasn't. The only time he ever backed off anything was when someone offered him something he wanted more. And he'd already had everything she had to offer.

Dammit! Why couldn't it have turned out right? Why couldn't Richard have listened to her and accepted the deal with Kyle? Why couldn't he have fallen for her instead of some frigid little blonde who probably wouldn't know what to do even if she *did* let him in her bed?

Staring into the swirl of snow and sleet, Mavis imagined a face with eyes as pale as the ice chinking against her windowpane.

Victoria had no idea how long she stood staring after Richard, immersed in memories and regrets and futile wishes, as well as a sense of shock at being back in the scarlet room once more. Sometime after he disappeared, her feet began to move, taking her on the logical errand of returning to the truck for the luggage.

As she stepped into the hall she glanced up. Sheryl Fontaine was standing at the open door of the room directly across the way. It occurred to her that Richard's "very dear friend" must have heard every angry word he uttered. But it didn't matter. Victoria didn't care. Everything was so totally out of control, a little thing like eavesdropping didn't make any difference. With a cut nod of acknowledgment, she swept past the doctor and down the stairs.

The wintry night enfolded her as she stepped outside and started across the courtyard. Snow continued to fall at a whirling pace, the flakes interspersed with particles of ice. The freezing wetness helped to clear her head, though her emotions continued to knock about in a way that kept her feeling slightly off balance.

Retrieving her own bags and Missy's small suitcase, Victoria trudged back to the lodge and came across Eric and Miles in the entrance hall. Declining their quick offers of help, she was pelted by their questions.

"I'll fill you in later," she muttered evasively, and continued on her way. By the time she returned to the steam-filled bath, Hilda was wrapping Missy in a fluffy towel.

"There you go, little one," the old woman murmured in a kindly voice, though the look she turned on Victoria from behind the child was far from kind.

"I've laid your nightgown on the bed, Missy," Victoria said. "Why don't you go on out and get dressed? I'll be there in a minute to dry your hair."

As Missy walked obediently into the bedroom Hilda moved

to the tub and reached for the drain. Victoria could hardly miss the scathing "hmmph!" as she passed.

"Okay, Hilda. What's the problem?"

The small woman straightened, her beady gaze swerving up to Victoria's. "What you do is your own business, miss. But I don't like seeing Mr. Richard hurt the way he was tonight."

Victoria tried to swallow the lump that sprang to her throat. "Sometimes we can't help but disappoint people, Hilda."

"I didn't say 'disappoint,' I said 'hurt.' When the two of you came back from the mountain, his feelings were clear enough for anyone to see. So were yours, or so I thought. Then you just took off without so much as a fare-thee-well! How could you do it?"

"Maybe I had no choice."

Hilda walked stiffly to the doorway and glanced over her shoulder. "We've always got a choice, miss. That's what separates us from the animals."

The stinging comment echoed in Victoria's ears, making it harder still to summon a believable smile as she left the humid bath and went to join Missy.

Seating the child at the foot of the bed, Victoria settled cross-legged behind her and turned on the hair dryer. As she attended the shining tresses her thoughts finally left Richard to center on the little girl before her. Missy was warm now, her face flushed with healthy color. She would be all right, but as Victoria thought back to the wet shivering body that had huddled against her in the truck, she knew things could have turned out differently. An hour or so more in that snowstorm and Missy Rochelle would have frozen to death—her life forfeited to the mere chance of escape from Shine Valley.

Thinking back on the occasions they'd met and talked, Victoria heard the child's cry for help quite clearly. At the time, she supposed, she'd been so caught up in her own troubles that she simply hadn't listened. It wouldn't happen again. Victoria turned off the dryer and ran a palm over the shimmering hair.

"Okay, Missy. You're done. Let's get you tucked in."

When she crawled beneath the covers, Missy looked up, her laurel-green eyes suddenly alert. "This is your room, isn't it?"

"Yes," Victoria answered.

"Will you stay with me while I sleep?"

Victoria tucked the sheet over her shoulder. "For tonight."

"And you won't call my stepfather?"

Victoria straightened, her eyes meeting the hopeful ones of the child. "He'll have to be called sometime, Missy. He *is* responsible for you, after all."

"You mean you won't take me with you to the island?"

"Missy, I can't just disappear with you. . . ."

She trailed off as the child's eyes filled with tears. Sinking to her knees beside the bed, Victoria put a gentle hand on her shoulder. "Tell me what's wrong," she urged. Missy shook her head. "I can't help you if I don't know what's going on."

"If I tell, will you promise not to send me back?"

"I can't promise until I hear what you have to say."

The bright green eyes peered into hers, the tears gradually receding to a sheen that made the look of courage that came over the child's face all the more moving.

"All right, I'll tell," Missy finally said. "They think I'm too little to understand, but I do. Mr. Sweeney looks at me funny. He looks at all the girls funny. Then last month it happened to my friend Emma."

Once again the name Sweeney chimed with familiarity in Victoria's ear. "*What* happened to your friend?" she asked.

"The men took her away. She didn't want to go live in Parkersburg, but they took her anyway. And the same thing's going to happen to me. Mr. Sweeney says the Big Boys like girls with blond hair. That's what he means when he says it won't be long. He means he's going to send me to Parkersburg with the Big Boys."

Victoria rocked back on her heels, a feeling of sickness erupting in her stomach, rocketing to her throat.

Sweeney! Now she remembered. She'd seen the name on page after page of the ledgers four years ago. He was the Big Boys' connection in Shine Valley! Maker of moonshine! Procurer of young girls! Dealer of debauchery! *Sweeney!*

Just then Rosemary the raccoon waddled into the room and jumped up on the bed, delighting Missy when, after a welcoming sniff of the child's face, she sat down by her side.

"Can she stay?" Missy piped. "We've been friends a long time, you know."

"She can stay," Victoria replied absentmindedly, her thoughts roiling with faces and names—Sweeney . . . Darlene Potter . . . Cal Stevenson. Once again she saw a silver-haired man leading a young girl to the back of a limo.

"This is how home should be. Safe and warm and friendly-like."

Looking swiftly down at Missy, Victoria snapped back to the present. The child's head was bowed, her little-girl fingers extended to Rosemary's curious snout.

"Please don't send me back to Shine Valley," she added.

"I won't," Victoria replied fervently. "In fact I'll do everything I can to prevent your going back ever again."

Missy looked up, her eyes wide and shining. "You will?" Breaking into a smile, she threw her arms around Victoria's neck. "Thank you," she murmured.

"You're welcome." After a moment Victoria disengaged the clinging arms from about her neck and tucked Missy beneath the covers once more. "Now it's time to sleep," she added.

"And have happy dreams," Missy said.

"That's right. Only happy ones allowed here."

Rising to her feet, Victoria turned off the bedside lamp and gazed down at the form beneath the velvet spread. In the dancing light of the fire, she appeared so small, so fragile.

"You won't leave me, will you, Victoria?"

"No. I won't leave you."

"Promise?"

"For as long as you need me, I'll be here. Now close your eyes."

As the child complied Victoria's mind filled with the magnitude of the vow that had rolled from her mouth. She'd just promised to stay on the Black Top, within reach of her most formidable enemy, her most vengeful foe. *What the hell was she doing?*

As she looked at Missy the answer came without the gloss of words or phrases, just a simple sense of rightness that couldn't be misconstrued.

Something had to be done. Now. There would be no more Darlene Potters, and not a single Missy Rochelle would take the luxurious ride to Parkersburg.

Hilda was wrong about choices. Sometimes there were none; for now that she understood the villainy that had Missy in its clutches, Victoria could no more desert her than she could leave behind a piece of herself.

"Night," Missy mumbled, and turned on her side.

"Night, Missy." Bending down, Victoria pressed a small kiss to the top of her head. "Sleep well."

Telling himself his single purpose for going down the hall was to check on the child, Richard had started to tap at the open door and make his presence known.

But the scene had arrested him—the fair-haired girl looking up with such hope, the golden-haired woman gazing down with such tenderness. . . .

You won't leave me, will you, Victoria?

No. I won't leave you.

Promise?

As long as you need me, I'll be here.

The sound of her voice filled his ears, the image of her face filled his mind, and the swell of emotion that overtook Richard was like a tangible weight dragging his heart to his feet.

The fifteen minutes when he believed he'd lost Victoria had been the longest of his life. Now, after slapping him with the fact of just how quickly she could slip through his fingers, she was back.

But not for you, Richard reminded himself as he watched her bend to Missy with a good-night kiss. Backing silently away, he returned to his rooms.

With Rosemary lodged staunchly in the curve of her back, Missy was sleeping soundly, her rhythmic breathing showing no signs of congestion. It was past midnight when Victoria stepped out of the bedroom and closed the door.

The lodge was quiet and dark, but for the light that showed beneath the door at the far end of the hall. Richard's quarters. Turning in the opposite direction, Victoria moved onto the landing and sat down at the top of the stairs.

Beside her the giant Christmas tree came to a peak above the rail, filling the air with the pungent aroma of fir, the star on top catching the twinkle of tiny lights.

Incredible, she thought. First Richard; now Missy. No matter how she sought to leave the Blue Ridge behind, it somehow brought her back at every turn. She gazed blindly down the stairs as a corrupted image of Missy's face began to form—framed by the fluttering of pink-and-white curtains, painted in a way meant to disguise the fact that she was a child.

Victoria released a shuddering breath. Maybe there *was* such a thing as destiny after all. Maybe this was why she'd been born, to be directed step by shameful step to this mountain, this stand, this challenge to even the scales and save a childhood for one long lost.

Reaching into the breast pocket of her robe, she produced the key and held it up so that the Christmas-tree lights glinted off the metal. It was a common-looking thing, innocuous in fact. But it was a tangible link, a solid tie, the kind of thing she'd spent most of her life taking care not to leave behind.

She tucked it back in her pocket. Just a simple key, but once the door to her life was opened, there was no telling what demons might fly out.

"Looks like I'm not the only one who can't sleep." Dressed in an elegant robe of black satin, the raven-haired woman melted out of the shadows. "Mind if I join you?" she added.

After an immobilized moment of surprise, Victoria slid over and made room on the top step. The doctor sat down and offered a hand.

"I'm Sheryl Fontaine."

"I know," Victoria replied after a brief handshake. "I have a feeling you know my name as well."

"How's the little girl?"

"Missy's sound asleep. She'll be fine, I believe, though I shudder to think what would have happened if she'd stayed out there much longer."

"It was kind of you to bring her here. Almost heroic, in fact."

Victoria surveyed the pretty, dark-eyed face. "Wouldn't you have done the same?" she asked.

"I suppose so," Sheryl answered. "But then *I* wouldn't have been well on my way to a successful escape."

"Escape . . . an odd choice of words."

"Come on, Victoria. What do you expect people to think?

That you were out joyriding in a broken-down truck in the middle of a snowstorm?''

Sheryl waited, but the only response was a slight narrowing of silvery eyes. ''Richard pressured you into coming here, didn't he?'' she added.

''He told you about me, didn't he?'' came the sharp reply.

Sheryl caught her lip before answering, ''A little.''

''Great.''

''He spoke to me once in confidence.''

''How reassuring.''

''It was after you disappeared from Pawleys Island, Victoria. He felt responsible. In his eyes it was *his* fault. *He* had messed up. And believe me, that's not a feeling that sits well with Richard. He was frustrated, angry, didn't know where to turn. . . . I gather he managed to find you, after all.''

''Yes,'' Victoria returned in a tight voice. ''He seems quite the master at that.''

''Richard wants to help you.''

''Richard lives in a dreamworld.''

Cocking her head to one side, Sheryl studied the profile of the woman beside her. Robed in simple white terrycloth, she'd scrubbed her face clean and tied her hair back in the simplest of fashions. Nonetheless she exuded an air of refinement. Victoria Blackwood was lovely and well-spoken, and suddenly Sheryl caught scent of the mystery that had so bewitched Richard.

''I advised him not to follow you,'' she said. ''I urged him to go home and forget the whole thing. You sounded dangerous, Victoria. That's why I came here—to see you for myself.''

Victoria looked up. ''And now that you have?''

''I'm not sure what to think. Why do you do it?'' Even in the dim light Sheryl could see the color that flooded the picture-perfect face.

''If you're referring to my vocation, I'm afraid your clinical curiosity will have to go unappeased, Doctor.''

She rose briskly to her feet. Sheryl followed slowly.

''You said Richard spoke to you in confidence. I assume that means you'll keep whatever he said to yourself.''

''Yes. And the same would apply to you.'' Reaching into her

pocket, Sheryl offered a business card. "I want you to have this."

"No, thank you."

"Take it, Victoria."

Though the doctor was a good six inches shorter, the authority that streamed from her dark eyes was overwhelming. Reluctantly taking the card, Victoria stowed it in her pocket with the key.

"Someday you may want someone to talk to," Sheryl added. "I'd like for it to be me . . . though *why* I feel that way is quite beyond me. Pardon the pun, but I ought to have my head examined."

"I don't understand what you're saying."

"I'm saying that I love Richard."

"Doesn't everyone?" Victoria asked after a moment.

"Don't you?" Sheryl returned.

The two women gazed at each other through the soft, twinkling light of the Christmas tree.

"If you're worrying about me standing in your way, don't," Victoria said quietly. "As it happens, I need Richard's help for the child. After that's arranged, I'll be gone."

Folding her arms, Sheryl released a sigh. "He won't be happy about it."

"I'm afraid that doesn't matter a hell of a lot."

Looking up, Sheryl found that the pale eyes had turned suddenly, glitteringly opaque.

"You were right about me, Doctor," she said, her gaze lifting into the distance. "I *am* dangerous. And the sooner I'm away from here, the better it will be for all concerned."

With that, Victoria Blackwood stepped around and headed down the hallway, toward the strip of light at the end that marked Richard's domain.

Richard dropped a log on the fire, straightening and stepping away as the dry wood caught in a shower of sparks. A knock sounded at the door.

"Stay, Lobo," he commanded, and pushed the coyote back to a reclining position by the hearth. Tucking in his shirttail as he went, Richard crossed the room and pulled open the door.

"I'm sorry to bother you at such a late hour," Victoria said, "but we need to talk."

He treated himself to an up-and-down study. He'd never seen her this way—the lace of a high-necked nightgown ruffling at the throat of a long white robe, beneath the hem of which peeked the toes of fuzzy slippers. Her face was scrubbed to a glowing pink, her hair pulled back in a ribbon. All fresh and pure and ready for bed. The sight of her stoked his anger, and sent his pulse racing.

Richard extended a palm toward the interior of his chamber. When she'd taken several stiff steps inside, he derived a measure of satisfaction from sending the door flying. It closed with a bang, and she spun around.

"Look, Richard. I realize you can't stand the sight of me, but do you think you can get past that for a few minutes? I want to talk to you about Missy."

Despite the urge to grab and shake the woman, he couldn't shrug off the picture of the child begging her not to leave. Burying his hands in his pockets, Richard met Victoria's haunting eyes. "What's the problem?" he asked.

"Missy can't return to Shine Valley. Not tomorrow. Not ever."

"When did you come to this conclusion?"

"Tonight. You told me yourself what Shine Valley is like. We can't send Missy back there."

"It's her home, Victoria. What do you expect me to do?"

"Take protective custody."

"What?"

"Missy has no family but her stepfather, and he isn't fit to raise a little girl. I intend to call Anita about enrolling her in the school, but in the meantime she needs a court-appointed guardian. Much as I'd like to be that for her, we both know I'd never stand the inspection. It has to be someone settled in the community, a taxpayer, a law-abiding citizen. It has to be you."

"And you decided all this in the past two hours," Richard commented, a caustic tone in his voice.

Her chin rose. "I know exactly what needs to be done. Social Services must be notified, along with the local authorities, although in Missy's case the locals might very well be prejudiced. It's my opinion they should be circumvented.''

"Is that right," he murmured with a lift of his brows.

"She's a minor who needs emergency protection granted by the court," Victoria went on briskly. "A judge must issue an *ex parte* order naming you her temporary legal guardian. Later, it will take a court hearing to make the appointment permanent, but at least for now her well-being can be ensured.''

"Sounds like you've got this all figured out."

"As you once pointed out, I specialize in the legal profession. I saw a case like this once. The little girl was seven years old, and she'd been beaten and sexually abused. I'm sure you don't want anything like that happening to Missy.''

"Of course not," Richard snapped. "I don't like the idea of Missy living in a place like Shine Valley any more than you do. But so far I haven't heard anything to justify my intervention—"

"Let me ask you something," Victoria broke in, her eyes leveling on him, forcing him to uncomfortable silence. "If you found out a despicable man was going to throw a little girl off a cliff, would you intervene?''

Richard's gaze shifted between her eyes.

"Well?" she prodded. "Would you take the child and run? Would you do everything in your power to make sure she wasn't returned to the monster?''

"What the hell's going on?" he demanded.

Turning on her heel, Victoria walked restlessly toward the hearth. Lobo remained uncharacteristically still as she approached, watching with pricked ears, waiting, it seemed—just as Richard was—for the woman of mystery to unleash yet another cryptic plot.

"I gather this stepfather isn't really going to throw Missy off a cliff," he said to her back.

"Sweeney. His name is Sweeney."

"All right, Sweeney. Whatever he's doing, it had better be damn good if you expect the court to take the girl away from him.''

Victoria turned. "Is white slavery good enough?"

The look on her face arrested Richard as much as her words.

"It sounds like something from another world, doesn't it?" she added. "A world of waterfront bars and shanghaied sailors, not towering mountains and virgin forests. The truth is it can happen anyplace evil gains an upper hand. And it's happening here."

"Would you stop philosophizing for a minute and tell me exactly what you're saying?" Richard barked.

"That Sweeney sells young girls into prostitution. That Missy will become one of them if something isn't done to protect her."

"How do you know this?"

"The things she told me tonight convince me that's exactly what he has in mind for her."

"That's not good enough, Victoria. If you intend to charge the man with such a crime, you need proof."

"What if I told you I have it?"

Richard's brows furled in a dark line. "I don't mean to shoot holes through your theory, but I have a certain grasp of what the court accepts as proof. In a matter of this magnitude, the hearsay testimony of a child wouldn't be enough."

"I'm not talking about hearsay. I'm talking about ledgers, black-and-white records of sale. Sweeney has been doing this for years, and it's all fronted by the Big Boys."

"The Big Boys?" Richard repeated with a look of disbelief. "What do you know about *them*?"

"I know that for generations they've held the Blue Ridge in a suffocating, self-righteous grasp—taking what they want, twisting people's lives to their own ends. I know that behind a facade of good works, they finance operations of bootlegging and gambling and prostitution."

As she spoke Richard had backed mindlessly to the foot of the bed. Now he sank to its surface. "God," he murmured. "Every time I think I'm beyond being shocked, you do it all over again. Who the hell *are* you?"

Victoria studied his face, and a number of feelings grabbed for the surface—the most powerful of which was the insane urge to race the few steps to the bed and crawl up on his lap, to push the world away and be held close as he'd held her scant hours ago. Instead she remained where she was—reminding herself that as of this moment, she alone stood for Missy Rochelle, and it wasn't enough. She needed Richard.

"Who am I?" she said, her voice uncontrollably bleak. "Just someone who's been here before."

"Here?" he questioned. "On Black Top Mountain?"

"Not the Black Top. Devil's Rock. Years have passed, but there are still people in town who would remember me. Need I say the circumstances of my departure were rather . . . hurried?"

Richard continued to regard her through a haze of surprise. "Hurried, you say. But still you had time to abscond with evidence of federal charges implicating not only this Sweeney, but also the Big Boys?"

"Yes."

"Where is it?"

"In a safe-deposit box in a bank."

"What bank?"

Reaching into her pocket, Victoria produced the key. "First Tennessee Mutual. In a small town about a day's drive west. The box is in the name of Veronica Bates. I want you to have the key, Richard. Sweeney must be stopped, and I figure of all the people I've known in my life, you're the one to do it."

"Why can't *you* do it? You're the one with the ledgers."

She shook her head. "I can give you the evidence, but I can't stay around to see this through. It'll be up to you."

"Up to me."

"My being in the picture would only damage Missy's position. Believe me. I should leave as soon as possible."

He nodded, though the gesture seemed somehow to negate his slightest participation in what she was suggesting.

"Take the key, Richard," she prodded.

His thoughtful gaze lifted. "And if I do, does it mean I subscribe to this wild plan of yours?"

"It might sound wild," she said, "but it's the only way. Otherwise I wouldn't be here. Take the key."

After a moment's hesitation he grabbed the key and stuffed it in his pocket.

"Good," she said in a relieved voice. "Now I can rest my mind."

"Rest your mind?" he repeated so sharply that she looked at him with renewed wariness. "What do you think this means? That everything's hunky-dory? That because you've stepped forward on behalf of a needy child once again, you end up getting away with murder once again?''

Her expression turned fierce. "Why would you use such a term?''

"Because I'm sick of this, dammit!" Richard exploded. "Because I'll do what I have to to protect the child, but I'll be damned if that means I'm giving you carte blanche! What the hell do you think you're doing, Victoria?''

"Asking your help for Missy," she returned in a like tone. "But nothing else. I'm not asking your permission regarding anything I might do, Richard. I never have and I never will. I only ask that you consider what I'm trying to tell you—that things can only get worse if I remain here.''

Richard rose from the bed and strolled up to her. "Works out nice and neat, doesn't it?''

"What do you mean?''

"I think it's fairly clear. You couldn't turn your back on Missy, so you've come up with a scheme designed to gain my sympathy . . . a ploy that will safeguard the child and lead me to bid you a cheery farewell while you take off for who-knows-where.''

"It's not a scheme or a ploy.''

"Why should I believe there even *are* any ledgers?'' Richard fired. "The whole story is fantastic. You're right about the Big Boys. For all practical purposes, they run this part of the mountains. Nobody could get close enough to get that kind of dirt on them.''

She had to make him believe her. Victoria steeled herself against a shiver of foreboding as the door to her past opened another notch.

"Somebody might get close enough if she worked for one of them.''

"If she . . .'' The look of incredulity returned to Richard's face. "You mean you ran your con on one of the Big Boys?''

The crass words struck hard, as did his expression, which suggested he was regarding some strange specimen that both surprised and horrified him. Victoria stiffened as a stinging sensation raced up her spine. "I suppose that's one way of putting it," she replied.

"Who?'' Richard demanded, his eyes round as an owl's.

She flung exasperated arms wide as she whirled away from the shock in those eyes. "It doesn't matter who! The point is the files are real, Sweeney's name is all over them, and I've got them. . . . Or rather you've got them." Her voice fell as she added, "Regardless of what you may think of me, Richard, I happen to hold you in the highest regard. I know you'll do the right thing."

"Don't try a snow job on me, Victoria. There's enough of that going on outside." His gaze drilled into her back.

Victoria turned slowly, suffering his penetrating look as she gave a final warning.

"If I were trying a snow job, I wouldn't say that this will probably end up being both expensive and dangerous. Sweeney's name is there, all right, but so are the names of the Big Boys. When the records go public, this part of the Blue Ridge could be in for the biggest feud it's seen in a hundred years."

"I see. Well, thank you very much for involving me in it."

Stalking to the window, Richard pulled aside the curtain. Beyond the glass the wind whipped the snow into maelstroms that danced across eerily illumined grounds. Behind him he felt more than heard Victoria's gradual approach.

"Look at that," he said in a rumbling tone. "The question of your leaving is a moot point, Victoria. Nobody's going anywhere for a couple of days."

"Then only one question remains. Will you do this, Richard? For Missy's sake?"

He turned his head, their eyes locked, and something about the look that came over Victoria rocked Richard from head to toe. There was an ethereal quality about it, something sad and glowing all at once. If he didn't know better, he could almost swear—

"It will mean dealing with Social Services and the juvenile courts," she said. "Papers being served, hearings—"

"It will mean taking responsibility for Missy's life."

"That's right," she replied softly. "So she can have the chance for one worth living."

Richard's heated gaze moved over her. She was standing there like innocence incarnate, hands demurely clasped, patiently awaiting his answer. Damn! The woman had abandoned him mere hours ago; now here she was, asking for his help and a roundabout blessing to take off again. But there was one thing he simply couldn't get around, and that was the picture of Missy Rochelle in the hands of some hillbilly pimp.

"I'll call Bill in the morning," Richard answered finally. "He'll know the proper channels and he's got connections. Maybe he can pull a few strings."

Victoria broke into a beaming smile. It flashed over Richard like the lick of a flame.

"I knew you'd come through," she said.

"Yeah," he grumbled. "I guess it's pretty obvious who's got who pegged around here."

Richard was still staring, still trying to make heads or tales of the strange radiance about her, when Victoria startled him by stepping forward and catching his shoulders in light fingers.

Her lips brushed his cheek, and she was gone, gliding away on a waft of powdery fragrance, quietly closing the door, leaving the room suddenly still and silent, but for the crackling of the fire and the thunder of his heart.

=TWELVE=

December 23

Snowed in. Victoria had never fully grasped what the phrase meant until now. Drifts billowed about the lodge in the shapes of clouds, muffling landmarks, turning familiar grounds into a foreign arctic place. And still the snow came down in a sheet of white, blurring the edges of sky and earth until it was impossible to determine where one ended and the other began.

The idea of traveling through such a blizzard was ludicrous, unless perhaps one had access to a team of huskies. Once again Victoria felt the Blue Ridge reaching out to hold her, this time with fingers gloved in the binding fabric of winter.

From another point of view, however, the snowfall was beautiful. Missy, who was elated already for having escaped Shine Valley, was so excited that her glee was contagious. Victoria hadn't traipsed in the snow in years. Now she found herself unable to resist it. Dressing warmly and borrowing pairs of oversized galoshes, she and Missy set out from the kitchen at noon with a bag of goodies for the deer.

Outside, the cold stillness peculiar to snow enveloped them—chilling and wet and clean. Clasping hands, they stumbled, laughing, through the white blanket that crunched up to their boot tops. When they entered the toolshed, they were surprised to find the doe standing just inside. She skittered away at first, but quickly lost her shyness as Missy offered a piece of apple.

"She's all well, isn't she?" Missy asked brightly.

The deer's harnessing bandage was gone, replaced by a white square of gauze. Richard's attention was apparent.

"She certainly looks it," Victoria replied, her thoughts hovering on Richard. She'd seen him that morning from a distance, from the back, as he headed down the hall toward the library. The thrill that such a mere glimpse provoked was still a marvel.

"I guess one day soon she'll go away," the child commented with a note of sadness.

Victoria turned to look at Missy—her long blond hair streaming from beneath her cap, her small hand extended to the deer. She was such a picture. "So will you," Victoria commented.

Missy looked up. "I will?"

"Come over here, Missy. I want to talk to you." They sat down in a couple of chairs near the worktable. "You like Richard, don't you?" Victoria continued.

"He's the greatest."

"I'm glad you feel that way, because if things go right, he's going to become your guardian."

"What does that mean?"

"It means Mr. Sweeney won't be responsible for you anymore, Richard will."

"Really?" The child's face lit up. "That's nice. Does that mean I get to live here at the lodge?"

"Not exactly. Although I'm sure you'll come for visits. Remember when you said you'd like to live on Pawleys Island?"

"Yes."

"Would you still like that?"

"Sure!"

"There's a wonderful school there," Victoria went on. "The Dalton School. My best friend runs it. Her name is Anita. You'll like her. And there are lots of children. You'd live right there at the school."

"I would? I thought I'd live with you in your house."

"The school is much better. It has playgrounds and everything."

"You don't *want* me to live with you. Is that it?"

Reaching over, Victoria hugged her close. "No. That's not it. Listen to me, Missy. I don't think I'll be going back to Pawleys for a while, but it's the most wonderful place in the world for you to be. Anita and the others are the best. That's what you deserve, and that's what I want for you. Do you believe me?''

Leaning back, the child looked up. "Yes. But will you visit?''

"Of course I will. Does that mean I should call Anita when we get back to the house?''

Missy nodded, a look of excitement rising to her face. "Do you think they have one of those merry-go-round things on the playground? You know, you push it around and around until it goes really fast?''

Victoria smiled. "It's entirely possible. Now, let's say good-bye to the doe and get going. It's freezing out here.''

When they returned to the lodge, they found most of the folk gathered in the kitchen. Eric and Cainey were wrapping up to go outside. Miles was on his way to the aviary to feed the birds.

"Could I go, too?'' Missy piped.

As Missy eagerly followed Miles out of the room, Victoria removed galoshes and gloves and muffler while casting a discreet glance across the cozy kitchen. Beyond the chef, who stood patiently stirring a giant pot on the stove, Gertrude, Hilda, and Sheryl Fontaine were seated at the breakfast table, exchanging companionable chatter over steaming mugs.

Perhaps Victoria shouldn't have felt like such an obvious outsider, but she did. Yesterday she'd been in Richard's arms. Last night his very pretty friend had turned up. And today that friend was ensconced in the chair Victoria had claimed, however temporarily, as her own.

Her hooded gaze told her that Sheryl—in white jogging silks that contrasted strikingly with her dark coloring—was attired as impeccably as she'd been the night before. Hanging a striped, woolen muffler on the hat rack, Victoria glanced down the front of herself and beheld layers of socks folded down over laced-up boots and the unglamorous lines of faded jeans and a bulky fisherman knit sweater. Once again she compared herself to the chic doctor and came up lacking.

She did her best to shrug off a mounting sensation of jealousy, but couldn't resist walking across the room and throwing a gauntlet on the breakfast table. "Has anyone seen Richard?'' she asked straightforwardly.

"I believe he's in the game room, miss. Taking in a game of pool."

"Thank you, Hilda," she said, and started to turn.

"I'd think twice, Victoria."

She turned to meet the doctor's flawlessly lined eyes.

"Richard's in a touchy mood," Sheryl continued. "I've known him a long time. When he takes to the pool table, it's because he's working something out. Or trying to, anyway."

"Thank you," Victoria replied. "I'll keep that in mind."

In a sense, she supposed, her oblivious departure was a slap in the doctor's face. On top of that, Sheryl Fontaine had shown her nothing but courtesy. Concern, in fact. As Victoria walked along the corridor toward the game room, she felt petty and peevish—the very portrait of a woman she'd never want to be. But dammit, she couldn't help it. She was trying to go, trying to leave Richard to the kind of future he deserved. No one should expect her to do it with a damn smile on her face.

She marched into the game room with a full head of emotional steam. Richard was poised over the billiard table, getting ready to take a shot. As she blustered in he miscued and sent the eight ball flying across the room. With methodical slowness he straightened and began chalking the end of his cue.

"Well, I guess that takes care of that game," he said.

"Sorry," Victoria muttered. Walking over to the corner, she retrieved the ball, set it respectfully on the felt tabletop, and looked up. He was positively breathtaking, his black jeans and turtleneck giving his sun-kissed looks a distinctly sexy air.

"Have you talked to Missy?" she asked.

"Not really. But I did speak with Bill a couple of times."

"What did he say?"

"It was no small feat, but he called in a favor from someone in Social Services, who pushed a petition through juvenile court, and so on. The upshot is the papers should be served on Sweeney by the end of the day."

"What do you think he'll do?"

Richard shrugged. "I don't know Sweeney. I have no idea."

Their eyes met and held, speaking silent volumes of the riotous questions going unanswered between them.

"I told Missy about the school," Victoria said, glancing away. "I think I should call Anita."

"Get on with it then," he replied with a curt nod to a table across the room. "There's a phone over there. The last time I was on with Bill, the line was acting up. If this storm continues, we could lose it altogether."

There was, indeed, static on the line. Still, Victoria received the warmth of Anita's voice and couldn't help but smile.

Yes, she would anxiously await Missy Rochelle's arrival. Yes, things were going well.

"And what about you?" Anita probed. "What are you doing tucked away in the mountains with Richard Adams?"

A burst of static interrupted, granting Victoria the clemency of no reply.

"Wait a minute!" Anita's voice boomed finally. "Darcy's here, and she has something to tell you!"

There was a slight pause, and then Darcy's laugh chortled across the line.

"What is it?" Victoria asked with an answering chuckle.

"You won't believe it, but guess who's getting married?"

"Darcy!" Victoria exclaimed in a high-pitched squeal. "You're getting *married*!"

"Got the diamond and everything. Bill said he thought about waiting for Christmas, but couldn't. He gave me the ring last night, and the date's set for a month from now. You'll be here, won't you, Victoria? I can't get married without you!"

Another round of static granted the seconds necessary for Victoria's spirits to plummet, and for her to regain control.

"Of course I'll be there," she answered when the line was clear. "Listen, Darcy. We'd better get off. There's a snow-storm going on up here."

"You won't get off that easy," came the flip reply. "What's going on between you and Richard?"

"Nothing."

"Victoria! You're infuriating. Obviously there's something going on, or you wouldn't be there!"

Victoria cast a sidelong glance to where Richard stood at the end of the pool table. He was racking up for a new game, wearing a stern expression.

"He's . . . different," she said finally.

"Different," Darcy repeated. "Is that all you've got to say?"

"Yep. That's all."

"Okay, Miss My-Lips-Are-Sealed, have it your way. I'll see for myself sooner or later." A frenzy of static attacked the line.

"I'm going now, Miss Engaged-to-Be-Married," Victoria retaliated. "Talk to you soon."

Hanging up the phone, she turned as Richard dropped the final ball into the rack.

"Missy's in," she announced. "For the term beginning after the holidays. Classes start the first week of January."

"That's good," he said without looking up.

"And Darcy's getting married," Victoria added.

"So I gathered. When?"

"The end of next month."

"To the guy she was with at the dance?"

"Yes. Bill Jacobs."

"I met him. He's a nice guy." Giving the rack a few short rolls, Richard abruptly positioned the lead ball on the black point at the far end of the table.

"I appreciate what you're doing for Missy," Victoria offered after a moment. "The school is my idea, and I want you to know I intend to take care of all expenses. I'll arrange it with Anita."

"No, you won't. I agree it's the best thing for Missy."

"Even so—"

"I don't care about the money, Victoria. Missy's a good kid. I *want* to do it." Lifting the rack with a deft stroke, he left the billiard balls in an undisturbed pyramid. "Care for a game?" he asked.

Victoria succumbed to the urge to lift her eyes. How she loved the man. "Eight ball?" she questioned.

"I've set it up that way. But it can be your choice."

"Believe it or not, I know my way around a pool table."

"Yeah?"

"My father had a table when I was growing up." Stepping over to the cabinet, she almost reached for a stick.

"Careful," Richard cautioned. "You revealed something about yourself there. Let's see, a father with enough income to afford a table and a house big enough to hold one? A definite clue.''

Withdrawing her hand, Victoria kept her back to him as a sharp pain sliced its way from her head to her toes. "I made a mistake," she murmured, and started for the door.

"Victoria, wait!"

She stopped and turned.

Stuffing his hands in his pockets, Richard ambled around the table. "I'd like to say, 'I'm sorry. Don't go,'" he muttered after a moment. "But after that I'm not sure what to say."

"Maybe that's because there's nothing left to be said between us, Richard."

"You're wrong."

"Then allow me to rephrase," Victoria said, a throbbing hurt pounding at her chest. "There's nothing that can be said that will change anything."

Spinning around, she made swift progress to the doorway and brushed past Sheryl Fontaine, who was on her way in.

"Excuse me," the doctor uttered in a startled tone.

"My fault," Victoria returned, and continued along the hall.

Walking into the game room, Sheryl found Richard staring morosely out the doorway. Folding her arms, she moved to join him. "You were right," Sheryl commented. "She *is* a puzzle. I find her lovely and bright and extremely sad."

"Sad?" Richard echoed with a hint of surprise.

"If you think she's happy about what's going on here—or that she just doesn't give a damn—you're off the mark. She cares."

Looking up, Sheryl waited for Richard's eyes to settle on hers.

"She's not what I expected," she added.

"Nor I," Richard responded in a voice that sounded as doomed as he felt.

That night at seven o'clock every person in the lodge was seated at the banquet table. There was something about a snowstorm that made a person ravenous, and the chef had prepared a stew steaming with a beefy aroma that filled the halls, along with fresh-baked bread and apple cobbler, a mere sniff of which had everyone's mouths watering.

An hour later every bowl and platter on the expansive table was empty, and the diners were mostly leaning back in their chairs and shifting uncomfortably full stomachs when a round of banging sounded at the front door.

"Who could that be?" Eric rumbled, barely finishing the question before the noisy banging resounded down the hall once more, this time accompanied by a chorus of angry voices.

Suddenly alert, Richard leaped from his chair and stalked around the table to the cabinet at the end of the room. "Cainey, take the ladies to the kitchen, will you?" he said as he passed. "Eric. Miles. Chef. How about coming over here and grabbing a rifle?"

Murmuring among themselves, the women made a swift exit as the men gathered behind Richard.

"What's going on?" Miles asked as he reached for a weapon.

"I'm not sure. Maybe nothing." Swiftly loading his rifle, Richard snapped it to readiness. "But we could be in for some trouble from Shine Valley."

Eric, Miles, and the chef formed a three-man wall some ten feet behind Richard as he approached the double doors. The wood vibrated with noisy pounding as the voices outside escalated.

"Who is it?" Richard called.

"Jake Sweeney!" came the booming reply. "Open this door, or I'll break it down for ya!"

Calmly drawing the door wide, Richard stepped back as the wintry night swept into the entrance hall. For a moment the three men were silhouetted against a backdrop of white, their heavy jackets and ten-gallon hats making them appear tall and massive. Spotting a flatbed truck behind the snow-covered mounds of Sheryl's car and the old pickup, Richard had a fleeting thought of wonder at how they'd managed to get up the mountain in such snow. But they were, after all, mountain men in the truest sense, born and bred in the rugged hills for generations. Stepping inside, they slammed the door behind them. All three wore dark beards, an unmistakable look of meanness, and shoulder-slung rifles.

Two of them took a post by the door, eyeing Eric and Miles and the chef as the man in the middle moved forward.

"That's far enough," Richard continued. "What do you want?"

"What do you think I want? Where's my kid?"

In the kitchen where the women huddled against the door listening, Missy stepped swiftly back, covering her mouth with her hand as tears started to her eyes. Victoria put a quick arm around her shoulders.

"It's all right," she whispered to the child. "Don't worry."

"She's not really *yours,* is she?" Richard challenged.

"Well, she sure as hell ain't yours! Hand her over, Adams! You ain't got nothin' on me!"

Shifting his weight to a casual stance, Richard continued to cradle the rifle in a position of readiness. "Oh, I don't know about that, Sweeney. If I were you, I'd think twice about making things tough for Missy. You wouldn't want the authorities looking into what happens to little girls who turn up missing from Shine Valley, would you?"

Sweeney's eyes narrowed so sharply they nearly disappeared beneath his bushy brows. "What the hell are you talkin' about, boy?"

"I'm not a boy," Richard returned steadily. "And I think you know what I'm talking about."

"Let's say I don't."

"Let's say that whatever has happened in the past won't be happening to Missy. Let's say that it's time for you to get out of my house and out of my sight."

Sweeney grabbed for his sidearm, but Richard was faster.

"Don't," he cautioned, swiftly cocking the rifle and aiming it at the man's barrellike chest.

A peal of clicking filled the air as every rifle in the room was brought to alertness. After a long moment of consideration, Sweeney backed away, though his expression remained threatening.

"You won't always have your boys backin' you up, Adams."

"Get out, Sweeney," Richard replied. "And take 'your boys' with you."

Reaching the door, Sweeney flung it open and looked over his shoulder. "You ain't seen the last of me," he growled.

"You'd better hope I have," Richard returned.

With a final glare Sweeney stomped out into the snow, followed by his two companions, who backed slowly out and kept their rifles trained on the entrance hall all the while. Taking long strides to the door, Richard slammed it in their faces.

Eric, Miles, and the chef erupted in cheers and moved to clap him on the back as he returned. Then everyone else spilled out of the kitchen to encircle Richard in a chattering mob.

"He sounded so mean!" Gertrude exclaimed with wide eyes.

"Did you hear how Richard handled him?" Eric replied proudly. "Cool as a cucumber."

"Hey," Richard objected. "Sweeney was right about one thing. It would have been a different story if you guys hadn't been backing me up."

"I guess Shine Valley will think again before coming back on the Black Top," Miles observed gleefully.

Moving up beside Richard, Missy took his hand, drew him away from the throng, and beckoned as though she wanted to whisper a secret. When he bent down, she kissed him on the cheek.

"Thank you for being my guardian," she said, her child's eyes round and solemn.

Breaking into a smile, Richard caught her under the arms and swung her around and around until her gay laughter had everyone else joining in. Planting the child on his hip, Richard anchored her with an arm around the waist.

"Have you ever shot pool?" he asked.

Missy shook her head. "Can girls do it?"

"Girls can do anything they set their minds to. Wanna learn?"

As the two of them moved off toward the hall to the game room, Sheryl glanced aside, her gaze passing and returning to Victoria. The pale eyes were shining like stars, the face positively glowing. Sheryl did her best to swallow down the sudden tightness that clutched her throat.

Whatever else Victoria Blackwood might be, one thing was sure. She was a woman in love.

On Christmas Eve morning the snow dwindled to a mist and finally stopped. Garbed in a plush velour robe and slippers,

Kyle stepped out on the porch for the newspaper and was greeted by the sound of a snowplow making its way along the road from town.

He glanced up at the sky. The storm had passed, but it was still cold as hell. Tucking the paper under his arm, he turned to go back inside, pausing when the sound of another vehicle joined the noise of the plow. Looking around, he saw Sweeney's flatbed making its way up the snow-covered drive. Kyle moved to the top step, holding his collar closed against the cold as he waited.

"What the hell are you doing here?" he greeted when Sweeney climbed out of the truck.

"Somethin's happened, Mr. Skinner. Somethin' I figger you oughta know about."

"What?"

"Two nights back, my girl turned up missin'. Then yesterday evenin' the damn sheriff from over Taylortown way showed up with papers sayin' she wasn't comin' back, that Mr. Richard Adams was her actin' guardian."

Kyle arched a brow. "Adams, huh?"

"Me and a coupla boys went up there last night. I figgered we'd just go in and take the kid. But he started talkin' mighty big about me thinkin' twice about causin' trouble for Missy, that I wouldn't want it gettin' 'round about girls missin' from Shine Valley. I didn't like the sound of it, Mr. Skinner."

"It's nothing but smoke. So the kid spilled a story. So what? There's no way he could prove anything."

"I don't know. He sounded pretty sure of himself."

"You losing your nerve, Sweeney? Forget the kid. There are bigger fish to fry on the Black Top. Don't worry. Adams is going to get his. In spades. Now get the hell back to your truck. I'm going inside. It's cold as a bitch out here."

By noon, the clouds were breaking up. Patches of blue appeared in the sky, and shafts of sunlight fell with blinding radiance across the snowscape.

When Eric and Miles came out to shovel the walks, they were pelted with snowballs hurled by Victoria, Missy, and Gertrude, who had built a stockpile behind the cover of Sheryl's car and the adjacently parked old pickup. A full-fledged fight ensued, and when Richard stepped innocently out the front door, he was bombarded from both sides. Scrambling to join the men behind the meager cover of a snow-flocked rhododendron, he crouched, fashioned a quick missile, and fired just as Gertrude bent over to scoop up ammunition. Richard's snowball smacked her square on the backside, and as she straightened with a squeal the men burst into laughter.

Standing inside and watching through the expansive front window, Hilda joined in with companionable chuckles.

Sheryl was coming down the stairs. "What's so funny?" she asked, and reaching the bottom, went to join the old woman.

"Look at those overgrown kids out there," Hilda replied.

Sheryl looked out just as Richard launched a huge snowball that exploded harmlessly against the side of her car. "That rogue," she pronounced smilingly. With a swift thought of joining in the fun, she glanced down at herself, noting the black cashmere sweater . . . and the toes of Italian leather pumps.

"But it's good to see him laughing again," Hilda added. "It's amazing, isn't it—the difference a child can make around a place."

Scouting for Missy, Sheryl looked across the courtyard just as Victoria heaved a round at the rhododendron and managed to hit Eric on the shoulder. Gertrude and Missy jumped up and down with excitement, and the beautiful blonde laughed up at the sky.

"Yes, of course," Sheryl replied thoughtfully. "A child makes all the difference."

The cold was so intense that even though the sun shone brilliantly, the top layer of snow remained frozen in a crust that made perfect snowballs. Swiftly bending and forming a half dozen or so, Victoria turned to Missy and Gertrude with a conspiratorial grin.

"You guys hold them down from here," she instructed. "And I'll try to sneak around to their unprotected side."

As Missy and Gertrude proceeded to throw with all their might, Victoria edged her way around the end of the pickup. It was all she could do to stifle a victorious laugh as she made it halfway across the courtyard and watched the men busily stooping and throwing, thoroughly unaware of her approach. When she moved within range, she fired six snowballs in quick succession and managed to hit each of them at least once. The three men looked up in unison, their faces wreathed with surprise, and she could restrain her laughter no longer.

Victoria dropped to her knees and started forming more of the frosty weapons, laughing all the while. It wasn't until she heard the crunch of rapidly approaching footsteps that she looked up and saw Richard coming toward her at a full run, a menacing smile on his face as he raised a gloved hand and showed a perfectly fashioned snowball.

With a startled whoop, Victoria leaped to her feet and took off across the courtyard, Richard in hot pursuit. The snowball splattered against her back. She kept running. He kept chasing— closing the gap in short order and tackling her when she would have darted around the garage.

She was still laughing uncontrollably when he turned her over and dropped down on top of her, his thighs pinning her hips, his position of mastery the instinctive one of a man on a woman—though the childlike game they were playing took the sexual sting out of it . . . for about a minute.

Reaching beside her head, Richard grabbed a handful of snow and held it directly over her, letting streams of the white stuff fall between his fingers to land on her face. Between chortling shrieks, Victoria squirmed and tried to grab for snow to retaliate. He caught her wrists and fell forward, effectively stilling her arms, but also bringing his face to within mere inches of her own.

Victoria looked up, and suddenly the cold was gone, as were the joyful sounds of the fight continuing nearby. His eyes twinkled with sunlight. His cheeks glowed. Behind the fast-puffing clouds of his breath, his smile shone . . . and then gradually faded.

Releasing a wrist, he moved a gloved hand to brush the snow off her brow . . . away from her mouth. Her arm was free. She could have grabbed a handful of snow and tossed it in his face. But the playful mood had gone out of the moment. Instead Richard peered into her eyes in such a heated way that she'd have sworn every bit of snow around her should have melted and run down the mountain.

He bent an inch's worth closer, and she caught her breath. Whether he noticed, Victoria couldn't be sure. Seconds later he got swiftly to his feet and offered a hand. After helping her up, he turned without a word and stalked back to the rhododendron.

"How about it, Eric?" she heard him say. "Playtime's over. Let's hitch up the snowplow and see what we can do for the road."

Sheryl was waiting in the entrance hall when Eric came striding in, followed by Richard, whose expression was a bleak contrast to the crisp sunniness of the outdoors.

"Richard," she said. "I need to ask you something."

"Can it wait?" he snapped. "We're going to change into some dry things and get the snowplow going."

"It won't take more than a few minutes."

"Dammit, Sheryl! I don't have time to entertain you right now. Can it wait?"

"*Entertain* me?" she exploded. "I've never been so *un*-entertained in my life. Believe me, Richard, if it weren't for this damnable snow, I'd have been long gone yesterday!"

Their stormy eyes met, and the fire gradually went out of Richard's.

"I'm sorry," he said, and started to reach for her.

With a quick accusing glance at his drenched garments and muddy gloves, Sheryl backed away.

"Really, Sheryl. I'm glad you're here, and I'm sorry I've been such an abominable host. I'm just . . ." Sputtering into silence, Richard peeled off a glove and ran a frustrated hand over his hair.

"I know what you're 'just,'" Sheryl replied sagely. "And I don't want to hear it."

"What was it you wanted to ask?" he added.

"Never mind," she replied, and turned for the staircase. "The answer is abundantly clear."

With that she scaled the stairs with a regal step and disappeared toward her room.

Victoria was still outside, building a snowman with Missy near the courtyard entrance, when Richard emerged once more, dressed in a fresh pair of jeans and the red quilted jacket he'd worn on their hike. The memory of the rescue station assaulted him, and he hesitated as his gaze lingered across the yard. But only for a moment. Mentally shaking himself, he continued on his way to the garage and keyed in the computerized code.

The door lifted, revealing the freezing interior of the unheated building. As he walked over to the plowing machine at the end, Richard became aware that Victoria had left Missy and was plodding in his direction. Doing his best to ignore her, he climbed up into the small cab and started the motor. He couldn't screen her out moments later, however, when she stepped up on the running board and tapped at the window. Releasing a heavy breath, he rolled down the glass and gave her a questioning look.

"So you're going down the mountain?" she asked.

"Maybe we can get some of this off the road before it freezes hard. Who knows? If the plows in town get on the stick, the roads could be passable by tomorrow. That ought to give you a thrill."

Looking sharply away, she stepped down off the plow and walked out. Richard's jaw set hard as he depressed the clutch and shifted into first gear. Sometimes he couldn't stop himself from lashing out at her, but he felt like hell every time he did. Propping his arm in the open window, he chugged up beside her.

"Hold on a minute," he said.

She stopped and looked slowly up, her eyes the color of the ice framing the trees behind her.

"I didn't mean to be short," Richard added. "Why did you come over just now? What did you want?"

"I was just wondering if you and Eric are going all the way down," she answered slowly.

"As far as we can get," he replied.

"Do you plan to go into town?"

"I don't know, Victoria. Why?"

"Because it's Christmas, and there are no presents for Missy."

The feeling sparked to the surface and lit up the whole of him in a matter of seconds. God, he loved her.

"Do you think any shops in town might be open?" she added.

"I'll do my best to see."

She smiled then. Although it was hesitant and limited, the sight of it sent the feeling racing through him all over again.

"What do you think a little girl like Missy would like if I can get it?" Richard added.

The beguiling smile broadened. "Ribbons," she said. "And barrettes. And a vanity set with a brush and mirror. Is there a toy shop in town? No, I guess not. But I'd love for her to have a doll or a stuffed animal or something to take with her to school. And, of course, clothes. Nightgowns. Sweaters. Jackets. Anything. I'd estimate she's a girl's size ten."

"I'll try," Richard responded slowly, quaking with the depth of feeling he had for this woman, writhing with the urge to hold her, kiss her . . . keep her.

"Thanks," she murmured, and started to turn.

"Victoria!" She looked up once more.

"I'm . . . sorry for the way I strike out at you sometimes," he said finally. "It's not like me."

"I know," she replied, the light look of question dying away, leaving her face inscrutable.

"I guess I just can't accept what you're saying."

"I realize that."

"I mean I can't allow to happen what you say *must* happen."

"I understand how you feel, Richard."

"No. I don't think you do," he said in a voice so thick with emotion it barely made it past his throat.

Eric approached then, interrupting the moment as he swung the passenger door open with a loud creak and started climbing up. Richard stared a moment longer into Victoria's eyes.

"Maybe when the moment slaps me in the face," he added quietly, "I'll know what the hell to do with you. Now, step back."

When she was a safe distance across the courtyard, the plow chugged into motion, sending snow flying in white wings on both sides as it moved off toward the road down the mountain.

It was well after nightfall when the two men returned. Having changed into the most holidaylike outfit she had with her—forest-green corduroys and a white sweater appliquéd with sprigs of holly—Victoria had been keeping an ear pealed for the sound of the snowplow as the supper hour came . . . and went.

Leaving platters of ham and turkey and an assortment of vegetables on the banquet table, the lodge group—minus two—settled around the Christmas tree. What could have been a rather awkward time, with everyone turning eyes toward the door every few minutes, was saved by Missy, who—displaying a God-given gift no one had suspected—joined the carols broadcasting from Gertrude's radio with a clear, ringing child's soprano that added an aura of magnificence to her movements as she looped final chains of popcorn around the tree.

She captivated them all when she threw back her head and sang:

"This! This is Christ the King, whom shepherds greet and angels sing. Haste! Haste! To bring him laud, the babe, the Son of Mary."

The sweet notes reverberated through the lodge, and everyone was spellbound . . . until the door burst open and Richard and Eric strode in. Clamoring to the front of the hall, the group enfolded the prodigals.

"How is it down the mountain?" Cainey demanded.

"Did anyone try and make it up the road?" Miles asked.

"What's going on in town?" Gertrude chimed in.

"They're clearing the roads," Eric supplied.

"Things are getting back to normal," Richard offered.

The questions continued, and Eric drifted with the group toward the tree. Victoria remained, hovering, as Richard removed his jacket and hung it on a peg by the door.

"Well?" she prodded when his eyes flickered to hers.

"Well?"

"Obviously you made it to town," she added quietly. "Were you able to do anything for Missy?"

With a slowness he was sure she found infuriating, Richard stripped off his heavy ski sweater and took his time pushing each sleeve of the thermal undershirt to the elbow. When he looked up once more, she was regarding him with obvious impatience.

"I nabbed Mr. Massey when he came to check on his store," he answered, surrendering a smile. "Needless to say, Massey's

Dry Goods and Notions doesn't have anything left that could possibly please a little girl. I figure when you put her to bed, I'll bring the stuff in.''

Her look of impatience melted into that strange glow that tended to come over her these days. Rising on tiptoe, Victoria brushed her lips across his cheek as she'd done two nights ago, and—without a backward glance—returned to the noisy crowd around the tree.

Richard watched her go, the fast beat of his heart settling to a heavy thud as he took in the scene. Christmas filled the room with the scent of evergreen, the twinkling of lights, the melody of a familiar carol mixing with familial sounds of chatter and laughter. A minute passed, and Victoria's musical laugh rose above the others, startling him with—what seemed at that moment—an amazing similarity to the laugh of his mother.

The past rose like a wave to break over him, showering him with all the old feelings of loss and guilt. Mother was gone. And all his instincts said that if he didn't figure out something pretty damn quick, Victoria would be gone as well.

Turning away from the festive group, Richard ambled down the hall to the solitude of the library.

'' 'Twas the night before Christmas,'' Victoria chanted as she pulled the covers over Missy, ''and all through the house, not a creature was stirring . . . not even Missy Rochelle!'' she concluded in a rush, and drew a lyrical giggle. Victoria smiled as she tucked the velvet spread around the child's shoulders.

''This is the best Christmas I've ever had,'' Missy said.

''It's not over yet. I imagine Santa Claus is just getting started on his rounds.''

Missy's brow puckered. ''There's no such thing as Santa Claus.''

''Who told you that?''

''Mr. Sweeney.''

Bastard! Victoria thought. ''I wouldn't take his word for anything,'' she said aloud. ''Santa Claus is the spirit of Christmas giving, and I know for a fact that such a spirit exists. Now go to sleep. Who knows? Maybe you'll be surprised in the morning.''

Rosemary arrived to claim her chosen spot at Missy's back, and the child went peacefully to sleep. Long after she was quiet, Victoria stood by the arched window and gazed down on the moonlit snow. The sky was clear, the road plowed. And time was up.

Tomorrow. She had to leave tomorrow.

In the old days, when it came time to move on, her mind had always clicked precisely from step one to step two to step three, on and on until every detail of a clean getaway had been neatly planned. But tonight the idea of leaving this place, these people, made it impossible to think clearly.

The distant sound of their voices drifted up from the entrance hall, and she found herself listening, distinguishing one from the other—Hilda, Gertrude, Eric, Miles . . . even Sheryl Fontaine, who had spent nearly an hour that evening with her and Missy, diligently folding and cutting newspapers into paper-doll chains. Through the medium of the child the two women had developed a surprisingly natural and spontaneous camaraderie—though barriers of mistrust and competitiveness had lurked in the back of Victoria's mind, and she sensed it was the same with Sheryl.

Richard had disappeared in the direction of the library shortly after he returned. Victoria hadn't seen him since then, and wondered if memories of that tragic Christmas long ago were haunting him again. The idea of his pain touched her once more, just as it had three nights ago when she allowed herself to be lured into believing one more day wouldn't make any difference.

Now, once again, the seductive phrase floated through her mind: *One more day* . . .

But it couldn't be. Richard had nearly been shot the last time she fooled herself. And Kyle would strike again. She knew it. The snowstorm may have held him at bay for the past two days. But he'd be back, and there was no telling who might get caught in the line of fire. Richard again? Or maybe Missy?

Tomorrow. She had to leave tomorrow.

Steeling herself to accept the inevitable, Victoria took a long hot bath and pulled on a favorite nightgown. But the soft flannel did nothing to comfort her; nor did the quiet that settled over the lodge as the hour crept past midnight.

As Missy slept Victoria paced the darkened room, trying to direct thoughts that remained stubbornly muddled. Should she take the truck again? Should she search for the BMW's distributor cap? Should she confront Richard and demand that he give it back? He'd never do it. In fact, she couldn't risk saying good-bye to him because he'd never let her go.

The only thing that might convince Richard of the necessity of her leaving was the truth. But even if Victoria could have forced a recitation past her throat, she refused to try. She remembered quite well the horrified look on Richard's face when she divulged her connection to one of the Big Boys. She didn't want to see, or even imagine, the look that might come over him if he knew she was wanted for murdering one of them.

It was after one o'clock when her frustrated thoughts drove her from the room. Taking a reassuring look at Missy's peaceful form, Victoria slipped into the terrycloth robe and went downstairs to the deserted foyer, halting in her tracks when she beheld the glorious array beneath the Christmas tree.

There was a beautiful doll dressed in a bridal gown . . . and a schoolbox with drawing pad and colored pencils . . . and a green hooded jacket about the shade of Missy's eyes with matching mittens . . . and a vanity set adorned with pink rosebuds.

Victoria lifted templing fingers to her mouth as she moved slowly around the giant tree, her gaze dancing from a stuffed bear nearly as big as Missy, to an assortment of shampoos and bubble baths, on to a pretty pink sweater and soft denim jeans, beside which lay a stream of satin ribbons in every color of the rainbow.

Once again the tears that had so long eluded Victoria welled up and spilled over, running past the temple of her fingers, slipping along the lines of her jaw. She had no idea how long she stood there staring at Missy's Christmas plunder, sealed in a vacuum of mushrooming emotion, before the odd noise reached her ears.

Like the distant whack of an ax on a tree, it came once . . . and then again. Victoria wiped her cheeks, waiting, listening, realizing as the staccato crack sounded out once more that someone was shooting pool in the game room down the hall.

* * *

Sinking the nine ball, Richard chalked his cue as he considered the shot on the ten. He looked up with surprise when he caught the sound of approaching footsteps. It was late as hell. Who else was up? Of all the faces that flitted through his mind, Victoria's was not among them. And yet it was she who walked in, looking much as she had two nights ago when she came to his room—muffling terrycloth robe, hair pulled back in a ribbon . . .

Only now the stirring radiance that shone from her face was like the glow of a full moon. She said nothing as she moved toward him, stopping when they were but a foot apart, gazing silently up at him. Her eyes were shining, too, as though something inside her was all lit up and there was no containing it.

"Victoria?" he greeted on a questioning note, and set the cue stick aside. "Is something wrong?"

"No," she mumbled. "Yes," she added.

"No? Yes? What is it?"

She shocked him by throwing her arms about his neck and landing against him with such force that he stumbled back a pace. For a surprised few seconds he couldn't think. As she buried her face against the side of his neck, his arms rose on their own, instinctively reaching to enfold her.

"Richard," she whispered eventually.

He started to pull back, but she clasped him more tightly.

"Don't look at me," she said. "I want to talk to you, and I don't want you to look at me."

"All right," he supplied slowly.

He waited, holding her, becoming acutely aware of the warmth of her body seeping through the fabric of his undershirt.

"I want you to know I wish things were different," she murmured finally. "Oh, God, I wish so much that I could be who you want me to be, Richard. You dropped out of the sky and into my life and changed so many things. You even made me wish you could change everything, but you'll have to take my word when I say you can't."

He tried to lift his head once more.

"I'm not finished," she objected, and clutched him closer still, so that he failed to capture even a glimpse of her face.

"I never thought I could feel this way for any man," she continued, her lips moving against his neck, threatening to stifle the words he strained to hear. "But then you're not just 'any man,' are you? Not by a long shot."

"What are you saying?" Richard managed, his chin stirring the shining crown of her hair.

"I'm saying that whatever happens, I want you to know I'll never forget you, Richard. Whatever happens, please remember that if things were different . . . if I had my choice . . ."

"What?" he prompted after an impossible few seconds. "If you had your choice, what would you do?"

"I'd spend the days watching you smile, and wish the nights away so I could wake up in your arms," she answered steadily. "I'd grow old with you, and take care of you, and be with you always."

A charge flashed down Richard's spine and along his limbs. This time he gripped Victoria's shoulders with irrefutable strength and forced her back so he could look in her eyes. "Don't con me," he warned in a rumbling tone.

"I'm not," she returned, her voice low but ringing with the same conviction that sparkled in her eyes. "You know I'm not. You can't help but feel the truth of what I'm saying. It's too amazing. Sometimes when I look at you, I have to turn away. It's like looking at the mountains or the ocean. I can't take it all in. I just—"

She halted as he scooped her up in his arms.

"Don't say anything else," Richard commanded, and started off toward the game-room door at a brisk pace.

"But what are you—"

"Don't . . . say . . . anything," he repeated, and moving swiftly through the entrance hall, started up the stairs at a pace belying the weight of the woman in his arms. When he strode into his chamber, Lobo trotted over and yipped at his heels.

"Out, boy!" Richard commanded, and kicked the door closed behind the coyote.

Taking a few more steps in the direction of the bed, he set

Victoria down, and suddenly it struck him—the closeness of the bed, the meaning of the moment. Richard backed off a pace.

"Well, here we are."

"So I see," she responded.

"Want me to light a fire?"

"In the hearth?" she questioned with the arch of a brow.

Cocking his head, Richard swept her with a head-to-toe look. "Listen . . . I'm not sure what you have in mind, but if you keep looking at me like that, and making remarks like that, I'm going to proceed as though you came here of your own free will."

"Please do," she responded, and said no other words, though her hands spoke volumes as they moved to the sash of her robe. A moment later the terrycloth fell in a pile at her feet, and she stood before him in the virginal white of a thin flannel nightgown with pristine lace about the collar.

Damn! Richard thought . . . or said out loud. He didn't know which as he backed to the door and reached behind himself to lock it, his gaze fixed on her all the while. In a quick move he pulled the undershirt over his head and tossed it aside.

She never flinched as he approached with burning eyes and a lifting hand. His fingers closed on the top pearl button of her nightgown as he bent to kiss her neck. Capturing her skin in his open mouth, he bathed and caressed it as his hand freed the top button and moved on. When his knuckles brushed across her breast, he felt a sharp intake of breath. But it was followed a heartbeat later with a scintillating trail of fingernails across his back.

Releasing the final button, Richard lifted the gown over her shoulders and let it fall about her ankles. As he surveyed Victoria with blatant intensity she reached for the snap of his jeans. Moments later their naked bodies melded as Richard gathered her up in a delving kiss. Her fingers grasped in his hair as her breasts nuzzled his chest, triggering the most irrepressible desire he'd ever experienced. Securing her hips, Richard pressed his hardness into her belly and tore his mouth from hers.

"Who the hell are you?" he demanded, heatedly plumbing her eyes. "Victoria? Valerie? Who?"

"Whoever I am, I'm yours," she replied breathlessly. "That's for damn sure."

Sweeping her up once more, Richard moved to the bed and crawled with her beneath the sheets. There was no romantic fire. No sexy sax wailing from a stereo. Just the ordinary lamps lit against the winter darkness, and the extraordinary music of Victoria's body moving beneath his. She was like silk, wrapping herself in a smooth caress around his hips and back . . . clasping him with contrasting heat as he pressed inside.

As though he were watching from some faraway place, Richard saw his head jerk back like that of a wolf releasing a howl. Maybe he *did* howl because the sensations that blasted through him could hardly be borne—exploding as they did not only along every inch of flesh, but through his brain as well.

His eyelids slammed shut, his ears were stopped. Silence and darkness engulfed him as he made her his own again and again . . . until it became clear, through the red haze of his mind, that it was not he who was claiming her, but the other way around. He might hold Victoria now in every sense and level of the word, but she held him just as tightly.

A couple of hours, or centuries, later Richard rolled on his side. He had no conception of how much time had passed. Not that he gave a damn. Never had he been driven to such feats of passion—not when he was an adolescent, not ever. No sooner had he spent himself than the craving started building all over again.

Surely there was no fluid left inside his body, and his limbs felt as though they'd never move again. But as Victoria snuggled up against his back Richard knew they would. When she reached, he'd respond. And he saw then and there that the free wandering of bachelorhood was over.

Some animals mated for life, and he was one of them. Never again would there be anyone but her.

God in heaven, Richard thought mindlessly.

Tucking a pillow beneath his cheek, he sank into its feathery depths, an unconscious smile spreading across his face as he sank into blissful slumber.

Thousands of feet below and miles away, Mavis woke with a start. The headboard banged against the wall as she sat

swiftly up, staring blindly across the moonlit bedroom, recalling the dream step-by-step—the fallen leaves dancing across
the yard as she strolled up to the Skinner house . . .
the jack-o'-lanterns grinning at each side of the door . . . the
crowd, the costumes . . . the icy eyes of a beauty dressed like
Marie Antoinette.

Vanessa? her voice echoed. *I love the name. So feminine.*

The familiar bedroom settled gradually into focus. Mavis
glanced at the clock. Nearly four A.M. Too bad. Kyle could like
it or lump it. Reaching for the pack on the bedside table, Mavis
lit a cigarette, climbed out of bed, and headed for the closet.

Santa had, indeed, left a plum in her stocking. And its name
was Vanessa Blair.

A hesitant knock sounded at the door. Glancing at Jeanette's
cuddled-up form, Kyle swung his legs over the edge of the bed,
stuffed his feet in his slippers, and stalked across the room.

"What the hell is it?" he demanded of Tibbs's anxious face.

"It's Miz Brewer, sir," the old man supplied, his eyes on the
floor. "She's downstairs and won't go on till she sees ya."

Grabbing his robe, Kyle stomped down the stairs and
tendered Mavis a flickering glance as he walked into the study.
Proceeding to his father's old cigar box, he lit a smoke and
propped back against the lectern. She strolled forward, her
hands buried in the pockets of the fur coat she was so fond of
wearing.

"This had better be good," Kyle greeted.

"I think you'll like it a lot."

"Do you?" His eyes probed like dark sentries through a
cloud of smoke. "Exactly what is it I'm going to like so
much?"

"The proposition I'm about to make."

"It's close to milking time, Mavis. And on Christmas
morning, no less. This proposition of yours had better be
damned good if it can't wait till sunup."

"I don't think you'll want to wait," she replied. Leaning
forward, she trailed a tapered nail along his stubbled cheek.
"Tell me, Kyle . . . Just what would you give in exchange
for the whereabouts of Vanessa Blair? The guaranteed safety of
Richard Adams, perhaps?"

Moments later the deal was made, and Richard was safe.

Sinking down in one of the many plush leather chairs appointing the room, Mavis quietly watched as Kyle scurried for the phone—hoping for a feeling of absolution that didn't come as he rousted Chief Matthews.

"Christmas Eve?" Kyle blasted into the receiver. "I don't care if it's the damn Eve of Destruction, get your butt out of bed and over here!"

Mavis lit a cigarette and leaned listlessly back against the leather headrest.

But then, she supposed, you shouldn't hope for absolution when you'd just made a pact with the devil.

$=$ THIRTEEN $=$

December 25
5:55 A.M.

Richard was sprawled against the pillows, head thrown back, one arm dangling off the edge of the bed, the other encircling her.

Settled warmly against his side, Victoria reached for the hand resting on her hip and lifted it up where she could study it. In the muted light of the rising sun, it was dark and perfectly outlined . . . like a hand in a painting. She'd always admired his hands; now she knew for herself the magic they contained.

Absently caressing his fingers, she thought over the past few hours, marveling at the sensations that had swamped her again and again . . . sensations she'd never even come close to imagining. Loving a man was a miracle. Making love to the man you loved was an experience for which there were no words.

"Excuse me."

Looking up, she found Richard had cracked an eye in her direction. "I'd better warn you," he mumbled. "If that's meant to be foreplay, you're going to give me a heart attack."

She laughed. Listening to the music of it, Richard shifted up on an elbow and looked down at her, the golden hair fanning across the pillow, the sparkling eyes turned up to his.

"How do you feel?" he asked.

"Too good," she replied lightly. "It feels dangerous, as though God may strike me down at any moment."

"You realize, of course, that you can never leave me now."

The look of merriment evaporated as she lifted a hand to stroke his hair. "I sure as hell don't want to," she said.

"Not the exact answer I would have liked," Richard replied.
"But I'll take it."

He bent to kiss her, gradually shifting on top of her as her
welcoming arms ignited his passion once more. Long moments
later Richard lifted his head as the distant sound of a ruckus
reached his ears.

"What the hell is that at this hour?" he muttered.

There were voices, a medley growing louder as it reached
the second floor . . . Hilda's high-pitched protests clearly
distinguishable now against a backdrop of masculine bellow-
ing.

Richard climbed out of bed, reaching for his jeans as a
tingling feeling of apprehension swept Victoria from head to
toe.

"Maybe it's Sweeney again," Richard said, and swiftly
crossing to the fireplace, removed the rifle from the rack over
the mantel.

Sweeney . . . The name sifted through Victoria's mind as a
mounting sense of alarm sent new chills coursing along her
limbs. No. It was something else. Something worse. She
lurched up, clutching the sheet over her breasts.

Just as Richard arrived at the door the banging began.

"Open up in the name of the law!"

"The *what*?" Richard mumbled in a tone of wonder.
Unlocking the door, he prepared to step out, but never got the
chance as Chief of Police John Matthews moved brusquely
inside.

"Get rid of the firearm, Mr. Adams."

Richard's surprised gaze turned beyond the sheriff to behold
two deputies and . . . *Kyle Skinner?* . . . along with Hilda
and everyone else spilling out of rooms and moving toward the
commotion.

"I said, put away your weapon!"

Applying the safety, Richard set the rifle aside and raised his
palms. "What the hell is going on here?"

"I understand you have a Miss Victoria Blackwood staying
here," the chief replied. Taking another step inside, he turned
a sweeping look about the room. "Well, what have we here?"
he added.

Richard looked over his shoulder. Victoria's face had turned as white as the sheet she was clutching.

"Now, wait a minute," Richard objected, starting for the bed.

"No. *You* do the waiting," the chief ordered, seizing his arm. "Come on in, Mr. Skinner."

Richard jerked his arm free, his violent gaze shifting from the chief to Kyle Skinner, who strolled casually into the bedroom as though he owned it. "Would somebody tell me what the hell's happening?" Richard thundered. "What's *he* doing here?"

"Mr. Skinner is here for the purposes of identification," the chief replied, once again pulling Richard back.

Kyle walked up to the foot of the bed. Victoria's gaze darted to his eyes. She was unable to make anything else move.

"I always knew I'd see you like this someday," he said with the remembered, evil smile. "Hello, Vanessa."

"Is she the one?"

"Oh, yes, Chief Matthews," he replied with the utmost courtesy, his black eyes raking Victoria's body through the meager cover of the sheet. "She most certainly is the one."

"*What* one?" Richard bellowed.

The chief glanced over his shoulder to one of the deputies. "Take my place here, will you, Tobin?"

A sheepish-looking, overweight officer moved forward, taking Richard's arm and looking uncomfortably away when he received a scalding glare.

"Vanessa Blair," the chief began, Richard's glare following the man as he joined Kyle Skinner at the foot of the bed. "I hereby place you under arrest on charges of grand theft, assault with a deadly weapon, and murder in the first degree. You have the right to remain silent. . . ."

Richard could see that the man continued to speak, but heard nothing more as the word "murder" exploded in his head. Minutes later the sound of Victoria's voice made its way to his ears. She said something about her robe. Bending down, Skinner picked up the white terrycloth and tossed it to her. As Richard watched her struggle to cover herself behind the meager shield of the bedsheet, he snapped back to sudden alertness.

"Listen!" he shouted, bolting forward despite the deputy's efforts. "I don't give a damn what you think you're doing here, but she deserves the chance to put some damn clothes on!"

She climbed out of bed then, clutching the neck of the robe about her throat as she stood straight and still. There was no color in her face, no life in her eyes.

In fact, she seemed oblivious to everyone and everything around her as the chief escorted her out of the bedroom and up the hall . . . until Missy came out of the scarlet room, rubbing her eyes. Without a word, Victoria looked sharply at Sheryl, who, in seeming understanding of the silent command, drew the child swiftly into her own room and closed the door.

"You've got five minutes," the chief said as Victoria walked into the bedroom.

Darting back inside his chamber, Richard pulled a sweater over his head, grabbed his boots, and pushed grimly past the questioning faces of Eric and Miles and the others, past the two deputies posted at Victoria's door, and on to where Chief Matthews and Kyle Skinner stood at the head of the stairs.

"Would one of you be so kind as to fill me in on a couple of things?" he demanded. "For instance, who the hell is she supposed to have murdered?"

Skinner stepped forward, his black eyes gleaming. "Four years ago, on the night of November fifth, your girlfriend in there killed my father, nearly killed me, and then made her getaway in a stolen car worth about fifty grand."

Richard felt as though he'd just been socked in the diaphragm. He drew a long, shuddering breath. "I don't believe it," he then replied.

Skinner reached up to his forehead and pointed to a thin scar stretching from his right brow to his hairline. "She killed my father, Adams. Then bashed me in the head and left me for dead while she went driving off in my Vette."

"I still don't believe it," Richard repeated.

"That's entirely up to you," Skinner returned with a cold smile. "What you believe doesn't make a damn bit of difference."

A moment later Victoria stepped out of the scarlet room, having tied back her hair and donned boots, jeans, sweater, and windbreaker. Handing a small bag to one of the deputies, she looked neither right nor left as the chief fastened handcuffs about her wrists. Swiftly pulling on his boots, Richard hurried down the stairs after them and reached for his jacket.

"Where do you think you're going?" the chief asked.

"I'm coming with you."

"No point in that, Mr. Adams. In fact I insist that you don't. The lady's a runner. There won't be any bail, and there won't be any visitors."

Stopping helplessly in the doorway, Richard peered into the freezing winter morning. If he lived to be a hundred, he would never forget the way she looked walking out of the lodge, distant and silent, the lifeless shell of a woman drifting across the snow toward the flashing lights of police cars.

A two-story structure built of stone quarried from surrounding hills, the Devil's Rock town hall housed the police station, along with a number of other public offices. The basement served as a morgue, the ground floor was used for administration, and the top story featured six jail cells that remained consistently empty.

The bitch would have them all to herself. Kyle's every nerve ending was twitching as he followed her and Matthews up the stairwell at the back of the station. Pushing open the door of the second cell, the chief removed the handcuffs. She turned and moved sedately inside. She had yet to say a word. Setting her bag inside, Matthews started to close the door behind her.

"Hold it," Kyle objected. "I'd like a minute alone with her."

"I don't think that's such a good idea—"

"Give me the keys, Matthews," Kyle broke in, extending a palm. "I'll lock up."

The chief walked grudgingly away. "I'll be at the foot of the stairs," he said.

Kyle barely heard as he walked into the cell, his hungry gaze starting at the toes of her boots and devouring her inch by inch. The outdoorsy ensemble of jeans and boots was out of sync with his memories of Vanessa, but the long legs and slender waist were the same. Beneath that bulky sweater was a pair of perfect breasts. He remembered the feel of them in his hands.

Flashing to her face, Kyle's gaze was filled with the lust of victory. She didn't see it, however, as she continued to stare woodenly into the distance beyond him. That, too, was Vanessa.

Kyle lifted a hand to her hair. "So, you're a blonde."

Snapping to life, she took a swift backward step. "Don't touch me," she commanded, her eyes pale and freezing, just as he remembered.

Kyle chuckled. "Now, *there's* the Vanessa I know and love."

"What do you plan on doing with me, you bastard?"

His look of mirth disappeared. "Whatever I damn well please." Stepping forward, Kyle grabbed her by the jacket collar and wrenched her up to him. "If I want to touch you, I will," he said. "If I want to *bed* you, I will. And maybe if you please me, you just might manage to stay alive."

Catching the back of her head, he planted his mouth on hers in a bruising kiss. She pushed futilely at his shoulders. When he was ready, Kyle released her with a shove. She backed away, rubbing the back of a hand across her mouth.

"Maybe we can make a deal," she said.

"A deal?" Kyle repeated with a hearty laugh. "What makes you think you're in any position to bargain?"

"The ledgers."

"Ah, the missing ledgers. You mean you've held on to them all these years?"

"Of course I've held on to them," she retorted. "As insurance against just such a day as this."

"I don't see your insurance as being worth much. With Vanessa Blair buried, the files will be buried as well."

"Don't count on it."

He arched a questioning brow.

"I have them rigged, Kyle. If I don't check in at the scheduled time, they'll be sent to the U.S. attorney."

"You're bluffing."

"Am I?"

"Either that or you're a fool. If you dared to come into the arena against me and the Boys, you'd be gobbled up so fast you'd never know what hit you. Remember the Christians and the lions?" Kyle clucked his tongue. "Not a pretty picture."

With a slight toss of her head, she looked away.

"Face it, Vanessa. I caught you. You're mine. And there's not a damn thing you can do about it."

Staring at the wall, she made no reply.

"But for now," Kyle proceeded in a cheerful tone, "I think I'll just let you get used to your new surroundings."

He glanced around the gloomy cell. There was a cot, a straight-backed chair, a sink, and a toilet. The light of the newly risen sun streamed in through a single, barred window.

"Not exactly plush," he remarked, "but I think you have everything you need."

She continued to look askance.

Walking out of the cell with a jaunty stride, Kyle slammed the iron door. "Oh, by the way," he said, glancing back through the bars, "Merry Christmas."

As the day passed, Richard felt as though he were enveloped in a cloud. Beyond the mist he was aware of Sheryl and Hilda and Eric and the others. But their images were dim, their voices distant.

Murder? The word kept ringing in his mind. *Murder?*

Before he knew it, night had fallen. He was sitting at his desk, the library growing dark around him, when Missy walked in and turned on a lamp.

"They're wrong," she said. "Victoria wouldn't hurt anybody. She *couldn't* hurt anybody."

Richard's head snapped up, and with a brief look into the child's steady eyes, he found relief so overwhelming that it sent chills down his arms.

"You know, Missy," he said, "you're absolutely right."

Turning swiftly to the computer, he flipped on the unit, picked up the modem, and waited impatiently for the whirring system to come on line.

"What are you going to do?" Missy asked.

"Research," he replied. "Would you do me a favor? Please ask Hilda to put on a pot of coffee."

The child turned away.

"Hey, Missy!" She looked over her shoulder. "Thanks," Richard added in a heartfelt tone of gratitude. She walked out with a smile, and he looked back to the computer's screen.

As soon as the menu came up, Richard scrolled through the

sophisticated list of services with which he was networked. Finally finding and selecting the volume he sought, he keyed in the password to the Library of Congress.

December 26

Sheryl quietly finished dressing and went downstairs to the kitchen. Missy was still asleep; everyone else but Richard was gathered about the breakfast table, still talking in the hushed tone of shock that had befallen them the previous morning.

Sheryl poured herself a cup of coffee. "Is Richard still in the library?"

"I don't believe he left it all night, miss," Hilda answered.

Pouring a second cup for Richard, Sheryl proceeded to the library, where she found him propped before the computer.

"Care for a hot cup of coffee?" she asked.

"Thanks, but no," he replied, bestowing a quick, smiling glance before looking back to the screen. "I think I've already had a couple of potfuls."

His hair was tousled, his beard a dark shadow, and he had not changed his clothes since the night before.

"You look as though you've been up all night," she said.

"I guess I have. What time is it?"

"Nearly nine. Exactly what is it that you've been doing, Richard?"

"Reading old newspaper texts."

"What?"

Flipping off the computer, he stood up and ran a hand over his hair. "I spent the night in the Library of Congress, Sheryl. First I keyed in Vanessa Blair and read everything published about her. Then I plugged in Judge Skinner, and finally Kyle."

Sheryl peered up at him. Obviously rumpled, the look about him was nonetheless bright and eager. "Apparently you're pleased with what you were able to learn," she observed.

"Yep," he replied with another quick smile, and pushing down the rolled-up sleeves of his sweater, started out of the room.

"Where are you going?" Sheryl demanded.

"Old Doc Hawkins is a GP, a justice of the peace, and the

town coroner. He's bound to be the medical examiner as well.''

"What?'' Sheryl piped up once more, scurrying after him as he strode down the hall.

Richard paused in the entrance hall long enough to pull his jacket off the rack and give her a quick peck on the cheek.

"She didn't do it, Sheryl. I know it.''

With that, he opened the door and stalked off toward the garage.

It was late in the afternoon. Tobin was coming on duty and the chief getting ready to head home when Richard Adams strode into the police station.

"What the hell does *he* want?'' Matthews muttered under his breath. "Can I help you?'' he added, raising his voice.

"I want to see her.''

"I told you yesterday, Mr. Adams. No visitors.''

"Chief Matthews, are you sure you're within the law here? What about inalienable rights?''

"Everything's being handled strictly by the book, Mr. Adams. Due to the severity of the charges, and particularly because of the lady's history as a fugitive, she's being held in solitary confinement. Her inalienable rights entitle her to an attorney, that's true—though if you can find one willing to take her case, I'll be mightily surprised.''

"Oh, she'll have an attorney, Matthews. You can count on it.''

Turning on his heel, Richard trotted down the steps and into the deserted lanes of Sky Road. Looking up, he shielded his eyes against the bright sunshine as he scanned the barred windows dotting the second floor of the building. "Hey, you up there!'' he yelled. "Victoria!''

She appeared at the second window. He could clearly see the palms she pressed against the glass behind the bars.

"It's going to be okay! Do you hear me? I've got a plan! You're going to be all right! Just hang on!''

Bustling out of the town hall, the chief and his deputy accosted Richard on each side and escorted him back to the walk.

Across the street at an upstairs window of the old Brewer house, the curtains fluttered closed as Mavis turned away from the sight.

* * *

When Richard returned to the lodge, Sheryl was waiting in the entrance hall. Granting her a preoccupied greeting, he hung up his jacket and headed once more toward the library. Following him in, she closed the door.

"I'm putting my foot down, Richard. You haven't slept in forty-eight hours, and as far as I know, you haven't eaten either. You're behaving like an obsessed man, and I want you to stop."

Sinking down in his desk chair, he gave her a weary smile. "You're right. I'm tired and I'm hungry. But I can't stop."

"Dammit, Richard! I admit she's intriguing. I can understand how you got caught up in this. But it isn't about stolen cars anymore. She's been arrested for murder."

"She didn't do it, Sheryl."

"You said that before. How can you know? Don't you think it's possible your judgment is a little clouded here?"

"This morning I knew it in my gut. Now that I've seen the medical report, I know it here," Richard concluded, tapping his forehead with a fingertip.

Sheryl folded her arms. "I have my theories about the bodily parts involved in *this* conclusion."

Cocking a brow, he got to his feet. "All right. I'll show you."

There was a ruler on his desk. Richard pushed it toward her.

"Judge Skinner was killed by a succession of blows to the head with a marble-headed gavel," he explained. "Obviously this ruler isn't as heavy or unwieldy as the actual murder weapon, but it'll do for the purposes of demonstration. Okay, Sheryl. I'm Judge Skinner, and you're going to kill me with that thing. You're going to swing with every bit of your strength directly at my temple. Go ahead. Pick it up."

"I don't see what this can possibly accomplish, Richard."

"Humor me," he challenged. "Go ahead. Kill me."

Slowly unfolding her arms, Sheryl eyed the fictitious weapon with obvious doubt.

"Go on, Sheryl."

With a shrug she grabbed the ruler, hauled back, and let fly a mock swing, stopping mere inches from the side of Richard's head.

"I presume you don't really want me to hit you," she said.

"Just look at where you *would* have hit me," Richard returned in a tone of consummate patience.

"You said to swing at your temple."

"That's right."

"Well, that's where I would have hit you, then."

"Squarely on the left temple, correct? Which is exactly where Judge Skinner received the first blow. That's the point."

Letting her arm fall, Sheryl tossed the ruler on the desk. "I must not have performed very well," she said, "because I certainly don't see the point."

"You performed fine. You did just what any right-handed person would have done. The point is Victoria is left-handed."

Sheryl met his eyes with a start.

"If she were going to swing at a full-grown man with the intention of killing him," Richard went on, "she would *not* hold the weapon in her right hand. Consequently the blow would *not* be delivered to the left side of the victim's head. The newspaper accounts say she struck Kyle Skinner with the same gavel that killed his father. Yesterday he showed me a scar near his *right* temple. Maybe that part's true. I'm not sure. But I'm convinced she didn't murder the Judge."

"Okay," Sheryl surrendered slowly. "Let's say you're right. But if Victoria didn't do it, then who did?"

"Interesting question, isn't it?"

Stepping around the desk, Richard opened a drawer and began sifting through its contents.

"I need your help, Sheryl."

"Again?" she questioned. "With what?"

"Ah, here it is." He held up the driver's license bearing the name Veronica Bates. "A little cut-and-paste job with your picture ought to do it."

"You're doing it again, Richard."

"Doing what?"

"Steaming away on a train of thought and leaving me behind at the station."

Tossing the driver's license on the desktop, Richard sank once more into the chair and looked up at her.

"Several years ago Victoria managed to obtain some files, records of illegal activities involving a ring of powerful men.

She stashed the papers in a safe-deposit box in Tennessee. Like you said, if Victoria didn't murder the Judge, who did? The only other able-bodied person in the house was Kyle Skinner. He's one of the Big Boys, and Victoria's files supposedly incriminate the lot of them. Evidence like that could be leverage.''

"So what do you want from me?"

"The safe-deposit box is in the name of Veronica Bates. I have a key, but it will take a woman to sign for the contents."

"Oh, no," Sheryl murmured slowly.

"All you need to do is practice the signature a few times."

"I'm sure you're not suggesting that I drive to Tennessee, pose as this Bates woman, and then falsify her signature."

"The roads have been salted. They'll do it again tomorrow. After that it should be completely safe to travel."

"So you've got this all worked out," she commented with a caustic note in her voice.

Richard's eyes settled on hers. Though tired and bloodshot, they still exerted the old familiar pull.

"Come on, Sheryl," he said quietly. "I'd go myself if I could. I need your help. Please don't turn me down."

Ultimately she released a long, defeated breath. "Could I ever refuse you?" she replied.

With a quick smile Richard pushed up to the desk and reached for his address book.

"What are you doing *now*?" she asked.

"Calling Bill. The way Chief Matthews is handling this, the only person who can get in to see Victoria is her attorney. God, I never thought about the remoteness of these mountains in any terms except their beauty. Now I see the downside. Matthews is right. There's no attorney within a fifty-mile radius who would touch Victoria's case."

"You said Bill. You mean Bill Honeycutt? Your friend who lives in Charlotte?"

"He's one of the best criminal law attorneys in the state," Richard answered, flipping through his book and finally targeting Bill's number.

"Let me get this straight," Sheryl said in a musing tone. "You're going to ask Bill to defend the woman who stole his Mercedes and disappeared pretty-as-you-please?"

Richard paused in the midst of reaching for the phone. "I never said it wasn't going to be a little sticky."

Sheryl arched a brow at his sheepish expression.

"Maybe I should get Bill up here first," he suggested, "and *then* explain."

"I find that idea disgustingly underhanded," Sheryl said. "And *definitely* the way to go."

Richard cracked a small smile. "Do you think that in spite of everything, I can talk him into this?"

"Why not?" Sheryl retorted. "You talked *me* into it, didn't you?"

Two days and hundreds of bumpy miles later, Sheryl drove a mud-streaked, salt-sprayed car into a small town in western Tennessee. Locating the bank on Main Street, she pulled over and parked.

"Richard," she muttered, though the derision in her tone was all for herself, "the things I do for you."

With a quick check of hair and makeup, she summoned her most professional, take-charge demeanor and went inside.

December 29

Victoria was washing her face when the treasured voice rang up from the street below. Leaving the water running, she dashed to the window and climbed up on the chair.

There he was, the smile on his face rivaling the sunniness of the winter morning as he waved up at her. Catching her lip, she waved back.

"Your attorney will be here tomorrow!" Richard boomed. "Tomorrow! Are you doing okay?"

She nodded, but had no idea if he saw her as a deputy appeared and swiftly hauled him out of the street. Climbing down off the chair, Victoria returned to the sink with a smile lingering about her lips. Ever since that first afternoon, he'd come by every day, yelling up at her from Sky Road until some officer or other dragged him away. Richard . . . her fondest fantasies had never even come close to the real man.

It was the fifth day, and it went by in the way of the others.

A deputy showed up at nine, twelve, and seven with a food tray. Other than that, she saw no one. When the lights went out promptly at ten P.M., Victoria lay down on the cot, fully dressed, and stared into the darkness.

Another day gone, and it seemed she'd made it through one more time. Kyle hadn't shown his face since Christmas Day. He'd be back, of course. Maybe tomorrow. Maybe the next day. For now, she surmised, he was enjoying a waiting game—sensing that every time she heard the door open below, she prickled with the dread that it would be his step that ascended. By staying away, he was taunting her with the inevitability of his coming, drawing out the kill like a hunter capturing a long-sought prize.

Kyle was right. She did tremble with dread at the mere thought of his return, the mere wisp of an image of him touching her. She wasn't sure if she could live through it if he raped her. But then that was probably his ultimate plan anyway. Rape her. Kill her. It was what he'd had in mind that night four years ago.

It had been a long time since Victoria had been so terrified of a solitary man. A very long time.

Still, in a roundabout way Kyle had provided her with a sort of serenity. Everything had been taken out of her hands. No more decisions. No more escapes. No more running. She had no choice but to exist day-to-day and wonder if each were her last.

Here in Devil's Rock Kyle Skinner had the power to make it happen in such a way that not the slightest ripple of suspicion would touch him. No one could fight one of the Big Boys on his home turf. Not even Richard.

Victoria closed her eyes. Richard. The talent she'd developed so long ago served her differently now. Now, instead of conjuring faraway places and the peace of aloneness, she sank into memories of his face, his smile, his touch.

Soon there were no stone walls, no iron bars, no distant sound of men's voices in the station below. Soon there was no sound at all but the rustle of sheets as Richard's body moved on hers.

December 30
2:00 P.M.

"I don't believe it," Bill mumbled.

From the vicinity of the kitchen came the light sound of Missy's laughter. But in the game room the cue sticks had been set aside, and the air was heavy. Richard peered across the pool table, his eyes locking with those of the man he'd known for a lifetime.

"I know it's a lot to digest, but—"

"A lot to digest?" came the resounding reply. "Why didn't you tell me, Richard? Why?"

Richard's face felt as though it had caught fire. "At first I thought I should substantiate what seemed to be happening before I called you."

"At first . . . Would that be when you spotted her in Atlanta two months ago? Let's see, how many days is that? Sixty or so?"

Ignoring the angry challenge, Richard went on bravely.

"Even when I followed her to Pawleys Island, it was still in my mind to get the goods on her so we could really nail her."

"A noble plan. What happened to it?"

"I uncovered her other life, Bill. Her real life. As Victoria Blackwood she lives the life of a beneficent recluse—taking in stranded adolescents, almost single-handedly meeting the financial needs of a school for damaged children. At first, I guess, I was just stymied by the paradox. And then . . ."

"And then?" Bill prodded curtly.

Richard looked up, the fire in his cheeks receding as the emotion within him rose like a booning tide. "The bottom line is I fell in love with her, Bill. I guess I've got a lot of nerve asking for your help."

"I guess so!" Bill sputtered after a moment.

Their eyes locked once more—Bill's wide with disbelief and accusation; Richard's humble but unflinching.

The tense moment was shattered as Sheryl's voice made its way down the hall, followed shortly by her straightforward entrance.

"There you go, Commander." Dropping a manila file on the pool table, she offered Richard a mock salute. "Any other impossible missions come along while I was away?"

Richard enfolded her in a smiling hug.

"Now I know why soldiers like homecomings so much," she murmured.

"What's that?" Bill asked with a nod to the file folder.

"Something I haven't had time to tell you about yet," Richard replied. "It might figure into the case somehow."

Backing out of Richard's embrace, Sheryl directed a curious gaze across the table. "Hello, Bill. When did you get here?"

"About a half hour ago."

The eyes he turned on her were bright with anger. "Although it feels like years have passed," he added. "I see Richard's drafted you into this thing, too."

"I'm his chief errand runner," Sheryl returned. "How about you? Are you going to sign up?"

Richard's eyes lifted to see how his friend would respond. Bill looked from one to the other. Richard and Sheryl. Sheryl and Richard. He'd often thought of them as a couple, and now the two of them had joined forces on behalf of Valerie Blake. It was crazy! Still, the mystery Richard presented was an intriguing one.

"The jury's still out on that one," Bill answered, unable to ignore the crestfallen look on Richard's face as he reached for the files.

"Did you take a look at these, Sheryl?" he asked.

"I looked. But I didn't really know what I was looking at."

Richard flipped swiftly through the pages. "Victoria was right. This is hot stuff. Sweeney's name is everywhere. So are the names of all the Big Boys, including Kyle Skinner."

"Skinner," Bill mumbled after a moment. "Isn't that the sole witness? The one who's bringing all the charges?"

Richard nodded. "Pillar of the community, town councilman, et cetera, et cetera. You could say he pretty much runs Devil's Rock. But I've done some checking on Mr. Skinner. If you dig into his background, you find things that paint a pretty violent picture. Tickets for reckless and drunk driving. And there was a scandal that got him kicked out of military school. The Judge used his influence to hush things up, but the fact is

Kyle Skinner beat another cadet to the point that he went into a coma. A couple of months later the kid died.''

"So, this Skinner has killed before," Bill observed.

"Looks that way."

"And he was the only other person on the scene when his father was murdered?"

"Yes," Richard confirmed.

Bill stroked his chin. "Interesting."

"Interesting enough to make you want to take the case?"

Once again Bill looked from Richard to Sheryl and back again. "Hell," he muttered eventually. "I guess I've lost my mind."

Breaking into a smile, Richard started to move around the table.

"Don't!" Bill commanded, and lifted a warning palm. "I may be in, but I'm not happy about it." Once again he could not ignore Richard's abrupt look of disappointment. "Not yet anyway," Bill added. "There's a lot I don't know."

Despite the hostility that continued to hang around the man like a thundercloud, Richard approached and offered a hand. "It feels good to have you in our corner, Bill. Thanks."

Bill surrendered a small smile along with his handshake. "Ever since you were a boy," he grumbled, "you've always known how to wrap me around your finger."

"I know exactly how you feel," Sheryl volunteered, and drew a peal of laughter from the distinguished attorney.

"I don't know why I'm laughing," Bill said finally. "This case is as impossible as the boy genius, here. Where the devil is my client? If we're going to do this, let's get on with it."

Victoria was lying on the cot when she heard the door below creak open. Her first thought, as always, was that Kyle was coming. Leaping to her feet, she stood poised and ready to confront him.

But the man who walked up to the cell door behind the deputy had silvery hair and . . . a familiar look about him and . . . it was Bill Honeycutt! Feeling as though the wind had been knocked out of her, Victoria sank down on the cot and buried her face in her hands.

There was the sound of the iron door opening and slamming, receding footsteps, and then approaching footsteps.

"You needn't look so distraught," he said. "I'm here to help."

All she could do was shake her head.

Setting down his briefcase, Bill took off his overcoat and laid it on the only chair in the room, a straight-backed affair that looked as though it had been claimed from a rummage sale.

"Richard led me to believe you were expecting a visit from your attorney," he said.

She looked up with those unforgettable eyes, and Bill was transported in time. It didn't matter that he was standing in a jail cell on some godforsaken mountain, or that her hair was fair instead of dark. Suddenly he was once again in his rose garden, staring at Valerie.

"Yes," she said finally, the sound of her voice washing over him with more memories. "But I didn't expect *you*."

"Politics makes strange bedfellows," Bill replied. "I guess murder charges tend to do the same thing, particularly if Richard Adams is involved."

"Of course," she murmured. "Richard."

The sound of the name on her lips took him to a more recent memory. Once again Bill saw the tortured look on the kid's face: *The bottom line is I fell in love with her, Bill.* . . . Did this woman return the feeling? Could this woman—whoever she was—love *anyone*?

"Do you have objections to my defending you?" Bill asked.

"Do *you* have objections to your defending me?" she countered.

Folding his arms, he slipped into an uncontrollable smile. "You always were bright," Bill pointed out. "I always said your intelligence was being wasted on a clerical position. Remember?"

"I remember," she acknowledged.

The fleeting smile faded. "Of course I found out later such a waste was not, in fact, occurring."

Rising to her feet, she regarded him with a regality that belied the casual jeans and sweater she was wearing, as well as the sordidness of her surroundings. "Let's get it out in the open, Bill. You want to know why I masqueraded as your assistant . . . why I took your car . . . why I've done the same thing before and since to other men.''

"All right," he responded curtly. "Why?"

"I can't tell you."

"Can't or won't?"

"A little of both. So if your decision about defending me rests on some lengthy explanation of who I am and why I've done the things I've done, I'm afraid you'll have to decline. What I will say is that it's over."

"You mean that if you get out of here, you don't intend to go right back to the same thing?"

She thought of Richard's smiling face, the integrity that lay behind it, the fierceness of the love in her heart. He'd changed everything, as she sensed he would from the beginning.

"It's just not . . . right anymore," she said.

"Oh, and it was 'right' before?"

"There was never anything personal in it, Bill."

"Nothing personal?" he exploded. "I fell in love with you!"

"I never wanted that."

"I asked you to *marry* me!"

"I never wanted that either."

"Damn! You make it sound like *you've* been the victim!"

"I *have* been," she replied. "On that you can depend."

Planting fingers at the juncture of his brows, Bill spun around and paced the length of the cell in frustration. Finally he whirled to peer at the woman once more. "Did you cross state lines with my car and sell it?" he asked.

"Yes."

"Did you do the same with Renfield's Jaguar?"

"Yes."

"Did you steal Kyle Skinner's Corvette?"

She rolled her eyes at the ceiling. "Yes," she confirmed. "And I hit him with that damned gavel of his father's. I only wish I could have made it count for something."

Bill walked toward her, his gaze drilling, searching. "Did you kill the Judge that night?" he demanded.

Her brows settled in dark streaks above her pale eyes.

"No," she replied. "But why on earth should you believe me?"

"Because," Bill began, and expelled a heavy breath of surrender. "Because I can always smell the truth, and I smell it now. And because Richard pointed out something I remember to be true. You're left-handed."

"Yes," she admitted slowly. "Does that mean something?"

"It means you're innocent . . . of murder, at any rate."

"Really," she murmured, as though considering some completely innocuous idea.

"Yes, really. And Richard knows I can never turn away from an underdog fight with an innocent client."

She smiled then, and Bill was stopped in his tracks for he'd never seen such an expression on her face. There had never been anything so spontaneous, so unguarded. This was something new, something that seemed to shine beyond her control.

"Is that smile because I've agreed to take your case, or is it something else?"

"What else would it be?"

"Something to do with Richard, perhaps?"

"I can't talk to you about Richard."

"More secrets?"

"No," she replied, the glimmering smile growing brighter and brighter until it seemed to light the cell. "It's just that when it comes to Richard, I have no words."

So, she *did* love him! Something died in Bill at that moment—a fantasy that had never been quite right, never been quite able to take the place of the life he'd known with Ann. And something else was born—a feeling of happiness for a man he'd always looked on as a son, a feeling of impending doom if he couldn't do something to straighten out this mess.

Tossing his coat on the cot, Bill turned the straight-backed chair around, sat down, and propped his chin on the top rail.

"You're going to have to tell me everything that happened that night. Every single thing, all the way down—"

"I know," she interrupted, still smiling. "All the way down to the last detail."

Fifteen minutes later they were still talking when a deputy came upstairs to inform them that time was up. When Bill went down, he found that another officer was waiting below, this

ne wearing a cap with an ornate insignia on it, along with an
ir of authority.

"I'm Chief Matthews," he greeted without the offer of a
andshake. "Am I to understand you're the prisoner's attor-
ey?"

"The name's Bill Honeycutt. Yes, I'm her attorney. And I'd
ike to know what's being done about setting a trial date."

"Not much," the chief replied with an ill-disguised smirk.
'Reckon we'll just have to wait for a circuit judge to make a
pot for us. See, we used to have a district court judge right
ere in town, but the lady upstairs took care of him."

"*Allegedly* took care of him," Bill corrected stiffly. "Good
ay, Chief Matthews."

Stepping out of the town hall, he took refreshing breaths of
he late-day mountain air as he strode to the Jeep where
Richard was waiting. As he approached, Richard started the
ngine; and when he climbed in, the kid pinned him with a
esperate look.

"How is she?" he demanded.

"She's all right, Richard. And the case is suddenly stream-
lined. The assault was in self-defense, and charges of theft
could be dismissed the same way if only we can prove what
she's saying—that Kyle Skinner came after her because she
saw him kill his own father right before her eyes."

"I knew it!"

"It's only her word, Richard."

"Along with reasonable doubt. She's left-handed, remember?"

Bill shook his head. "In this neck of the woods, reasonable
doubt won't mean much against Skinner. Like you said, he
seems to run things around here, and if I can't get the trial
moved out of this county, we're in trouble. Take me to the
scene."

"The Skinner place?"

When Bill nodded, Richard pulled away from the curb and
headed for the outskirts of town, where he pulled over beside
a sprawling estate. Tall and impressive, the Skinner house sat
back off the road and was protected by iron gates on both
entrances to the circular drive.

"I can't tell anything from here," Bill said. "But I suppose a look inside is out of the question."

"Maybe not," Richard replied with a bright look. "The invitation came about a month ago when I was away, but the Skinners are having a New Year's Eve party tomorrow night."

Bill turned, a slow smile spreading across his face. "I *knew* there was a reason I packed my dinner jacket," he said.

That night after supper everyone remained gathered around the banquet table as Missy entertained them with a medley of folk tunes. After an enthusiastic round of applause, she curtsied like a seasoned performer and beamed at her audience.

"Aren't you the little star?" Hilda said with a wide smile. "You look entirely at home on a stage." Getting to her feet, the old woman began collecting dishes, aided by Gertrude.

Missy looked curiously down at the floor. "Is this a stage?"

"Anyplace can be a stage," Eric answered.

"That's right," Miles confirmed.

"The entire world is a stage," the chef put in, and with an expansive stretch, followed Hilda and Gertrude to the kitchen.

"I do believe she has one of the loveliest voices I've ever heard," Sheryl said, looking across the table to Richard. "Does the Dalton School offer any sort of program in music?"

"I don't know," he replied. "I'll find out. How about it, Missy?" he added, his smiling gaze turning to the child. "Do you think you might like to grow up to be a singer, and get extremely rich so you can take good care of your old guardian?"

"You mean people pay other people money to *sing*?"

Bill chuckled. "If they sing as well as *you* do, people pay." Propping his elbows on the table, he considered the child. "Tell me about this new school of yours."

"It's got playgrounds and lots of other children," she replied. "And it's on the island where Victoria lives." Her bright expression turned suddenly dim. "Or *used* to live," she added.

During the brief solemn lull that befell the table, the phone rang, and a moment later Hilda called out for Richard.

Summoning a cheery smile, Sheryl reached out to Missy and drew her close to her chair. "Classes start next week, don't they?" she asked. "I used to love the first day of school. I'll bet you can't wait to get there."

"I guess so," the child replied as Richard rose to his feet and rounded the table toward the door to the kitchen. "Rosemary will miss me," Missy added.

"She's not the only one," Richard tossed with a smile as he pushed through the swinging door. "Who is it, Hilda?"

"Mr. Walters."

"Walters?"

"You *know*," she added, her beady eyes wide. *"FBI."*

"Oh!" Richard grabbed for the phone. "Ben! How are you?"

"Good, but busy. The wife wants to know when you're going to bring your pretty face back up here to Washington."

"Tell Helen if I'd known she thought I was pretty, I'd have stayed up there years ago."

Ben laughed. "I got the information you wanted," he then said.

"Information?"

"Was it or was it not Richard Adams who sent me a nice little set of prints to be analyzed ASAP?"

"Yeah," Richard responded eagerly. "Did you find out anything?"

"Just who she is. Damn, Richard! You send in an innocent-looking set of prints, and they turn out to belong to a society girl who's been missing from McLean, Virginia, for over a decade."

"You're kidding."

"No. Vicki Buchanan, only child of *Superior Court Judge* Montgomery Buchanan, disappeared in her daddy's Lincoln the night of her high-school graduation. Everybody assumed she was kidnapped, but nobody ever sent a ransom note. It was pure luck her prints were on file. A year before she disappeared she was brought in on a misdemeanor. Nothing serious, nothing the other rich kids didn't do. She got caught joyriding with a boyfriend in a 'borrowed' car. The cops would have let them go with a warning, but her daddy insisted the thing be handled by the book. Both kids were fingerprinted, charged, and spent a night in a juvenile facility. I remember the judge. He could be tough in a courtroom. I guess he was tough on his kid as well.''

"Anything else?" Richard asked.

"What else would you like?" Ben returned flippantly.

It was Richard's turn to laugh. "Nothing. Thanks a lot, buddy.''

"Well?"

"Well, what?"

"Are you going to tell me how you stumbled across Vicki Buchanan when nobody, *anywhere*, has been able to ascertain whether she's living or dead for nearly fifteen years?"

"Nope," Richard returned blandly.

"Are you going to tell me anything at all?"

"Just that this is important to me, Ben. And I'd appreciate your keeping a lid on it."

"You'd appreciate it. Fine. No problem. Happy New Year."

Richard smiled. "Happy New Year. Give Helen a kiss for me.''

Richard returned to the banquet hall to find that everyone had cleared out except Bill and Sheryl.

"How do you like that?" Richard greeted. "I just heard from an old friend of mine at the FBI. It turns out Victoria is the only child of a prominent judge in McLean, Virginia. She was presumed kidnapped years ago and never heard from again.''

"A *judge*?" Sheryl echoed, the question in her voice repeating the look in her eyes.

"So that little town someplace in Virginia turns out to be McLean," Bill mused. "One of the wealthiest, most exclusive suburbs in the country. I knew there was something about her . . . a kind of polish that—"

Bill's musing came to a halt as he noted Richard and Sheryl's eyes drilling into him. "No matter," he added brusquely. "Interesting as all this is, it doesn't do a damn thing to help us at the moment. Her position is extremely precarious, and I'll tell you what I see that can hurt her more than anything else.''

"What?" Richard asked.

"You."

"Me!"

"Use your brain, Richard. What are you going to say when the prosecutors put you on the stand, and they most certainly will—the woman was arrested in your house. Hell, she was arrested in your *bed*! Do you intend to perjure yourself?"

"No!"

"Well, then, what will you say when they ask how and where you met her? Will you tell them you spotted her first at my house, after which she disappeared with my Mercedes, and then again in Atlanta just before she took off with Renfield's Jaguar?"

"Damn! What should I do? Leave the country?"

"There's another way."

"No," Sheryl breathed, a look of horror forming on her face.

"What?" Richard demanded in a shrill tone. "What is it?"

"You could marry her," Bill said blithely.

"*Marry* her?"

"No," Sheryl murmured once more.

"Spousal privilege," Bill explained. "They can't force a husband to testify against his wife."

"*Marry* her," Richard repeated, this time with a look of consideration on his face.

Sheryl leaped to her feet. "This has gone too far," she snapped.

Bill's gaze flickered from Richard to her and back again. "Of course you could always get an annulment after the trial," he added. "If you wanted one."

"Marry her," Richard murmured once more, his brows lifting.

"Stop saying that!" Sheryl exclaimed, and stalked forward. "This makes no sense at all, Bill."

"You're wrong," he replied in a mild tone. "In terms of the case, it makes perfect sense. What do you say, Richard? Is there a justice of the peace around here?"

"There's Doc Hawkins."

Sheryl turned wild eyes to Richard. "No. Don't do this."

"Sheryl . . . I . . ." He lifted his shoulders as he searched for the words. She couldn't bear that searching look.

"This is insane!" she exploded, and whirled out of the room.

When Richard ventured up to her room, he found her packing—flitting from dresser to bed, dresser to bed, filling the open suitcase on the spread. Stuffing his hands in his pockets, he leaned against the wall by the doorway.

"Are you leaving?" he asked after a moment.

"Tomorrow," she answered briskly. "You know me—in from Tennessee one day, out the next. I've got a few days' vacation left, and it's nearly time for Missy to go to school. I thought I could drive her down to Pawleys, maybe do a little shopping on the way. Remind me to get you to give me a blank check."

"Sheryl, will you look at me for a minute?"

She turned and met his eyes, her own glaring. "Some things are sacred, Richard. I can't believe you're doing this—and all for the sake of some rigged jury."

"That's not the only reason," he said.

She held up a quick hand. "I don't want to hear it."

"I'm in love with her, Sheryl."

"I said I didn't want to hear it!"

Richard studied the floor for a minute before lifting his gaze once more. "I was hoping you could find it in your heart to be happy for me," he said.

"Yeah?" she blazed. "Well, I'd *try* to be, Richard—if this woman weren't a compulsive thief and felon charged with murder!"

"That's not all there is to Victoria," he said quietly.

Sheryl's smoldering gaze darted between his eyes. Slowly, gradually, the fire within her seemed to die in a pile of ashes.

"I know," she admitted in a hollow tone. "I've known from the first time you said her name. I just didn't want to think—"

Breaking off suddenly, she turned back to the suitcase and started folding her clothes swiftly into piles.

"You know I was thinking about what that FBI guy said. Her father could be the key to Victoria's puzzle. He's a judge, right? I'll lay you even money this aberrant behavior of hers has something to do with him."

Richard walked up to her and put a caressing hand on her shoulder. "Sheryl . . . don't leave like this." He could feel her stiffen beneath his touch, though the frenzied movements of her hands never stopped.

"I've stayed longer than I planned," she said. "I've become more involved than I ever dreamed. And now you're getting married. Please don't ask me to stay and watch."

December 31

It was nearly one in the afternoon, the sun high and shining on the banks of snow that continued to stand in the forested glens of the mountain. But despite the sunshine it was frigidly cold, and predictions were that the temperatures would dip into the teens that night.

Loaded on one side with the giant teddy bear and on the other with a couple of bags, Richard walked with Missy out of the lodge. Bundled up in her new green jacket and clutching the bridal doll for all she was worth, the little girl seemed too small to be taking such a trip.

"Are you sure you've got everything?" Richard said.

"Yes. Sheryl's awfully nice. She loaned me a suitcase, and I took special care packing everything Santa Claus brought."

They walked along a few more steps.

"Are you happy, Missy?" he asked with a searching look.

She looked up with eyes as steady as they were bright. "Yes, Richard," she replied. "I'm very happy."

And suddenly she didn't seem so little anymore. There was something about females, whatever their age. Just when you thought they should crumble, they held their own with the tension of steel.

"I talked to Mrs. Dalton this morning," he said. "She's expecting you the day after tomorrow and already has your room picked out. She and Victoria's good friend Darcy are going to help you settle in. You'll like them both a lot."

"If they're Victoria's friends, I'm sure I will."

Coming to a halt, Richard dropped to crouch before her. "I know Victoria would like to be here to see you off, Missy. She'd probably like to drive you down to the school herself, but—"

The child stopped him by placing a mittened hand over his mouth.

"You don't have to explain," she said solemnly. "Victoria doesn't have to see me off. She doesn't have to say a word. She's the reason I'll never go back to Shine Valley, and I love her."

Throwing her arms around his neck, Missy added in a near whisper: "Please help her."

"I'll do my best," Richard mumbled around the lump in his throat.

"And tell her I said good-bye, but I'll see her soon."

With that, Missy released him and backed away. "Don't worry," she added, apparently noting the moisture in his eyes. "Everything's going to be fine."

"Thanks," Richard said, rising to his feet. "I needed that."

Settling the bear and luggage in the back of Sheryl's car, he strapped Missy into the passenger's seat and turned to find Sheryl standing behind him. Atop a tailored white blouse and slacks, she wore a black duster that reached her ankles and matching shoes, gloves, and bag. As she studied him her raven hair shone in the sun along with her eyes. She was stunning.

And a chapter of the life that had existed between them for so long had come to an irrevocable close. The wondering was over. He knew it. And so did she.

"Beautiful as ever," Richard said.

With a slight grimace she opened her arms as she so often had. Richard caught her up and held her close.

"You lied to me, you know," she murmured.

"Did I?"

"You promised that when you grew up, I'd be the first to know. Now I see you've done it overnight, and you never said a word. Good-bye, Richard."

With a quick kiss to the side of his neck, Sheryl walked around the car and never looked back as she drove away from the lodge.

=FOURTEEN=

"Could I see your invitation, sir?"

The man at the gate was one of the deputies who had been at the house the morning they took Victoria away. Richard didn't know his name, or care to. He flashed the card out the window.

"Very good, sir. If you'll just continue up the drive, you're welcome to park on the side lawn wherever you can find a space."

"I had no idea they were this formal up here," Bill observed as they drove through the gate.

"Money is money wherever you go," Richard replied.

Up ahead every window in the massive house was alight. And on the side lawn bordering the forest, a row of cars stretched from the road nearly up to a garage with a cupola on top.

"Nor did I think there were this many people within a hundred miles," Bill commented.

"Everybody who's anybody attends parties at the Skinners'," Richard returned wryly. "Or so I've been told."

"Get a spot as close as you can to the garage," Bill instructed. "That must be where Victoria took off in the infamous Corvette."

Nosing the Jeep into an uphill space between the trees and the garage, Richard killed the engine, and the two of them got out. The last night of the year was freezing cold and dark as pitch, the floodlights of the house failing to reach the recesses of the grounds bordering the garage. Stepping nosily up to a window, Richard peered into the structure, swiftly followed by Bill.

Car after car was parked in sedate splendor within—a Lincoln limo, a Mercedes, a vintage MG, and more.

"Looks like Skinner's got quite a collection here," Bill observed. "Don't take it the wrong way if I say that it looks like a happy hunting ground for our favorite lead-footed lady."

Richard turned with a scowl.

"Relax," Bill said, cracking a smile. "She already told me she's a reformed woman."

"She did?" Richard questioned, his brows flying up.

"Yes, she did," Bill supplied. "Somehow or other it seems you managed to make an impact. Come on. Let's go in the back way and see what we can see."

Crossing immaculate grounds, they walked a brick-lined path to the backdoor and entered a sprawling kitchen where a covey of servants were scurrying around.

"My word!" a maid in uniform exclaimed. "You're not supposed to be coming in this way!"

"No matter," Richard responded, smoothly collecting Bill's elbow and pushing him forward. "We're friends of the family who've been in the kitchen a hundred times. Haven't we, Bill?"

"Oh, at least."

Richard smiled encouragingly as they hurried through the kitchen, stared at by a half-dozen people who'd come to a sudden standstill in the midst of their tasks.

"Happy New Year," he added, and received a murmuring response from the serving staff as he and Bill hurried into the hall.

There was music coming from the front of the house, along with the roar of voices. They made their way up the hall and gradually broached the outskirts of the crowd, no sooner arriving than a pretty blonde in a white dress descended upon them.

"Mr. Adams!" she chortled. "I see I've finally enticed you to attend one of my little affairs! And who is this?"

"Good evening, Mrs. Skinner. Allow me to introduce a friend of mine who's here for the holidays, Bill Honeycutt."

Bill responded to the lady's offered hand by kissing it in continental fashion and bringing a blush to her cheeks. "Mrs. Skinner," he greeted.

"Jeanette," she corrected.

"Jeanette," he responded, smiling. "It's so kind of you to allow me in your home. I hope you don't mind my crashing your party."

With a toss of her head, she bestowed the desired response. "Why, heavens, no! Any friend of Mr. Adams is a friend of mine, and such a courtly one, too! Are you enjoying your time in our mountains, Mr. Honeycutt?"

"I can say without equivocation that I'm having one of the most interesting times of my life," he answered.

"I'm so happy to hear it. The Blue Ridge has much to offer, if one can only take the time to look."

"Would I be out of line if I asked permission to look about your lovely home?" Bill asked pleasantly. "I don't believe I've ever seen such antebellum grace set against the mountains."

Once again the lady responded like a well-trained thoroughbred to his lead. "*Do* make yourself at home, Mr. Honeycutt. You too, Mr. Adams. You've never found time to visit us before. Please take this opportunity to stroll the rooms however you like."

Glancing over her shoulder, she pointed to a room leading off to the left of the hall. "The party is centered in the ballroom and parlor," she added. "But if you'd care to look behind any closed door along the way, feel free."

"You're very kind," Richard said.

"Not at all," she replied with a gracious smile. "And now if you'll excuse me, I must see to the hors d'oeuvres."

With that she bustled past them toward the kitchen. Exchanging a discreet arch of brows, Richard and Bill moved up the hall, passing clusters of guests, smiling and wishing "Happy New Year," both of them looking for a door that might mark the entrance to the room where Judge Ray Skinner met his death.

Finally they came upon double doors opening into a spacious study with draped windows, a lectern that looked as though it belonged in a courtroom, and an unmistakable air of both privacy and masculinity.

"This is it," Richard said quietly.

"Let's go," Bill murmured, and with a smiling glance over

his shoulder at some passing guests, followed Richard inside.

"This must be where it happened," Bill said, moving up to the mahogany table. "Victoria said he was thrown back upon a table, and she watched from the cover of drapes about . . ." Trailing off, he scanned the windows. "About there," he supplied, pointing to a window adjacent to the sweeping table.

"She watched from there, Richard. Like she said, from a vantage point like that, she would have seen it all."

Bending to the table, Richard picked up a gavel from its resting place on a pedestal of honor. "Look at this, Bill." Shifting it between his hands, he gauged the weight. "Oak shaft, marble head. It must weigh ten pounds."

Bill joined him and held out an open palm, preparing to experience the weight for himself. . . .

"You're right. That's it."

Both men spun around as Kyle Skinner strolled into the room, pulling Mavis along with him. Dressed in a daringly low-cut red gown covered with bangles, she appeared pale and ill at ease.

"The murder weapon," Kyle went on. "The police confiscated it, of course, but after time passed and there seemed no reason to keep it, they allowed me to bring it home. It's rather an heirloom, you see. A favorite possession of my late father."

"I can see why it's so important to you, then," Richard snapped, and received a warning glance from Bill.

"Your father," Bill repeated, moving forward and extending a hand. "Then you must be Kyle Skinner."

Kyle joined him in a brief shake. "And you must be Bill Honeycutt—attorney extraordinaire."

Bill arched a brow. "I'm flattered . . . and surprised. I only arrived yesterday afternoon."

Kyle smiled. "Not much goes on in Devil's Rock without my learning of it, Mr. Honeycutt."

"Bill."

"Kyle," he returned, still smiling. "Allow me to present Mavis Brewer, another favorite possession."

With a damning look for Kyle, she proffered a hand. "Hello, Bill . . . Richard," she added, though she didn't offer to shake his hand, or to meet his eyes.

"Hello, Mavis," Richard responded. "It's been a while."

"Yes," she murmured. "I suppose it has."

"So, here we are," Kyle said, as though summing up the situation with immense satisfaction. "The accusers and defenders all in one room. Interesting, isn't it?"

"Extremely," Richard answered, unable to hold his tongue, though Bill gave him another glare. "One thing I don't understand, Skinner. How did you make the connection? How could you know Victoria and Vanessa were one and the same?"

Kyle put an arm around Mavis and pulled her to his side. "I have to credit this little lady with that. She spotted Vanessa at your place a couple of weeks ago. It took her a few days to realize where she'd seen her before, but she finally did, and voilà!"

"I see," Richard commented, his mild tone doing little to disguise his anger.

Despite the scalding heat that rushed to her face, Mavis did her best to look Richard squarely in the eye. "She murdered the Judge," Mavis commented defensively. "What did you expect me to do?"

When Richard made no reply, Bill moved suavely forward.

"I'm sure you did what any upstanding citizen would have done. Although I must point out, Mavis, that my client has merely been charged with the crime. She's innocent . . . until *proven* guilty, of course."

"Of course," Kyle joined in. "But although I hate to sound pessimistic on such a festive occasion, *Bill*, I don't see how a jury could possibly find any other verdict."

"We'll see," Bill replied with a smile.

"Indeed we will," Kyle returned.

An interval of silence followed—Kyle and Bill regarding each other with rivaling smiles, Richard pegging Mavis with a look of accusation that ultimately made her drop her gaze to the floor.

"Well," Bill said after a moment. "I appreciate your hospitality, Kyle, but I guess Richard and I should be heading back up the mountain."

"So soon?" their host inquired.

"As you point out, I've got my work cut out for me. Better get back to it, but thanks for a lovely evening."

"My pleasure," Kyle returned, maintaining smooth grace as the two men walked out of the study, stopped to say good night to Jeanette, and made their exit.

"He seems almost as smart as Richard," Mavis observed.

Taking his arm from around her, Kyle straightened his tie. "No matter," he replied briskly.

"He's a big-time lawyer, Kyle. There's no telling what kinds of tricks he might pull in a courtroom."

Kyle's black eyes shifted her way, gleaming with the malicious light that so often lit their ebony depths. "I have special plans for Miss Blackwood," he said. "And none of them includes a courtroom."

With that he went back to his guests and left Mavis shuddering with the doubt and guilt that had plagued her ever since she came to his damnable house on Christmas morning.

"So what do you think?" Richard asked as he and Bill hurried out of the house and through the freezing night toward the Jeep.

"I think Kyle Skinner murdered his father."

Without breaking stride, Richard looked around with a smile bright as day. Bill held up a palm as he walked along.

"Don't look so pleased," he warned. "Proving it is another matter, particularly here in Devil's Rock. I knew the trial should be moved out of this county. Now, after meeting Skinner, I realize it's an absolute necessity. Whether Victoria is innocent or not won't matter much if she comes to trial anywhere near this place."

Starting up the Jeep, Richard drove away from the Skinner house and turned onto Sky Road, slowing when he neared town, and finally pulling over in front of the town hall.

"What the hell are you doing?" Bill asked.

"I'm going to call up to her. Tell her good night. Tell her everything's going to be fine."

"No."

Richard's head snapped around. "But I've been by every day," he objected. "She's up there all alone, Bill. I don't like the thought of her up there all alone."

"It'll have to wait," Bill commanded. "If we're going to pull off what we plan for tomorrow, I think it's in our best interest not to create a scene tonight, okay?"

Reluctantly, begrudgingly, Richard shifted the Jeep into gear and headed back to the Black Top.

January 1, 1993

It was Friday night, and most folks were home nursing a dose of too much celebrating the night before. A single guard was posted at the desk in the police station. Bill strolled into the place as though he owned it.

"Good evening, officer."

The man leaped out of his chair. Apparently he'd been dozing.

"I'm Miss Blackwood's attorney, Bill Honeycutt," he said, offering a hand. "I don't believe we've met, Deputy . . ."

He trailed off, looking for the name on the badge.

"Tobin," the man supplied, eagerly shaking his hand. "Freddy Tobin. I'm the only one here right now."

"So I see. Well, you're in luck. Something special is about to happen here."

"What?" the deputy asked with round eyes.

Holding up an index finger and donning a look that promised the greatest of surprises, Bill stepped to the door and ushered in Richard and Doc Hawkins. "There's going to be a wedding," he then announced.

"A *what*?" the deputy exclaimed.

"The lady upstairs is going to marry this fine young lad."

"But nobody's supposed to go up there!" the deputy objected.

"Except me, of course," Bill replied with a smile. "I'm her attorney. I go up there all the time. Don't worry, Deputy. If you'll just unlock the door to the stairs, Richard and the justice of the peace will remain at the bottom while I alone go up to stand with the lady."

"I don't know," the deputy hedged.

"Come now," Bill urged. "Surely you don't mean to stand in the way of true love?"

Finally the deputy shuffled across the room and unlocked the stairway leading up to the cells. "I'm still going to have to call the chief about this," he said as Bill hustled the other men to the foot of the stairs and hurried up.

"Victoria?" he called as he stalked to the second cell.

She was standing there waiting, her beautiful face flushed with color. Bill thrust a bouquet of holly through the bars. Though prickling with the stickers of the wild, the greenery was bunched and tied with a white, nuptial ribbon.

"Hilda and Gertrude sent this along with best wishes," he said hurriedly.

"How sweet," she murmured, cradling the thorny branches as though they were orchids.

"I have a feeling we should get through this as quickly as possible," Bill pressed. "Are you ready?"

"Are you sure this is necessary?" Victoria returned.

"Yes."

"Are you sure Richard doesn't mind?"

"I think it's safe to say he doesn't mind," Bill returned glibly. "Now, let's get on with it."

The groom and magistrate stood at the foot of the stairs yelling vows; the bride and witness called down from above. Hardly a picture-perfect wedding, but the deed was done before Chief Matthews blustered into the town hall and ordered immediate dispersal.

January 2

Saturday was cool but sunny, the snow melting in muddy columns along the edges of the street, running toward the drains in swollen streams.

As the days since Christmas passed, Mavis had developed a fixation on watching the barred window on the second story of the town hall across the street. And she was watching that morning when Kyle's limousine pulled up in front of the jail.

Acting on impulse, she shrugged into her fur coat and hurried across the street. The only officer in attendance was one of Matthews's deputies, Freddy Tobin. He was middle-aged and pudgy and had been trying to get in her pants ever since Harry died.

Opening the front of her coat to reveal the clinging lines of her sweater and slacks, Mavis sashayed into the office. "Hello, Freddy," she said, and perching on the edge of his desk, gave him one of her best smiles.

"M-Mavis!" he stuttered, his chubby cheeks turning red. "What are you doing here?"

"There's nothing to do, and I'm bored," she said with a pouting look. "What's going on with our little jailbird up there?"

Her gaze turned across the room. The door to the stairs had been left unguardedly open.

"Mr. Skinner just went up to see her a few minutes ago," Freddy offered. "Other than that it's been quiet."

"Just like everything else in Devil's Rock," Mavis responded on a sighing note.

"Last night she got married! Did you know that?"

"No."

"I about got my head chewed off for that one," Freddy added with a sheepish look. "That's why I'm here again today. *Disciplinary* detail. But, shoot! What was I supposed to do? This fancy lawyer comes in, and he's got everything lined up. I called Chief Matthews quick as I could."

"Who'd she marry?" Mavis asked idly.

"That Adams fella."

"Richard?" came the shrill question.

"Yeah. That's the one. What's the matter, Mavis?"

"Oh, nothing," she responded with an admirable show of carelessness. Scanning Freddy's desk, she noticed his coffee cup and had an idea. "You wouldn't happen to have any more of that coffee in the back, would you?"

"Gosh. I'm sorry, Mavis. This is the last of it."

"Oh," she mumbled, her face a picture of disappointment.

"I could make a new pot," Freddy suggested.

"Could you, honey? There's nothing I like better than a fresh cup of coffee. Well . . . ." Mavis added with a seductive wink. *"Almost* nothing."

Freddy fell all over himself scampering around the corner, and Mavis slipped across the room. At the foot of the stairs she could pick up the deep resonance of Kyle's voice. Halfway up she could hear both of them quite clearly.

"You may think you have me around a barrel, Kyle, but you don't. I have friends, and evidence of the corruption the Big Boys are spreading across the mountains like a plague. Hard evidence."

"Are we back to the infamous ledgers?" he returned. "Your bluff has run out, honey. Those things are rigged, and I know it."

"Rigged or not, it's all going to come out in the open. When this thing goes to trial, I intend to tell everything I know about you, Kyle."

He laughed. "First of all, nobody would believe you. Secondly—or finally, I should say—there isn't going to be any trial."

There was a moment of silence before he went on.

"I've enjoyed thinking this whole thing through. I could have had you *here*, but let's face it—these surroundings aren't up to my standards. No . . . what's going to happen is this. Tonight, during the Boys' meeting at my place, Victoria Blackwood will ingeniously escape. Jeanette and the girls have already gone. We'll have the house to ourselves. It'll be just like old times. Only this time you'll give *me* what you gave Adams."

"There is nothing you can say, nothing you can threaten, that will *ever* make me do that." Although the words were quietly spoken, the voice had a quality of granite about it.

"Are you sure about that?" Kyle questioned. "What if I told you I can have Richard Adams wiped out in the blink of an eye?"

Mavis ground her teeth. *Bastard!* she thought. *Bastard!*

"I see I struck a nerve," he added. "How does it feel to hold your husband's life in your hands? That was quite a coup, by the way. Although it doesn't change one iota of what's going to happen to you."

"What do you mean, 'wipe him out'?" the woman rallied.

"What do you think I mean? I mean I'll have him killed."

"I don't believe you."

"Hell, I've already been *this* close. I understand now that you were the one who was with him that day on the mountain.

Ironic, isn't it? There I had my boys shooting at Adams, never dreaming that Vanessa Blair was in the line of fire.''

"But I thought—"

"You thought what? That it was poachers?"

"But why? What do you have against Richard?"

"He has something I want, and he's not willing to sell. In a way you could say he brought it on himself. But I'm a businessman. I've always got an eye for a fair trade. How about it, Mrs. Adams? Is the life of your husband worth a night with me?"

"You're revolting."

"So you've said before."

"And I still don't believe you."

There was a pregnant pause, and Mavis could picture the cold, dangerous smile forming on Kyle's face.

"You watched me bash my own father's head in," he said finally. "Do you really think I'd hesitate to kill Adams?"

Mavis's entire stomach seemed to lurch to her throat. Clapping a hand over her mouth, she inched her way down the stairs and darted for the door just as Freddy came in bearing a cup of coffee.

"Sorry," she mumbled. "I'm not feeling well."

Bursting into the sunshine, she took deep gulps of fresh air as she hurried around the side of the building. It didn't prevent her from getting sick in the bushes.

Ten minutes later she was waiting by the familiar limo when Kyle came out of the town hall. "We've got a deal, haven't we, Kyle?" she challenged.

He arched a brow. "Deal?"

"About Richard."

"What about him?"

"Don't play dumb," Mavis snapped. "The only reason I turned Victoria Blackwood over to you was to guarantee Richard's safety. You *said* you agreed."

"I say a lot of things."

"Are you telling me you don't intend to stick to our bargain?"

"And if I don't, what are you going to do about it, Mavis?"

She started to swing at him. He caught her arm before her palm could strike his cheek.

"You forget yourself," he muttered, his grip turning cruel. "I'll do *what* I want, *when* I want. If I want Richard Adams dead, he *will* be, and there's nothing you can do to stop me. The only place you can hold your own with me is in the sack, Mavis. Don't ever forget that. And don't ever try to stand in my way."

With that he pushed her away, got into the limo, and drove off. Mavis waited until the car was out of sight before running back to the house, grabbing her keys, and setting off for the Black Top.

Richard was sprawled in an easychair reviewing the ledgers as Bill pored over papers at the adjacent desk.

"Gambling, prostitution, bootlegging, transportation of illegal substances across state lines," Richard mumbled. "I keep thinking there must be a way to capitalize on these records."

"If you're imagining blackmail, I don't think Kyle Skinner is the type," Bill returned. "More than likely you'd wake up some morning with your throat slit by one of his Shine Valley buddies."

"Victoria wants me to use them to put Sweeney out of business, along with the notorious Big Boys."

Bill looked up. "If you're going after the Big Boys, you'd better have some pretty big guns."

"I know. That conversation with Ben Walters keeps coming to mind. Don't you think the FBI is the right place to take something like this? Isn't it possible they might even be willing to work a trade?"

"What kind of trade?"

"This evidence in exchange for immunity from prosecution on several counts of grand theft auto."

Bill leaned back in his chair. "You want her free and clear, huh?"

"Yeah," Richard answered with a smile. "Free and clear."

"It's possible," Bill admitted eventually. "It sounds like the kind of thing the FBI might go for."

"Maybe I'll give Ben another call."

"The more I think about it, the more I'd say you could probably trade out all the charges," Bill surmised slowly.

"Except one. I don't believe they'll let her off on murder, Richard. Especially the murder of a district court judge."

"That's the one thing she *didn't* do," Richard returned irritably. "We're just going to have to find a way to prove it."

Removing his glasses, Bill massaged his eyes. "That's what I'm looking for, but damned if I can see any way of doing it—short of tripping Kyle up on the stand. And once again he doesn't seem the type. It's his word against hers, Richard. A lot's going to depend on the jury, and the location of the trial."

"There isn't going to be any trial."

They looked up with a start as Mavis walked into the library. Rising quickly to his feet, Richard greeted her with a scowl.

"What are you doing here, Mavis?"

"I came to tell you something."

"What do you mean, 'no trial'?" Bill demanded.

"Tonight during the Big Boys' meeting at the Skinner house, Victoria will conveniently 'escape.' The chance that she'll ever be heard from again is entirely doubtful."

"How do you know?" Bill and Richard barked in unison.

"I overheard Kyle talking to her no more than an hour ago. After the meeting, no one will be around except Chief Matthews and Kyle's Shine Valley boys. He intends to rape her, maybe worse."

"*Rape* her?" Richard thundered. "What the hell are you saying?"

Mavis walked slowly forward. "Please, Richard. Just hear me out. Believe it or not, when I turned her in, I did it for you. Kyle has been plotting against you for months. He wants this land. You know that much, but I don't think you know what lengths he'll go to for what he wants. Those poachers on the mountain a couple of weeks back weren't poachers, they were Kyle's men. He had in mind to have you killed and make it look like a shooting accident."

"Dammit, Mavis! Why didn't you tell me before?"

"Because he threatened me as well. He said I was in on the deal, and I was staying in, or else. I was terrified. I didn't know what to do. And then I realized who Victoria was. I thought she was a murderess, and I traded her for you, Richard. Kyle promised you'd be safe, and I thought I'd done the right thing. But then today I heard him say—"

Her voice broke, and she rubbed her fingertips anxiously across her forehead.

"What?" Bill questioned. "What did he say?"

Mavis glanced his way. "Richard isn't safe. Not at all. Kyle intends to go right ahead with his plan. And on top of that, he's using Richard to threaten Victoria into submission."

"Is this on the level?" Richard demanded.

"I understand why you might not trust me," she replied, "but believe me, I'm not Kyle's girl anymore. In fact, the thought of him makes me physically ill. I always knew he was a bastard, but I never realized how completely evil he is until today. I heard him say . . . I couldn't believe it, but . . ."

Once again she stumbled to a halt. Richard pulled up a chair, and she sank heavily into it.

"Go on, Mavis," he prodded, this time in a gentler tone.

She looked up, her dark eyes brimming with tears. "Victoria wasn't the one who killed the Judge. It was Kyle. He killed his own father. I heard him say so."

"You heard him say so?" Richard repeated in a tone of wonder.

Straightening away from Mavis's chair, he took on an ethereal look Bill had seen before—the same look he remembered from years ago, just before the bright-eyed boy moved the queen into deadly position and declared: "Checkmate!"

"Hold on, Richard," Bill cautioned. "It's hearsay. And hearsay carries no weight in a court of law."

Richard turned to him with glazed eyes. "But don't you see?" he murmured. "She heard him say so. . . . That's it!" He began pacing to and fro, his voice dropping to a mumbling monologue. "It'll be risky, no doubt about it. But there's no other way, and besides it could solve everything."

When he dropped to a sudden crouch before her chair, Mavis shrank back with surprise.

"So, when Victoria supposedly escapes, she'll be abducted to the Skinner house. Who do you think will take her?"

"I'm sure it will be Matthews," Mavis replied hesitantly. "Kyle wouldn't trust such a thing to anyone else."

"What can you tell me about the Big Boys' meetings, Mavis? Have you ever been around for any of them?"

"A few. Never inside the house, though. Kyle always makes

sure it's cleared out. Jeanette and the girls are already on a trip somewhere. I imagine the servants are gone by now, too."

"What time will the meeting begin?"

"It probably already started."

"What time will it be over?"

"Sometime in the evening. Eight or nine o'clock maybe."

"And then only Matthews and the Shine Valley boys will be there, you said. You mean Sweeney?"

Mavis nodded. "He's usually there, along with a couple of others."

"Inside the house?"

"Usually at the front door."

"How about Matthews?"

"Parked by the garage, watching the back."

"I'll have to try and slip past him," Richard mumbled, rising to his feet. "And I'll have to bank on the fact that Victoria's 'escape' won't take place until after nightfall."

He glanced at his watch. "That still doesn't leave much time," he added. "Bill, you'll have to get to Victoria this afternoon."

Bestowing a dazzling smile, Richard bent and kissed Mavis resoundingly on the lips. "You're the best!" he pronounced before turning toward the doorway. "Hilda?" he called. "Where's Hilda?"

Mavis watched with astonishment as Richard stalked away. "What the hell's going on?" she demanded, turning confused eyes to Bill. "I came here with bad news, I thought."

"Shhh," Bill responded. "I've seen him do this before. Come on."

Dropping her fur, Mavis followed with Bill Honeycutt as Richard strode through the entrance hall and on to the kitchen, calling for Hilda. He found her by the stove with the chef. The others were gathered around the breakfast table.

"There you are, Hilda," Richard greeted cheerily. "Where's that old hearing aid of yours?"

"Why, Mr. Richard!" she objected, her wizened cheeks turning a bright pink. "You know perfectly well I never needed a hearing aid in my life!"

"I know perfectly well you used to hide it in the side drawer of your bureau in the old house. Is that still where you keep it?''

"Why, of all things!" she sputtered.

"And Gertrude," Richard said, his gaze swerving to the breakfast table. "Where's that transistor radio of yours? I need it."

Silence ensued. Richard looked from Miles to Eric to Gertrude to Cainey . . . on to the chef and Hilda . . . Bill and Mavis. Eight pairs of eyes stared at him.

"Let's get moving, ladies," Richard urged. "I don't have much time."

"Time for what?" Eric asked as Hilda and Gertrude scurried from the room.

"To build a bug."

"I think I'm following you now," Bill said. "You're going to wire Victoria, and get Kyle's confession on tape."

"Confession to what?" Miles asked.

"Kyle Skinner killed the Judge," Richard replied. "Mavis heard him admit it no more than an hour ago."

As the men around the table erupted in a chorus of "I knew it's" and "I told you so's," Bill strolled forward. "It's a great idea except for one thing," he said. "The Skinner house will be virtually a fortress—guarded on all sides, like Mavis said. How are you going to get in?"

"I'll have to come through the forest," Richard replied, "and hope I can get close enough with a makeshift receiver to pick up Victoria's signal."

"What about Matthews and the Shine Valley boys?"

"Shine Valley?" Eric chimed and rose to his feet. "You mean Sweeney and his lot?"

Bill nodded. "Mavis says they're usually guarding the front."

"Well, well," Eric said, folding his arms over his massive chest. "I've been hoping for the chance to come up against Mr. Sweeney again. You can count me in."

"Me too," Miles and the chef joined in.

"Now, wait a minute," Richard cautioned, lifting his palms. "I can't ask for help here. This could be dangerous."

"The more alone you are, the more dangerous it'll be," Eric pointed out to the enthusiastic confirmation of the others.

"Well," Richard acquiesced with a smile. "I guess if you concealed yourselves in the front yard, you could keep the mountaineers busy if something went wrong."

"Damn right we could," Miles said.

"How about me?" Bill asked.

"You're going to have to smuggle the wire in to Victoria, along with a roll of surgical tape, and explain what she has to do. That's enough."

"I'm not going to sit tight like an old man while all the action is going on, if that's what you're thinking."

Richard lifted his shoulders. "Well, maybe you could stick with me, and take off with the tape as soon as we've nailed Skinner—make sure it gets safely away while I go in for Victoria."

"You're going up against Kyle alone?" Mavis questioned.

"I'll have a rifle," Richard answered. "But I hope I won't have to use it. I'm hoping I can bluff my way out with her once I can hold a confession over his head."

"What can I do?" Mavis added.

"You've done enough already. Further involvement is too dangerous."

Planting her hands on her hips, Mavis moved forward and looked up, her eyes shining with conviction. "Nobody wants to bring Kyle down more than I do, Richard. He's degraded and threatened me long enough, and he says there's nothing I can do to stop him. Let me prove him wrong."

Richard's eyes moved to hers.

"Please," she added quietly.

He reached out and stroked her cheek. "All right, then. I don't believe I've ever met anyone more capable of keeping a man's mind off what's happening around him than you. Think you can keep Matthews occupied while Bill and I close in on the house?"

"Hell, yes," she agreed, breaking into a smile.

"Looks like we're all in on this citizen's arrest together," Bill observed.

"So it does," Richard agreed, his smiling eyes circling the group as Hilda and Gertrude hurried back into the room, Gertrude eagerly handing over her radio, Hilda still pink-cheeked as she surrendered the hearing aid.

"One more thing," Bill said. "By taking on Skinner and Matthews and Sweeney, we're basically taking over the town. Before you start building that bug, I suggest you go ahead and get that FBI friend of yours on the phone. If everything's about to hit the fan in Devil's Rock, it would be nice to know the cavalry's on its way."

Two hours later Richard was busily at work in the library lab while Mavis and Bill looked on.

"What did your friend Walters have to say?" Bill asked.

"That he's setting the wheels in motion. He hopes to have a U.S. marshal here by tomorrow morning. It'll probably be the day after that before he can get any of his own team down here." After a moment's pause Richard added, "The Big Boys will be meeting in the study, right, Mavis?"

"That's right."

"We'll just have to hope that's where Kyle brings Victoria— to the scene of the crime that occurred four years ago."

"It seems the kind of irony that would appeal to a son-of-a-bitch like Skinner," Bill commented.

"You'll have to tell Victoria to maneuver him as close to the outside wall as possible, Bill. That's where we'll start, anyway. If we don't pick up a signal, we'll have to try and track them down the best we can."

"With a little luck this just might work," Bill observed.

"If Victoria can do her part and get Skinner to confess," Richard replied. "I'm making the device as small as possible, but I don't exactly have access to an electronics store here. She'll need to wear something like a bulky sweater to hide it. Do your best to explain what she has to do."

"I will," Bill replied. "This isn't the first time I've worked with a wire, you know." Glancing at his watch, he added, "It's nearly three o'clock. Are you getting close?"

"Almost there," Richard mumbled. "The only thing that's taken any time is converting this transistor into a transmitter. There, I think that'll do it."

Setting aside the stripped-down radio, Richard reached for a length of audio cable and sliced the coating off the end of the wires.

"Once we hook up our hearing-aid microphone to the

transmitter, I'll set an AM frequency, tune the receiver to match, and we ought to be in business.''

"Brilliant," Bill murmured.

"You think so?" Richard asked somewhat absently. "I don't know how strong the signal will be. That's why we'll have to be as close to the transmitter as possible." He applied a final twist to a wire and sat back. "That's it," he muttered. "The best I can do on short notice."

"Then I'd better get going," Bill said. Carefully collecting the device, he stashed it with the surgical tape beneath a pile of papers in his briefcase.

"The sun goes down early these days," Bill added, heading to the door. "And I've got to get down the mountain and back before it's time to go to Skinner's."

"I should be heading back, too," Mavis said. "When it gets dark, I'll drive to the edge of town and pull over near the estate. As soon as the Big Boys leave, I'll take my post with Matthews. How does that sound?"

Rising to his feet, Richard took her hand. "It's not too late to reconsider, Mavis. Are you sure you want to do this?"

She gave him a glowing look. "As far as I'm concerned, it's come down to us against Kyle. It feels good to be on the side of the angels for a change."

Richard pressed a kiss to the back of her hand. "You are one hell of a woman, Mavis Brewer."

Caressing the hand he freed, Mavis gave him a smile and sighed. "If you only knew," she replied. "There's just one thing I've got to ask."

"What?" Richard questioned, his brows lifting.

"Did you have to *marry* her?"

"Get outta here," he said with a playful swat to Mavis's bottom.

"Good luck," she called as she sashayed out the door.

"Yeah," Richard murmured. "Good luck to us all."

As the sun disappeared behind the mountains Victoria stood in the most private corner of the cell. Having donned a body shirt that conformed to her shape in a thin sheath, she applied a final piece of surgical tape to plant the makeshift microphone between her breasts. The modified transistor radio was already secured at the hollow of her waist by round after round of the white tape, and as she pulled on a camouflaging sweater and her torso barely moved, she imagined this was how someone felt after being taped up for broken ribs.

She considered starting all over again and going not quite so heavy on the tape, but then decided against it. She'd rather be stiff than run the risk of losing Richard's ingenious device at the wrong moment.

A century seemed to have passed in the space of a day. First there had been Kyle's arrival, the evil he spouted even worse than she'd imagined; for he threatened not just her, but also Richard. She's spent slow-moving hours in hopelessness— wondering if Bill would come, willing him to come so she could bequeath a warning. Bill loved Richard, too. Bill would safeguard him, she knew, even if nothing could be done to save her.

When the silver-haired attorney finally appeared at the iron door, she'd nearly pounced on him. But he'd shushed her with a calming hand, a calming voice, and as he spoke she'd gradually melted in hypnotized silence to the support of the cot.

It was the most outlandish, the most inspiring scheme . . . Richard's scheme. Once again, despite the dreary confines of the cell and the chilling prospects of the evening in store, Victoria dissolved in a smile. Damn, he was something.

As darkness settled over the mountains and the artificial lights switched on in the jail, she clasped her hands and sat down on the cot to wait. It was nearly eight o'clock when Chief Matthews came up the stairs and opened the cell door.

"Stand up and extend your hands," he commanded.

When she did so, he pulled handcuffs from his belt and started fixing them about her wrists.

"I've been expecting you," she said. "Tell me, Chief. How does it feel to be one of Kyle Skinner's goons?"

His bushy brows gathered in a swift frown. "There's no need for smart talk, young lady."

"Young *lady*?" she repeated. "How can you call me that and do what you're doing at the same time?"

Fastening the cuffs with a distinct click, he caught her by the shoulder and turned her toward the door.

"Do you have family, Chief Matthews? A wife? Daughter? Maybe a granddaughter? I wonder how you'd feel if something like this were happening to one of them at this moment."

"Shut your mouth, hussy!" he boomed. "None of mine would do anything to get herself in such a fix! Anybody with sense knows better than to cross a Skinner. Like my daddy before me, and his daddy before him, I keep the peace. You disrupted it with all you pulled, and now it's time to pay the price. So don't come crying to me. Get going!" he concluded with a shove toward the cell door.

And yet with all of his handcuffing, and all of his shoving, he gained not the slightest suspicion of the time bomb she carried about her waist. There was no one in the station house below, no one to see as the chief shuttled her out the rarely used rear exit of the town hall.

Sitting in the back of the police car, Victoria peered out the window as Matthews drove her toward the confrontation she now anticipated with every fiber of her being. As they approached the Skinner estate her vision climbed to the distant rocky crest.

Against the star-filled mountain sky, Devil's Rock was a clearly defined dark presence—poised and still above them all, seemingly waiting with the greatest of interest for the night to unfold.

=FIFTEEN=

The review was over, the meeting drawing to a close. Kyle sat back in the chair that once had been his father's and cast a sweeping look along the table. The Boys were closing up briefcases and exchanging comments about the meeting that had just taken place, as well as projections of business for the next monthly review, which would take place in Parkersburg.

"What about that offer on the Black Top?" Angus Mac-Gregor asked. As his nephew echoed the question all eyes turned to Kyle.

"That matter will be concluded soon," he answered.

"Seems like you've been saying that for quite a while now," Tuttle observed.

"Yeah," Boggs put in. "Is that Adams fella gonna do business, or what?"

"Don't worry," Kyle returned. "By the time we meet in Parkersburg, the Black Top will be taken care of. The past week or so I've had something else on my mind."

"What's that?"

"Be patient. She should be arriving any minute."

"Something new from Shine Valley?" Stevenson asked eagerly.

"Shine Valley never saw the day it could match this," Kyle replied.

A minute later Matthews walked in, pushing Victoria ahead of him. Jerking away from the man's touch, she walked up to the table on her own and took a stand before the six of them. It didn't matter that the hands before her were cuffed, or that she wore boots and jeans and a bulky old sweater, the majestic air she exuded as she lifted her chin to peer over their heads was that of a queen.

"That'll be all, Matthews," Kyle said. "You can wait out back."

"Hold on," Stevenson said, his gaze racing over the woman as the chief disappeared through the doorway. "The clothes are different, and the hair, but . . . Damn! It's *her*, isn't it? The one who killed the Judge and ran off in your car!"

"And the one who took those missing records!" Tuttle exploded.

An uproar of exclamations ensued as the Boys ogled and stared, and Victoria seemingly held herself above it all—refusing to look at any one of them.

"We needn't worry about those records," Kyle said in a mild tone. "Victoria—as she calls herself now—has secreted them where they'll never see the light of day. Isn't that right, Victoria?"

Again she remained silent, continuing to pin her gaze on the wall beyond them.

"What are you going to do with her?" Harley MacGregor asked.

"I've got a suggestion," Stevenson put in. "Let her go with me to Parkersburg. I've got a room at the house that would be a perfect setting for a jewel like her."

Finally the woman moved, but only to turn her head a mere inch and look down her nose. "I thought you preferred little girls, Mr. Stevenson," she said.

Stevenson's silky smile faded. "She doesn't say much, but when she speaks up, she's got a right smart mouth," he accused.

Again a round of exclamations rippled down the table, this time peppered with suggestions of what should be done with the upstart female. Finally Kyle rose to his feet.

"Gentlemen, gentlemen," he chided, raising palms of truce as all eyes turned his way. "It was *my* car and *my* father. And now it's *my* decision."

At his last words, Kyle finally drew her icy eyes to his.

"I merely brought her in so you could pay your last respects," he added with a smile.

* * *

While he and Bill remained crouched in the trees by necessity, Richard had clenched his jaw along with his fists as Matthews ushered Victoria in the backdoor of the Skinner house. He guessed he should have realized she'd be handcuffed again, but he hadn't, and the sight of her being callously pushed along by the police chief had been almost more than he could take.

They'd been in position for nearly an hour when Matthews showed—Eric, Miles, and the chef having slipped into cover behind giant trees on the front lawn; Richard and Bill hovering on the edge of the wood behind the garage.

But with the Big Boys still inside, their chauffeurs were gathered in the drive—a group of husky-looking, uniformed, presumed-to-be-loyal hired hands who would be all too eager to join in a fight should one erupt. Then there was the trio of mountain men led by Jake Sweeney. Strolling about on the softly lit porch, all three cradled rifles.

There had been too many eyes to avoid—too many potential disasters lying in wait—to attempt approaching the house as Matthews walked away with Victoria.

Now he was back outside. And *she* was in. Richard's scalp was crawling, but there was nothing he could do without blowing the whole plan.

Even as the Boys came out of the house and the last of their cars disappeared from the drive, it remained too risky. Sweeney and his men were still on the porch. And near the garage where Richard could clearly see the side drive they had to cross, Chief Matthews leaned against the side of his police car and lit up a smoke.

Come on, Mavis, Richard thought fervently. A moment later a pair of headlights appeared in the drive. Moving straight to the garage, she pulled up adjacent to the police vehicle and got out of her car.

Richard and Bill were close enough that they could clearly hear the voices against the quiet mountain night.

"What are you doing here?" the chief asked.

"Kyle's going to call for me when he's ready."

"Call for you? I thought—you know—the blonde . . ."

"The more the merrier, Chief."

Richard could picture the seductive smile she slipped into as Mavis tucked the front of her fur coat behind a shapely hip and leaned forward.

"Married men have been known to enjoy something out of the ordinary now and then, you know. It's cold out here," she added, offering a bottle. "Have a drink?"

"Well," the chief replied, clearly hooked. "I don't guess I'm really on duty."

Sashaying along the side of his car, Mavis held out the bottle like a carrot dangled before a horse, and adroitly led the chief into turning his back.

"One hell of a woman," Richard whispered to Bill. "Come on. Let's go."

The snow had melted almost completely away, and the grounds were dark. *Are they out there?* Mavis wondered while she smiled at John Matthews. Then, beyond the chief's shoulder, she saw a couple of shadows separate from the forest and move across the grounds. Her smile broadened as they melted into the shrubbery alongside the house.

"Tell me, Chief," she said. "Why is it we've never gotten to know each other any better?"

Followed a second later by Bill, Richard sidestepped through the bushes and plastered himself against the outside wall of the study. Setting the tape deck on the ground, he pulled on the headphones, turned up the volume, and stared blindly into space.

"How about a brandy?" came Kyle Skinner's voice, so close in his ear that it triggered chills of both victory and disgust. Looking up to Bill's questioning eyes, Richard broke into a smile.

"I've got her," he whispered, his smile disappearing as he tuned in for more.

Pouring two snifters without waiting for an answer, Kyle turned and walked toward her.

"No, thank you," Victoria said when he offered a glass. "I prefer not to touch anything you've touched."

He chuckled. "You're going to touch plenty," he said. Tossing down the contents of his glass, he set both snifters aside.

Victoria strolled slowly toward the window where she'd taken cover so many years before. There she turned and gave him a look of loathing. "Tell me, Kyle. I want to know. After you've had your way, do you plan to dispose of me as expediently as you did your father?"

"Oh, no," he purred, moving in her direction. "I plan to take my time with you. I've had four years to imagine how to do it, four years to remember every detail about that night—the way you felt lying on the floor beneath me . . . the look on your face just before you brought that damn gavel crashing into my skull."

"That was self-defense," she returned, looking him squarely in the eye despite the terror that consumed her as he brought his face to within inches of hers.

"Like I said," he murmured, his breath fanning her skin. "I remember it all." Placing a swift palm on her shoulder, he attempted to run it down the front of her sweater.

"Get your hand off me!" Victoria commanded. Slapping the offensive thing away with her cuffed wrists, she started backing away. "I may be handcuffed," she added. "But I'm not helpless."

"Good," Kyle said, following her step for step. "You intend to fight. That's the way I always dreamed it would be."

"Is that what it takes to turn you on, Kyle? Violence? Did it give you a thrill to beat your father to death?"

"Not particularly. If it had given me a thrill, I would have gone on hitting him. As you recall, two strikes were enough, and the old man deserved them. There hasn't been a day that's gone by that I haven't rejoiced that he's dead."

Victoria's back came up against the wall. There was no place left to go as he loomed close, his black eyes gleaming.

"Enough reminiscing," he said slowly, and with contrasting speed grabbed her up and forced his mouth on hers. One hand closed cruelly in her hair as the other roamed boldly down her body.

Suddenly breaking away, Kyle shoved her to arm's length.

"What the hell is this?" he demanded, grabbing the bottom of her sweater and snatching it up to her breasts.

"What the hell!" he repeated, this time his voice booming like thunder. "You've got me *bugged*?"

* * *

"He found the wire," Richard announced, ripping the headphones off his head and the cassette out of the deck at the same time. Planting the tape in Bill's hand, he commanded: "Get going!"

As Bill moved out of the bushes Richard hurried along the wall of the house.

"Hey!" Chief Matthews called out as Bill darted across the drive.

Freezing at the corner of the house, Richard looked across the drive in alarm. Bill kept running for the trees.

"Halt!" the chief yelled, this time reaching for his holster.

Then many things happened at once. Answering voices called out from the porch, and Richard could only assume Sweeney and his men made a move toward the drive as gunfire erupted in front of the house. At the same time, just as Chief Matthews drew his pistol, Mavis stepped up and brought the liquor bottle smashing across the back of his head.

The chief started to fall. Richard didn't wait to see him land as he dashed to the kitchen door and ran through the house to the study.

"Do come in, Adams."

Richard came to a skidding halt just inside the doorway. Holding Victoria firmly against the front of his body, Skinner had the chain of the handcuffs planted fiercely on her throat.

"Hand over the rifle, or I crush her windpipe," he said.

Richard looked from Kyle's black eyes to Victoria and back again.

"I said, hand it over!" Kyle thundered.

Lowering the rifle, Richard took a slow step in his direction. "It's over, Skinner," he said. "You murdered the Judge, and we just got your confession on tape."

"Nothing's over," Kyle retorted. "Except maybe the life of the little lady here. That's up to you. Give me the rifle, Adams. And then I'll take the tape."

"I don't have the tape. Bill's long gone with it by now."

"Honeycutt can be caught up with. Give me the damn rifle now!" he boomed, jerking the cuffs so that Victoria's head snapped back and she gasped for breath.

"All right, all right," Richard said, quickly offering the weapon.

Anchoring one arm securely about Victoria's neck, Kyle snatched the rifle and brought it with one hand to a threatening position.

"Just back off, Skinner," Richard added. "It won't do any good to hurt Victoria or anybody else. It's over, I tell you. A U.S. marshal will be here by tomorrow morning."

"Morning is far away, Adams. Right now there's nobody in my sights but you."

Just as he started to pull the trigger Victoria wrenched violently against his imprisoning arm. Richard leaped and rolled to the right as the shot split the air, the bullet smashing the window beyond him. Scrambling behind the cover of a chair, Richard looked up as Kyle planted a hand on the scruff of Victoria's collar and yanked her forward while using the other to point the rifle at her back.

"The next one will go right through her if you follow," Kyle warned, pushing her toward the door. "I'm going after that tape, Adams. And after I get it, I'll be back for you. Nothing's over. Not by a long shot."

With that they backed through the doorway. Richard started to move around the chair.

"I mean it, Adams!" Kyle yelled as he propelled Victoria into the hallway. "She'll get it right through the heart!"

As the blast of gunfire continued in front of the house, Kyle went out the back with Victoria, once again planting a forearm around her throat and dragging her as she sputtered and struggled against his hold.

"Watch it, bitch," he muttered as they started toward the garage.

"You won't be going anywhere, Kyle," Mavis announced.

Kyle looked up with a start. She was standing there beside Matthews, who was lying on the ground, unconscious or dead. He didn't give a damn which.

"Between the chief's car and mine, the garage is blocked," Mavis added.

Pushing Victoria ahead of him, Kyle peered over his hostage's head. "Give me your keys, Mavis."

"No."

Kyle kept pushing, his arm planted across Victoria's windpipe like a vise.

"Then get out of my way," he said. "I'll take the chief's car."

"No, Kyle," Mavis replied defiantly. "Everything stops here."

Continuing to close the gap between them, Kyle came within ten yards. "I warned you, Mavis," he said with a smile. "Don't ever try to stand in my way."

As he raised the barrel of the rifle Victoria clamped her teeth on his wrist and bit with all her strength. The gun went off, and Mavis grabbed her left thigh as she fell atop Matthews. Kyle threw Victoria to the ground and, looking back to Mavis, continued in her direction. Mavis frantically fumbled behind her back, her hands searching and finally closing on the chief's pistol as Kyle came to a stop mere feet away.

"Best damn piece of ass in the Blue Ridge," he muttered. Lifting the rifle, he took aim once more.

"No!" Victoria screamed.

The shots rang out in unison. For a shattering few seconds Kyle backed away. And then he toppled like a fallen tree.

Emerging from the house at a gallop, Richard ran to Victoria.

"I'm all right," she choked, her eyes wide with horror as she nodded toward the garage. "Go there! Hurry!"

Scrambling away, Richard dashed to the drive. Kyle was lying on his back, his eyes opened fixedly to the sky. Passing him by, Richard moved swiftly to Mavis. The fur coat was open, the white sweater beneath blooming with a dark, ugly stain.

"Oh, God," Richard mumbled, and stripped off his jacket. Dropping to her side, he applied pressure to the wound with one hand and cradled her head in the other.

"I stopped him, didn't I?"

"Yeah. You stopped him."

"Maybe I'll get to heaven after all."

"Hold on, Mavis," he urged. "Just hold on."

"Shut up and kiss me, will ya?"

Richard's eyes searched hers and saw a tear slide from one of the corners.

His lips were on hers when she expelled her final breath.

302 / Marcia Martin

* * *

It was nearly midnight when Doc Hawkins arrived. Having fetched the BMW from down the road, Richard loaded Victoria in the car, and they left the morbid scene in the Skinner drive, the flashing red light of the ambulance following them all the way to Sky Road.

A long hour and a half had passed since Kyle dragged Victoria out of the house only to meet his destiny with Mavis. Sweeney's cohorts had fled to the woods, but Sweeney himself was in jail, along with Chief Matthews. Eric and the others had volunteered to keep watch at the town hall until the U.S. marshal arrived.

Richard cast a look at the building as they drove past—it was all lit up as if a party was going on. "Look at that," he suggested. "I guess the good guys are celebrating."

But Victoria didn't budge. In fact, she hadn't moved a muscle since he looped an arm around her and she settled quietly against his side. They were nearing the turn to the Black Top when she finally spoke.

"It seems strange to be riding in my own car again."

"It's black," Richard pointed out. "You'll note from my matching clothes that I didn't especially want to be spotted tonight."

"I can't believe what's happened," she said. "I just can't believe it. Two people are dead, and it's all because of me."

"I don't think that's the right way to look at it."

"It's the only way to look at it. I can't say I'm sorry Kyle Skinner is no longer alive, but Mavis . . ."

"I'll miss her," Richard said, his voice deep with regret. "Maybe I should have put my foot down more firmly. I tried to persuade her not to come, but she refused to be excluded. She wanted Kyle brought down—maybe more than any of us. I've got to believe she thought the risk was worthwhile."

They started up the curving mountain road to the lodge.

"All of you could have been hurt," Victoria commented eventually. "Or killed."

"Everyone knew the risks," Richard replied. "And everyone involved wanted to be—for your rescue, yes, but for other reasons, too. Things are going to change around here. The days of the Big Boys' control in Devil's Rock are over. Did Bill tell you we got those ledgers of yours from Tennessee?''

"No.''

"It's all going to come down the way you wanted, Victoria— Sweeney out of commission, the Boys under investigation. A friend of mine at the FBI has dispatched an agent to pick up the ledgers. He should be arriving in a day or so, and once the Bureau is involved, I have every faith the Blue Ridge Big Boys will get what's coming to them.''

"You're amazing," she said softly.

"There's something else," Richard went on after a moment. "I cut a deal with my friend. In exchange for the evidence you provided, the FBI is guaranteeing you immunity from prosecution on all charges of grand theft auto. You'll have to be debriefed by that agent I told you about, but after that you'll be basically in the clear.''

Reaching up, Victoria hooked an arm around his neck and buried her face in his shoulder.

"Did I do the right thing?" Richard asked.

"Yes," she whispered, and said nothing more for the rest of the ride, although she continued to hold on to him for dear life.

Ironically, the tighter she clutched him, the more Richard sensed her slipping away.

When they walked into the lodge, Hilda and Gertrude greeted them with a barrage of questions.

"Everyone's all right," Richard replied wearily, his arm planted around Victoria, who mutely regarded the two women.

"Well, someone might have called!" Hilda scolded.

"Where are the others?" Gertrude asked.

"They're staying at the jail until the marshal arrives.

"Are you all right, miss?"

Victoria nodded.

"It's been quite an ordeal," Richard said. "But everything's going to be fine now. Why don't we all get some rest?"

As Gertrude and Hilda started off toward their rooms, still chattering, Richard turned Victoria in the opposite direction, looking over with disappointment when she stopped at the door to the scarlet room. "I thought . . ." He trailed off, his gaze darting down the hall to his own chamber before returning to her eyes.

The barest blush of pink rose to her cheeks. Other than that her face was like marble. "I need a bath," she said. "And some time to myself."

Richard reached up to brush a lock of hair over her shoulder. Although she never moved, he somehow got the impression that she flinched away. "Sure," he replied, his arm falling to his side. "I understand."

But he didn't. Long after she closed the door quietly in his face, Richard lay in bed alone, wondering what the hell was going on behind that flawless expression of blankness.

Early the next morning the men returned from town. The U.S. marshal was ensconced in the town hall and would keep order until a new regime of law could be established in Devil's Rock. Red-eyed but victorious, Eric, Miles, the chef, and Bill retired to various rooms as Richard went downstairs to the kitchen.

Pouring himself a cup of coffee, he looked across the room, where Hilda and Gertrude were sitting at the breakfast table.

"I'll be in the library," he said. "Do me a favor, will you, Hilda? Let me know when Victoria comes down."

He called the Dalton School to tell Anita and Missy the good news, and for a while was uplifted by the joy in their voices. But as the hours rolled by, and Victoria remained secluded in the upstairs room, there was no escaping the feeling that something was wrong. It was the middle of the afternoon when Hilda came scurrying in, her face a picture of doom.

"You told me to let you know when she came down. Well, she's down. But she wouldn't take time to chat or eat, just poured a cup of tea and went out back. She's like she was at first, Mr. Richard. Only worse."

Richard rose to his feet. "Worse? What do you mean?"

"I don't know," Hilda replied, hugging herself against a shudder. "Like there's a misery inside her so big and black, it's putting out a light that wants to shine."

Picking up a jacket, Richard went out back. She was standing near the toolshed, seemingly absorbed in studying the doe, who was sniffing around remaining patches of snow a short distance away. Victoria was wearing only a white turtleneck sweater over her jeans. Halting in the midst of pulling on the jacket, Richard planted it around her shoulders as he arrived.

"You're not dressed warmly enough to be out here," he said.

"Sorry," she said with a flickering glance, and an even briefer hint of a smile.

She looked back to the doe, and Richard followed her line of vision. The deer was straying farther and farther from the shed, closer to a trail that led up into the forested wilderness of the mountain.

"It's time for her to go," Richard observed.

"Yes. I suppose it is," Victoria replied in a tone that drew his sharp attention.

"Are you all right, Victoria?" he demanded. "You're acting strange as hell."

"I know. I'm sorry. A lot has happened. I guess I'm a little . . . stunned."

"That's understandable," Richard replied gruffly. "If that's all it is." Without replying, she looked once more into the distance.

"I heard from my FBI friend a while ago," he added. "The agent will be here at ten tomorrow morning."

"How about Mavis's funeral? Have you heard anything about that?"

"It's at three," Richard responded solemnly, and stuffed his hands in his pockets. "Stay with me tonight, Victoria."

She looked up, her eyes catching the light of the descending sun, reflecting it like frozen pools.

"I've missed you," he added. "If you don't want to do anything else, that's okay. But I need to hold you through the night."

A tremulous smile curved her lips as she nodded.

It was after nine o'clock when she walked into his room, scrubbed to a glowing pink and wearing the white terrycloth robe. Lobo actually wagged his tail upon her arrival. Richard sent the coyote quickly packing, closed the door, and turned, suddenly finding himself at a loss for words.

"Make yourself at home," he managed finally, and felt like an idiot. They were *married,* dammit! This was *their* bedroom!

"I'll just wash up," he added, and escaped to the adjoining bath.

As the sound of running water came from the neighboring room, Victoria wandered around the chamber, noting things she never had before—photographs of Richard with famous people, diplomas from a number of universities, certificates citing awards for one thing or another. As she passed the small desk near the hearth, she noticed a leatherbound journal, picked it up, and looked curiously inside.

When she grasped the meaning of the notations, she sank into the nearest chair. Honeycutt's Mercedes . . . Renfield's Jaguar . . . Charlotte . . . Atlanta . . . Columbia . . . and linking them all a dark puzzle that had fascinated Richard as surely as one of his constructions in the library. As she saw herself through his eyes, the truth that had been glaring at her since the previous night became blinding.

Richard came out of the bath wearing a towel around his hips and a hopeful smile. The smile froze as he saw the journal Victoria held in her hands, and the look on her face.

"Hold on, Victoria. I wrote those things long ago. That's not how I see you. It's not who you are."

"Yes, it is," she said, and setting the journal aside, rose from the chair and started for the door.

"Where are you going?" Richard asked, and stalked after her.

"Back to my room."

Catching her by the arm, he turned her around. "Why?"

The hurt in his voice pulled at Victoria, heightening the ache of the dreadful inevitability swelling through her heart and mind.

"I don't expect you to understand, Richard. But I'll try to explain what I can. For a very long time I haven't looked at myself. Now all the curtains have been ripped away, and I'm all I can see. It's not a pretty picture."

"You know, this whole thing seems to have backfired," he replied heatedly. "I thought you'd be happy, and instead you're further away than ever."

"I'm sorry."

"I don't want you to apologize, Victoria. I want you to smile and laugh and . . . kiss me."

He bent to her, but she turned her head. He was losing her once again. This time Richard couldn't bear it.

"I love you," he announced.

"I love you, too," she replied so readily that his mouth dropped open.

"You do?"

She looked up, the enigmatic look on her face knocking down the swift hope that had risen within him.

"I love you beyond all reason, Richard. Beyond all I ever imagined the feeling could be. But I have to be able to love myself, too, or at least like myself a little bit. And I can't. God, I can hardly stand being inside my own skin." She started to pull away.

Richard's grip tightened. "You're my wife, dammit!"

"Get an annulment," she replied softly.

"No!" he responded in a contrasting boom. "I love you. You love me. That's what it's supposed to be about, isn't it?"

"You are so invariably sweet, Richard. And so naive."

Rising on tiptoe, she brushed her lips across his cheek and would have pulled away once more.

Richard yanked her back. "I can remember two distinct occasions when you did that, walked away, and left me staring," he announced, his feverish gaze darting between her eyes. "It's not going to happen again. I'll have an answer, and I'll have it now. You're leaving, aren't you?"

"Yes," she replied quietly. "Tomorrow. After Mavis's funeral."

"I won't let you."

"You've seen to it that no one can stop me," Victoria returned. "I have to work through this on my own, Richard. If you care about me, you'll let me go."

Dropping from his eyes, her gaze fixed on the fingers he'd latched about her arm. After a moment Richard released them with a quick jerk and brought his arm to his side. Her eyes lifted, brimming with the glow he knew now to be love.

"You must know that I'd like nothing more than to stay with you, be your wife, share your life. Maybe someday . . ."

She peered into his eyes as she searched for an ending to the optimistic phrase. Apparently none came. A moment later she was gliding off in that inimitable way of hers, leaving him shut off once more as she gently closed the door.

Richard had said she wouldn't leave him staring. But she did—staring and shaking and swaying on his feet as the fierce knocking of his heart threatened to crumple his knees.

The next morning a brisk young man introducing himself as Agent Keyes sequestered himself with Victoria in the library and recorded her statement. She found it ironic that it took only an hour to tell the story of years—to quote the names and towns she'd told herself she'd forgotten, and never had. As she finished she felt purged, but also drained of anything that could help her fight the battle that remained.

When it was over, Agent Keyes shook her hand and wished her well. Directives had to flow through all the proper channels. But for all practical purposes, when Victoria walked out of the library, she walked out a free woman, cleared of all criminal charges.

Two hours later when she insisted on driving herself to the cemetery—beneath a scowling look of consternation from Richard—the BMW was packed with all she'd brought to the Black Top.

Everyone from the lodge attended Mavis's funeral. After the service Victoria made the rounds of the people she'd come to know and care for—Hilda, Gertrude, Miles, Cainey, the chef. What started as another quick parting embrace for Eric turned into a bear hug.

Backing away from the giant man with a smile, Victoria glanced across the lawn where Bill and Richard were talking near the line of cars parked outside the cemetery fence. As she walked toward them she thought how handsome the two of them were—all dressed up in dark suits, like father-and-son models for some chic magazine. Their conversation dwindled into silence as they noted her approach.

Richard's eyes fastened on her, and he could no more have torn them away than he could stop her from doing what she was about to do. Fair hair pinned in a sleek twist, she wore a navy suit with the ruffle of a white blouse at the throat. Navy shoes and bag. White gloves. A picture of classic beauty, she could have been a princess making an appearance at a lawn party. Richard's throat went dry as she stepped up and offered a hand to Bill.

"There's no way I can ever repay you for what you've done," she said as he joined her in a shake.

Bill smiled. "Two weeks ago I would have liked to string you up. Now the only payment I want is for you to be happy." With an arched look toward Richard, he added, "And I mean both of you."

Victoria's gaze fell to the toes of her pumps. They were the only heels she'd packed in Pawleys when she set off for Columbia a lifetime ago. Drawing a deep breath, she made herself meet Richard's searching eyes.

"Walk me to my car?" she asked. "I suppose I should try and thank you, too," she said as Richard fell in beside her. "But anything I could say would fall so terribly short of what you deserve."

"Don't worry about it," he mumbled.

They ambled along in silence, Victoria's hands gripping her purse, his buried in the pockets of his trousers until he reached to open the door of the BMW.

"Going back to Pawleys?" he asked then.

She looked up, once again trying to record for forever the sight of his face. Now the brows were furling, the eyes sparkling with an anger belying the conversational voice.

"Richard," she began in the gentlest of tones, "if I could abide being around anyone I care about, I'd stay here with you."

Hanging an abrupt arm on the ledge of the door, he looked swiftly across Sky Road. "I don't get this," he muttered. "Every time I think we're rounding the home stretch, you throw out a new hitch. The hard part's over, Victoria."

"No," she replied. "The hard part's just beginning."

Richard's head snapped around, his eyes probing, impaling. She endured the scutiny for only an instant before pressing a quick kiss to his lips, climbing into the BMW, and starting the engine.

Lifting exasperated palms to the sky, Richard slammed the driver's door and stepped away from the car. She rolled down the window.

"Just remember that I'll always love you," she said, and left him staring once again as she scratched off the dirt bank and disappeared up the curving mountain road.

=SIXTEEN=

January 24
Pawleys Island

The school chapel had been transformed by a garden of greenery and white flowers, the tall candelabra standing on each side of the altar lending a cathedrallike aura to the simple sanctuary.

As an usher escorted Victoria toward the front she nodded to students and faculty members, who looked up with quick, welcoming smiles. It was a small crowd. She knew almost everyone. And when the usher stopped at the pew where Anita and Missy were seated, the child emitted a joyful squeal that triggered a ripple of comradely laughter through the group.

Minutes later Bill Jacobs came out of an anteroom with the chaplain, and the pianist began the rousing chords of the wedding march. The crowd stood and turned, and as Darcy came down the aisle—a petite, picture-perfect bride all in white—Victoria could do nothing to prevent the tears that filled her eyes.

Though brisk, the January day was sunny, and after the ceremony the wedding crowd spilled out of the chapel to gather on the lawn. Victoria walked out holding hands with Missy and flanked by Anita, who was studying her with a quiet intensity Victoria knew would erupt as soon as a moment of privacy presented itself.

Victoria focused on Missy. Garbed in a pretty pink dress, her hair pulled back in a matching ribbon, she had roses in her cheeks and the light of happiness in her eyes.

"How do you like school, Missy?"

"I love it," the child replied enthusiastically. "It's just like you said. Even better."

A dark-haired girl about the same size as Missy darted up to them then. "Want to come with me to the cafeteria?" she asked eagerly. "There's a wedding cake in there. And cookies and punch."

"This is my best friend, Samantha," Missy announced. "We do everything together."

"Hello, Samantha," Victoria greeted with a smile.

"Hello," the child replied, her eyes swiftly returning to Missy. "Well? Do you want to come?"

Missy squinted up at Victoria. "Are you going to stay?" she asked.

"Not this time," Victoria replied, and watched the child's expression turn dim. "Come here, Missy. Give me a hug." As the child complied she added, "I'll be back. Don't worry. Go ahead, and have a good time. I'll talk to you soon."

Her spirits restored, Missy sprinted off with her friend just as Darcy came running across the grass, the long white skirt of her gown billowing in the breeze.

"I knew you'd be here!" she exclaimed, and threw her arms around Victoria's neck.

"Of course you did," Victoria replied with a laugh, giving her a heartfelt squeeze before backing away to peer into Darcy's face.

Studying the smiling countenance framed by the white lace of a bridal veil, Victoria flashed upon the memory of the first time she'd seen Darcy—a mere slip of a girl in faded jeans and a ragged shirt. Once again, her eyes began to sting.

"You're radiant," Victoria whispered.

"Thanks," Darcy replied in a similar voice.

Summoning a bright tone along with a smile, Victoria asked, "How about a honeymoon? Do you and Bill have plans?"

"We're driving down to Charleston in a little while. Bill has made arrangements at a bed and breakfast right on the Battery. It's got a fireplace and a four-poster bed, and you can see the ships passing right from the bedroom window."

"It sounds very romantic."

"Yeah, I know," Darcy replied with a familiar, perky wink. At that moment the groom approached, wearing a happy face almost as radiant as his bride's. "Hello, Victoria," he greeted.

"Hello, Bill. Congratulations."

"Thanks," he said, his eyes turning to Darcy. "The photographer whats us back inside the chapel for pictures."

"Okay." Darcy looked swiftly back to Victoria. "Will I see you later at the reception?"

"No. I've got to get going, but listen, you two. I'm sure you have quarters of your own, but I want to offer you the use of the canal house until the lease runs out next fall. And I want you to have the BMW, too. I'll leave the keys on the bureau in the living room."

"Victoria!" Darcy chimed with a note of objection.

Victoria held up a gloved hand. "That's the way I want it," she said. "And no argument. Now, go on. I intend to have plenty of pictures to look at the next time I'm here."

Grasping her by the shoulders, Darcy shifted up to press a quick kiss to her cheek.

"Be happy," Victoria whispered as the bride walked away on her husband's arm. She watched until they disappeared through the chapel doorway, then turned to Anita, who continued to watch her with piercing eyes. "They make a lovely couple, don't they?" Victoria asked.

"Yes. They do."

"And it seems Missy is settling in."

"Missy's doing beautifully," Anita replied, and waited no longer to plunge into the issue. "The past few weeks I've learned a great deal about the mysterious Victoria Blackwood. I thought we were the best of friends. Why didn't you ever confide in me, Victoria? I would have tried to help."

Victoria released a heavy breath. "I know you would have tried, Anita. But there was nothing you could do then, and there's nothing you can do now."

"Now?" Anita piped. "I was given to understand that everything was settled, all the hurdles behind you."

"All but the biggest," Victoria replied, and watched the look of questioning in Anita's eyes grow even sharper. "I love you, Anita," she added quietly. "And I'll be in touch, but for now I really must go."

As she drove away from the school Victoria surveyed the

seaside highway with a feeling of longing. The cypress and Spanish moss were the same, as was the wild beauty of the marsh. But Pawleys was no longer a haven. Now that she'd confronted herself, it seemed there was no place to which she could escape.

Turning up the familiar canal road, she let herself in the familiar house, but still she found no comfort. Even the clocks had turned traitorous. Now, instead of consoling her with their ticks, they shouted of all the time that had been lost, all the minutes and hours that continued to slip away.

Changing into jeans and a warm sweatshirt, Victoria spent less than an hour collecting some favorite things in a garment bag. Then, with a last sweeping look about the kitchen, she locked the side door behind her and started down to the dock. She came to an abrupt halt when she spotted Richard waiting by the stairs.

Dressed in jeans and a leather jacket, he was propped against the rail, his hands stuffed familiarly in his pockets. The sight of him stole her breath, along with the capacity for movement. As Victoria stood there, silently staring, he moved forward and took her bag, slinging it effortlessly over his shoulder.

"You took me by surprise," she said finally.

"I knew you wouldn't miss Darcy's wedding."

"You came all the way down here on that chance?"

"And for the chance to visit Missy and the others. I was on my way to the school when I had the impulse to swing by here and spotted your car." His gaze shifted to her eyes. "I'm glad I did. It's good to see you."

"It's good to see you, too." Shaking off the mesmerizing effect of his nearness, Victoria looked away and started down the stairs. "But I really can't linger."

He fell in beside her as she proceeded to the dock, watching in silence as she stripped the cover off the Chris-Craft.

"How's everyone at the lodge?" she asked, tossing the tarp aside.

"Why don't you come back with me and see for yourself?"

The challenge was out before Richard knew it was coming. As she straightened and gave him a haunted look, part of him was sorry he'd said it. Part of him wasn't.

"Actually I'm renting a little place up the waterway," she

answered finally, and hoisted her bag over the side of the boat.

"Up the waterway?" Richard repeated. "Where?"

"North," she responded evasively.

"What about this house?"

"I've given it to Darcy and Bill for as long as the lease lasts. I gave them the BMW, too."

"What are you doing? Divesting yourself of everything you own?"

"Like you said long ago—a clean slate, a fresh start."

"I want that fresh start to be with me," Richard announced, and watched her look uncomfortably away. "I'm your husband, after all," he added anyway.

"You haven't gotten an annulment?" she asked, still gazing across the canal.

"No. And I'm not going to. If you want an annulment, you're going to have to handle it yourself."

She turned to face him once more, the first smile he'd seen playing about her lips. "I guess I should scold you," she said, "but I can't deny that something inside me is pleased."

"That's a start. Let's build on it."

Her smile faded. "I meant it when I said it's good to see you, Richard. But it's hard, too. Don't waste your life waiting for me," she concluded, and stepped back to the boat.

"I want you more than ever, Victoria. That's the waste."

She hesitated for only an instant, then crouched at the stern and began untying the lines as though he'd never spoken.

"I can't stand this," Richard said to her back. "Haven't you learned anything in the past few months? Things can be worked out. Problems can be solved."

"That's what I'm trying to do."

"Don't shut me out again," he said as she tossed the final securing line on deck.

She looked over her shoulder. "Richard," she muttered in a weighty tone, "there is no other way. Now please stop making this excruciatingly painful for both of us." Dropping surefootedly into the Chris-Craft, she moved to the wheel.

"Vicki Buchanan!" he called.

Halting in the midst of turning the ignition, she turned veiled eyes up at the dock. Richard took slow steps to the edge.

"How do you know that?" she demanded.

"I did some checking."

"Well, well. I always did say you were a master at tracking me down. What do you know?"

"That you grew up in McLean, Virginia, the only child of Elizabeth and Montgomery Buchanan—distinguished Harvard graduate, dynamic district attorney, and finally prominent superior court judge. He didn't die like you said, Victoria. He's in poor health, but he's alive . . . and living in the same house where you grew up."

"Alive?" she repeated in a wooden tone. "That's funny. He'll always be dead to me."

With that she turned the key, and the engine blasted to life. A moment later, in blatant disrespect of the strict laws governing the canal, the Chris-Craft was heading for the waterway at a speed that sent a wake sailing higher than Richard's head.

February 27
Raleigh

The sun disappeared early as a cold rain fell. Sheryl was making a pot of tea when the doorbell rang.

Looking through the doorpane, she saw a bareheaded woman, her shoulder-length hair shedding rivulets of rain down a dark slicker. Sheryl opened the door. "Yes?" she voiced on a questioning note.

The stranger held forth a calling card. Dripping and bedraggled, it was nonetheless a business card that Sheryl recognized at once as her own.

"You gave me this once," the woman said. "I hope it's still good."

"Victoria!" With the explosion of the name on her lips, Sheryl stepped onto the rain-swept porch and drew her inside. "For God's sake, you're drenched!" she added. "Take off that wet wrap while I get a towel for your hair."

When Sheryl bustled back from the linen closet, she found Victoria standing in the exact spot where she'd left her, a puddle gathering about her sneakered feet. Taking the towel she offered, Victoria wiped her face and lifted troubled eyes.

"What the devil's going on?" Sheryl asked.

"I've tried to deal with this alone, and I can't," Victoria answered. "Help me, Sheryl. Please. I'm a complete mess, and I must get myself straight. I'm going to have a baby, you see."

March 4

"Hello, handsome," she greeted when Richard answered the phone.

"Hello, Sheryl."

There was no life in his voice, and she knew why. His heart was aching in the same hopeless way her own had ached for years.

"Victoria asked me to call," she said.

"Victoria?" he repeated, his tone at once sharp and alert.

"She's been with me for about a week now."

"Been with you? For God's sake, Sheryl, why didn't you call before? You know I've been worried sick—"

"Shut up, Richard. I have something important to talk to you about. Something to do with Victoria."

"Okay," he supplied after a moment. "What is it? And what's she doing at your place?"

"She came to me for help, and I think I can give it to her. Although I have no idea how long it will take before there are promising results. Victoria is trying to work through a tremendous problem, Richard. I'd say she's working harder than any patient I've ever had. But maybe that's because she has such a great incentive—a future with you . . . and your baby."

"Baby," Richard mumbled mindlessly as his brain seemed suddenly to polarize and fly off in opposite directions. "What baby?"

"The one that will be born about nine months from last Christmas morning."

His gaze darting to the closet, Richard took several quick steps in that direction. Forgetting the phone, he let it fall from his ear and bang to the floor. The clatter pierced his stupor. Grabbing the receiver, he jammed it to his ear.

"Sheryl? Sorry. I dropped the phone."

"I've heard fathers-to-be do that sort of thing," she observed.

"Listen. I'll just throw a few things in a bag—"

"No."

"*No?* What do you mean *no?* I'll be there in four hours!"

"*No*, Richard. You can't come now. It's not what she wants, and as her doctor I must say it's not what she needs. Victoria has a long way to go, and no one else can help her get there. I'm doing all I can, but as for the really hard work, she's going to have to do it alone."

"What is it?" Richard exploded. "What the hell's wrong with her?"

"She was victimized as a child, Richard. And it was from that trauma that the aberrant behavior of her adulthood stemmed."

"Victimized," Richard mumbled. "You mean abused?"

Silence followed, and Richard broke out in a cold sweat.

"You were right, weren't you, Sheryl?" he pressed urgently. "It was her father, wasn't it?"

The silence bloomed.

"Dammit, Sheryl! Is it what I'm afraid it is?"

"Yes," came the whispering affirmation.

"Oh, God," Richard murmured, his quiet tone belying the consuming urge to beat the hell out of something.

"She's always hidden behind the mask of a Valerie or Veronica or Vanessa. Now, for the first time in her adult life, she's staring this thing in the face. It's hard enough for her to look at, much less talk about. That's why she asked me to call you. She wanted you to know about the baby. She wanted you to know the truth about herself. But she can't bear to discuss it with you. Not yet anyway."

"When?" he barked. "When can I see her?"

"When she's ready."

"How long will that take?"

"There's no way of telling, Richard. Every woman is different, and every woman reacts differently. The one thing I believe such victims universally experience is that the scars remain for a lifetime. They may work through it to the point of accepting themselves; they may lead perfectly normal, loving lives. But the scars of the past remain."

"I know where she is," Richard mumbled after a moment. "I know she's hurting. How can I stay away?"

"If you love Victoria, you'll wait."

"All right then, dammit! I'll wait!"

"I thought so," Sheryl replied mildly. "She also wanted me to ask you a question that I believe to be totally unnecessary. But she insisted, so I'll ask. Now that you know everything about her, do you still want her?"

"Tell her . . ." Richard began after a moment, and from the sound of his voice, Sheryl could picture the strained look on his face. "Tell her I'll always want her. And I'll wait as long as it takes. Tell her all she has to do is call, and I'll be there."

She worked with unflagging fortitude and courage. During the day when Sheryl was at the office, Victoria read articles and research books she was assigned. At night she secluded herself with the soul-searching, autobiographical journal that was more grueling. Through it all she tackled the misplaced feeling of shame that belonged not on her shoulders, but on her father's.

When therapy first began, Sheryl had expected the typical periods of backsliding that often went hand in hand with such a trauma. Then she learned better. Whatever expectations she had, Victoria surpassed them, and at one point Sheryl thought there was nothing they couldn't accomplish together, no goal toward which she would spur Victoria and be refused. Until they came to the wall—her father.

He had abused her sexually from the time she was eight years old, possessed her as his secret lover until she escaped at seventeen. Over the course of months Victoria grew to be able to talk about him, even to cry angry tears about him, but when it came to Sheryl's belief that the only way to really put the experience in the past was to face the man in the present, she balked like a horse at an impassable fence.

Finally one May night as they waited together in the kitchen for tea to brew, Sheryl brought up the taboo subject once again. But this time there was a difference; this time she pushed a button she'd never dared to press before.

"How about Richard?" Sheryl asked. "Are you considering him at all?"

The pale eyes lifted. "I always consider Richard. You know that."

"Have you considered that if you can't get past this, he'll have to live with it, too? Richard would do it, no questions asked. But is it what you want for him? Or your baby?"

Early the next Saturday morning Victoria came downstairs dressed in a traveling suit.

"Will you take me to McLean?" she asked bravely.

Crossing the kitchen, Sheryl put a strong arm around the taller woman. "Of course I'll take you," she replied. "I'll walk every step of the way with you if you want me to."

But it didn't turn out that way. That afternoon, when they drove up to a white mansion bearing a striking resemblance to Mount Vernon, Victoria walked the long path to the door alone.

Eyeing the doorbell, Victoria lifted a hand and watched it begin to shake. She had to force her trembling fingers to make the connection, then clasped them tightly in front of her as she waited and listened—swallowing hard as she heard footsteps and the door opened.

Expecting to look up into her father's face, she felt a flash of relief when a gray-haired woman in a nurse's uniform looked curiously out.

"May I help you?" she asked.

Victoria drew a deep breath. "I'd like to see the Judge."

The elderly face took on a kind smile. "Judge Buchanan doesn't see visitors, my dear."

"I think he'll see me," Victoria returned. "I'm his daughter."

"His . . ." The nurse paused, her brows lifting with surprise. "You mean you're Vicki?"

At Victoria's affirming nod, she drew the door wide and stepped aside. "Come in, my dear! Come in! Why, I had no idea!"

Victoria walked slowly into the foyer, her gaze traveling the remembered room, sweeping up the remembered banister.

"Vicki Buchanan!" the nurse chattered as she followed

along. "Your father speaks of you all the time, but I thought . . . you see, I was led to believe . . . well, my goodness, this is quite a shock."

"Yes," Victoria agreed. "It is."

"The Judge always spends this part of the day in the sunroom," she announced, her face taking on a sudden look of worry. "But I have to warn you, my dear, your father is not how you must remember him to be. He's been ill for many years. Frankly he may not know you."

"Maybe it will be enough for me to know him," Victoria replied, and drew a puzzled look. "I think I'll take a look upstairs first," she added. "Excuse me."

Ascending the staircase, she was assaulted by memories— carefree days when she'd run down it in joy to throw herself into her mother's embrace, terrorized nights when she'd climbed it in dread on her father's arm.

Moving steadily along the hall, she opened the bedroom door and walked into the past. Nothing had changed. Everything had been kept exactly as it was the day she left it. Same pink-and-white curtains at the windows. Same furniture. Nothing had been moved so much as an inch. Even the sweater she'd tossed across the chair fifteen years ago remained in the exact same spot.

Meandering to the bedside table, Victoria reached out to caress the Swiss clock. This, alone, was different. The whirring timepiece had stopped, its silence blanketing the room with the stifling quiet of empty churches and deserted shrines.

Closing the bedroom door behind her, she went downstairs and proceeded along the sweeping hall to the rear of the house. As she drew near the sunroom it was all she could do to make her feet keep moving. And yet it was with an admirable lack of hesitation that she threw open the double doors and walked inside.

Expecting to find him seated in the easy chair looking through some legal volume or other, Victoria faltered as she spotted the wheelchair by the window. He looked up as she moved forward.

His hair was silver and sparse; his face sagging; eyes vacant. "Did you bring my tea?" he asked in a trembling voice only vaguely reminiscent of the one she recalled.

"No," Victoria replied. "I imagine the nurse will be bringing your tea anytime now. Do you know who I am?"

The staring eyes moved over her, and he grinned—a sad, lopsided parody of the old, confidence-inspiring smile that some said would land him on the Supreme Court one day.

"You're Kitty's mother," he rasped. "Pretty little Kitty who lives down the street. I had a little girl once, you know. But somebody took her. Somebody took her far away."

To her horror, he burst into wailing tears. Lifting a hand to her mouth, Victoria backed away as the nurse bustled in.

"There now, Judge," she said. "It's all right. Everything's all right. . . ."

Victoria barely heard the woman as her gaze trailed over the broken effigy in the wheelchair. He had always been so big, so important. Superior Court Judge Montgomery Buchanan—all-knowing, all-powerful.

Along with the feeling of pity that swept over Victoria came a sense of release. The man she remembered was gone. The things she remembered were over. She couldn't escape the memories, but their writhing hold on her was dead.

The nurse looked up with concern as he continued to weep. "I'm afraid you'd better go now, my dear," she said.

"Of course."

"Perhaps you could come back another time?"

"No, I don't think so. Good-bye, Father," Victoria murmured, and walked out of the mansion, pausing on the porch to notice the fallen cherry blossoms dancing across the lawn with the breeze, accelerating her pace when she noticed Sheryl peering anxiously up from the car.

"You're quite a doctor," Victoria commented as she settled carefully into the passenger's seat.

"Is that good or bad?" Sheryl demanded in a desperate tone.

Victoria flashed a smile. "Let's get going," she suggested. "I have a phone call to make to Black Top Mountain."

The morning sun was bright in a clear sky. It was just past nine, and Sheryl was pouring a cup of coffee when the bell rang.

Glancing out the side pane, she saw it was Richard—dressed in a tailored suit and tie, and carrying a bouquet of white roses.

He must have left the Black Top at four in the morning to arrive at such an hour.

"I don't believe it," Sheryl murmured, and quickly opened the door.

"Hi," he said, his expression as stilted as his greeting.

"You must have gotten an early start."

"Couldn't sleep."

"Well, come on in," Sheryl invited as he continued to stand steadfastly on the stoop. Stepping inside, he looked wildly around as though expecting Victoria to leap out from a corner.

"Gee, you seem a little nervous," Sheryl observed. "Have a seat in the parlor. I'll go up and tell her you're here. And Richard . . ." He turned back with a start. "Relax," she added with a reassuring smile.

Moving into the familiar receiving room, Richard perched for a moment on the edge of the sofa. But damn, he couldn't sit still. He paced the room and had paused by the window when he heard a noise and spun around.

There she was—fair hair waving about her shoulders, face glowing, eyes sparkling. The radiance he remembered from long ago was back. His hungry gaze raced over her. Dressed in white slacks and a long white overblouse, she retained a look of slender grace despite the fact that she was obviously with child.

"I guess I look a little different from the last time you saw me," she said.

Despite Richard's best efforts, the flowers he was holding started to shake. "You look beautiful," he replied.

She smiled and moved into the room. "Are you sure you aren't just saying that to be polite?"

"I'm sure."

She came to stand before him. "Are those for me?" she asked, her gaze shifting to the roses.

"Oh," Richard muttered, hastily handing over the flowers. "I thought . . . well, you never had a proper bridal bouquet."

"Thank you," she murmured, and cradled the flowers as though she already held a child in her arms.

"How are you feeling?" he asked.

"Very well. Actually I seem to be having what they call a

charmed pregnancy. No sickness. No problems. And the baby is as healthy as I am.''

"The baby . . ." Richard repeated, and suddenly couldn't contain himself. Throwing his arms around Victoria, he drew her close and buried his face in her hair. "God, I'm glad to see you," he whispered.

"I'm glad to see you, too." Letting the roses drop to the floor, she stretched both arms around his back. "Not that I don't appreciate the flowers," she mumbled against his shoulder. "But I need this more."

"Take as much of it as you want," Richard replied, and they stood quietly holding each other as long minutes passed.

"You know everything about me now," she said ultimately. "Are you sure it doesn't make a difference?"

"Only in that I'll do everything I can to make it up to you."

"I'll allow that," she replied, shifting back just enough so that she could smile up at him.

At that moment the child inside her stirred. Richard felt it against his own belly, and a feeling the likes of which he'd never known flashed through the length of his body. "I felt that," he announced with a look of awe. "I felt the baby move."

"She's doing it more and more these days."

"She?"

"I had the test done. We're going to have a daughter, Richard." Lifting a hand, she trailed loving fingers along the side of his face. "And I hope she looks like you. Same eyes. Same smile. If she gets those, she'll be the most beautiful girl in the world."

"Listen to you talk," Richard murmured. "If she looks like her mother, I'll have to be guarding her with a vengeance from the day she's born."

Victoria released a light laugh. "Would you mind?"

"No, I wouldn't mind. She'll be kept safe, and nothing bad will ever happen to her. Nothing bad . . ." Richard hesitated as his eyes filled with tears. "She'll have a life so beautiful . . ."

Once again he trailed off, and this time was so overcome by emotion he couldn't continue.

"I know she will," Victoria murmured, and lifting her mouth to his, she kissed him with all the love and passion he'd brought into her life. "Let's go home," she said then, and smiled into the prince's glistening eyes.

Long after the car faded from view, Sheryl continued to see Victoria's head turn, her hand lift in farewell. Although Sheryl had been unable to see the pale blue eyes, she could imagine the look within them—happy, yet laced with the ice that threatened to spread in a concealing glaze. Perhaps it would never go away entirely. But with Richard on her side—along with her own determination—Victoria had a better chance than most women who'd been through the kind of trauma she'd suffered.

Closing the door on the warm May morning, Sheryl moved through the quiet town house.

It had been hard to watch them drive away together, but not as hard as she'd expected. She'd thought no woman could ever love Richard more than she, and yet she'd come to believe that Victoria did—loved him with all the desperation and joy of someone who'd locked up the feeling for a lifetime and finally set it free.

Going into the office where they'd spent so many hours, Sheryl sat down at the desk, idly perusing the notes and papers that had accumulated over the past three months—pieces that came together to sketch the portrait of a grown woman still struggling with her childhood.

On the night of her graduation ball, Vicki Buchanan—all dressed up in the finery of a formal white gown—hot-wired her father's limousine and disappeared. After that came Vanessa Blair . . . Valerie Blake . . . Veronica Bates . . . In all, there had been seven different aliases through which she'd vented her anger—seven screens though which she compulsively struck out at a past she was unable to face. Even Victoria Blackwood had managed to keep Vicki Buchanan buried for the most part.

The damage inflicted on her as a child could never be undone, but she was fighting back as hard as anyone Sheryl had ever known to reclaim her life—fighting to create a future for herself, her husband, and her child.

Applying a clean sheet of paper to the top of the pile, Sheryl reached for a pen. *Victoria Adams,* she wrote, and closed the file. It seemed the lady had finally found a name she liked well enough to keep.

=AFTERWORD=

This story was inspired by one of my dearest friends.

Over the course of twenty years, we'd been together through boyfriends and breakups, changes of plans, changes of majors, changes of goals for the future. There was nothing of any importance we didn't know about each other . . . I thought.

We were both settled down and married when she called me one day. The time to stop keeping the secret had come, she said.

I remember sitting back in my chair and losing touch with everything around me. I remember begging her pardon, putting down the phone, and trying to muffle the sobs. She'd always called me the strong, level-headed one, but on that day it was she who did the handholding.

Like many childhood victims, my friend had buried what happened to her, but she couldn't bury it so deeply that it ceased casting a shadow on her life. I understand now about traits that I thought were simply *her*—withdrawals that could come on without provocation, periods of depression so dark that no well-meant words of comfort could shed the slightest light. Now, after she's invested several years in therapy, pieces of the past continue to surface . . . and pieces of our conversations continue to show me how pervasively this trauma once imprisoned the friend I thought I knew inside and out.

Depending on the study cited, current estimates are that one of every three (or four) American women is a victim of childhood sexual abuse, often inflicted by a family member or friend, and commonly extending for a period of years. Statistics always sound so distant. It's painful to imagine what they mean in closer terms—to think that maybe somewhere out

326 / *Marcia Martin*

there tonight, one of every three or four little girls is being led to a secret place by a smiling father, uncle, or grown-up friend.

Confused and exploited by a trusted adult, the victimized child can develop a number of maladies in adulthood, including: paranoia; schizophrenia; phobias of every description; compulsive behaviors of every description; sexual frigidity, passivity, promiscuity; and more.

If you're trying to deal with such a problem alone, or know someone who is, please consider the suggestion to seek psychological help. If you don't know a therapist, your local mental health board can recommend one.

As for today's children . . . I wish they all could have carefree afternoons and homecomings that mean simply that—coming home. Sadly, I know that's not reality and I'd like to invite everyone who reads this to join me in keeping eyes and ears sharp. In my opinion, minding one's own business has no place in a situation where a defenseless child could be damaged for a lifetime.

There are hundreds of thousands of secret places out there; if even one goes unvisited, it will be a great victory.

—Marcia Martin
September 1992